Elig
GREEKS

April 2014

May 2014

Eligible
GREEKS
Sizzling Affairs

Kate *Robyn* *Sabrina*
WALKER DONALD PHILIPS

MILLS & BOON

Published in Great Britain 2014
by Mills & Boon, an imprint of Harlequin (UK) Limited,
Eton House, 18-24 Paradise Road, Richmond, Surrey, TW9 1SR

ELIGIBLE GREEKS: SIZZLING AFFAIRS
© 2014 Harlequin Books S.A.

The Good Greek Wife? © 2010 Kate Walker
Powerful Greek, Housekeeper Wife © 2010 Robyn Donald
Greek Tycoon, Wayward Wife © 2010 Sabrina Philips

ISBN: 978 0 263 24606 3

012-0514

Harlequin (UK) Limited's policy is to use papers that are natural, renewable and recyclable products and made from wood grown in sustainable forests The logging and manufacturing processes conform to the legal environmental regulations of the country of origin.

Printed and bound in Spain
by Blackprint CPI, Barcelona

THE GOOD
GREEK WIFE?

KATE WALKER

Kate Walker was born in Nottinghamshire and grew up in a home where books were vitally important. Even before she could write she was making up stories. She can't remember a time when she wasn't scribbling away at something.

But everyone told her that she would never make a living as a writer, so instead she became a librarian. It was at the University College of Wales, Aberystwyth, that she met her husband, who was also studying there. They married and eventually moved to Lincolnshire, where she worked as a children's librarian until her son was born.

After three years of being a full-time housewife and mother she was ready for a new challenge, so she turned to her old love of writing. The first two novels she sent off to Mills & Boon were rejected, but the third attempt was successful. She can still remember the moment that a letter of acceptance arrived instead of the rejection slip she had been dreading. But the moment she really realised that she was a published writer was when copies of her first book, *The Chalk Line*, arrived just in time to be one of her best Christmas presents ever.

Kate is often asked if she's a romantic person, because she writes romances. Her answer is that if being romantic means caring about other people enough to make that extra-special effort for them, then, yes, she is.

Kate loves to hear from her fans. You can contact her through her website at www.kate-walker.com, or e-mail her at kate@kate-walker.com.

For Lee Hyat
Thank you for the reviews, the publicity,
all your help over the years, but specially
for your friendship

CHAPTER ONE

THE setting sun only barely lit the winding path that Penny was following, making it impossible for her to walk fast, however much she wanted to.

No, the truth was that deep down inside she wanted to run. She wanted to get away from the villa as quickly as possible, to run as far and as fast as she could possibly manage. She wanted to run and run and never come back, to get away from the poisonous atmosphere in the house she had left behind. But the truth was that up until now any such action had been impossible.

And now?

Well, now she knew that she could leave—perhaps she ought to leave. But doing so would be to admit to herself that there really was no longer anything more to hope for. That her dream of love and a future was over, gone for good. Dead like her fantasies.

Dead like…

No, even now she still couldn't put Zarek's name, her husband's name, at the end of that sentence. If she did that then she was admitting that everyone else was right and she was the foolish one, the only one who had taken so long to let go.

To admit that she no longer had a husband. That the man she had adored and married was never coming home again.

Reaching the spot where the path petered out onto the shore, she kicked off her sandals and paced onto the pebbled beach. Out at sea, she could just make out the dark shape of a small rowing boat and the man who sat in it, broad shoulders hunched away from her, his head just a black silhouette against the sunset. He was wearing some sort of hat—a baseball cap pulled down low so there was no way she could decipher any of his features.

Even now the thought of someone on the water made her shudder inwardly. Out there, somewhere thousands of miles away, Zarek had lost his life. The depths of the ocean were his only grave. That was what she had had so much trouble coming to accept.

And she was going to have to accept one further, even more hateful truth. The fact that even when he had been alive Zarek had never truly loved her. Their marriage had been a lie, on Zarek's part at least. To him it had been purely a cold-blooded plan for an heir, never the love match she had believed it. So why was she still holding onto his memory when it was so obvious that he wasn't coming back?

Finding a smooth outcrop of rock just above the tiny horse-shoe shaped harbour, she plonked herself down on the make-shift seat and rested her elbows on her knees, supporting her chin in them as she stared out at the small craft bobbing on the restless waves. Sitting there, just staring out into the darkness, she let her unwilling memory go back over the scene she had just left behind.

'Penelope…'

The voice had come from behind her, just as she reached the front door of the villa and had her fingers on the handle, ready to turn it. It made her freeze into stillness, keeping her eyes directed away and fixed on the heavy wood in front of her.

'Are you going somewhere?'

There was no mistaking just whose voice it was. Only one woman had that cold, distant tone that made her sound as if she were speaking through a cloud of ice, freezing the words in the air as they came out.

And only one woman called her *Penelope* in quite that way. Using the full version of her name to make it sound like a criticism or a reproach when everyone else—her own family or everyone who liked her—only ever used the shortened form of Penny or even Pen.

Not her mother-in-law. Or, to be more correctly precise, her stepmother-in-law.

'I thought I'd go out for a walk.'

'At this time of the day?'

'It's cooler in the evenings. And I prefer it that way.'

Still she didn't turn round. She didn't need to, of course, but more than that she didn't want to. She could already see Hermione Michaelis' elegant figure in her mind's eye. Slender to the point of emaciation, her hair kept unnaturally jet black with the constant use of hair dye, so that the few streaks of grey that were starting to appear were carefully disguised in an attempt to look so much younger than her fifty-nine years.

'I still haven't really adjusted to the heat in the daytime.'

'After so long?' her mother in law queried, making Penny bring her sharp teeth down on the softness of her bottom lip in an effort to bite back the instinctive retort that had almost formed on her tongue.

'So long' was only a relative term, depending on who used it. To Hermione maybe the past two years or so had seemed like an age. An age in which she had to live with her unwanted daughter-in-law, who now stood between Darius Michaelis' second wife and the full control of Odysseus Shipping, which was what she had been aiming for from the very first moment she had met Zarek's father.

And 'so long' barely described the past two years that Penny had lived through ever since the news about Zarek's fate had come through to the island. The news that had turned her life upside down, destroying the hope of future happiness, and taking away with it any chance of being able to tell her husband how she truly felt about him.

The brief time of her marriage seemed to have flashed by in the blink of an eye, but the two years since then had taken an eternity to live through. An eternity that had dragged out to seem longer and longer with every day of hope that perhaps this was the day he might return. And then the dreadful, appalling moments that had killed all hope of that for ever. Since then her life had been something to be endured, a desert to live through. Empty and arid, without the love she had once hoped for.

No, who was she kidding? Even before he had vanished— been killed, they said—Zarek had never offered her the love she dreamed of, Penny told herself with bitter realism. He had married her in a cold-blooded business arrangement, entering into a marriage of convenience because it suited him to do so, because he wanted an heir. And she was the one who had been fool enough to think it was something else.

'My skin is sensitive to the sun—and I don't want to burn. That can be so aging.'

The faint hiss of Hermione's breath in between clenched teeth told her that her deliberate dart had hit home. The older woman was paying the price for a lifetime of sun worship-ping and the effects that none of her hugely expensive facials and even a recent facelift could really eradicate.

'So are you taking the dog?' Hermione turned the last two words into an expression of total distaste.

There was only one dog that she could mean. Argus, the great black and white hound who had once been so devoted to his master Zarek and who seemed to be the only other living soul who along with Penny mourned his loss. In the first few weeks after Zarek had gone missing, she had feared that they would lose Argus as well as the big sheepdog had pined for his owner, turning his head away from all food. But in the end he had transferred his devotion to Penny herself and now followed at her heel almost everywhere she went, lying under her desk when she had to work.

'I think not. He's already had a long walk today and the last time I looked he was fast asleep.'

Fast asleep on her bed if the truth was told but there was no way she was going to admit as much to Hermione. Her mother-in-law was only looking for an excuse to get rid of the big dog and Penny wasn't going to take any risks that way. Argus had kept her company when she had needed a friend most. His warm, reassuring bulk was there by her side in the darkness of the night. His long, shaggy fur had absorbed the tears she had shed on that dreadful night when the appalling truth that Zarek was in fact dead had been reported to them. The dog was the one living link to her lost husband and she would always love him for that.

'Nasty flea-bitten creature.'

Penny could practically see Hermione's mouth curl in disgust but she wasn't going to turn and check if she was right.

'There's one thing I can assure you and that is that my dog does *not* have fleas.'

Wrenching the handle roughly, she pulled the door open and stepped forward, enjoying the rush of air, scented with the tang of the sea, that flooded into her face. She felt trapped and confined—a feeling that was becoming the norm in a way that made her lungs constrict so that it was almost impossible to breathe naturally.

'Don't be long. It's getting dark already.'

Concern? Now that was new in a way that brought her head finally swinging round to meet Hermione's black glittering eyes. Immediately she knew that if she had been thinking that the older woman had her safety at heart, she was wrong. The light that was in that gaze was cold and predatory. The look of a cold-blooded buyer eyeing up her investment to check that all was well. Or a breeder with plans for producing a number of prize-winning offspring from a rather skittish brood mare.

No, that had been Zarek, Penny forced herself to acknowledge inwardly. He was the one who had seen her only as breeding stock for his dynasty.

'I'll be fine…'

'We need to talk to you…'

Penny's voice clashed with Hermione's, the sound of that 'we need to talk to you' making Penny's heart clench and thud roughly against the side of her ribs.

She knew only too well just what that 'need to talk' would entail. She had to. It was the one thing that Hermione and the rest of the family always wanted to talk about.

'I'll be back when I'm back,' she flung in defiance, pushing herself out of the door and into the freedom of the garden before Hermione could do anything to prevent her.

She almost ran down the path, her feet flying over the pebbles as they carried her as quickly as possible. She actually feared that Hermione would come after her, grab at her arm and drag her back, hauling her back inside the house to face 'the family' and the things they wanted to talk about. The older woman was capable of it.

Out at sea, the man in the small boat had given up on the fishing or whatever it was that had taken him onto the dark ocean this late. He was reaching for the oars, the powerful muscles in his arms and shoulders tensing under the white long-sleeved tee shirt as he began to pull against the waves. He must be a strong man, Penny reflected privately. Only someone with a great deal of muscular power could make that much progress against the swell of the tide. Watching him, she felt an unexpected shiver of awareness wash over her skin, perhaps as a result of the cooling breeze that blew in from the sea.

Or possibly it was the effects of the unhappy feelings that plagued her at the thought of that 'talk' that awaited her when she got back to the villa. When Hermione and her sons, Jason and Petros, would start on at her again, trying to persuade her to make the decisions they had been itching for her to come to for so long. At least they had had the sensitivity and the tact to let the last month go by without ever saying a word. They'd let her have the second anniversary of Zarek's disappearance, the day that marked the announcement of his death, without their insistent demands that it was time to look ahead instead of back, to plan the future, to 'move on'.

'Oh, Zarek…'

Dropping her face into her hands, Penny pressed her fingers hard against her closed eyes. Sometimes the misery could still grab her by the throat and make her wonder how she could live the rest of her life without ever seeing him again. He might not have loved her but she had adored him.

'I'll never forget you…'

But the realisation of the truth made the words catch in her throat even as she whispered them behind her hands. Because the truth was that with each day that passed she was finding it harder and harder to recall exactly the devastating attraction of her husband's forceful appearance, the powerful bone structure and sexual appeal of his stunning features. If she tried to visualise him against the darkness of her closed lids she found that the image danced and blurred before her and she could no longer form that once-beloved face in her mind.

The banging of heavy wood against wood jolted her out of her reveries. The fisherman had reached the land, his boat thudding against the pillars of the small jetty as he came up close. As she lifted her head to watch she saw him reach out to pull the vessel even nearer, his oars taken from their locks and dropped at his feet.

He really was a big man, Penny told herself, watching as the lean, powerful frame was silhouetted against the last of the sun, now sinking finally beyond the horizon. Tall, but not bulky—his rangy figure had a controlled power about it as he vaulted easily onto the jetty, bringing with him a coil of wet rope, the drops of seawater that fell from it glistening in the lingering remains of the light. It was the first time in so very long that she had even been aware of a man and how his body looked that she felt her heart kick hard against her ribs in a sense of shock at what she was thinking.

This much closer, she should have been able to see his face but the baseball cap that was pulled down low over his forehead hid so much. And the little that was left was concealed by the thick growth of a dark and bushy beard, which together with the overlong black hair falling onto the straight, strong shoulders gave him a wild, rather primitive look that made her toes curl into the pebbles in slightly shocked response.

Perhaps it was time that she made him aware of her. Let him know she was here.

'Good evening…'

No response. Clearing her throat carefully, she tried her amateurish Greek.

'*Kalispera.*'

That brought his head swinging round in her direction. She caught the flash of dark eyes narrowed against the setting sun and he adjusted his hat, tugging it down even lower as a defence against the glare.

'*Kalispera.*'

His voice was rough and unexpectedly non-friendly. Not aggressive; not hostile. Just very clearly not welcoming her approach. Which was unexpected and unusual. In all her time on the island never once had she approached the small town of Kioni without being greeted with warmth and friendliness from the locals so that her stumbling attempts at the Greek language had been no barrier at all to communication.

'Is the fishing good?'

What had she said now to make him stare at her for a moment so searchingly and intently that she felt almost as if his hidden gaze were a laser directed straight at her, threatening to shrivel her where she stood? Suddenly apprehensive, she found she was tensing, nerving herself for some sort of attack—not knowing what or why. Too late she wished that she had bothered to take the time to go and collect Argus and take him out with her on this evening walk. Not for nothing had the big dog been given a name that meant vigilant guardian, and if he had been with her then this disturbingly cold and unapproachable male would very definitely know to stand back, keep his distance.

Not that he showed any sign of actually wanting to approach her, because having considered her question for an inordinately long amount of time he suddenly shook his head abruptly.

'No,' he growled, tossing the word at her like a discarded piece of litter. 'Not good.'

And, turning away from her, he tugged hard on the rope to draw it up onto the jetty before looping it through an iron ring nailed into the wood and pulling it tight to fasten the boat to its mooring. A moment later he was crouching down to check that the knot was secure, the movement making the long, strong muscles in his legs and thighs bunch and flex as they took his weight

Again that disturbing shiver of response that Penny now knew had nothing to do with the cool of the evening in spite of the chill from the wind off the sea crept over her skin.

What was happening to her? Penny's head seemed to swim under the impact of the unexpected sensations, the unwanted thoughts that assailed her.

Was it really possible that the senses she had thought had died with Zarek were now coming awake again? Was she, as everyone had told her she would, finally really starting to take an interest in life again—in other men? But why would this man, this scruffy bearded, rough-voiced fisherman pique her interest so much? Or was it just that tonight she felt so lost, so alone that any man would act as a distraction from the bleakness of her thoughts?

Feeling uncomfortable and restless, she pushed herself to her feet but then found that she couldn't move, couldn't get away. Instead her gaze stayed locked on the strong, lean form of the man before her. Her throat felt dry and tight too, her heart thudding disturbingly so that she found it hard to breathe.

She should never have come out like this. Her tense mood and the uncomfortable meeting she had had with Hermione, the 'talk' she knew was coming, had all combined to knock her off balance so badly that she was no longer able to think straight. In fact she wasn't thinking at all, sitting here in the gathering dusk, her gaze hooked and held by a complete stranger. Yes, he had a good body—a great body—but was that enough to scramble her brain this way?

But then the fisherman stood up again and some movement of his head brought the little of it that was not concealed under the hat or the growth of beard into the light of a lamp at the side of the harbour. The sight of the jagged line of an ugly scar had Penny's breath hissing in sharply between her teeth, a faint sound of shock and horror escaping her involuntarily. White against the tanned darkness of his skin, it marred the line of dark beard on the right side of his face, skimming his temple and disappearing into the shadows thrown by his cap.

'Oh, my…'

The shocked exclamation died on her lips as something in her voice brought him swinging round to face her again. And everything about his stance, the way he held himself, the tension in the long straight spine and the way his hand clenched over the end of the rope that he held warned her that he had heard her response and that for some reason he didn't like it.

'That—that must have hurt…' she managed, her own body tensing warily under the burn of his dark-eyed glare.

'It did.'

His tone made it plain that he begrudged her the answer.

'And n-now?'

'*Ohi.*'

A shake of his head emphasised the denial.

'So how—?'

Hastily Penny caught herself up. What was she doing? Had she actually been about to ask him what had happened, how he had come by the injury? She must be crazy. Here she was alone in the darkness with a dark, powerful and clearly unwelcoming stranger and she was pushing him for answers he clearly did not want to give.

And why, why, was she even remotely interested? What was it about this stranger that had so unsettled her that she had actually wanted to know what had caused the injury that had marked him so badly? Wasn't the fact that it was so evidently the result of some terrible violence enough to clamp her foolish mouth shut?

'So many questions,' the fisherman mocked now, and the low voice carried over the silence to where she sat on her rock, some dark edge in it making her spine tense, her stomach twisting in sharp apprehension. 'Why so curious?'

'I…'

She was halfway to her feet, but the need to keep her eyes on the big, bulky figure silhouetted against the setting sun meant that she didn't dare to move too fast or too obviously for fear that she would show him how keen she was to get away.

'You…?' he queried, that disturbing note in his voice deepening worryingly. And he took a step forward, towards her. Pushing her to her feet in a rush.

'Penelope?'

Another voice broke in on them, coming out of the darkness along the shoreline. A male voice; a voice she knew and recognised.

'Penny?'

'Jason!'

She would actually have welcomed the arrival of any member of those she privately labelled The Family at this stage of things. But Jason was the only one of Zarek's stepbrothers who was actually kind to her. Closer to Penny in age than any of the rest of the family, and startlingly handsome—conventionally good-looking where Zarek had been dark and devastating—he had been approachable, even warm and sympathetic from the moment she had arrived on Ithaca as a young, naïve bride.

And it had been Jason who had warned her that Zarek's marriage plans had been the cold-blooded hunt for a wife who would give him an heir. A fact that Zarek himself had confirmed when she'd challenged him, asking why he'd proposed to her.

'Isn't it obvious? I couldn't keep my hands off you,' her husband had said. 'And I knew we would make beautiful babies together—and that's all that mattered.'

'You OK, *agapiti mou*?'

The term of affection was new, but it was what she needed. It was enough to have her on her feet and swinging round to him, nervous steps taking her towards him in a rush that had her almost tripping over herself on the slipping sand. Like a bird winging home to its nest, she ran straight for Jason, un-thinking, hands reaching out to him.

Jason opened his arms too so that she ran into them, almost collapsing up against his hard length and burying her face in the crisp cotton of his shirt. Long arms came round her, holding her tight.

And that was when second and then third thoughts forced themselves into Penny's whirling brain, taking the instinctive, mindless fear that had pushed her into movement and pushing it aside, replacing it with a sudden feeling of having made a terrible mistake. Fear of the stranger was one thing, but from Jason's reaction he had taken her response to mean much more than she had meant. He was holding her too tight, too close.

Too close for what she really wanted.

'Penny…'

And that tone had altered, putting something new into the use of her name, a thickness she had never heard and certainly wasn't meaning to encourage. The fisherman might have spooked her, twisting her nerves into fearful response, but a sudden slow crawl of unease down her spine gave her the unwanted sense of out of the frying pan and into the fire.

'Jason…' she tried experimentally, aiming to lift her head from where it was pressed against his chest, ease herself away from the limpet grip he had on her.

As she had feared his arms tightened round her, holding her still. Already unsettled by her encounter with the fisherman, and painfully aware of the fact that he must still be watching her, she felt as if her head was about to explode with stress. She didn't want this and if Jason thought he had found the perfect time to make a move…

Suddenly she knew she had had enough. Enough of this situation, this family. She didn't belong here and she never had. She had always been second best, unwanted and unpopular with Zarek's stepmother and stepbrothers. And second best to Zarek too.

So why was she so determined to stay here where she wasn't wanted? To cling onto memories that had never really been true, no matter how much she might wish they had. Perhaps if she escaped, she could leave, go home. She could be by herself and try to find another way of living. She could always take Zarek with her in her heart.

And that gave her the perfect way to distract Jason, to turn his thoughts onto other, more important things—more important to Jason, anyway. Even if Hermione's aggression was not Jason's way, he was every bit as hungry for control of Odysseus Shipping as his mother.

'I want to call a board meeting for tomorrow,' she said, raising her voice so that she could be heard over the crash of the waves.

It worked. She felt the change as soon as she spoke, the new and different tension in Jason's body, the gleam in his eye that he couldn't disguise as he looked down at her. He even loosened his hold on her so that she could step back away from him.

'Why?' he asked, not sounding at all as if he believed there was any reason other than the one she knew he was hoping for.

'I'm sick and tired of this whole business, Jason.'

The tension that had gripped her earlier pushed the words out in a rush, giving them far more emphasis than she had planned.

'I want to get away from here, start living again. I'm tired of treading water. It's more than time this whole business was sorted out and everything finalised so that we can get on with our lives. I can't inherit unless we have Zarek's death declared and legalised. So let's do that. Let's put it all behind us—'

'I'll get onto it right away,' Jason broke in on her, his tone revealing only too clearly how much her words had pleased him. He even gave her another hug but thankfully it had lost the sexual overtones of the earlier one. His ambition and greed were a more powerful force—or perhaps, more likely, the sexual flirtation had only been used with the hope of bringing things to this point. Another reason to be glad that she had made her decision.

'Exactly how do you want to play this?'

But Penny had had enough. Painfully aware of their silent watcher, the unsettling atmosphere he had created, she just wanted to get back inside, seek the privacy of her room.

'Not now, Jason. Not here. He—'

'Who?' Jason questioned sharply. 'Who's "he"?'

'That man…'

Flinging out her arm, Penny gestured wildly in the direction of the harbour and the spot where the fishing boat was tied up.

'What man?'

'He…'

But Penny's voice died away as she turned in the direction

she'd indicated and saw only the boat bobbing at its mooring, the water lapping against the harbour side and the lamp illuminating an empty and silent space where the mysterious man had once been. He had gone silently and secretly, and she had no idea just what he had heard or seen or why it should bother her that he had overheard any of their conversation. But all the same, something uncomfortable and uneasy nagged at her mind at the thought that he had been there at all, and the rapid, uneven beat of her heart was the lingering effect of her unnerving and unsettling encounter with him.

CHAPTER TWO

HE WOULD need to be more careful in the future, the fisherman told himself as he headed away from the harbour and towards the small, single-storey, white-painted house that he had made his home since he had arrived on the island a few days before.

He had almost given himself away there, speaking English—speaking at all when it was so possible that Penny might recognise his voice and know that he was alive. Alive and back on Ithaca for the first time in over two years.

And he didn't want her to know that. Not yet. Not until he had had a chance to check the lie of the land, see just how things were. It might only have been two years—just twenty-four short months—since he had been on Ithaca, and a much shorter space of time since he had realised that the place even existed, but to him it felt so much longer than that. It seemed as if it were a whole lifetime since he had set foot on the island. Then he had thought that he would be back within the week. He had never anticipated that it would be years before he saw his home and his wife again.

But now he was back. And not before time it seemed, he told himself as the door to the cottage slammed shut behind him and he marched into the single, cramped living room. It appeared that the reports he had been hearing were true. His stepmother and her family were moving in on the business. Hermione had always had her eyes set on Odysseus Shipping and now it seemed that his absence had given her the encouragement she needed to make a play for control. And he knew just how that control would be won. Through one of Hermione's sons.

And Penny had run straight into *Jason's* arms. She had been planning having him declared dead with his detested stepbrother. And the wild fire of fury that had flared inside him at the sight had been a struggle to bring under control. It was fierce, it was unthinking, it was irrational, but the sight of the woman—the *wife*—he had come back to find enfolded in the arms of the man he knew had been scheming his downfall for all of his adult life had had him fighting with himself not to react in anger. Unable to stay and watch, he had turned on his heel and marched away before the urge to declare himself there and then had got the better of him.

Shaking his head, he fixed his eyes on the now moonlit sea as it lapped against the edge of the beach below the cottage, the slow, dark swirl of the waves suiting his mood completely.

Jason had already taken the first steps towards acquiring what he and his mother had always wanted. His elder stepbrother had barely waited for Zarek's disappearance to be confirmed before he had been trying to apply for power of attorney to run Odysseus Shipping. He hadn't hesitated to make his move as soon as the opportunity had presented itself. But of course the legal control rested with Zarek's wife.

With Penny, who had had a far greater return on her investment of time in their marriage than she could ever have hoped to achieve.

Or thought she had.

He rubbed at the ugly scar that marked his temple, grimacing as the wound throbbed with the ache of memory.

That was one of the reasons he had come back to Ithaca in total anonymity, his true appearance obscured behind the wild growth of beard and hair. And it seemed that it had worked. Tonight he had come face to face with his wife for the first time in years and she had shown no sign of recognising him.

But just hearing her voice again had brought it all back.

'Go, then!'

The memory was so clear that he actually glanced up and in the mirror over the fireplace almost as if he expected to see that the door had opened while he had been absorbed in his thoughts and Penny had walked into the room.

'If you're going, then go! I don't know why you're even telling me this. It's not as if you're asking my permission!'

Shaking his head to try and drive the sound of his wife's voice, still shrill even after all these years, from his mind, he paced across the room to the window to stare out at the now moonlit sea where it lapped against the pebbles of Dexa beach. The wind was getting up, making the olive trees sway wildly in the breeze.

He was damn sure he hadn't been asking for permission or anything like it. The truth was that after the way their marriage had all but disintegrated in the short time they'd been together he'd firmly believed she would be as grateful for a break as he was. She'd even backed away from him sexually, and sex had been one of the things that had been right between them at the start. The glue that had kept them together.

'Just go—' she had flung at him, her sexy mouth distorting in the force of her rejection of him. 'But be warned, if you go, then don't expect me to be here waiting for you when you return.'

So had she waited? He'd thought she had when he had discovered that she was still here on Ithaca. He'd even allowed himself to wonder just for a moment whether she might hold out some hope that he would come back. From what she'd just said it seemed that it was the legalities resulting from his disappearance that had kept her here, not any lingering loyalty to her marriage.

But then she'd made it only too plain exactly why she'd married him in the first place. He'd been fool enough to believe her declaration that she wanted children—longed for them, she'd said—when in fact she'd been lying through her teeth. She'd even been taking the pill and when he'd confronted her with the evidence she'd thrown it back in his face.

'Bring children into this marriage—you have to be joking. Where did I sign up for that? Where was that written into the pre-nup you got me to sign?'

He'd never thought he'd need to do that. He'd signed and sealed the financial details, but never made them dependent on the one reason he'd determined on marriage in the first place.

And Penny had proved herself nothing but a scheming little gold-digger. She'd married him for those financial details and never intended to carry out her part of the agreement. Never intended to give him the heir he so longed for. Even if he had come back safe and sound from the *Troy*, she would still have come out of their brief marriage a millionaire in her own right. He had been happy to agree to very generous terms, never thinking he would have to fulfil them before he had even celebrated his first wedding anniversary. For ten short months of commitment, Penny would walk away with a huge profit.

But not as much as she would profit from his supposed death. From the will that he'd changed in her favour when they had married. One thing was clear. She wanted to realise her assets, get her hands on the company.

It must have felt like the answer to her prayers—as if all her birthdays had come at once—when he had done exactly what she'd wanted. He hadn't come back, leaving the field wide open to her. She hadn't even had to go to the trouble of divorcing him and so risking losing half the money she had married him for.

Pushing his hands through the long mane of hair, he faced his reflection in the mirror and saw the darkness in the eyes that stared back at him, the tautness of the jaw line under the thick growth of beard. Remembered anger tightened his lips until they almost disappeared. There was a way to deal with this that would have much more impact, and it seemed that Penny herself had just given him the perfect opportunity he had been looking for.

He'd been away too long—an absence he had not been able to do anything about—but the last week or two he had spent waiting and watching, just to see what he would be walking into when he made his return. That was all over now. The time for waiting and watching was past.

Heading into the tiny, primitive bathroom, he opened a cupboard and reached for scissors, a razor. It was time he came out from behind his concealing disguise and made his presence known.

Zarek Michaelis was back. And very soon the whole world would know it.

And so too would his errant, untrustworthy wife.

He was looking forward to seeing the look on her face when she realised that she was not going to get her greedy fingers on the fortune that she had hoped—believed—was hers. Or that the new life she had declared that she wanted would not be on the cards any time soon.

When she discovered that the husband she had believed

was dead and out of her life for good was in fact very much alive and ready to take back the reins of his previous existence.

'Penelope, it really is time to make a decision.'

Hermione leaned forward as she spoke, dark eyes boring into the face of the woman opposite her, long fingernails tapping on the polished wood of the boardroom table to emphasise the point she was making.

'We can't let things go on any longer as they are.'

'We?' Penny questioned, determined not to let Zarek's stepmother run this meeting, have things all her own way.

There was no escaping the decision that she had known she had to face some time. The decision everyone had been demanding she make for a year or more now. And deep down she knew she'd already made it. But it didn't mean that she was happy about it.

'We are all shareholders,' her mother-in-law pointed out, the bite of acid on the words making Penny flinch inwardly.

'Minority shareholders,' she flashed back, determined not to show how her stomach was tying itself in knots; the fight she was having to keep at least some degree of composure in the face of the bitterness of the inevitable.

'But nevertheless Odysseus Shipping is a family concern.'

It was Petros, Hermione's second son and Jason's younger brother who spoke, shifting his bulky form on his chair in a movement that echoed the impatience in his voice.

'And you are blocking us from playing a part in running the company,' he tossed over the table at her. 'We all need to put our expertise to work to keep it running—and growing. Without Zarek it has become a rudderless ship.'

His stiff tone and totally focused expression gave no sign at all of even noticing the pun.

'It needs someone in charge.'

'*I* am in charge,' Penny declared, stiffening in her seat.

This was how it had been from the moment that Zarek had first been declared missing. The rest of the family had barely given her time to register the loss of her husband, let alone grieve for him, before they had been putting pressure on her to find a new head of the family firm, and at least once every month they had dragged the subject of his successor up again. She'd tried to hold it together, she really had. But she'd had enough.

'It's a shipping empire,' Petros dismissed her protest with a contemptuous wave of his hand. 'A man should be in charge because we all know Zarek isn't coming home. And until things are made official then the company will always be in a shaky state. A prey for rumour and scandal in the papers. An insecure bet for investors.'

'You know what has to be done.' Jason leaned forward now to distract her attention. Obviously he had seen the way her jaw had tightened, her breath hissing in between clenched teeth, and he was clearly worried that she was going to go back on what she'd told him last night. 'Penny, it's over two years since Zarek went missing. There has been no sign of him, no word in all that time. It's time we accepted what we all know as the truth and had him officially declared dead.'

There. It was out. The words seemed to land on the table with a deafening thud, lying there in front of her in an almost solid form. Too real to reject or deny. But now when it came to it she didn't know if she could go through with this.

'It takes seven years to have someone who's missing officially declared dead.'

'Not in a case like this,' Jason reminded her. 'Not when there is so much evidence as to what really happened and that you can file a petition to have him legally declared dead. You know that everything points to the assumption that Zarek died that day on the boat. Even the pirate chief himself said…'

'I know what he said!' Penny's tone was sharp as much from the knowledge that she really didn't have a leg to stand on as from the fear of hearing those words spoken aloud again.

'That's him,' the leader of the pirates who had boarded the *Troy*, the boat that Zarek had been on on the very last day he had been seen, had said when they had shown him a photograph of Zarek during the investigation into what had happened. 'That's the one. And, yes, he's dead. I put a bullet in his head myself.'

He had been so openly defiant, so proud at the thought that he had killed one of the hated Westerners, the rich who had so much more than he and his band had ever had, that he hadn't even cared that he had convicted himself of murder with his own words.

'And then I watched him fall overboard into the ocean… He's shark food by now for sure.'

Penny shivered in spite of the sun beating through the window at her back. She had had nightmares about those words for months, could still wake up in a cold sweat with them pounding at her head, making her heart race in panic. In her nightmares she had seen Zarek's face as he had walked away from her, his expression cold and hard, eyes dark and shuttered. The knowledge that she had lashed out in her own pain, using the words that were guaranteed to drive him from her, still haunted her with the thought that they had been the last words he had heard from her. And now, when she saw him again, in her dreams, she knew that the glaze on his eyes was put there not by anger but something far more devastating.

'Then you know that the lawyers told us that someone who had been exposed to "imminent peril" like that and failed to return can be declared dead well before the legal time limit is up.'

'I know…'

She knew but she didn't want to face it. Making that decision would mean admitting that Hermione and her sons had finally dragged her down.

Suddenly in the distance there was a faint scream and a crash that brought her head swinging round, eyes going to the door from behind which the sound had come.

'What…?'

'One of the stupid maids being clumsy, I suspect,' Jason commented dryly, shrugging off the interruption. 'I suspect that means that our coffees will now be delayed. Penny…'

'And the girl will have to replace the broken crockery out of her wages,' Hermione added snappishly, frustration at the fact that things were not going her way obviously showing in her voice.

Pushing back her chair, she got to her feet and headed for the door, obviously determined to reprimand the poor girl severely at the very least. And it was that small action that pushed Penny out of her inertia, reminding her forcefully of just why she had made her decision last night. Why she so wanted to get out of here.

'You're so right, Jason,' she declared with force. 'Zarek's gone and Odysseus Shipping is all mine to do with as I please. So once the formalities are over—if we can work out terms— then the company is yours, Jason.'

And she would be free to live her own life.

Reaching for the glass of water in front of her, she lifted it, tilting it in Jason's direction in mockery of a toast, not daring to lift it to her lips for fear that her throat had closed up so badly that the water would choke her.

'The king is dead,' she proclaimed, making her voice sound as light and careless as she possibly could. 'Long live the king.'

Her words fell into a strange and disturbing silence. A silence that seemed to reach out and enclose her, tangling round her throat and making it impossible to breathe.

Suddenly Jason wasn't looking at her. He had turned away and was staring in the opposite direction. They were all staring that way. Everyone in the room had their eyes fixed on where the door had swung open, pushed firmly but not violently from the other side so that it created a wide, wide space. And everyone was staring into that wide space, shocked, stunned, almost as if they had seen a ghost. Even Hermione had come to a complete halt, one long, elegantly manicured hand going up to her throat in a gesture of horror.

'Jason...' Penny began, but the name died on her tongue, shrivelled on it by the realisation of just what was happening in the same moment that a voice—an impossibly, unbelievably, shockingly familiar voice—spoke, cutting across her in a rough, sardonic drawl.

'Long live the king? I think not, *agapi mou*...'

A sensation like a blow to the head made Penny's thoughts spin sickeningly, the room blurring before her eyes as she struggled to turn and look too. To make her gaze focus on the dark, powerful shape of the man in the door.

It couldn't be. It just couldn't be! There was no way this was possible. It had to be a dream—or a nightmare—or both at once. Because there was no way it could be happening that...

'Because to make that follow, then, as you say, the first king must actually be dead...'

And fixing his eyes on her shocked face, his burning gaze seeming to be drawing out all the blood that Penny could feel had drained from her face so fast that she thought it must leave her looking like a ghost, the new arrival took a couple of steps forward, moving further into the room.

'And as you can see, *gineka mou*, I am very much alive.'

'I—you—'

Penny tried to get to her feet but abandoned the attempt after only a moment, finding that her legs were too weak to support her. Her feet seemed to be balanced on a floor that was strangely uneven, rocking and swaying beneath her as if a huge flood had suddenly come along and lifted the house from its foundations, carrying it out onto the wildest swirling sea. And the look Zarek turned on her was cold and dark, one that killed any impulse to fly into his arms, even after the distance of these two dreadful years. It was a silent, black reminder of the fact that the last time they had been together they had ripped the fragile camouflage covering off their marriage and exposed the lies and deceit that were at the centre of it. Exposing it for the lie it was.

Slumping back into her seat, she shook her head faintly, sending her hair flying out around her face, then passed a shaking hand in front of her eyes, rubbing at them to clear them of this impossible hallucination.

But when she blinked hard and looked again he was still there. Dark and powerful and strong as ever with a forcefully carved face and deep burning eyes that seemed to flay off a much needed layer of skin, leaving her feeling painfully raw and vulnerable, totally exposed.

It had been so long since she had seen him in the flesh, rather than in the photographs she studied every day, that it was almost like seeing him for the first time. Seeing how devastatingly attractive he was, how big and powerful, his lean, rangy figure in the plain white shirt and steel-grey suit easily dominating the room and making everyone else look so very small and insignificant.

'Zarek …' she croaked, her throat closing up around the sound so that she could barely get it out. 'Y—you…'

'Indeed, *agapiti mou*…'

His response was a small, cynically mocking bow of acknowledgement, his probing gaze not leaving her face for an instant.

'Zarek Michaelis. Your absent husband. Home at last.'

CHAPTER THREE

HOME at last.

Who was he trying to kid? Zarek wondered. Even as he spoke the words he knew that there was no way this return felt at all like coming home.

Of course he was back on Ithaca, back inside the family house, the place where he had lived from his childhood and where he'd always looked forward to returning to whenever he'd been away. But somehow this time nothing felt the same. Nothing had that feeling of rightness, of completeness that it had had before.

Which was hardly surprising. After all, he had just walked in on a discussion of a plan to have him legally declared dead. With that on their minds, none of them was going to be glad to see him walk through the door large as life and infuriatingly, unfortunately alive.

Not even Penny.

Not even his wife, who had actually been toasting the fact that he was dead as he opened the door. And was now staring at him as if he was her nightmares come to life.

But what had he expected? That she would run to him on a cry of delight, fling herself into his arms? He'd be every kind of a fool if he'd even dreamed of that. She'd told him as much to his face. And last night would have taught him that dreams of her waiting for him were nothing to base his future on.

But forewarned was forearmed and so there was little to surprise him in the way that she just sat in her chair, slim and elegant in a dark green sleeveless linen dress, eyes wide, staring at him as if he had indeed risen from the dead right before her. If anything she seemed worse—even more appalled than Hermione, and his stepmother looked as if the devil incarnate had just risen up from hell to appear before her.

'So,' he drawled cynically, injecting dark mockery into his voice as the silence lengthened and dragged out. 'Is this any way to greet the prodigal son? I was expecting the fatted calf at least.'

'Then you should have let us know that you were coming!'

Hermione had managed to regain some control but the hiss of fury in her words betrayed the way she was feeling deep inside.

'Or even that you were alive—it would have been nice to know.'

'I did not know myself—that I was coming.'

Zarek couldn't be unaware of the way that his answer had only incensed her further, the flare of her nostrils, the flash of fury in her eyes revealing just what she thought of his response. But quite frankly he didn't give a damn. And he had no intention of launching into the lengthy and complicated explanation of how he came to be alive, and why he hadn't let them know about it until now. Not here and not in front of everyone including Odysseus Shipping's lawyer, their accountant and half the assembled members of the board, it seemed.

'I thought that I might wait awhile longer—and learn as much as I could about the home I was to return to. It has been an interesting experience to say the least. But suffice it to say that I am here. And I am staying. So…'

Leaning forward, he picked up a pen that was lying on the polished wood of the table together with a sheet of paper that held, as he knew it must, a precise order of business as prepared by Leander, whose obsessive concern for detail had not, it seemed, eased up any in the time he had been missing.

'So this…and this…'

With a rough slashing movement he scored the pen through the first point of business and then another and another. All of them dealing with the plans to have him declared dead and transfer the management of Odysseus Shipping to his step-brothers, just as he had expected.

'…can go—and this…'

A couple more decisive strokes of the pen and the entire pro-ceedings for the meeting had been obliterated apart from…

'"Any other business",' he quoted cynically. 'Well—is there any other business?'

One swift glance at the stupefied faces all around him gave him his answer and he screwed up the agenda into a tight ball and tossed it in the general direction of the waste-paper bin, heedless of whether it actually landed there or not.

'Then I now declare this meeting at an end. And you…'

His pointed look was directed at everyone not the imme-diate Michaelis family.

'Can go home.'

It was as if the command, and the general flurry of movement, with chairs pushed back and people getting to their feet, had broken the spell that had held almost everyone frozen in shock. Suddenly Jason—*Jason*—was coming towards him, his hand held out in greeting.

'It's good to have you back. Amazing.'

He actually sounded as if he meant it, Zarek reflected cyni-cally, and if the grip that enclosed his hand was just a little too much, a degree over the top, then that was only to be expected. Jason had always been good at playing the brother card, the friendly smiling brother, when Zarek knew that deep down the younger man hated his guts for being the oldest son, the real son. The only one who would inherit.

Petros on the other hand, like his mother, could not conceal his displeasure and disappointment at the return of the man he must have hoped had gone out of his life for good, leaving the way open to a far wealthier future than he had ever dreamed of. He looked as if he couldn't get out of there fast enough and quite frankly Zarek would be glad to see him go. To see all of them go and leave him alone.

All of them except Penelope.

His wife was still sitting just where she had been when he had walked into the room. In that very first moment she had made a tiny movement, a sort of jump in her seat, and all colour had drained from her face as her eyes widened in shock. That was all.

And now she might as well be carved from marble, she sat so still and pale. It was impossible to read what was going on in her head, behind those clouded eyes. And it was almost impossible not to turn and walk out of the room, leaving all of them—but most of all leaving her—behind him.

Was that the face of an innocent woman? A woman who had been mourning the supposed death of her husband, living with his loss for the past two years? Or was it the face of a woman who, if the scene he had witnessed last night had anything to do with it, had been looking forward to moving on, taking with her the fortune she had earned through a few short months in his bed?

Where was the warm welcome that any husband had a right to expect under such circumstances? Where was the gasp of relief, the rush into his arms, the ardent embrace that told him how much he had been missed? That she was so glad that he was home safe. That she was so glad that he was alive and had come back to her.

But this was just what he should have expected from her on his return. Hadn't she threatened—promised—him that this was how it would be?

'If you go, then don't expect me to be here waiting for you when I get back!'

Once again Penny's angry voice, the furious words she had flung at him, echoed down through the years from the day he had left Ithaca and set out on the *Troy*.

'This marriage isn't worth staying for as it is. If you walk out that door then you are saying it's over...'

But he had walked out of the door. Of course he had. The trials for the *Troy* were important, vital if they were to get the new design completed and on the market. And he'd thought he was giving them both room to breathe, to think. But then he'd believed he'd be gone and back again in a couple of days. Not a couple of years.

So why was *she* still here? Why had she stayed? For him in the hope that he would come back and they could start again, try to do something to redeem the hell that their marriage had become? Or had the news of his 'death' reached the island soon enough to stop her from leaving as she had said she would? And what had she stayed for? The vast inheritance that would now be hers rather than the part-share that would have come to her in a divorce settlement? Or the closeness with Jason that perhaps had been there all the time, but he had been too blind to see?

The scar along his right temple throbbed and ached, making him rub at it in discomfort, and he caught the sudden twist of Penny's head in sharp reaction. So if she hadn't known who he was last night, she did now.

And it worried her, that much was clear from the look— of guilt?—of apprehension that flashed across her face.

'Welcome back…'

'Good to see you safe…'

The conventional greetings, the slightly tentative slaps on the back, a shake of his hand, were the instinctive responses of the men who had worked for him. But he barely really heard them, acknowledged them only in an abstracted way. His attention was focused solely on the woman at the opposite side of the room.

'And what about you, sweet wife?'

Zarek turned towards where Penny still sat at the far end of the table, an empty water glass gripped in a hand that was clenched rather too tight, with the knuckles of her fingers showing white.

'Wh—what about me?'

'Nothing to say?' he challenged.

'No…'

Nothing she could manage to get her thoughts under control enough to put into any sort of order, Penny told herself privately. Her head was still spinning, her mind totally unfocused. Now she knew exactly why the maid whose scream they had heard had reacted as she'd done, dropping the tray of coffee cups in shock at Zarek's unexpected and unbelievable appearance. In that first moment that he had walked through the door, Penny felt she might actually do the same and send the glass she held flying to the floor to shatter into a thousand tiny pieces, and it was only the polished surface of the table underneath it that saved it from destruction.

She had reacted on a violent sense of shock in the moment she had first seen him, half rising to her feet and then sinking back down again just as sharply, frozen in a whirling storm of complete disbelief, bewilderment and not knowing what to do. And just like the maid who had reacted so forcefully to Zarek's arrival home, she didn't know if she wanted to scream out loud in an ecstasy of joy or express a wild rush of fear at what she saw.

The first impulse—to get to her feet, dash towards him and fling herself straight into his arms—had barely formed when a sudden powerful blast of reality hit her in the face with the memory of how they had parted. The shock of it was what had had her staying in her seat when every yearning sense in her body wanted to drive her close to this man, to feel the warmth of his body, inhale the scent of his skin. She wanted to have his arms close around her, know their strength supporting her as they had done in the past.

But the terrible sense that she had no right to do that any more, not after what had happened, kept her fixed in her place. The fear that if she even tried then he would reject her with cold and hostile disdain weighted her down even more. She couldn't make herself move though her heart raced in confused excitement and her eyes were fixed in hungry yearning on the dark, lean—too lean, she noted in some distress—form of the man before her.

'There's nothing I want to say here.'

Because now it seemed as if just holding onto the tumbler was the only thing that was keeping her under control. As if the hard glass were some sort of lifeline that she was clinging onto in desperation and if she let go then the tidal wave of emotions that had been building up inside her all day would break loose and swamp her completely.

'I don't think we should discuss our private business in front of everyone.'

'No, you're right.' Zarek nodded unexpectedly. 'What we need to talk about is private and personal. We don't need to share.'

The last remark was made with pointed emphasis and an equally pointed flick of black, thickly lashed eyes in the direction of Jason and his mother and brother. The three members of the Michaelis family were lingering between Zarek and the door, clearly unsure as to what their next move should be. In public, before the other members of the meeting, they had needed to show a united front, to make it look as if they were delighted to see Zarek back and welcomed him unreservedly. That they were glad to have his hands back on the controls of Odysseus Shipping. But now, when everyone else had left, an uneasy calm descended on the room. An uneasiness that Zarek was aggravating by his comment about keeping things private.

'We all need to talk…'

It was Jason who put the words into the silence, the disquiet that Penny felt she could actually breathe in from the atmosphere.

'We need to know what happened…'

'And you will learn—in good time.'

Zarek spoke without taking his darkly burning gaze from Penny's face, the words almost tossed over his shoulder at his stepbrother. Jason was saying the things she should be saying. The words she couldn't find the strength or the courage to form on her tongue.

'But for now you will surely acknowledge that there are some things that are private between husband and wife and are not to be shared with anyone else?'

Was she deceiving herself, Penny wondered, or had that deep, slightly husky voice subtly emphasised that 'husband and wife' as if deliberately driving home the fact that here was something in which Jason's presence was not at all welcome? Staking a claim, so to speak, like some powerful wolf moving in to demonstrate possession of his mate, the wild hairs along his spine lifting in open challenge.

'Of course, but—'

'In good time,' Zarek repeated, reaching out a hand to the edge of the door and pulling it open wide, the meaning of his message clear. He wanted everyone out of here and Jason would be a fool to ignore the signs. They were dismissed and that was it.

But still he lingered, looking across at Penny, a question in his eyes.

'Penny?' he queried, appearing to check how she felt.

How *did* she feel? She supposed to some it would seem wonderful that her husband, this man who had been away missing for so long—who had once been believed to be dead—would lay claim to her like this. To them it might appear that he was still so ardently in love that he couldn't wait to be alone with his wife, to restore the links of their marriage, renew their relationship.

But recalling what had happened between them before he had left, the rifts that had opened up between them, dividing them from each other, she knew she couldn't see it that way at all. Oh, yes, Zarek wanted to be alone with her but for his own personal, darker reasons rather than any loving reunion. And she could only begin to guess at just what those reasons might actually be.

But, 'It's fine, Jason,' she said, exerting every ounce of control she could manage to keep her voice firm and even when inside her nerves were quailing at the thought of how far from fine everything was. 'Absolutely fine.'

Was there some light of approval in the flash of the dark eyes he turned in her direction? The niggling worry that there was also something else had her shifting in her seat, finding herself able to move at last. Her brain seemed to have started working again too, sending the message *Zarek is back*—Zarek is *back*!—into her thoughts in a mixture of wild delight and shuddering apprehension. What was she to think? Yes, Zarek was back—but just who was this man who had been missing for two years? And what had happened to him while he had been away?

Exactly who had come home to her?

CHAPTER FOUR

PENNY pushed herself to her feet as Jason, Hermione and Petros made their way out of the door, tight knots forming in her stomach at the thought of being alone with her husband for the first time in so long.

She had never felt like this before, not even in the very beginning when she had first known him and had become his bride so very soon after that. Then she had been fizzing with excitement, just waiting for everyone else to go and leave them alone so that she and Zarek could become truly man and wife.

She had been so sure then. Sure that he wanted her—that he loved her. After all, he'd married her, hadn't he? At barely twenty-two she had been so very young, so naïve in matters of the heart, and even more innocent of the force of physical desire. It was only later that bitter disillusionment had set in and she had come to realise that Zarek was more than capable of *wanting* without any sort of love.

The door was shut, everyone else was gone. Shifting from one foot to another, Penny nerved herself for whatever was to come. At least standing upright she felt better equipped to face him. She had always been considered too tall by most men, but never for Zarek Michaelis. Somewhere in his past family history there had been an ancestor—probably his Irish great-great-great-grandfather who was always referred to as The Giant—who had brought a gene for height into the family and Zarek had inherited that in maturity. Even at five feet ten, Penny had to tilt her head back slightly to meet his eyes.

'So now…' she said as he closed the door a little too firmly for her mental comfort. 'What…?'

But the words caught in her throat as if a knot had tied tight around them, preventing her from getting them out. She could only stand and stare as Zarek lifted a hand to the right side of his face, just by his temple, and rubbed at the skin as if something there was troubling him.

'Are you all right?' she questioned sharply. 'Is something wrong?'

When he didn't respond but simply stood, back stiff, shoulders tight, head turned away from her, she felt the rush of memory like a sort of stinging mental pins and needles flood into her mind.

Someone else had done just that. And not too long ago. The memory seemed to dance at the corners of her thoughts, slipping away whenever she tried to get a grip on it. But right now she had other, more important concerns on her mind.

'What is it? Zarek? Do you have a headache?'

Still he didn't answer but stood motionless as a statue so that she launched herself towards him, covering the short space between them in a matter of seconds and whirling round in front of him.

'Tell me what's wrong?'

Without pausing to think, she reacted instinctively, lifting her hand to cover his where it still lay against his face, pressing her fingers over his as she looked up into his dark, shuttered face, seeing the way his heavy lids had come down over the darkness of his eyes. Hiding them from her.

'Tell me!'

For the space of a couple of jerky heartbeats he didn't move a muscle, but then at last he shifted slightly, moving the weight of his body from one foot to another, and drew in his breath on a slow, deep sigh. The warmth of his flesh reached her through the fine cotton of his shirt and the movement brought a waft of a deeply sensual scent, the ozone from the sea, sunshine on skin, and underneath it all the warm, musky scent that was personal to Zarek alone.

And in a split second the mood of the moment had changed. Where there had been nerve-twisting apprehension there was suddenly a heart-stilling tension. In Penny's veins the blood seemed to pulse infinitely slowly, shockingly heavy. Her breath too seemed frozen, leaving her with her mouth slightly open, unable to inhale, unable to think.

All she was aware of was the feel of Zarek's skin under her fingers, the heat and the softness of it, with the power of muscle and bone beneath the supple flesh. It was as if sparks had flown from his skin to hers, holding her melded to him, unable to move.

And the burn along her nerves reminded her only too painfully of how it had once been between them. The way that she had never been able to resist his touch, his kiss. The way that her body was yearning for it, reaching towards him even now.

'Zarek…'

His name was just a whisper across lips that were suddenly parched and dry, her tongue seeming to tangle on the sound so that she had to swallow hard to ease the discomfort in her throat. 'Zarek…'

'No…' Zarek said, his eyes still closed against her, his voice rough and seeming slightly ragged at the edges. 'Don't…'

'Don't what?'

But then he opened his eyes and looked down into her face and she knew exactly what he meant. What exactly he did not want her to do.

He didn't want her to touch him. He was rejecting without words the feel of her hand on his, the connection of skin on skin. He didn't have to say a word; it was there in his face, in his eyes.

And that was when she realised just what a terrible mistake she had made. Impulse and concern had made her break through the barriers that she had felt between them. The barriers that she had erected in her mind in self-defence because of the need to protect herself from the shock of his sudden arrival, the memory of all that had been between them before he had left.

'So your wife is not allowed to touch you?'

'My wife… Were you ever truly my *wife*?'

His eyes burned into hers as he raised his other hand to fasten around her fingers, clasping them tightly under the warmth and roughness of his palm. And as he pulled at it, bringing it down and away from his face, the force of his hold made her wince as her fingers were squeezed together.

But a moment later the slight discomfort was forgotten as shock ricocheted through her thoughts, making her head spin.

'You!'

She spat the word at him as she fought for control, struggled with the need to lash out with the hand that was free or launch herself straight at him, pounding her fist on his chest.

'It was you!'

She had seen the long white line of the scar before but then it had gleamed in the cold burn of the moonlight, the only visible part of a face that had been hidden by a cap, the fall of long dark hair, a heavy beard. The last time she had seen that scar it had been on the face of the man she had believed was a fisherman.

'You were spying on me!'

The memories of the previous night, the recollection of Jason's arms around her, and the thought of those dark burning eyes watching her put a new tension into her voice.

'Spying?' Dark cynicism rang in Zarek's voice. 'That word implies that you have something to hide.'

'As opposed to you who was hiding from me.'

She shouldn't be doing this, Penny told herself. She shouldn't be taking the conversation down this route. What she should be doing was asking Zarek where he had been, what had happened to him. She should want to find out—she did want to find out—just how he had come by that dreadful scar and what had happened to him. But she couldn't make her mouth actually form the questions. Her tongue seemed to have frozen and her throat wouldn't work on those words. Instead she heard the provocative and aggressive words come out as a challenge.

The thought that he had come home earlier but had not let her know that he was alive burned in her heart. That he had hidden from her, watched her, waiting—for what?—for her to betray herself in some way, was like a knife twisting in the wound. She had once been convinced that when she knew that he was alive and well she would be so happy, and had even allowed herself to think they might just have a chance to start all over again.

And now this…

Did she need further proof that, whatever else had happened while he was away, nothing had changed his mind about their marriage? He still regarded her with suspicion, as someone who was not to be trusted. Not as the woman he had loved and missed. But then of course she had known that that was the case from the start.

'Don't you think that I had the right to find out just what had been happening while I was away?'

'You didn't want to see me? Ask me.'

Another of those darkly blazing looks told her that he didn't need to ask. That in his mind she was already tried and condemned without a chance of appeal.

'"I want to get away from here, start living again,"' he quoted cynically, leaving her in no doubt that he had heard every word of her talk with Jason. '"I'm tired of treading water."'

'You really shouldn't listen in to other people's conversations,' she flashed back, knowing with a sinking feeling in the pit of her stomach just how he would have interpreted it. 'Don't you know that it's a fact that eavesdroppers never hear good of themselves?'

'I'm sure that most never actually overhear their wife planning to have them declared dead.'

'You were dead! At least—I—we thought you were.'

'And that was how it suited you.'

His grip on her tightened as he spoke, crushing her fingers. But it was not the biting pressure that shocked her, rather the rush of wild electricity up her arm, tracking a burning pathway along her nerves that frightened her with its instant and shocking reaction. How could he still affect her in this way when deep inside she knew the truth about the coldness of his heart?

'I don't want this,' she managed, tensing her muscles against his hold, pulling herself away from him as far as she could while he still kept her hand prisoner.

She had to get away, to find some space and quiet in which to collect her thoughts and decide how to go forward.

'Let me go!'

If he reacted against her, if he held her tighter, pulled her close, then she did not know what she would do. The swirl of ambiguous feelings inside her head was like a tornado, throwing her off balance and leaving her unable to think.

'I said let me go!'

The speed with which he released her added to the sense of shock, making her sway and stumble, almost fall. But it was fear that he would come for her again that had her reeling away, grabbing out at a nearby chair for support.

'Don't come near me! I don't want you near me!'

Oh, you liar, you liar, her conscience reproached her bitterly. You weak, cowardly liar. She wanted nothing so much as his arms around her, his body close to hers, to hold her and comfort her, to warm her and melt away the hard core of ice that seemed to have formed at the centre of her heart.

But Zarek simply folded his arms across his broad chest and regarded her coldly through eyes that seemed to have been formed from burnished steel, polished so hard that they were opaque and closed off against her.

'Of course not,' he drawled with bitter cynicism. 'After all, you never really wanted me back.'

It was only what she'd told him. If you go, don't expect me to be waiting here when you come back. Bitter pain had made her lash out at the time, knowing she would rather die than have him realise just how much she had loved him when he had seen her only as a willing body to warm his bed—and a brood mare to conceive his child. But it still stung viciously to have her wild, unthinking words turned against her in this way.

'You've sprung this on me—appearing from the dead. I— need some time,' she managed, trying for appeasement but getting nowhere with it if the cold burn of his gaze was anything to go by. And the way those powerful arms were crossed tight over his chest was like a rigid shield, deflecting any appeal she might direct at him.

'Then take it.'

'What?'

With her own defences ready formed for battle, his sudden capitulation was so unexpected that it took all the defiance from her, leaving her limp as a deflated balloon.

'Take it.'

It was more of a command this time, snapped at her with contempt that was like a slap in the face. It seemed that he had had enough of baiting her, for now at least. That shocking, taunting mood seemed to have evaporated, leaving instead something that sounded disturbingly like a cynical weariness.

'If you need the time to adjust to the fact that the husband you hoped was dead—'

'Never *hoped*!'

She couldn't let that pass. No matter how terrible things had been between them, she had never once hoped he was no longer still alive. And she was appalled that he might even think so.

'How could I ever hope that?'

'Hoped was never coming back…' Zarek amended without even the tiniest amount of a concession in his tone. 'Then take that time. I know that I sprung my arrival on you and heaven knows I too need some space.'

It was like a slap in the face, making pain twist in her stomach. She felt as if the room were closing in on her, crushing the breath from her body, making her feel sick with distress. He had been back—what?—barely an hour, and already he wanted space—to escape from her.

'To accustom myself to being here again. It has been a long time.'

Something in his tone brought Penny up sharp, made her look at him more closely. Only now did she see the evidence of new lines about his nose and mouth, the tiniest flecks of grey in his hair at the temples. Evidence that hinted at the fact that his life hadn't been totally easy while he had been missing. She had forgotten everything that the counsellors had told them, the advice they had been given at the beginning of all this, when they had believed that Zarek might be found and might be on his way back to them before the end of the year.

Wherever he's been, they'd said, whatever has happened to him, he will need time and space to adjust. He was held hostage, his life was in danger. It was unlikely that he would be able to just walk into the house and take up his old life where he had left off.

The wave of reaction that swept over her at the thought made her feel sick and ashamed, a terrible sense of guilt pushing her into rash, unguarded words.

'I'm sorry—I should have thought—do you need anything—want anything? Have you eaten? A sandwich? Some coffee perhaps?'

She sounded like the most inexperienced and gauche hostess greeting a complete stranger for the very first time. And obviously Zarek thought so too from the way that his beautiful mouth twisted and his dark eyes gleamed with something dangerous and cruel. One long, tanned hand lifted in a flicking gesture of dismissal.

'No—nothing. If I need anything, I can find it for myself— or get one of the staff to see to it. I do still have the staff in the house, I take it?'

'Of course you do.'

Flinging the answer back at him, she emphasised the *you* so as to make sure he realised that she had heard and noted that arrogant *'I'*, which made it plain that he was back here in his role as owner of the villa, MD of Odysseus Shipping, lord of all he surveyed.

And her husband.

And what of her then? As his wife did she still have a place in this house? And for how long? While Zarek had been missing she had had a role to play, but now that he was back…

Did he even still want her as his wife?

'Then you have nothing to worry about.'

And with that she was dismissed. As if she needed the message rammed home he turned his back on her, walking across the room to stare out of the window, one hand pushed deep into his trouser pocket, the other lifting once again to press against the scar above his eye.

In the doorway, Penny paused, half turned back to him.

'Zarek…'

But his only response was an impatient gesture of his dark head, repulsing without hesitation the tentative approach.

'Go!' he said and it was a command she would be a fool to ignore. 'Just go.'

Well, what had she expected? Penny asked herself as reluctantly she turned away again and made herself move away, letting the door fall shut behind her.

Zarek Michaelis. Your absent husband. Home at last.

The mocking words he had tossed at her sounded in her head as she walked down the long, sunlit hall, heading for the stairs.

He was home, but it was obvious that nothing had changed. And because of that the wonderful joy and delight she should have been able to find in his return were totally missing. Zarek was back in body perhaps, but in his mind, and most of all in his heart, he was as lost to her as ever.

Perhaps more so. Because at least the Zarek who had gone away had put on a good pretence of being her husband when they were together. He had made it plain that in one sense at least—the sexual one—he wanted her.

He had wanted her in his arms, in his bed. He had barely been able to keep his hands off her and at least that way she had been able to get close to him. Able to keep him with her.

But that had been before the dreadful row they had had; now it seemed that even that had waned, taking with it the only chance she had of holding him.

'Don't,' he had said when she'd touched him. And he'd kept his eyes closed to reinforce the rejection in his words.

Zarek had only ever wanted her sexually, never loving her. He had hidden it in the past, but it seemed that he was no longer taking the trouble to hide anything any more. His cold dismissal of her just now proved that. Even that wanting seemed to have died in the time he had been away.

She had got him back from the dead and finally lost him for ever all in the same moment, it seemed.

CHAPTER FIVE

THE sound of Argus scratching at the door and whining to be let out was what woke Penny from the deep, dark sleep into which she had tumbled, how long later she had no idea. Night had fallen while she had dozed and the room was now in almost complete darkness, with only the glimmer of the moon coming through the cloud-hazed sky to throw any light onto things.

'Argus—no!'

The words came automatically, the result of so many other mornings being woken like this, and feeling afraid that Hermione would hear and be outraged both at being woken so early and the damage she would declare the dog was doing to the door.

'Stop that! Give me a minute and I'll…'

The words faded as she came more fully awake, sitting up on the bed and looking around her, her thoughts blurring as the truth of reality hit home.

It wasn't morning, she realised, it was evening. Late evening on the day that her life as she knew it had been turned upside down.

Late evening on the day that Zarek had come back from the dead.

'Zarek!'

Just the thought of him had her almost leaping from the big double bed, whirling round to stare at the side of it where, during the days of their marriage, Zarek had always slept. This was after all his bedroom, so wouldn't it be logical that he would come in here if he wanted to sleep? She had been so deeply unconscious that he could have come into the room, into the bed, and she wouldn't have noticed. She couldn't begin to decide if the shiver that ran down her spine at the thought was one of excitement or dread. How would she have felt if she had woken to find her husband lying beside her in their marriage bed?

'No!'

Shaking her head to drive the tormenting thoughts away, she pushed herself into action, hurrying across the room to open the door and let Argus out. Freed, the dog hurried off down the corridor, claws pattering on the polished wooden floor. The whole upper part of the house was in total darkness and she had to grope her way along before she could find a switch to bring some light to the place.

'Argus—wait…'

She should have checked the time before she'd left the room. Her watch was still on the bedside cabinet and she felt so disorientated that she had no idea how late in the night exactly. The last thing she wanted was to disturb the household and have Hermione and her sons descend on her, full of complaints.

And Zarek?

Once again her nerves twisted so sharply that she almost missed her footing and went tumbling down the wide, curving staircase. She had no idea where her husband was or what he might have been doing while she had been asleep. And not even knowing how long—hours, or just minutes—she had been away from him, she couldn't even start to guess.

She had never intended to fall asleep. The only thing she had wanted was some time to herself, in peace and quiet, to try to adjust to what had happened and to bring herself to some sort of acceptance of the way that her life had been turned totally upside down in just a few short minutes. But the way that Zarek had dismissed her, ordering her from the room with that aggressive movement of his head, had shaken her to the core. She had sunk down onto the soft surface of the bed with a sigh, then flung herself back against the pillow and closed her eyes, meaning to force herself to try and think...

But the images that had floated across the screen of her eyelids had made any sort of rational thought impossible. All that she saw was a stream of snapshots of Zarek, the man she had adored, had loved to call her husband, in the days before the terrible realisation that she had never truly been the wife of his heart. Her mind had taken her back to their wedding day, not quite three years before, when she had walked down the aisle towards where he stood by the altar, tall and proud, devastatingly handsome—and totally secure in his own skin.

She hadn't been able to believe that this man had even noticed the insignificant junior secretary in the import and export business that worked so often with Odysseus Shipping, let alone asked her to marry him. And that he was here, now, prepared to go through with the ceremony. Only the previous night, for the first time since their engagement, he had let slip the cool, courteous mask that he wore when he was with her, and had finally revealed a burningly sensual, fiercely passionate man underneath.

That night had shown her that Zarek did at least want her with a desire that had stunned her. A heated hunger in which the words cold and rational had no place at all. And then she had been happy to give herself to him because she had believed she really was loved. It was only later, when she had come to know the truth, that she had started to withdraw from him.

Remembering it again now, Penny felt her legs tremble beneath her and she had to grab at the banisters for support. She'd fallen asleep on the memories of her wedding night and as a result her dreams had been filled with wild, erotic fantasies that had had her tossing and turning in the throes of burning need.

She hadn't felt like that since the first lonely time when Zarek had left for the test voyage for his yacht, the *Troy*, walking out on her in anger, to give her time to think, he had said, to get her head together. And then later, when he had been declared missing, and when she had believed he was never coming home. The yearning hunger, the aching need—the physical need, at least—had slowly subsided over the last year, but it seemed that all Zarek had to do was to walk into a room and once again she was swamped by a tidal wave of need, one that had hit her with its full strength in the moment that she had touched him, and that now had sent disturbing echoes through her dreams.

But Zarek had clearly not felt the same.

'*No,*' he had said. Just a single word. But there had been such total rejection in his tone, and in the coldly burning look that had accompanied it, that she could have been in no doubt that total rejection was what he meant. And rejection was all he felt. Even the burning passion that had once flared between them had gone now, dying as a result of whatever had happened in the years he had been away.

But would it have been any different if the hijack had never taken place? If he'd come back three days later as had been planned. Penny felt as if something cold and nasty had just slid down her spine at the thought. Zarek had married her because he wanted a child, an heir who would ensure that Odysseus Shipping stayed in the family and there was no risk that it would ever come under the control of his stepmother and brothers.

The ground floor of the villa was in total darkness too, still and silent as if everyone had left, abandoning the place. But going where?

And where was Zarek? Would he have actually left, so very soon after arriving home again? A cold hand seemed to squeeze at her heart at the thought that he might just walk out and never come back again. Simply leaving her with the knowledge that he was alive and so was their marriage. But a marriage that it seemed he did not want any more.

'Zarek?'

Uncertainty made her voice wobble as she called out into the darkness.

'Anyone there?'

A deep bark startled her, making her jump as Argus suddenly lifted his head and pointed his narrow black nose in the direction of the garden room. Another bark, shorter and sharper this time, before the dog took off at speed towards the scent or the sound that he had detected. Not for Argus the indecision and hesitation that came from not knowing what his reception would be. He was totally sure of his welcome and he bounded through the partly open door, his joy and excitement evident in every movement.

But then Argus had it exactly right, Penny reflected, following the big dog at a much slower pace. Zarek would of course be overjoyed to see him.

'Argus!'

The delight in Zarek's deep voice reinforced her belief that he would be more than happy to see his hound and prepared Penny for what she would see as she went into the room herself.

The moon was shining through the big patio doors that were open to the sight of the gleaming waves that swayed and tossed between the cliffs and the horizon, the sound of them breaking against the rocks on the shore. Zarek sat in a wide comfortable armchair just inside the room, his face, his whole body, in shadow.

'Argus!' he said again, slapping one hand against his thigh to call the dog to him. A moment later he was cradling the animal's big black and white head in both his palms, rubbing the rough fur and crooning softly in low-toned Greek. And Argus, instead of bounding round his master in overwhelming joy at his return, as she had expected, simply gave himself up to the bliss of being reunited. His eyes closed and the only thing that moved was his big tail that was wagging furiously.

It was foolish to be jealous of a dog, Penny told herself. But at the same time she couldn't help envying the hound's simple pleasure in the moment. And his total confidence that he would be welcome, that Zarek would be as delighted to see him as he was to see his master.

It would all have been so much easier if she could have run straight into her husband's arms in the moment that he had first walked into the room. But of course Argus had endured none of the distance, the arguments, the stand up fights that had marred the days before Zarek's departure. He was loved for what he was, not given house room simply because of what Zarek wanted from him. And, besides, he was happy to acknowledge the man as his master and to obey his every command.

Penny couldn't help feeling that if, like the dog, she had come when called, or at the slap of a hand against a thigh, then things might not be so tense and awkward. Instead they were like two opposing armies, facing a stand-off, waiting for the instruction either to attack or stand down. And she didn't know which one was most likely.

But how she longed to hear the gentleness in her husband's voice that he now directed towards the hound, or to feel his hands on her, stroking, caressing as they were moving over the animal's big head and down his long back.

'You kept the dog.' Zarek's voice broke into her uncomfortable thoughts, making her start slightly, lifting her eyes from the dog's black and white head to look into her husband's face. Not that she could see anything of Zarek's expression. The darkness of the shadows by the wall was too intense, hiding everything.

'Of course I kept him,' she managed stiffly. 'What else did you think I'd do?'

'He wasn't your pet. And you were never that much of a dog person.'

'No. But of course I kept him at the beginning when we still thought that you might come back.'

She wasn't yet going to admit that at the beginning the dog and his needs had seemed to be the only things that had kept her going. That the reason he slept on her bed was because she hadn't been able to sleep alone and that most nights she had wept into the dog's shaggy fur. Zarek might never have loved her but she had loved him and the thought that he was lost or dead had torn at her already wounded heart.

'Besides, he pined for you so I had to look after him—and after that Argus and I—came to an understanding.'

'Thank you for that.'

Zarek's strong fingers were still buried in the rough fur, Argus' head on his knee, the dog looking up into his master's face with such blind devotion that she felt tears sting at her eyes. Once she had felt like that, hungry for Zarek's attention, desperate for any casual word that fell from his lips, any caress he offered her. But that had been before she had realised that she was only ever second best and that the man she loved didn't feel the same way about her.

'It's very dark in here,' she said abruptly, needing to break the mood.

Swinging away, she searched for the light switch, found it. Her fingers were on it when Zarek spoke sharply from behind her.

'Don't!' It was a command not a request but a moment later he softened it slightly by adding, 'I always loved the sight of the moonlight on the waves. I missed it.'

This was her cue to ask where he'd been while he'd missed the sea, but even as she opened her mouth to do so her nerves failed her. She was manoeuvring in the dark, both physically and mentally, and she was having to grope her way slowly through the shadows, trying to find some sort of a path that would help her.

'Whatever you want.'

She moved to a chair opposite him. At least this way the light from the moon gave her some hope of being able to read the expressions on his face.

'What time is it?'

'Around eight.'

Zarek didn't even trouble to glance at his watch. It seemed that the hour was a matter of total indifference to him. He couldn't care less if it was night or day.

'So late?'

How had she come to sleep so long? Was it the exhaustion after the stress of the day? Or the rush of relief at knowing that Zarek was home. That he was safe. She still couldn't quite absorb the fact for all that she was sitting looking at him with the sound of his voice in her ears, the scent of his skin reaching her nostrils. Her fingers itched to reach out and touch, to reassure herself that he was real. To feel the warmth of his flesh under her hands. But the fear of how he might react held her back.

She didn't feel she could take another of those cold-eyed rejections. Not now with what seemed like several layers of her skin flayed away, leaving her nerves raw and exposed.

'Where is everyone?' she asked to distract herself.

Normally at this time the staff were busy preparing the evening meal. The family would meet for drinks before dinner. But of course there was no way that this was any sort of an ordinary day.

'Gone.'

'Gone where?'

Zarek's shrug dismissed the question as unimportant.

'Home—or wherever they spend their evenings.'

'Everyone?'

This time his only response was a curt nod.

'Even Jason—and Hermione?' Penny found it hard to believe that Hermione would relinquish her place in the family home after she had been so determined to move in.

'Even Jason—and especially Hermione.' Zarek didn't give either of the names any particular emphasis but all the same it seemed to Penny that they had a dark underlining to his tone.

'How did you persuade Hermione to leave?'

She hadn't been able to achieve that herself in almost two years, even when she had asked Zarek's stepmother point blank to go. Since then Hermione had been a constant, nagging presence, critical of everything she did.

'If she wanted to keep the generous allowance she receives

from Odysseus Shipping then there was no argument.' The cynicism that twisted Zarek's mouth sounded darkly in his voice. 'She was very easily persuaded.'

'So there's no one here?'

Was that slight shake in her voice apprehension, relief, or even a strange sort of anticipation? Penny couldn't begin to decide for herself and, from the faint frown that she saw draw Zarek's dark brows together so briefly, neither could he.

'No one but us—and Argus.'

Zarek moved at last, getting to his feet to open the big glass doors to the garden so that the dog could go outside. Once again Penny felt an affinity with the hound as he padded reluctantly forward, obviously needing to get outside, but wanting to be sure that Zarek would not disappear again if he turned his back. Did she look at him like that? she wondered. Could the sense of disbelief, the fear that it might all be an illusion after all, show in her eyes when she watched him?

'But why?'

'I thought we had a lot of catching up to do. We need to talk. And that we would do it better if we were on our own.'

'Oh.'

It was all she could manage, and the gulp as she swallowed down the word gave away more than she was at all comfortable with.

Zarek turned from the door, leaning back against the wall and pushing his hands deep into the pockets of his trousers. Penny knew it wasn't possible but he really did seem to have grown bigger in the last few moments—taller and stronger and darker. And definitely more dangerous, with that ominous 'we need to talk' sounding like a warning bell for what was coming next.

CHAPTER SIX

SHE WOULD HAVE LIKED to have got to her feet. At least then, standing up, she would have been more on a level with him. But she would also betray her discomfort, scrambling to her feet like a frightened child, and moving uncomfortably from one foot to another.

'Don't you think you should eat first?'

That at least would give her an excuse to get up from her chair. And if she could spend some time on practicalities like preparing food in the big kitchen then it would be a distraction from his threatening presence, the discomfort of being here like this with a man she knew so well in some ways and yet who was a total stranger in others.

'I'm not hungry.'

It was a dismissal of what he had recognised as her attempt at diversion, she knew. He had no intention of being dissuaded from the path he was determined to follow.

'Though I wouldn't mind a drink,' Zarek conceded.

'Of course…'

She was on her feet and turning towards the dresser where the wine was kept when the foolishness of her actions hit home. This was Zarek's home after all.

'No, I haven't forgotten,' Zarek murmured dryly seeing her

hesitation, the embarrassed look she turned on him. 'Two years is not so very long.'

'It seemed long enough!' Her temper flared again, setting her off balance once more. 'No sign of you, no word from you. I didn't know what had happened—'

'I was hardly in a position to give you a phone call,' Zarek cut across her, breaking into the flow of reproach like the slash of a knife. 'How did Hermione end up living here? Did you invite her to move in?'

'No, I did not! She invited herself and wouldn't take no for an answer. Have you ever tried to get your stepmother to do something she didn't want to do?'

'As a matter of fact I have.'

Zarek expertly removed the cork from a bottle of rich red wine and poured a generous amount into a couple of glasses.

'Well, I don't happen to have the promise of a generous income—or the threat of withholding one—to dangle over her head like a carrot. Hermione arrived when the news of your disappearance had just broken—I didn't know what to do for the best. I thought it might after all be an idea if we were all in one place until we found out just what had happened.'

And she had been reeling in shock and distress. It didn't matter how she and her husband had parted, learning that his yacht had been hijacked by pirates and Zarek himself taken hostage had left her unable to think straight, so that she hadn't had the strength to fight Hermione over anything.

'And Jason…'

Something in the way that Zarek reacted—or, rather, his complete lack of reaction—sent her a warning signal that she was entering dangerous territory. She knew what Zarek had seen and heard on the harbour front only the day before. Her husband might not love her but he was her husband and a traditionally possessive, jealous Greek husband at that. He would not take at all kindly to seeing his wife in the arms of another man. Particularly if that man was his hated stepbrother.

'And Jason...' Zarek prompted almost casually, holding out one of the glasses of wine towards her. Because of the darkness in the room, she couldn't read his face properly but the stiffness of his long spine, a clipped edge to his use of his stepbrother's name, made all the little hairs on the back of her neck lift in wary apprehension.

'Jason dealt with all the practical things—liaising with the police, the press. He was very—helpful.'

Besides, Jason had been kind and considerate then and his support had been welcome at a time when she most needed it.

'Good for Jason.'

It was impossible to interpret the strange note in Zarek's voice as he lifted his glass to his mouth and took a deliberate sip of the wine. But Penny didn't care what his mood was. If there was any doubt in his mind about what he had seen then it was time she made things perfectly clear. His opinion of her was low enough as it was. She didn't want to add any further complications to the already explosive mix.

'We're not lovers,' she said starkly and saw his head come up very slightly, though he controlled the movement almost at once.

'Did I say anything?'

'No—but you're thinking it.'

'Oh, is that what I'm thinking?'

Another slow deliberate sip of his wine, but, watching him, Penny saw how long it took him to swallow it. The burn of his eyes challenged her with the fact that he could have been thinking something else entirely but she wasn't yet ready to go there. Better to clear the air with the things she could deal with here and now rather than rake up old problems and risk ripping open old wounds.

That would have to come, but it was early days yet—not even days! She was still feeling her way with this man who was her husband and yet, after the time he had been missing, now seemed like a stranger to her. She knew his face, his stunning features, his voice, his mannerisms. But was the Zarek she had married, the Zarek she had been intimate with, made love with—no, no—the man she had had sex with—still inside this façade that was so well known and yet somehow totally unfamiliar to her? For now she would do better to stay on safer ground. If Zarek's detested brother could ever be considered safer.

'I know how it might have looked to you, but if you'd stayed around last night then you'd have seen how I pushed him away.'

'Forgive me—' the twist to Zarek's mouth, the cynical emphasis to the words made them anything other than a genuine apology '—but I was still trying to absorb the fact that my wife wanted me declared dead.'

'Not wanted. It was the only practical thing to do.'

'And of course you have been carefully planning the most practical way of dealing with things. With Jason's help.'

'I needed someone's help.'

Penny drank some of her own wine, feeling the rich red liquid burn its way down her throat. The kick of the alcohol entering her blood gave an added spark to the volatile cauldron of emotions bubbling inside her. Sick and tired of managing in the dark—in all ways—she ignored Zarek's previous command and moved to click on the nearest lamp, flooding the room with light before swinging round to face him with a challenge.

'And as you said, *you* were hardly in a position to do anything.'

She was not sure if the light was now helping or actually making matters worse. Yes, she could see Zarek's expression, but did she really want to know just how intent his eyes were on her face? Did she want to look into their dark depths and see the burn of suspicion, the coldness of contempt? And in the light her eyes were once more drawn to the ugly scar that marked his temple, twisting and distorting the beautiful bronzed skin.

Impulsively her free hand lifted again, needing to touch it, to touch him. She wanted to reassure herself that he truly was real, and at the same time she had a crazy, irrational need to smooth her fingers over that scar as if by doing so she could ease the long-ago pain the wound must have caused him.

But something that flared deep in those stunning eyes had her wrenching her hand down again, clenching it into a fist at her side. She took another swift, snatching drink of wine to bolster her courage.

'What did happen to you?' she asked brusquely, not having enough self-control to try and think of some more careful way of phrasing the question. 'We were told you were—dead.'

'You heard about the pirates?' Zarek asked, moving to the open patio doors where he leaned against the wall and looked out into the garden, watching Argus, who was happily investigating something that clearly smelled very appealing.

Penny nodded.

'I found it hard to believe at first. It doesn't sound at all twenty-first century. But since you were taken, there have been several other ships that have been boarded by pirates. We saw the reports on the television—saw the pirates get into that small boat and leave the yacht. But at the time we didn't know that you were with them—that they'd taken you hostage.'

'No one knew.'

Zarek sipped at his wine again, staring out into the moonlit garden, his attention, his focus, seeming to be totally elsewhere. In an absent-minded gesture he lifted his free hand and rubbed at the ugly scar on his temple, making her shiver in distress at the thought of how he had come by it. She hated to see the evidence of that hurt, was saddened by the way that it marred the male beauty of his face. But, at the same time, in some way it only added to rather than detracted from the powerful impact of his forceful features.

'The small boat they tried to get away in was covered so the troops who were going to board the ship couldn't see inside. It was pitch black in there—foul.'

With another swallow of his wine, Zarek frowned at the gleaming path the moonlight made along the sea.

'They were all nervous, panicking—possibly high on something…'

Penny found that the glass she held was shaking violently as her hand trembled in reaction to the stark, matter of fact way he was reporting the story. He might have been talking about someone else entirely—or recounting a story he had heard. She could only imagine with horror how it had felt to be in that situation. To be trapped in that small, dark boat, bobbing on the expanse of the ocean in the middle of the night, with a group of pirates who were all out of control and even more dangerous as a result.

And the last memory he would have had of her was of the angry, lying words, she had flung at him before he had left for the *Troy*.

'They were arguing amongst themselves. Some of them wanted to use me as a hostage—to try and get a ransom out of the company at least.'

With an effort Penny tried to raise her glass to her lips.

Perhaps a taste of wine might calm her nerves, reduce the sense of revulsion she felt at the thought of Zarek being trapped in that situation. But her hand was shaking even more, so that she couldn't manage it.

'And then when the shooting started all hell broke out.'

'Oh, my—'

Zarek's head swung round as Penny finally lost her grip on her feelings and slammed down her drink on the nearest window sill, crashing it against the window.

'Penny?'

'They said…'

Her throat closed over the words, refusing to let them out, and her eyes were wild as she looked into his dark gaze. Swallowing hard, she tried again.

'They said—he said—that he p-put—'

It was unbearable to think of the words, let alone say them. And even with Zarek standing there before her, whole and safe, making a lie of the pirate leader's claim, she still found the idea too horrific to contemplate.

'He said that he put a bullet in you—your head.'

Burning tears were swirling in her eyes, blurring her vision, but she recognised rather than saw the now-familiar gesture as he rubbed at the scar once more. And the thought of how he had come by it made her dig her teeth in hard to her lower lip to hold back the moan of distress that almost escaped her.

'Then he gave himself rather too much credit.' Zarek's voice seemed to come from a long way away. 'And exaggerated his success. He might have planned to do that but the truth is that he missed. His aim was off. The bullet grazed my head and knocked me flying—out of the boat and into the sea. Penny?'

His question was sharp, urgent, his tone changing completely. And suddenly he was right beside her, having moved up close, his powerful body almost touching hers as he stared down into her face. And when Penny ducked her head to dodge that searing, probing gaze, he dumped his wine glass down beside hers and put a strong warm hand under her chin, lifting her face towards his.

'What's this?'

It was impossible to resist his control as he turned her face to the left, into the light, and she could sense the frown that drew his dark straight brows sharply together.

'What's this?' he demanded again, his voice rougher now and his accent deepening on the hard-toned question. 'Tears?'

Penny fought to twist her chin away from his forceful hold, to hide her betraying expression. But finding she wasn't strong enough, instead she lifted a shaking hand to dash roughly at her eyes, brushing the moisture from her lashes.

'Yes, tears,' she flung at him furiously, determined to face it out now.

Of course he hadn't expected tears. They had never had that sort of a marriage—at least not in Zarek's mind. And the bitterness of that bit so deep that she was almost out of her head with the agony.

'And what's so shocking about that, hmm? What did you expect? Laughter? Three cheers?'

'You would have cared?' He actually sounded stunned.

'Of course I would have cared! And not just "cared" in the past but still care now! I might not want to be married to you any more, but I sure as hell would never, ever have wished you *dead*!'

The last word came out on a choking gasp. One that was as much from the sensual shock of realising just how close he was now as from the anguish that came with the memory

of how it had been when she had really thought that he had
died in the pirate attack.

'So you thought of me once or twice in the time I was away?'

'Yes, I thought of you! We might not have had a marriage
worth saving but there were—things—about you that I—
that I missed…'

Her throat dried in a sudden rush of heat as she foolishly
looked up on those words and met the burning fire of his gaze.
Her heart skipped a beat then lurched into a rapid, thudding
rhythm that was almost painful as it slammed against the
sides of her ribcage, sending the blood pounding through her
veins, pulsing round her head.

How could something so dark blaze so fiercely? she
wondered as she felt herself come close to melting in the intensity of his eyes. The effect was doubled, strengthened all
the more because it met with exactly the same feeling inside
her own body. The same hotly yearning hunger. The aching
need that drove all rational thought from her mind and left just
a burn of molten desire.

'Penny…' Zarek said slowly and his voice was ragged at
the edges so that she knew the need that had her in its grip
had taken hold of him too.

So what had happened to that cold command of 'Don't'?
There was no rejection, no distance in the look he turned on
her. It was pure fire and lightning, searing where it landed.
And it landed on her hair, then on her eyes, then burned across
her mouth so that she opened her lips in a gasp of much-
needed air.

And then forgot to breathe at all as Zarek reached out his
hand and touched her cheek. Still holding her eyes locked with
his, he let his fingers trail down to the side of her jaw, following the line of the bone until his touch reached her still-open

mouth. His thumb rested on the lower lip, pulling it down very slightly, very softly. And she couldn't resist the temptation to slide out her tongue to taste it, taking the essence of his skin into her mouth as she did so.

Which immediately made her want more. Her breasts felt tight against the lace of her bra, her skin seemed to ache for the touch of his hands and she knew that her eyes were heavy-lidded and sensual, her pupils dark, telegraphing her feelings without the need for words.

But of course Zarek had no use for words. Even after two years apart, his senses were totally attuned to the signals she was unable to control. She saw his body still, the tension in the long muscles communicating a need that was like a visible force, reaching out to enclose her. His fierce, unblinking eyes were black as night, his touch on her face a brand that marked her out as his, and the hiss of his breath in between his lips was a sound that seemed to shiver all the way down her spine as she heard it.

'I missed things too,' he murmured, low and rough. '*Mou elipses*—I missed you—but most of all I missed this...'

And his head bent to take her mouth with his.

CHAPTER SEVEN

SHE had forgotten the sensation of drowning, Penny thought hazily as Zarek's mouth closed over hers, the heat and hardness of his kiss making her senses swim. She had forgotten how it felt as if a dark wave of sensuality was breaking over her head, taking her down into the depths of passion where she lost her last grip on control, gave herself up to the sensation that possessed her.

One touch of Zarek's mouth on hers and she was once more the naïve young virgin he had first taken to bed, at the mercy of her hunger for him. A hunger that no other man had ever been able to awaken in her. And waking up was what it felt like. Waking from a deep dark sleep in which there had been no sensation, no light, no warmth, no joy.

Now she was flooded with heat and hunger, a sensation of coming back to life and seeing the glory of delight that was possible.

Her head fell back under Zarek's kiss, her hands going up to clutch at his arms, hold him near to her. Her lips opened under the pressure of his and she felt the heated, sensual slide of his tongue as he invaded the moist interior of her mouth. No amount of wine could have more of a head-spinning effect than the taste of him, no tantalising appetiser could stir her appetites as swiftly and as powerfully as it did.

'I have missed this,' Zarek muttered again, his voice thick and raw, his accent deep on every word. 'Missed it and thought about it so often at night. Longed for it. Hungered for it.'

He had gathered her up into his arms, crushing her tight against the heat and hardness of his body. Her head was pressed to his chest, feeling the wall of his ribcage under the soft cotton of his shirt. The race of his heart was like thunder in her ears and at the base of his strong neck she could see the heavy pulse that gave away how fiercely he was aroused. The force of his response sparked off an answering reaction in her own body. Moist heat pooled between her legs, in intimate evidence of the hunger he made her feel so easily.

'Zarek…'

His name felt strange on her tongue even though she'd used it before in the time since his sudden shocking arrival back in her life. But then it had been just a sound of shock. Now she was using it as a term of endearment, a recognition of something special, the name of her husband.

The man who had had the right to touch her as he was doing now. To stroke his hands over the shape of her body, sliding down her back, fingers tracing the line of her spine, until they splayed out over her hips, curved over the swell of her buttocks to press her even closer to him. His hips cradled her pelvis, the heat and swell of his erection hard against the softness of her feminine mound. Acting purely instinctively, she moved seductively against him, brushing against his arousal and hearing him groan low in his throat.

'*Gineka mou, gineka mou…Ise panemorfi.* You are so beautiful,' Zarek translated his muttered Greek, obviously needing her to understand.

Penny snatched in a shaken breath on a sound that even she was not quite sure whether it was a tremulous laugh, a gasp, or even an uncontrollable sob of response.

'I know. I know.' She whispered the words against his lips. 'You told me, remember?'

They had been some of the first words in his language that he had ever taught her.

Gineka mou…my wife. *Ise panemorfi.* You are so very beautiful.

And he had spoken them to her on their wedding day. Murmured them to her as they lay in bed. Whispered them in her ear as he took possession of her body for the very first time, took her virginity and made her his completely. And finally he had cried them aloud, in the heat of his passion and the throes of his climax as the thundering orgasm took them both right over the edge of the world, it had seemed, and out to spin in the wilds of uncharted space beyond.

At the time she had had no idea of what sexual fulfilment could possibly mean. She had dreamed and fantasised of course, yearned for Zarek's kiss, his touch. But she had had no concept of just how powerful a force of need could overwhelm her, the ecstasies that were within her reach when she abandoned herself to the skilled and knowing touch of her forcefully passionate lover. She only knew that she had given herself to him happily and willingly because she loved and had believed herself to be loved. She had thought that that was what made the difference.

Ten months of marriage had taught her all she needed to know. Ten months of marriage had given her time to learn, to discover her own latent sexuality and find herself as a sensual woman. A woman whose needs and desires were as hot and responsive as the man who made love to her each night.

And those needs, those hungers now rushed to the surface in a surge of demanding, stinging need in response to the caresses, the kisses of the man who had taught her everything she knew. Her one, her only lover.

She'd missed these sensations, missed him, and she couldn't hold back the ardent response that shuddered through her as she gave herself up to them for the first time in so long—far too long.

Zarek's hands were at her breasts, cupping their soft weight through the fine material of her clothing, making her moan aloud in a sound of hunger that she could just not hold back. It was not enough. She needed more. She needed the full sensation of his caress against her skin and she almost felt that she would have torn open the front of her dress to give him access if he didn't give her what she wanted.

But at the same time she wanted to use her hands to unfasten his clothing too. To wrench the buttons of his shirt from their fastenings, strip the fine cotton from his powerful torso, expose the muscled lines of his chest and shoulders to her hungry touch, her seeking mouth.

And Zarek was there ahead of her anyway. He needed no urging, no impatient encouragement as he used his mouth to ease the delicate straps of her green dress aside, fastening his teeth on one and tugging it down and over her shoulders. At the same time his hands were busy with the front of the garment, sliding it down over her straining, aching breasts to expose the creamy curves, the pink, tightly budded nipples that curled and hardened even more under the arousing caress of his knowing hands.

'Oh, Zarek…'

This time his name was a long, sighing cadence of delight as his thumbs swept over the swollen tips. The rough caress

sent burning arrows of pure pleasure along every nerve
pathway to centre in the most feminine core of her being,
where they piled further hunger, built even more need on the
yearning that was already driving her to total distraction.
She couldn't take much more of this, couldn't take any
more…the thought was like a beating refrain inside her head,
making her feel as if her mind would blow apart if she was
subjected to this onslaught of sensation for very much longer.
She couldn't take much more and stay in one piece and yet
she knew that if Zarek so much as considered stopping then
she would disintegrate, would fall into pieces in a totally different way.

'I want you…'

She wasn't sure which one of them said the words first. The
truth was that the declaration was torn from both of them in
almost the same moment so that the rough-voiced assertion
sounded as if there hadn't been two single people speaking it
but one of them as a whole, both male and female proclaim-
ing the overwhelming primal need that had them in its grip.

'I want you…' Penny managed again, her low, shaken
voice sounding like an echo that had fallen from the very first
pronouncement and was now fading away into a broken
whisper, almost drowned out by the crash of the waves against
the cliffs beyond the open door. 'I want you.'

'And you shall have me,' was Zarek's ardent response as
he lifted her from the floor, swinging her up into his arms and
carrying her swiftly from the room.

The hallway and stairs were still in almost total darkness
but Zarek seemed to have eyes like a cat so that he didn't
hesitate for a moment but strode swiftly up the stairs, even
taking them two at a time at one point, in his haste to reach
their bedroom. Kicking open the door, he hurried her across

to the bed where he tumbled her down on the covers, coming down beside her in an instant.

'*Ise panemorfi...Ise panemorfi.*'

He was muttering the phrase over and over again, punctuating each word with a kiss on a different part of her exposed body. Her face, her shoulders, her arms, down the slopes of her breasts. And then, at last, at long, long last, his mouth closed, hot and hungry, over one tight nipple. Sharp teeth scraped it so gently for a moment, before he suckled hard to relieve the tiny pain, making her arch against him with a low, wordless cry of pleasure.

'Z-Zarek...'

His name was all she could manage as any thought and the ability to find coherent words were obliterated by the sheer force of the sensual storm that took her. Acting blind, she had managed to pull open his shirt, tug it part way off his shoulders, so that at least her hands could explore the warm, tight contours of his chest, tangle in the rough haze of black body hair that tickled her palms, curled around her fingertips.

Zarek's hands were dealing with her dress, taking it down further at the front, tugging it up at the skirt to expose her legs, the plain white knickers that were now her only covering apart from the band of bunched material at her waist. And they didn't last for long under the determined assault of those powerful hands that tore them apart as if they had been made of nothing more substantial than tissue paper.

She had barely time to gasp in shocked excitement when those wicked fingers, gentler now, were stroking through the dark curls he had exposed, finding the moist cleft between her legs, the tiny bud that pulsed with hungry need.

She was so aroused that the first intimate touch of his hand on her had her crying out and throwing her head back against the pillows, her eyes closed so that she could focus on the shock waves of pleasure that rocked her world.

'I missed this…' Zarek's rough mutter close to her ear echoed her own private thoughts and all the time that knowing hand teased and tormented her, building the desire to the point where it almost broke her, then easing back to take her away from the edge just for a moment. 'And I know you did too. Missed what we had together…'

Penny had no idea where the sudden change of mood came from. The abrupt and totally unexpected switch from blind and greedy passion to a new and very different frame of mind, one that shocked her out of the heated sense of oblivion into which she had fallen. It was as if someone had suddenly opened a window, letting in an icy rush of cold night air that feathered over her exposed skin, cooling her blood and making her shiver in shocked response. As if a cold, cruel voice had spoken out of the blue, and the words she heard inside her head had the force of a slap in the face, jolting her back to bitter reality with a rush.

Missed what we had…

Missed what we had…

And what had they had? Blazing passion, true—a burning physical desire that had blinded her to everything else. But nothing more. There had been nothing between them but sex. At least on Zarek's part.

And was she going to let him just walk back into her life— and into her bed again—without so much as an argument? When Zarek had left for the *Troy* she had known that she had never meant her wild and hurting threats that she would not wait for him. She'd told herself that if she stayed, then when he returned she had to stand up to him. That there had to be more to make this marriage work, her love alone wasn't enough to sustain it, and something was going to have to change.

Two years was a much, much longer wait than the few days she had been expecting, but her resolve needed to still be so much the same. More so if she was to be able to survive as Zarek's wife ever again.

Nothing would change if she gave in at the first kiss, the first caress.

'Zarek…' She tried to speak but it seemed that all strength had drained from her voice and nothing audible came out.

'*Gineka mou…*'

Zarek had no such trouble and as he pressed his mouth against her breast again his words were perfectly audible. As was the darkly possessive note in them.

*Gineka mou…*My wife.

He was staking his claim on her once more, using sex to do so. That was how he'd won her, how he'd held her blind and deceived for the first six months of their marriage. But then she'd learned the truth…

'No!'

This time she had no trouble in making herself heard. The cry of rejection was loud and clear, echoing round the empty house. In the same moment she tried to push at Zarek, push him away from her. Free herself from his possessive and dangerously enticing hold. His hands still caressed, his mouth pursed to press another kiss against her breast and she could feel the hot, moist touch of his tongue against her skin. Another moment and she would be lost again. Already she could feel the tidal waves of dark desire sweeping over her, threatening to drown out the frantic voice of sanity and self-preservation.

'I said *no!*'

With urgent, desperate hands, she pushed at him but he was too big, his powerful body too heavy for her attempts to move him. So throwing caution to the wind she resorted to desperate measures. Reaching out, she grabbed a handful of his black hair—two—twisted her fingers in it, refusing to let herself think about the silky slide of it in her grip, and tugged. Hard.

'*Gamoto!*'

She didn't have to know much Greek to understand that Zarek's violent explosion of sound was definitely a swear word. She only had to see the way his head came up, his eyes flaring sharply.

'What the…?'

'I said no!'

Surprise gave her an advantage she hadn't expected and with a frantic wriggle, another push, she was free of his confining weight, out of the bed and thudding onto the floor. Panic carried her halfway across the room, almost falling as she struggled to keep her balance and get as far away from him as possible so that he couldn't reach out and grab her, use his superior strength to hold her, keep her prisoner.

'What the hell…?'

If Zarek's eyes had been sparking irritation before, now they were positively incandescent. They burned with fury, turning a look on her that she felt really should have shrivelled her into a pile of dust where she stood, silhouetted against the window, the moonlight lighting her from behind.

'You…'

Zarek stopped abruptly, clearly fighting to bring himself under control. With an effort he drew in a long harsh breath between his gritted teeth and raked an angry hand through his hair, sweeping it back from his forehead so that the harsh white line of the cruel scar showed up so much more clearly in stark relief.

'What the hell is this?' he demanded again, his words

falling ragged and raw into the shocked stillness of the night.
'What sort of game—?'

'No game!' Penny put in frantically, suddenly terribly
afraid that he might still consider this some risky sort of
foreplay, designed to heighten anticipation, increase appetite,
and decide to go along with what he thought she wanted.

She had had a narrow enough escape as it was, barely
managing to escape before the dark seas of need had closed
over her head completely, drowning her for ever. If he
touched her again she didn't know if she had the strength to
resist him.

'No game at all! I'm deadly serious…'

The look he flung at her almost totally destroyed what
little was left of her self-control, but, heaving in a desperate
breath, she forced herself to face him with as much strength
and defiance as she could muster.

'This has gone far enough—too far. I don't want it. I
don't want you.'

'Liar!'

It was low and deadly and this time his eyes burned molten
with rejection of every word she'd said.

'You little liar. You wanted me every bit as much as I
wanted you. You said so—'

'I was wrong…'

'And your body said so too. It's still telling the same story.'

A wild, contemptuous gesture in her direction emphasised
the angry words.

'You can't deny—'

'Oh, but I can—I will!'

Her voice was pitched too high, too shrill. It sounded too
despairing, too desperate to protect herself. Which was hardly
surprising when she could barely bring her whirling senses

back under any degree of control. Her pulse was still pounding in her veins, sounding like thunder in her head.

'You would?'

Cynical disbelief rang rough in Zarek's voice, making her shiver because she knew that she couldn't refute. He knew that she was lying and so did she.

'You'd deny this…'

Before she could even realise that he had moved he was at her side in three long strides. Hard hands clamped around her naked shoulders, bruising fingers digging into the skin as he swung her round in front of him. This way she faced the big full-length mirror set into the wardrobe on the opposite side of the room.

'You'd deny *this*?' Zarek repeated savagely. 'Look at yourself!'

Penny closed her eyes tight. she didn't want to look—didn't need to look. She knew what he meant; knew what she would see. But a rough shake of her shoulders forced her to open them again. When she did so the first thing she saw was Zarek's dark eyes looking over her shoulder, meeting hers in the glass. That was bad enough but the burn of something dangerous in that glittering stare made her drop her gaze and face her reflection squarely, wincing in embarrassment as she did so.

It was worse than she had expected.

The green dress was bunched up around her waist, her wildly disordered clothing exposing her breasts. The creamy flesh still marked with red as the result of his kisses, the abrasion of his late evening stubble against the sensitive skin. Her hair was a wild bird's nest around her face, tumbling in tangled chaos on to her shoulders. Her nipples were still hard and flushed with pink, faintly gleaming with the moisture left on them by his tormenting mouth.

Her breasts stung where they were now exposed to the air and rapidly cooling from the heated response of just moments before. And between her legs the throbbing need his deliberately provoking caresses had awoken and then stoked with every touch was still a burning torture of demand. One that made her feel it might actually drive her to lose consciousness from the agonising frustration of having to fight it. Just for a second she felt weak enough to sag back against Zarek's strength and support, but realised in time how appalling a mistake that would be.

'I mean—I can't deny that it happened. That I responded.'

It seemed that was not the response Zarek was expecting. The grip on her shoulders eased slightly, becoming loose enough for her to twist away. At least this way she didn't have to look at herself, or meet his darkly accusing eyes.

'I'd be a fool to try and do that—wouldn't I? I mean— look at me…'

No, that was a mistake. Bringing his eyes to her exposed body, reminding him of how she looked, how he had made her look, was not going to help her in this. With a flare of hot embarrassment flooding up into her cheeks, she tugged at the skirt of her dress with one hand, the top of it with another, both movements having very little practical effect.

'Here…'

To her total shock and consternation, Zarek moved across the room, snagged a blue silky robe from the back of the door, shook it out and held it open.

'What?'

'Put it on…'

At the sight of her wary-eyed hesitation, he muttered an imprecation in savage Greek.

'I am not going to harm you.'

'I know…'

Whatever else there might have been between them—or not—Penny knew Zarek was not was physically cruel or hurtful.

But these were not normal circumstances. She still had no idea at all what had happened to Zarek while he had been away. The whole time of his absence had started with the violence of the hijacking of the *Troy* by the pirates. Then there had been the ordeal of being held hostage in the tiny, enclosed boat, the bullet that had been meant for his head and had only by some miracle missed by inches.

And after that? That had all been in the very first week— God knew what had happened in the years afterward.

Oh, but the truth was that even when they had been together, she had never truly known him. She had married him in a rush, in the heat of the biggest crush she had ever had in her life. She had been wildly in love, with the emphasis on *wild*, but she had never really known the man she had married. That had been proved to her by later developments.

'I'm sorry—I know you wouldn't harm me under normal circumstances!'

It was meant to be a peace offering, a verbal olive branch, and although Zarek nodded in acknowledgement it didn't subdue the blaze in his eyes or ease the tension in his jaw and shoulders.

'Then cover yourself up and perhaps we'll be able to talk— *normally.*'

The bitterly cynical emphasis on the last word made Penny wince, as did the bleakly efficient way he was setting about restoring his appearance to—that word again—normality. The way he buttoned up his shirt, tucked it in where she had pulled it adrift at the waist, smoothed the disordered hair her clutching fingers had tangled, spoke very clearly of his instant withdrawal from her.

What had happened to the hot-blooded, fiercely passionate man who had carried her up to his bed just a short time before? Had he really existed? Or had she been deluding herself? Had that been just another sign of cool calculation on Zarek's part? Like the way he had decided to marry her in the past.

The way he had chosen her as the potential mother for his heirs.

CHAPTER EIGHT

SHIVERINGLY cold in spite of the warmth of the September evening, Penny stumbled across the room to where Zarek still held out the blue silk robe and pushed her arms roughly into the sleeves. It was all she could do not to snatch the robe away from him as he pulled it up around her shoulders, but the ordeal didn't take long. A moment later she was back over the other side of the room, dragging the sides of the robe together and belting it as tightly as possible around her waist. It was made of soft and thin material, so it was little use as protective armour against him, but at least she was covered and felt more secure that way.

'You never needed to armour yourself against me.' Zarek's drawl stunned her with its hint of dark amusement. Even more so with its uncanny echoing of the word in her own thoughts. 'And you never used to play games in bed—at least not those sort of games.'

'I wasn't playing any sort of game.'

'No?'

With the blue robe wrapped round her, Penny felt a little more secure and able to face his cold-eyed derision.

'I wasn't playing at anything. I know I responded—there was always that spark—OK, more than a spark—of passion between us.'

'As I recall, you couldn't keep your hands off me. And vice versa. But then I'm not the one denying the blatantly obvious.'

'I'm not denying it,' Penny persisted. 'I'd be a fool to even try. It's there, obviously it is—but that doesn't mean I'm going to act on it.'

Whatever else Zarek had been expecting, it was not that. His dark head went back sharply, his eyes narrowing till they were just gleaming slits in his tanned face.

'I'm not someone who just jumps into bed with any man in the first moment I see him, no matter how strong the provocation.'

He knew that. She saw the acknowledgement of it in his eyes even though he said nothing in response. She'd come to him a virgin and, in spite of an almost overwhelming longing to change that situation before then, she had been a virgin on their wedding night.

'I'm not just any man.'

'But I don't know you.'

'I'm your husband!'

It was a sound of fierce exasperation blended with total disbelief of what she was saying. Penny took several steps backwards, away from him, stopping short when she found that her back had come up against the wall. She could see from his face that he thought she had gone completely mad, right before his eyes, and even in her own mind her argument sounded weak and unsubstantial. But then he had got exactly what he wanted from their marriage. She wasn't yet prepared to open up her heart to him and confess the truth—that he wasn't the husband she needed.

She had more pride than to admit that until she knew more clearly exactly where she stood.

'So you keep telling me.'

'Are you saying you don't believe I am who I claim to be? What do you want—a DNA test?'

Penny flinched at the malign humour in his dark tones but, pushing her hands into the pockets of the silk gown and curling them into tight, defiant fists, she managed to find the strength to continue in spite of feeling that she was suddenly desperately fighting for her life.

'N-no—I don't need that.'

'Then start acting like you know me. I'm your husband—the man you married—and you damn well know it. And if you need any further confirmation—something we both know—then let me remind you that I am also the man who made sure that you—or at least an image of you—was added to the carving on our bed.'

One long tanned hand pointed back at the dishevelled bed they had just left.

'Yes—as a mouse!' Penny flung back at him.

She knew he was referring to the ornately carved wooden headboard that had been one of the wedding gifts at their marriage. Apparently these carvings were a tradition in the Michaelis family and were usually made up of symbols and images to represent the bride and groom, their families and elements from their lives. When the headboard had been given to Zarek and Penny it had all seemed to be about boats and the sea, with very little that related to her personally. When she had protested, Zarek had said that he would make sure she was added. She had come back from her wedding reception expecting at the very least to see a rose or two for her English nationality, or even a soaring oak tree as a play on her maiden name of Wood.

It had taken her a long time to find the tiny field mouse almost hidden in one corner of the ornate bed head.

'Was that what you thought of me? As a mouse? A creeping, sneaking, terrified little mouse?'

'Well, certainly not now,' Zarek replied dryly, strolling over to a chair by the window and dropping down into it. 'Right now you are—what is it that old film was called?— The Mouse that Roared.'

Was that actually a gleam of humour in the darkness of his eyes? Penny couldn't be sure and because of that she didn't dare risk rising to his teasing.

'You have changed, Penny.'

If only he knew how much.

'I've had to change—had to learn how to stand on my own two feet. One moment I was a new wife, embarking on a very different sort of life in an alien country—with in-laws who weren't exactly pleased to see me arrive in their home, but with my husband by my side to help me through. The next I was…'

Breaking off, she could only shake her head, twisting the tie belt of her robe round and round her fingers, tying it in knots and then tugging them free again.

'The next you were what?' Zarek prompted when she couldn't find the words to go on. 'You didn't seem to be struggling quite as much as you would have me believe. Certainly not with the in-laws.'

'You think so?'

Outrage had Penny letting drop the narrow belt as she put her hands on her hips and faced him defiantly.

'You want to try living with your stepmother complaining about every thing every minute of the day. With everything you do being wrong—and everything that dear Jason and Petros do is absolutely perfect.'

It was only when Zarek's mouth quirked up into an unexpected and totally unguarded smile that she realised just how rigidly he had controlled his features from the time he had arrived until now. Even when he had been intent on seducing her, no trace of true emotion had shown through the tight muscles, only the burn in his eyes giving away any sort of feeling. It had been almost as if he had been determined not to show anything. So now she felt her insides twist, her heart lurch as she recognised the unexpected softening in his face.

'I did,' he acknowledged dryly. 'I lived with that constant carping from the moment my father first brought Hermione home. And then when he married her and moved her and her sons into the house…'

He shook his head slowly, mouth twisting again at the memories.

'I was glad to escape to boarding school in England.'

'How old were you?'

Penny knew that her voice sounded slightly breathless because she was struggling with a tightness in her chest that came from the fact that Zarek had actually opened up about something in his past. When they had married he had always insisted that the past was irrelevant. That it was the here and now that mattered.

'Seven.'

'So young!'

At seven she had gone to the small village school just down the road. She couldn't imagine how it would have felt not to be able to go back home at the end of each long, tiring day.

'But I suppose you had Jason and Petros for company? No?' she questioned when Zarek shook his head again.

'They never went away to school. They had private tutors here on the island.'

Catching the sound of her swiftly indrawn breath, he switched on another smile, one that was totally different from before.

'I much preferred it that way. And if I could have stayed at school through the holidays I would have preferred that too.'

The words were flat, emotionless, but all the same Penny felt that she saw something of the reasons why Zarek had always been so totally set against his stepfamily, his unyielding resolve that they would never get their hands on Odysseus Shipping.

And that perhaps was some part of the explanation why he had been so determined on having a family—an heir—as soon as possible. But it did nothing to ease the sense of being used, seen not as a wife but as a womb to carry that child, which was how she had ended up feeling in their marriage. And that was why she had resorted to taking the contraceptive pill, the discovery of which had sent Zarek incandescent with rage just before he had left for the *Troy*.

'And your father?' she asked and once more Zarek shook his head.

'He gave Hermione whatever she wanted. He just wanted a quiet life and, to get that, he had to let her run things the way she wanted them.'

'Then you'll understand why I was ready to get out of here. You walk back in and assume that I've just been sitting here quietly, waiting for you to return. Perhaps doing a little embroidery to pass the time.'

The realisation that she had in fact been doing something like that made her heart skip a little uneven beat. She didn't really expect an answer to her question and she didn't get one. Instead Zarek continued to sit as motionless as a statue, even his eyes hooded and opaque.

'How do you know that I hadn't decided I'd had enough long ago and divorced you?'

'On what grounds?' Cool and swift, it had a bite as lethal as that of a striking snake.

'Desertion?' she parried sharply, refusing to let herself think of the way that he had never meant his marriage vows. Never intended to *love* and cherish. 'You haven't been in contact for two years.'

Something had changed. She couldn't tell quite what it was, only that something in the atmosphere in the room was suddenly very different. Zarek hadn't moved or spoken but everything about his long, still body communicated a new and very different form of tension.

'I believe that we have already established that I was hardly in a position to phone you or to send many text messages.'

The dry, slightly mocking words only added to the already strung-out way she was feeling, knocking her over from irritation into full-blown exasperation.

'When you were captured originally, perhaps! But you got away from them. That same week, if I have it right. And after that? There are two whole years with not a word, not a message. Nothing to let me know that you were still alive.'

'Perhaps that's because I didn't know that I was.'

'What…? What do you mean? That doesn't make sense.'

But even as she asked the questions Zarek moved at last, getting to his feet and prowling restlessly across the room to stand by the window, staring out at the now moonlit waves. And as she saw his hand come up to rub at his head, at the ugly scar that marked his temple, she felt her heart thud just once, hard and cruel, at the reminder that he had been literally just inches away from death. How long it would have taken him to recover from that she had no idea.

'I mean that for a long time even I did not know who I was,' Zarek said, still not looking at her so that he didn't see the way that her hands had gone to her mouth as if she could wish her foolish words back. 'When I hit the sea I had already blacked out. I have no idea how long I drifted. I was just lucky that I was eventually picked up by a man in his yacht. He took me back to his home in Malta.'

'Malta!'

Penny felt she might choke on the word. Was that where Zarek had been all this time? When she had been imagining all sorts of horrors, the thought of his lifeless body tossed into the ocean with a bullet in his head, he had been on that beautiful Mediterranean island.

So near and yet so far.

And what had he been doing all that time while she had been left stranded, neither a wife nor a widow? Not knowing whether to mourn him or to wait for him.

'Don't they have phones in Malta? Writing paper? Envelopes? A post office?'

That brought Zarek swinging round to face her, a faintly wry smile twisting his beautiful mouth in his shadowed face. That smile twisted a knife in her insides with its memory of how he had once looked, in the early days of their marriage, when he had been smiling at something she had said.

'I wouldn't have known who to contact. At the start, when I was unconscious and ill from exposure, I had no identification on me, no way of anyone knowing who I was. And when I did come round, I was no help.'

'Oh, come on…' Penny began, but then the full impact of just what he had said hit home to her and the words faded into nothing as her mind reeled in shock. 'Do you mean…? Are you saying…?'

'I'm saying I had amnesia—the wound on my head—the shock—exposure—any of it could all have caused it or added to the effect—but I couldn't remember a damn thing. I knew I was alive—I was male and…'

He threw up his hands in a gesture expressing resigned acceptance of defeat.

'That was it. So I couldn't help anyone by telling them who I was or who might be looking for me. I didn't know if I was married or single. If I had any family and where they were. I spoke English—that was what my rescuer spoke to me—but not Maltese. I also spoke French, Greek, Italian—so in which of those countries did I look for any clues?'

'Amnesia…'

Penny could only echo the word in a sense of shock and bewilderment. It was so obvious now that she knew. It explained so many things, which was a relief.

And it also took away that feeling of outraged injustice at the thought that she had been left abandoned, suffering the torment of believing him dead when all the time he had been alive and well and living in Malta.

Suddenly it was as if that sense of outrage had been all that had been holding her upright. As if the removal of the indignation had been like tugging a rug from under her feet, throwing her totally off balance. Was it possible that her own lingering anger and hurt at all that she had found out about him just before he had left for the *Troy* had coloured her judgement, making her see hurts where none was intended, cruelty where he had never planned any?

But all the same he had come back to the island incognito, if not in disguise. He had come in secret, concealed behind the big beard, the long hair. And he had set himself to watch her, to observe what she was doing. For how long? Just how many days—weeks—had he been there?

'Wh-when did you start to remember things?'

'Only slowly. I'm not sure if I fully recall everything yet. For perhaps the first year I didn't know anything. But occasionally I would have flashes of memory or dreams—'

He broke off abruptly as an unexpected sound interrupted his words. A sound that made Penny blush and made a rare, stunningly genuine smile of real amusement cross his face.

'What was that?'

'What?' It was an attempt at distraction, one that didn't work as her empty stomach growled again, more loudly this time.

'Are you hungry?'

It was so long—too long—since she'd seen that teasing smile on his face. And having seen it resurface, she felt she would do anything to keep it there. There had once been a time when they were happy together, even if, underneath it all, Zarek had only been pretending.

'A little,' she admitted. 'No—a lot…'

It was the first time she had sounded genuine, unconstrained, since she had leapt from the bed as if all the hounds of hell were after her, Zarek reflected. The first time she had sounded at all like the woman—little more than a girl—that he had married. And she pressed her hands to her belly as if somehow she could silence the growl of hunger that sounded once again.

'Me too, now,' he admitted, finding he could say it to this softer, younger-looking Penny. 'I haven't eaten all day.'

'Neither have I.'

She said it with a sort of astonishment that made him smile at her obvious sudden self-discovery.

'I didn't manage anything this morning because—the meeting was on my mind. And since then, well…' she shrugged, her expression becoming almost shame-faced '…things rather intervened.'

'They did. For me too.'

It seemed ridiculous to be having this rather inane conversation about food in the darkness of the late evening in the silence of the big house. Especially in the heated atmosphere that had been boiling between them earlier. But privately Zarek found that he was admitting he was actually rather enjoying it. It was a relief to have a slight lull in the tension and abrasive aggression of the rest of the day. The constant need to keep his focus on what was being said and how it was being expressed. After his investigations of the past weeks, the sense of always looking over his shoulder had become so much a part of his life that he was glad to let it drop for a while.

And not just in the time since he had rediscovered who he was. The worst thing about getting his memory back had been recalling the way that had been a part of his life for so long. Knowing that Hermione and her poisonous sons were always waiting and watching, just hoping for a chance to stab him in the back. They had tried their damnedest when his father had been alive, putting any barrier they could between him and his parent, and in the two years since Darius had died had redoubled their campaigns in the hope of moving in on Odysseus Shipping.

And they had almost succeeded. If he had not walked in on the board meeting when he had…

But exactly what part had Penny played in that?

'Let me get you something.'

'There's no need…'

'Well, who else is going to do it, seeing as you've given the whole staff the night off?'

She made the comment sound light but he could still read the tension in her eyes, the faint quiver of her bottom lip. She obviously felt vulnerable and exposed alone in the house with him like this. Which was exactly how he wanted it. How he had planned it all the way along. Until he knew exactly what his lovely wife had wanted...

She had declared to his face that she and Jason were not lovers—had not been lovers. And he found that he believed her. How could she respond to him as she had just done if she had ever been intimate with his stepbrother? She had been as much at the mercy of frustrated hunger as he had felt after two long years away.

Which meant that the passion they had just shared still blazed between the two of them, though she seemed determined to deny it. For the life of him, he couldn't see why. Unless she had something else to hide.

And she had been good at hiding things. A sudden flash of memory reminded him of the way, the last time he had been in this room, he had planned to leave a gift, some of her favourite perfume, in a drawer in her dressing table for her to find while he was away. Instead, the perfume had ended up in the waste-paper basket, thrown there in a dark fury when he had found the packs of contraceptive pills...

For a moment the memory of the bitter disillusionment that had savaged him then came back to slash at him. He had married Penny because she had driven him half mad with wanting but also because she had seemed different. Because she had appeared to offer something so unlike the poisonous atmosphere of lies and greed. Because she had seemed innocent and open. So when he had found that she had been deceiving him all along, he had vowed that never again would he let a beautiful face, an innocent air, mislead him.

But, oh, dear heaven, she *was* lovely.

The sensual thought sprang from nowhere into his mind, knocking him sideways mentally, and very nearly physically.

It had such a force that he actually almost staggered under it, taking a single involuntary step to the side to steady himself as he did so. His body was still burning with the heated response that had seared through him such a short time before. He might have himself back under control but the hungry ache just would not go away and it left a throbbing bruised sensation along every nerve that still came close to making him want to groan aloud.

Now he knew why he had never been able to touch another woman in the time he had been away. Never had the inclination even though there had been plenty of opportunity, plenty of chances on offer to him. But even when he had still been struggling with his memory, when he hadn't yet recalled just who he was, some inner instinct had created a restraint that had held him back from taking advantage of any of them.

And, looking back, he knew that the only women who had ever interested him had shared his wife's sleek dark hair, her tall, willowy build and huge deep blue eyes. The brutal kick of sexual hunger that thought brought made him rush to force his mind onto other, less provocative matters.

'A meal would be welcome. As would a shower.'

He even managed a smile. It wouldn't hurt to be civilised for a while, even if the feelings he was burying behind the smile were very far from civilised and only just barely under control.

'The plumbing at the cottage was very much on the primitive side.'

The rush of relief into her eyes was one that set his teeth on edge. Did she really think that she had got away with it after all? That everything was now sweetness and light between them? If she did then she had no real recollection of the man her husband was. She had lost out on a lot when he had come home, her plans to leave and start a new life ruined by the fact that she could not have her husband declared dead as she had planned. He had rushed into a relationship with her once before and lived to rue the day he had met her. He was not going to let himself get trapped that way again. But he could afford to take things rather more slowly for a while.

'It must have been. Well, you can take this bathroom while I...'

Belatedly she realised how she sounded, the gracious lady-of-the-manor act she was putting on with a welcome guest. But he was no guest in his own home and whether he was actually welcome was something he had yet to finally prove one way or another. That burned in his gut so viciously that he knew it must show in his eyes, in the uncontrolled glare he turned on her suddenly smiling face.

It had her stumbling over her words, coming to an abrupt halt and snatching in a raw, ragged breath before she made herself go on in a very different tone altogether.

'I'm sorry—I mean—I'll use one of the other bathrooms. Of course.'

'Of course,' Zarek echoed dryly.

In the past they had shared many showers in the big luxurious wetroom that formed the en suite bathroom to the master suite in the villa. Long, indulgent showers that had often ended up with them back in bed at least once before they ever decided it was time to dry off and get dressed again. Now she looked as if she couldn't wait to get out of the room and...

Or did she? OK, she looked edgy as hell, already moving a careful step and then another towards the door. But there was a darkness in her eyes that didn't fit with the image of careful retreat. It was the sort of darkness that he suspected was still in his eyes too, making his pupils huge, swallowing up all the colour of his irises. It was the darkness of awareness, of arousal. And just to see it made his throat ache with the effort of holding back everything he wanted to say.

The way her arms were folded tight under the soft swell of her breasts, pushing them up and forward, sent his blood pulsing hot and heavy through his head. And her hands curved to cup their softness in a way that made the bite of sensual jealousy a torment he could barely keep under control. He wanted to stride forward, to tug her arms away from their defensive position, hold them prisoner high above her head, keep them there while he plundered her mouth with his, tasting her sweetness, taking her lips' hungry response into his own.

The blue robe might be fastened tight around her slender frame in a way that spoke of determined defence, of protection from his touch, from his kisses, but it was no defence against his eyes or his thoughts. He could still see the outline of the rucked up dress, the pleats of cotton at her hips and waist. But below that the soft silk clung lovingly to the fine curves of her thighs, the shadowed place between them, reminding him, sharp as a cruel knife, of how close he had been to being able to bury himself in her and find the heaven of release he sought. The release of oblivion in ecstasy.

It was a cruel irony that he had only just come to remember his life and there was so much of it that he wished he had never recalled. An even crueller stab of fate was the fact that Penny had been the first memory to return. Thoughts of her had been there in flashes, haunting his dreams, just out of reach, even before he had known who she was. It had been the need to find her that had driven him to try harder and harder to remember.

And then, when he had recalled just who she was, he had felt that burn of disillusionment all over again.

'If you need a change of clothes…' Penny's voice broke into his thoughts.

'It's all right…'

This was something he had already decided he would have to concede on. He had been away for two years. The reports had had him dead. Anyone—everyone—would have thought that it was a crazy thing to do to hang onto his clothes for that long. After his mother had died, even his own father had had to acknowledge that, adore her as he had, he couldn't keep his first wife's wardrobe when she had been gone six months.

'I understand if there's nothing here.'

'No—'

She had crossed to the wardrobe that had always been his, was fumbling with the handle. Pulling it open, she stood back so that he could see. The sight of every item of his clothing still hanging neat and straight just as he had left them over two years before had an effect like a punch to his guts, driving all the breath from his body.

'You kept them…'

But that had her lowering her face as if in embarrassment, brushing off his comment with an awkward little flick of her head.

'You know where the towels are…'

She almost ran from the room, leaving him staring after her, his mind see-sawing sickeningly as he tried to adjust to what had just happened.

She had kept all his clothes. In spite of the fact that she had been told he was dead, she had kept all his clothes as carefully and as well cared for as she had done when he was there. She hadn't cleared them out or packed them away, but had kept them here, in their bedroom. The room in which she still slept.

So what did that mean?

But he had seen her with Jason that first night. Seen the way she had run into his stepbrother's arms. And heard her...

'I want to get away from here, start living again. I'm tired of treading water... I can't inherit unless we have Zarek's death declared and legalised. So let's do that. Let's put it all behind us...'

And then, just as he reached the door this morning, that final, dismissive toast she had made, obviously with Jason in mind.

'The king is dead. Long live the king.'

So how did that square with the same woman who had kept every item of clothing he possessed for the time he had been gone? Did this mean that Penny had actually been hoping that he would come back?

In which case, why the hell had she bolted from his bed as if his touch appalled her?

Shaking his head, Zarek headed for the bathroom, discarding his clothes as he went.

He had taken his time about coming back, had sent a private investigator to check out the situation here on Ithaca first, before he had even made the journey from Malta and then moved onto the island incognito because he had wanted to watch and see for himself. Because, face it, the return of his memory had brought with it bad memories as well as good. Memories of feelings that the intervening two years could only have added to, made worse, dug in deeper.

And the woman he had come back to—the wife he had found waiting for him—was not at all what he had expected. For a start, he had never expected her to be here at all.

Turning on the shower full force, Zarek stepped under the rush of water and let it beat down on his head.

In fact there was just one way in which she was just the same as when he had left. And that was that she was the sexiest woman he had ever seen. The woman who only had to walk into a room to crank the heat up by one hundred degrees. Whose smile was an enticement to seduction. The woman who could make him burn with heat and hunger with one look, one word in her beautiful voice falling from her sexy soft lips.

She was a temptation strong enough to distract him from the way he really needed to be thinking, the things he had wanted to find out before he took up his old way of life again. His marriage was going to be so very different this time, or it was not going to exist at all.

But even as he told himself that the all-too-familiar heavy tightening in his groin warned him of what just thinking about Penny could do to him. The sort of reaction that stopped him thinking, drove the blood away from his brain and down to other, much more basic parts of his body. He'd already almost been caught that way once tonight. And thinking, not responding, was what he needed to do.

With a heavy sigh he reached up and turned the control on the shower to *cold* and forced himself to stand under it for far, far longer than he needed to get clean.

CHAPTER NINE

'THAT was wonderful, thank you.'

Zarek pushed his plate away from him, reached for his wine glass, and leaned back in his chair to sip at the golden-toned liquid with a sigh of contentment.

'It's so long since I tasted baked feta with peppers that I had almost forgotten how much I enjoyed it. And baklava...I didn't know that you knew how to make it.'

'Marta taught me,' Penny said, referring to the cook who usually ran the villa's kitchen with a rule of iron. 'I've been having cooking lessons with her—for something to do.'

She didn't add that she had specially learned how to make the simple dish and others like it because her instructor had told her that they were Zarek's favourites. She'd already given far too much away by revealing that she had kept all his clothes in the wardrobes since the time of his disappearance.

'So that's how you spent your time.'

'Part of it anyway.'

Once again Penny couldn't look at him but fixed her eyes on the dark line of the horizon. Even after ten o'clock at night it was still warm enough to sit out on the terrace beside the swimming pool and that was where she had served the quick and simple meal she had put together for them after she had emerged from the shower.

She hadn't stayed under the water for long. Once safely in the sanctuary of a bathroom belonging to another bedroom, at the far end of the landing from the master suite she and Zarek had once shared, she had been quick to strip off the blue silk robe, tossing it onto the bed and then freezing in horror at the sight that confronted her in another full-length mirror.

'Oh, my… No!'

Had she really looked such a shocking mess? With her dress dragged down and pushed up, actually torn in one place, she looked more like the victim of an assault than a passionate lover happy to give herself to the man she adored. Her underwear had disappeared, lost who knew where, and her hair was a complete bird's nest falling in wild and knotted disarray around a shock-pale face. Even the untypical light traces of make-up that the thought of today's dreadful board meeting had driven her to put on were smudged and smeared around her eyes, the soft tinted lipstick totally kissed off.

'No!'

Penny put her hands to her face, covering her eyes to block out the sight, then almost immediately snatched them away again. She couldn't bear to stay like this a moment longer. A long, hot shower would make her feel better, restore some sense of balance, repair her damaged self-esteem.

At least that was what she hoped for. What actually happened was that as she removed and discarded what little was left of her clothing all she could think of was the way that it had felt to have Zarek's urgent hands on her dress, snatching aside the straps, dragging her skirt up high to expose her legs… She could almost still feel his touch everywhere on her skin, on her face, her breasts…her thighs. Somehow those hungry fingers had seared a path over her flesh, one that would not vanish even when she was many metres away from him, separated from his presence by the thickness of several walls.

Even diving under the shower and turning it on full force hadn't helped. The heat of the water had followed the path of the heated touch, trickling between her breasts, sliding down to the dark curls between her legs, along her thighs… Making her freeze under the rush of the water as she felt it pound down on her head, seeming to thump out the syllables of Zarek's name against her skull. Over and over again without a pause.

Za—rek. Za—rek… Until she could bear it no longer but lurched out of the shower, water stinging her eyes. She had no way of knowing if it was the flow from the shower or the tears that threatened, only that she was half blinded by it, groping roughly for her towel before snatching from the rail at it and rubbing her face hard.

How was it possible that she had gone into the shower to feel clean, to wash away the scent of Zarek's body on hers, the feel of his touch, and yet now she felt worse than before, tainted, marked for ever? It was as if his caresses had been a brand, his kisses scarring her for life. She would never be free of the darkly sensual hold he had over her, the fetters of sexuality that had bound her to him from the very first.

And was that all that it was? she couldn't help wondering now. She had fallen head over heels for Zarek when she had first met him, and she had truly believed herself in love at first sight. But had it been anything more than a hugely powerful crush, the first stirrings of her female sexuality? She hadn't known what sexual desire really meant and so she had only thought of the way she had felt for Zarek in terms of love and giving her heart.

But her time married to this man had taught her that he, at

least, was capable of claiming her as his in purely sexual terms. Of wanting her only for the wild and white hot passion that flared between them every time they touched. Every time they kissed. He had wooed her, won her, seduced her, married her, made her his, without a single trace of love for her. He had wanted her in his bed, to warm and satisfy his body and to create an heir for the company that was really the only thing that touched his heart, or what part of a heart he actually possessed.

'I married you for a child!' The last angry words he had flung at her before leaving for the *Troy* came back to haunt her once more. 'If you want this marriage to continue then that is non-negotiable.'

A sensation like the trickle of something slow and icy slipped down her spine at the thought. And that sense of creeping cold was made all the worse by staring out at the moonlit sea and remembering all those other nights she had sat out here on the terrace, doing exactly that. Then she had had to fight so hard against the nightmarish thoughts of Zarek's lifeless body tossed overboard from the pirates' boat and left abandoned in the water. Just the memory she had of those thoughts made Penny shiver convulsively in spite of the warmth.

'Cold?' Zarek shocked her by the speed and focus with which he reacted, turning his attention—the attention she had believed was fixed on the view before them—onto her in the space of a heartbeat.

'No—not really,' she managed on an awkward laugh. 'Someone just walked over my grave.'

Then, when his dark brows drew together in a frown of confusion and incomprehension, she had to force herself to continue and explain the superstition.

'When you get a shiver like that it's said to mean that someone somewhere is walking over the spot where you're going to be buried. It's just an old wives' tale. I think the scientific explanation is that the shiver is a response to the release of stress hormones.'

She was rambling and betraying her nervousness by doing so. She could see it in the darkness of Zarek's eyes, shadowed in the flickering light of the candles she had set on the table around them. He was back to watching her too closely for comfort and the steady, intent observation he subjected her to made her shift uncomfortably in her seat.

'And are you?' he asked at last, lifting his wine glass to his lips again but not swallowing as he studied her over the top of it. 'Stressed, I mean.'

'Of course I am!'

This at least she could answer with total honesty, for a moment or two anyway. She still found it almost impossible to believe that he had come back from the dead. That he was here, sitting with her in the warmth of the evening with the sound of his breathing in her ear, the scent of his skin in her nostrils.

'Why wouldn't I be stressed? I started this morning as I have done for the past two years, thinking that I was alone—a widow—that my husband was dead. And then suddenly the door opens and there you are—large as life and twice as ugly. And—and…'

'And?' Zarek prompted when she stumbled over the words, unable to go on. Setting his glass down on the wooden table top, he leaned towards her, elbows resting on his thighs, chin supported on his hands. 'And?'

He was too close. Too dangerously close in every way. She could see the way that his chest rose and fell with each breath, the shadow at his jaw line of the growth of that black beard even though he must have shaved only that morning. This close, and looking into his eyes, she could see how they were not totally dark but the deep brown was flecked with gold, like sparks flying up from a fire. And the scent of his body was like some spice in her nostrils, making her blood heat, her heart pound.

'And now my life is upside down and inside out and I don't know where I'm going or who I am.'

'My wife.'

He inserted the words with smooth precision, like sliding the point of a stiletto into her ribs, so smoothly and easily that at first, at the start, she didn't actually feel any of the pain it was inflicting on her.

'You are my wife.'

It was so calm, so controlled, so totally sure that that was all that mattered. And the absolute certainty, the note of dark possessiveness, made her skin chill once more, the tiny hairs at the back of her neck lifting in tension as she managed to control another of those shivers this time.

'Nothing has changed.'

'Oh, but it has!'

Talking with Zarek now was rather like skating over a deep, murky pond that was just covered with thin ice. She was sliding every which way, unable to quite get her grip on what was really happening, while all the time being aware that under the ice were the coldest, blackest, most dangerous depths, just waiting for the moment that her foot went through the surface and she tumbled in. Then she had the desperate feeling that the waters would close right over her and the icy cold would steal all her breath away and leave her to drown.

'Things have to have changed. It's been two years since I saw you—a lot has to have happened in that time. Two years in which I don't know where you've been, who you've been with, what has happened to you.'

'I could say the same for you.'

Was that darker note that threaded his voice the result of the same sort of careful control she was imposing on herself, the fight not to let the discussion tumble over into the anger that had destroyed them the last time? Or was it one of warning, telling her she was treading on treacherous ground?

'Oh, I've just been here, all the time. But you…'

'All you have to do is ask.'

Could it really be that simple? But life with Zarek had never been simple anyway. So why should it start being so now, with the weight of the complications of his disappearance added to the way things had been before?

Ask. OK, then…

'You said you had amnesia. You didn't remember anything?'

'Not a thing.'

Was she imagining things or had he actually leaned just a little closer? She was drowning in his eyes, her senses seduced by the warm, clean scent of him. But she couldn't allow herself to be enticed that way. That was how she had fallen into love—her juvenile childish love—with him at the beginning. She had to hold onto her heart until she knew if it was safe to give it ever again.

'So what was it that started to bring your memory back to you?'

He took just a moment too long before answering her. The space of perhaps two heartbeats instead of one in a way that set her even more on edge. But his answer when it came was calm, and apparently open enough.

'Believe it or not, it was those damn pirates who helped to break down the walls my mind had built around it. I couldn't believe that I was having images of an attack, hearing the word *pirates* in the twenty-first century. And so I started to look things up, track down stories about pirates in the press, on the Internet. At first it was like looking for a needle in a haystack.'

Needing to break the almost mesmeric hold his closeness had on her, Penny forced herself to sit back, reach for her glass.

'But then one name kept going round and round in my head—the *Troy*… Careful.'

The last word was a warning as Penny swallowed too quickly, too awkwardly, and almost choked on her wine. She had been hoping for another name—her own name. The name of his wife. But no, the first things that had come back to him were connected with his company.

'You never could handle retsina,' Zarek said in mild amusement. 'In fact I always thought you hated it.'

'It wasn't to my taste at first,' Penny acknowledged. 'But I have to admit that I've grown to like it better.'

'Another of those things that have changed while I've been away.'

'Well, you wouldn't expect everything to just come to a halt—stay there, frozen in ice because you weren't here.'

Pure nerves had pushed the wild words from her tongue. And she knew what was twisting those nerves into painful knots so that she couldn't think straight.

'Of course not.'

'Of course not!' Penny snapped. 'We couldn't just give up on things. Life had to go on. For everyone. I mean, even…'

'Even…?' Zarek prompted when her throat closed up and she couldn't finish the name.

Penny reached for her glass again, took another fortifying sip of wine. Nerves had made her slip on the words, but suddenly she was determined to have this out. Time it was out in the open and faced.

'Even for bloody Odysseus Shipping.'

Oh, she had his attention now. If she thought that nearly black gaze had been focused before, now it had the burn of a laser so that she expected her skin to actually scorch where it rested.

It was too much to see the sudden change from stillness to attention. To watch his face change, the sudden light of interest in his eyes.

But, "Bloody Odysseus Shipping?" was all he said and his tone was quite mild, enquiring. 'You were desperate to get rid of it,' he added in the same sort of tone.

'Is that so impossible to believe?'

Pushing her chair back with an ugly scraping sound on the stone-tiled terrace, she got hastily to her feet and reached for his empty plate. Stacking it on top of her own, she winced inwardly at the crashing sound it made. She wasn't deliberately clattering them together, it just sounded that way. Her hands weren't as steady as she wanted and she cursed how much they gave away of her inner turmoil.

'I mean, I'm no hot-shot businesswoman. I'm a secretary—a very junior secretary at that. And when a company loses its chairman to sudden death—an accident at sea—and there is no one ready and trained to take his place, then apparently the values of shares waver—people wonder about their connections with the firm. Didn't you hear? I mean, I assume that you did a lot of investigating, checking on facts— looking into things before you came back to Ithaca. Just so that you knew what was going on.'

She actually paused and looked up at him, waiting for his answer. Not that she needed it. She knew already that he must have checked out all the details of what was happening on Ithaca before he had even thought about coming home. That was the sort of man Zarek was. He never made a move until he had all the facts.

'You didn't know!' she exclaimed as his head went back in shock. 'You really didn't find out about that?'

'I knew.'

Zarek's confirmation was a low growl as she made herself turn and head towards the kitchen with the dirty plates. She wouldn't allow herself to look back but she heard the pad of his bare feet on the tiles as he came up behind her.

At least the simple task of loading the plates and cutlery into the dishwasher meant that she could keep her back to him, focusing hard on the job in hand. But all the same she felt as if she could sense the tension coming off him in waves and directed at the back of her head, so sharp that it almost penetrated her skull.

'Then you'll understand why it felt like a millstone round my neck. And all the time I had Hermione and your stepbrothers on my back too. Telling me that nothing I did was right. That the company needed a man in control. So, yes, in the end I gave in. I'd had enough. I was going to walk away, go back to England. Start my life over again. Yes, I know you never wanted them to have the company, but what else could I do? It's not as if I had a child whose inheritance I had to fight for too.'

Too late she realised just what she had said, the minefield into which she had wandered. And the silence from behind her was so deep, so intense that she could practically feel it closing around her, sealing off her lungs, taking the breath from her body.

'No, you made sure of that.'

His voice had turned to ice. Icy shards that seemed to slash at her exposed and vulnerable skin.

'You knew I wanted a child. You led me to believe you wanted one too.'

Washing-powder tablet…rinse aid… Penny forced herself

to focus on the mundane details to stop her mind going into meltdown as she hunted for an answer.

'I didn't want your heir.'

She could answer him this way while she had her back to him and he couldn't see her face. It meant that she couldn't see his expression but that hardly mattered. It was much more important that he didn't know her answer for the half lie that it was. She hadn't wanted only to provide him with an heir, but the thought of a small baby with Zarek's black hair and deep brown eyes almost destroyed her. Her eyes were blurred with focusing on the front of the dishwasher so fiercely rather than let any tears form.

'But that was why we married—why I became your husband.'

Slamming the dishwasher door shut—the noise and force deliberate this time—Penny pushed herself up from the squatting position and pressed the start button fiercely.

He was leaning against the worktop, arms folded across his powerful chest, but the tension in the long body showed the position to be anything other than the relaxed one it appeared to be.

'But there's so much more to being a husband than just declaring it.'

Did something change in those eyes or was it just the flicker of the candlelight throwing a different set of shadows into them?

'What was missing? Was I cruel to you? Did I treat you badly—not give you everything you wanted?'

'You gave everything I could have dreamed of.'

If they were talking about material things. But from the moment that she had known how much she needed his love, then marriage, his beautiful homes, all the riches he had were as nothing compared with what she wanted most in all the world. And she had more pride than to beg for something he couldn't give her.

'And yet you didn't want to stay—you didn't want a child.'

Just as she couldn't read his face, she couldn't interpret his tone.

'We didn't have a marriage to bring a child into. A child has the right to have two parents who are happy to be together, and not just because of the life they had created between them.'

Two parents who loved each other.

She'd finished drying her hands on a towel and now she tossed it down onto the marble surface beside the sink. She'd prevaricated for as long as she could, avoided meeting his eyes until she could do so no longer. If she didn't turn now and look him in the face it would be so obvious that she was avoiding him that she would not be able to dodge it any more.

'I was wrong to marry you. My parents married just because I was on the way and it was a terrible mistake. They tore each other apart—and I was always caught in the crossfire.'

'We didn't even get that far,' Zarek murmured dryly.

'No—because I realised I should never have said yes in the first place.'

'So why did you stay when I was declared missing?'

'Someone had to hold things together. I discovered that you had left everything to me in your will. And there was always just the possibility that you might come back.'

'And now that I am back?'

'I really don't know.'

Simple honesty was all that she was capable of. In spite of the sleep she had had earlier that day she was suddenly desperately tired. It was as if the tension that had been holding her upright and keeping her going in all the time that Zarek had been away had now totally evaporated, taking with it her spirit and the strength of her spine. Her mind seemed hazed, her thoughts muddied.

'You don't know why you married me?' Zarek questioned sharply, throwing her even further off balance.

How was she expected to answer that without bringing the L word into things? Right now, attack seemed the better form of defence.

'Don't you think it's a little late to be asking that now? It never occurred to you to ask it when you were about to put a ring on my finger? Well, no, I don't suppose you did. Because for you it was all cut and dried, wasn't it? A cold-blooded business deal. You wanted me and you wanted a child. Marry me and you'd get both.'

Zarek shifted his weight from one hip to the other, but apart from that his expression remained unchanging.

'Not all such deals are cold-blooded.'

'No, of course not—we were pretty hot-blooded most of the time. And that gives you the reason why I married you. Great sex.'

When he dared to frown as if he needed more explanation she lost her grip on her tongue and really let him have it.

'I was twenty-two. You're pretty gorgeous—and rich. What's not to like?'

'Yes, there was that.'

'There definitely was.'

Somehow the defiance she dredged up from deep inside her made it easier than she thought to face that dark-eyed gaze.

'But while you've been away I've had time to grow up. And…and…'

Watching him wipe the back of his hand across his face, she found she was stumbling over her words. If she was tired then he looked drained, and she recognised the way that he pressed his fingers to the scar at his temple as a warning sign.

Looking at him more closely, Penny saw the shadows under his eyes, the faint cloudiness in the polished jet gaze. She thought that she knew how he felt. It was now well past midnight and she felt as if she had lived through several life-times in less than twenty-four hours. Right now she felt as if she was losing her grip on being able to control where the con-versation went and what, underneath it all, it might mean.

'But I don't think now is the time to discuss it. It's been a long day. And we've both had so much adjusting to do since you came back.'

Dear heaven, was it only this morning? Just a few short hours before and yet she felt as if he had been back for ever. As if he had never been away. But he *had* been missing and that had had such an effect on her life that she had no idea quite when she would feel as if her existence was back under her control once more.

'We do need to talk more. But not tonight. It's late—and I'm—I'm tired.'

She accompanied the words with a stretch and a yawn to emphasise them but the truth was that she didn't have to put on any sort of a show. Now that she thought about it she was worn out, aching with tiredness right through to the bone, her head spinning nauseously.

Or perhaps it was the result of the stress of the day. A long day of trying to adjust to all that had happened, a day of shocks and bewilderment that had kept her feeling raw and on edge with every hour that passed.

CHAPTER TEN

SHE didn't expect that Zarek would allow himself to be diverted but to her surprise he nodded his head and stepped backwards towards the door.

'You're right. It is late, and I'll admit that I'm looking forward to sleeping in my own bed after all this time.'

Perhaps it was her own fatigue, or perhaps it was the way that they went up the stairs, Argus trotting beside her and Zarek switching off the lights behind them as he mounted the stairs, that blurred Penny's mind. They had done this so many other times in the past, when they had been married. Wandering upstairs in companionable silence at the end of the day, having shared a meal, a glass of wine and now heading for bed. But it was not until she reached the wide landing and turned towards the bedroom that reality hit home again re-minding her of the truth of how things really were and making her stumble slightly, banging into the wall as she fought to keep her balance.

'Careful.'

Zarek put a hand out to support her, taking hold of her elbow and helping her to straighten up.

'Thank you.'

It was stiff and tight, the muscles in her throat clenching

in response to the feel of the heat of his palm against her skin, the burn of his touch along every nerve. In flashes of memory the scene in the bedroom earlier that night came back to haunt her, overlaid by older but no less vivid memories of the nights that Zarek had taken her to bed in the past. During their marriage. Starting with the heated passion of their wedding night that had left her weeping with joy and disbelief that such stunning passion could ever exist.

And now Zarek clearly expected that he would share her bed again. That they would sleep together in the wide soft marriage bed with its huge, ornately carved wooden head-board. And after his casual, 'Yes, there was that,' that was more than she could bear.

Coming to a halt before she actually reached the master suite door, she half turned towards Zarek and tried for what she hoped was an appeasing smile.

'I'll get you some clean towels and bring them to your bedroom. The blue suite is made up and ready.'

'The blue suite?'

Appeased was the last thing Zarek looked. His black brows drew together in an angry frown and the flash of something dangerous in the depths of his eyes made her legs tremble beneath her.

'I think not.'

'Oh, but…'

Protesting was a mistake. As was thinking that he was ever going to be persuaded on this one. Ruthless rejection of what she had planned was stamped in hard, cruel lines on his face, burning in that cold-eyed glare that he turned on her.

'Oh, but nothing. Not if you are trying to say that you think I should sleep elsewhere.'

His hand was already on the door, twisting the handle with

a force that spoke of the anger he was working to hold in check. But what made Penny's stomach tense and twist itself into tight, painful knots was not the thought of the dark fury he might feel but the demonstration of the ruthless power he was determined to exert to control it. The force of will it spoke of made her quail at the thought of it being used against her.

And which way would it be used? Earlier today he had wanted to take her to bed and she had been unable to resist. Only at the last minute had common sense reasserted itself, the much-needed sense of self-preservation kicking in to make her react in the rational way at last. If Zarek turned the sheer power of his seductive persuasion on her once more she might not be able to hold out this time.

Just the memory of the feeling of drowning in his kisses, in his touch, gave her the sense of going down for the third time. She could feel the dark heated waters of sensuality swirling about her dangerously once again.

'Where else would I sleep, *glikia mou*?'

The bite on the last two words took them to a point light years away from any real term of affection.

'This is my home, this is my bedroom. My bed. The bed I have dreamed of sleeping in again ever since I realised just who I was. There is nowhere else I intend to sleep tonight— or any other night.'

And there was no way at all she could refute that argument even if she dared to try.

'So—what about me?'

'What about you?'

The coolly assessing stare he turned on her moved from the top of her head, down to her toes where they curled nervously on the polished wooden floor, then swept back up again to linger on her uneasy face, looking straight into her frowning eyes.

'Where—where am I expected to sleep?'

'Expected?'

There was a dark note of mockery in that single drawled word, one that scraped over her nerves like the sound of fingernails on a blackboard, making her wince inwardly.

'I expect nothing from you, *agapiti mou*. I would be all kinds of a fool if I did. But as to where you should sleep—'

If the faint shrug of one shoulder was meant to be casual then it failed completely. As Penny suspected it was meant to. Instead she was sure that it was an indication of the fact that he didn't give a damn one way or another.

'The normal place that a wife sleeps is at her husband's side.'

'Normal!' Penny's anger was like a red haze in front of her eyes.

Once again Zarek was staking his claim to everything as he had been doing from the moment that he had walked back into her life that morning.

Back into *his* life. Into his house.

His room. His bed.

His wife.

And as his wife she was expected to warm his bed because that was what was normal. For normal read that Zarek would get what he wanted.

'We never had a normal marriage. And even if we had, you've been gone a long time. Long enough for you to be…'

No, her tongue wouldn't frame the word and she choked to a halt, watching the black frown that snapped his dark brows together.

'Long enough for what?' He pounced on the words like a hunting big cat on its prey. 'For me to be *what*?'

Something in her face gave her away and she saw those brilliant eyes narrow until they were just hard slits in a drawn face where white lines of anger and rejection were etched sharply around his nose and mouth.

'Oh, no, lady,' he said with savage control, the bite of the icy fury in his voice lashing against her skin so that she shivered in miserable reaction. 'You are not going to accuse me of being unfaithful to you. I respected my marriage vows even when I did not know that I had made them.'

'All that time—on Malta...?'

'All that time. Even though there was temptation.'

Of course there had been temptation. Zarek was a gorgeous man. A glorious, devastating specimen of manhood. Wherever he was, women were drawn to him like moths to a flame. He had only to direct one burning glance from those stunning, heavy-lidded eyes or flash a single wide, brilliant smile and every breathing female within reach was reduced to a molten pool of honeyed sensual response.

'So you're saying...'

'Not saying.' Zarek's delivery was brutal. 'Telling you. I have never broken my marriage vows to you.'

Could he really mean it? Mean that there had been no one else. Not even when he hadn't known who he was, whether he was married or not?

'And you expect me to believe that?'

'Why not? I believed you.'

It was so unexpected it hit her like a slap in the face, making her reel back.

'I thought you were dead,' was all she could manage.

Zarek pushed one hand roughly through the shining darkness of his hair, shaking his head slightly.

'You thought I was dead. You believed you were a widow. Even if you had met someone new while I was away. I couldn't expect you to wait for ever.'

'But I didn't—' Penny began, but Zarek persisted, talking across her as if she hadn't spoken.

'I understand that Jason saw an opportunity to step into my shoes, in more ways than one. And I have no doubt that he was fully prepared to use you to do just that. If you'd let him.'

'He helped me run the company. I certainly didn't have the experience to do so.'

'And he was kind.' Zarek pronounced the word as if it were a foul, bitter taste in his mouth and suddenly Penny's temper flared out of control.

'Yes, he was kind—and because of that I might have been tempted. So perhaps you might like to stop and think about your part in that.'

Oh, that had got his attention. His head went back as if she had slapped him in the face and if his eyes had seemed to burn before now they practically seared off a fine layer of her skin, leaving her raw and unprotected underneath.

So raw that she no longer cared what she said or how she said it. She only knew that she had had enough for tonight. That she couldn't go on but she needed to escape to somewhere dark and private. To some silent sanctuary where she could lick her wounds for a while and try to come to terms with everything that had happened today. To face up to everything that had changed—and everything that had still remained so agonisingly the same. Perhaps after some time alone, time for thought, she might just be able to face whatever came next. Whatever the future—and Zarek—decided to throw at her.

'The reasons why I might want someone who could be *kind* rather than a man who is so determined to lay claim to his home, his bed—*his wife*. To have them all under his control like his precious company. Someone who thinks that he can walk back into my life and demand that the woman he married should be at her husband's side, in her husband's bed, whether she wants to be there or not.'

But she'd overstepped the mark there. From the way Zarek's lips thinned, his jaw tightening ominously, she knew exactly what was coming even before he shot the question at her viciously.

'And are you saying that you have no desire at all to be in my bed? Are you saying that what happened between us earlier this evening was totally what I *demanded*? That it was simply you *under my control*—with no say in what was going on? That it was not what you wanted at all?'

'No—yes…'

Oh, how did she answer that? The truth was that she had wanted it. Wanted it until she had felt she was going to shatter into tiny pieces with the yearning that was eating her up inside. And yet at the same time it was exactly what she did *not* want. The sensual enticement Zarek offered was such a blend of temptation and danger that it would destroy her if she gave into it as she had done when she had rushed into marriage with him without thinking about the possible consequences. But at the same time, somewhere deep in her heart she had the terrible feeling that it would also devastate her if she never knew it again, never experienced just once more the sexual magic that Zarek could bring to her body, the total ecstasy of fulfilment he could give her in the heat of their marriage bed.

'You can say what you like about our marriage, about the past—but don't ever lie to me about that,' Zarek stated with icy precision. 'What there is between us in bed is special. I've never known anything like it. And I at least am not going to deny that.'

'I…'

Twice she opened her mouth to answer him, and both times her voice failed her completely. She didn't know how she could explain it to him anyway without ever using the three words that explained everything. The three words he didn't want to hear. She couldn't share his bed knowing that she loved him and that he had no feelings for her other than the powerful desire he had just stated so coldly.

Unable to use the words *I love you*, and finding it impossible to tell the man who had just demanded that she didn't lie to him, she gave up totally on speaking and could only shake her head in silent, desperate despair.

She knew just how he had interpreted her response by the way that his lips compressed hard and a revealing muscle tugged sharply in the right side of his jaw.

'All right, *glikia mou*, tonight you have it your way. Tonight we sleep alone. I will allow you the fact that we have been apart for two years—that we are like strangers again—for tonight at least. But I suggest that you take the night to think—to decide whether you want this marriage or not. Because after this, if we stay as husband and wife, then we stay in a real marriage, with everything that entails.'

A real marriage. The words were like a slap in the face, making her head spin nauseously. To her, a real marriage was one that was made in love and caring. A union of equals who each had given their heart to the other, But to Zarek, a *real* marriage was one that gave him the sexual satisfaction he sought, and the precious heir he had wanted all along.

And once he had that heir, just how long would that 'real' marriage last anyway?

'Zarek…'

But she was speaking to the back of her husband's head. He had turned away from her, wrenching open the door and stepping into the bedroom, striding away from her without even glancing back.

'Goodnight, Penny,' he said, cold and hard and totally distant. 'Sleep well.'

With a firm movement of his hand he slammed the door shut right in her face, giving it an extra push when closed as if needing to be sure.

What had he expected? Penny wondered bitterly. Did he think that she would be unable to cope with one night without him and that she would start to beg to be let back in? To beat on the door with her fists, begging and pleading.

Well, if he did then he was going to be bitterly disappointed. She knew when she had been dismissed and she had more pride than to go begging for him to change his mind, to open the door to her. Besides, this was exactly how she wanted things, wasn't it? To be free from the sexual enticement that she seemed to breathe in with the air that surrounded her long-lost husband and that had come straight back to torment her from the moment that he had walked into the house? She had meant what she said—that she didn't know him, and that she couldn't sleep with a man who didn't care about her.

At least that was what she told herself. So why was it suddenly so very hard to force her legs to walk away from the bedroom and take her towards the blue suite that she had already told Zarek was fully made up and ready for someone to sleep in? Why was she weakly tempted to do just what he seemed to have suspected might happen and crawl back to the closed door and…?

And what? Humiliate herself by begging to be let in? Reveal what a total fool she was where Zarek Michaelis was concerned and go to his bed, willing to take the little he might toss her way instead of holding out for the love she knew she needed? The love she deserved.

Even Argus had managed to sneak into Zarek's bedroom without risking rejection or coldness. And however jealous she might actually feel, she was not going to bring herself down to the level of the dog at his master's beck and call.

Marching into the blue room, she pulled off her clothes and dropped them on the floor. Then, naked because her night-clothes were in her original room, she slid into the bed, shivering faintly as the cool soft cotton chilled her skin.

It wasn't a cold night, she told herself. She would soon warm up. And she did, but even being warm and cosy in the soft, comfortable bed didn't mean that she could relax or that sleep came anywhere near as she lay restlessly awake, staring sightlessly into the darkness.

How was this possible? she couldn't help wondering. She had spent so many long nights lying awake until the early hours of the morning, feeling lost and alone and wishing, praying, that Zarek would come back from the depths of the dark sea that she had believed had swallowed him. If only he would be found alive, she had told herself, she would never complain again, never ask for more.

And now Zarek was back in her life. He was lying safe and sound just a few metres down the landing, probably fast asleep in the bed that he had said he had been dreaming about for so many months. Her every wish had come true and yet she felt so little of the happiness and the joy that she had told herself would lighten her heart if this night ever came.

The night she had dreamed of was here and yet she felt more lost and abandoned, more miserable and lonely than she had even been in all of the seven hundred and fifty other nights of Zarek's absence.

And the most terrible part of it was that deep in her heart she feared that there was far more—and worse—to come.

CHAPTER ELEVEN

Penny had no idea what it was that woke her. She only knew that something had roused her from the shallow, restless sleep she eventually managed to find, startling her awake so that she sat bolt upright, shivering with a sense of shock.

'What? Who?'

When the sound came again, a harsh, choking cry, she knew at once that it was coming from the master bedroom just down the landing. The room where Zarek was sleeping.

Zarek.

His name was enough to push her out of bed, have her flinging open the door, running down the hallway.

'Zarek!'

The room was in darkness but the curtains had been left wide open and so the cold wash of moonlight lit up the bed where Zarek sprawled in a tangle of bedclothes. He was lying on his back, black hair wildly dishevelled against the fine white cotton, one arm flung up beside his head, the other stretched out across the bed. His bronzed chest was bare, the black hair that hazed it shadowy in the half-light, and the sheets were draped over the lower half of his powerful body, twisted and disturbed by his restless, fretful movements.

For a moment Penny froze in the doorway but as she watched

he stirred again, twisting from side to side and moaning in his sleep. It was all that she needed to push her forward, coming to the bed and dropping down onto the side of it. Reaching for his hands, she folded her own around them, stilling their agitated flailing as even in his sleep he felt her touch.

'Zarek,' she said softly. 'Darling—it's all right. I'm here.'

His deep, deep sigh seemed to come right from his soul, bringing tears to her eyes as she held on tight, willing him to know she was with him.

'You're not alone.'

Something in her voice got through to him. The lush black crescents of his eyelashes fluttered slightly then lifted slowly, his dark, unfocused gaze looking up into her watchful eyes.

'Penny? What…?'

His voice was rough and raw as if it came from a painfully sore throat.

'You were having a dream—a nightmare. I heard you call out.'

Zarek frowned for a moment, then closed his eyes again on another deep sigh.

'*Thee mou*, yes, I was—a dream… '

'Would it help to talk—can you tell me about it?'

She felt his shudder through the hands she held. Still keeping his eyes closed, he seemed to be reviewing the images his sleeping mind had projected, viewing them on the screen of his eyelids.

'The boat…' he began uncertainly.

'The *Troy*?'

But Zarek's response was a rough shake of his head.

'The small boat—the one the pirates came in.'

He'd been back in the boat where the pirates had taken him at gunpoint, Zarek recalled. In the hot, stinking, confined darkness of the small craft that pitched and tossed so violently on the waves that he feared that one of his captors' weapons might just fire by accident. All around him there had been panic and chaos, voices muttering savagely in a language he didn't understand, the wild arguments—obviously the debate over what they were going to do with him.

It had all been a form of wild confusion. He had no idea exactly in what order things had happened. He recalled the moment he had thought he saw an opening, the shouts getting louder, wilder. The explosive sound of a shot and the searing pain along his left temple. The icy cold that soaked into his clothes as he hit the water. And then the complete, the total blackness.

'Zarek?'

A voice called him back to reality. And it took a moment to realise that it was a voice here, now, in the present, and not the voice he could have sworn he had heard in the darkness, when he had drifted between waking and unconsciousness, never knowing where he was or what was happening.

'Penny?'

It was an effort to bring his mind back into focus. But the warm touch of her hands on his seemed like a lifeline to draw him back from the darkness. Slowly he opened his eyes, saw the pale shimmer of her skin in the moonlight.

'Penny! You must be freezing…'

'I'm O…'

But her protest was ruined by the small, uncontrolled shiver she gave. One that had him adjusting his position swiftly, pulling back the covers, flinging them open so that she could come into the bed beside him.

'But I—I've nothing on.'

'And neither have I. All the more reason for you to come and get warm. And it's not as if it's never happened before.'

Still she hesitated, and he thought she would actually refuse, but another involuntary shudder had her hurrying under the bedclothes, pulling them up around her. Her slender body was cold from the night air and she held herself stiff and straight, well away from him so they might have been miles apart rather than sharing the same bed. But in spite of that he knew a sense of relief. A real feeling of rightness that she should be there. The scent of her skin, her hair filled his nostrils, and the faint sound of her breathing helped him to relax.

'Do you want to talk about it?' Penny said quietly. Her eyes were fixed on the ceiling above her, deliberately not looking at him.

He opened his mouth to say no, it was over, done, he was fine…and found that instead he actually wanted to tell her about it. For the first time he wanted to share with someone the dark places that his mind could take him. To let out the memories that haunted his nights, disturbed his sleep, even when he hadn't known who he was or where those images had come from.

If she had said anything, asked a question, made a comment, then he felt he would have dried up at once, unable to go on. But she simply lay there, silent and receptive, and as he talked to her he felt the slow but definite softening of her body, the easing of tight muscles, the adjustment of her position. In the end she had curved towards him, her face turned to his and so close on the pillows that he could feel the softness of her breath on his cheek.

'I thought it was the end,' he said, and now he was the one staring up at the ceiling, eyes wide so that he didn't see the images of the black, black night, the empty, dark sea, even in his mind. But he felt the shiver that shook Penny's body and knew she was imagining it too.

'When you come close to death, you start to think about

what really matters and what doesn't. I realised then that there was plenty in my life that I could let go of.'

Weird how a silence could be more encouraging than any words. How even just the slight hitch in the smoothness of her breathing could tell him she was still listening.

'Ambition, wealth, success wouldn't have held much value then and there,' he said as if she had actually asked the question. 'Even Odysseus Shipping could have crumbled and it would have just been a challenge to start all over again.'

Beside him in the darkness, Penny stirred and he almost felt her gaze on his shadowed face as she drew in another soft breath.

'And what does matter?' she whispered.

She had broken the silence, and she was so near... He couldn't stay where he was and not touch her. Turning onto his side so that he was facing her, he reached out to pull her close, feeling her instinctive resistance, the tightening of every muscle.

'Relax, just let me hold you. Nothing else—I swear.'

He could almost hear the battle in her mind. But in the same moments he felt again the softening of her body, the way she inched forward until she was fitted against his side, and he knew in that moment that nothing had ever before felt so right. Folding his arms round her, he rested his head against her hair and tried to answer her question.

'Loyalty, trust...'

None of the words seemed right. None of them fitted.

'At a time like that you wonder just who would care if you didn't come back. Who would be waiting when you come... home.'

Home. That word resonated so hard in his thoughts that it stopped his speech. He had to wait, to let it sink in, absorb it.

'I felt alone,' he finally managed.

Beside him he heard Penny's breathing slow, deepen. The

warmth of the bed and the lateness of the hour were getting to her and he could sense her drifting. But just for a moment she stirred briefly, and he felt her eyelids flutter open against his throat.

'I would have…' she managed before sleep claimed her and she drifted into silence.

Would have? Zarek echoed in his thoughts. Would have cared? Would have waited?

Would she still have been here if the legal problems in finalising the declaration of his death hadn't kept her on Ithaca?

Of course I would have cared! The words she had flung at him earlier came back to him now, seemingly in response to the question, but not actually answering it in the end. *And not just 'cared' in the past but still care now! I might not want to be married to you any more, but I sure as hell would never, ever have wished you* dead!'

And that was when he knew there was one thing he hadn't been able to tell her. One thing that perhaps he could never tell her.

In the pirates' boat and then again in the dark, dark hours in the water. When he had drifted in and out of consciousness, there had been one thought that had always been there. The thought of this woman—his wife—and the difference she had made to his life. When he had thought that it would be easier to give up and just drift, let go, the thought of the way they had parted had somehow kept him from going under, made him hold on.

He had thought of Penny even when he hadn't known who she was. With his memory scrambled, and nothing of his life, this island—not even Odysseus Shipping—anywhere in his thoughts, she had come to him in his dreams when he didn't even know her name. It was the need to find out who she was that had kept him hunting for the truth.

He had wanted to come back to her. He had thought that then he would find what he was searching for.

It seemed impossible that in all the time he had spent away, even when he hadn't known who he was, he had dreamed of coming home—wherever 'home' might be. He had thought that when that happened his life would be changed. Complete. It would have the meaning that seemed so lacking while he was lost and wandering. He would finally know just who he was and where his place in life belonged.

'Belonged—hah!'

His low laugh was a sound of harsh cynicism, dark and rough, and it echoed round the silent stillness of the room in the empty house.

Empty all but for the woman curled up next to him in the bed asleep. The woman who had turned his life upside down from the moment he had first set eyes on her and who seemed determined to drive him out of his mind before he was very much older.

He was already part way there as it was. Half out of his head with wanting her and yet not knowing whether their marriage had a chance of surviving. When he had first come back to himself after long months of not even knowing who he was or where he lived, she had been the first person he had set himself to find out about. The wife he had left behind and who had now spent two years without him.

But that was before everything had come back to him. And what he had finally recalled, when put together with what he had heard, had left him determined to wait and watch.

That was when he had heard her state openly that she wanted him declared dead so that she could move on with her life. And when she had realised that her husband was in the room…

'Gammoto!'

Zarek's fist clenched tight as he recalled the way that Penny—that *his wife*—had looked at him in the moment that he had walked back into her life after two years' absence. Two years in which she hadn't known if he was alive or dead— and hadn't cared too much, if the way she had looked was anything to go by. Her whole face had frozen up, her eyes looking dead and emotionless, and she could barely get his name out when she spoke.

And since then she had played hot and cold depending on what suited her and the situation in which she found herself.

Or had she?

His hand twisted in the sheet that covered him, crushing the fine fabric ruinously as he recalled the way that the cool and distant woman who had offered him a sandwich and a coffee as if he had just come back home after a busy day at the office had suddenly turned into the passionate, fiery creature who had heated his bed and delighted his senses in the days, months, after their marriage. And then just as quickly turned back into the remote, unapproachable iceberg with the feeble excuse that she no longer knew him well enough.

And yet she was also the woman who had heard him cry out in the night and had come running so fast that she hadn't even stopped to put on any clothing.

He knew which woman he had wanted to come back to— but which was the real Penny? And had he ever seen her?

Dawn had barely broken but Zarek gave up any further pretence of trying to sleep. Moving carefully so as not to disturb the woman sleeping beside him, he slid out of bed and walked across to the window to stare out at the restless surface of the sea. The waves reflected his mood, looking edgy and agitated, swirling deep currents over the pebbled beach and lashing against the rocks on the shore.

This was where he belonged, where he lived. But home…?

A low plaintive whine broke into his angry thoughts and a cold black nose was pushed into the palm of his left hand where it hung at his side. Glancing down at the big black and white shape of Argus, Zarek smiled ruefully and ruffled the fur at the back of the big dog's neck.

'Had enough of being inside, hmm?' he asked softly. 'I know—you're desperate for a walk.'

And exercise might just help clear his own head. A run along the stony shore, drawing the ozone scented air into his lungs, pushing his body hard, driving himself until the sweat was dripping into his eyes, until he was too tired to think, too exhausted to care about the nagging ache that just lying with her—being with her anywhere—always created in his body.

Looking at her now, at the way she lay curled under the covers, her dark hair splayed across the pillows, her face relaxed, he was so strongly tempted to slide back into the bed and gather her close to him. To haul her up against him, and kiss her until they were both delirious with need just as he had wanted to do last night.

Then he had wanted to kiss the lying words 'I don't want it. I don't want you,' from her mouth and crush them back down her throat. And then he would have taken her to the bed—to their bed, their marriage bed—and made love to her until every last thought of 'not knowing' him was driven from her mind.

And he still wanted to do just that. Wanted it so much. All that was feminine in her called to every masculine sense in his own body, making him harden until he burned with need, ached with the frustration of holding it in check. But he was going to hold back if it killed him. He had been caught that way before, in the early days of their marriage. He'd rushed her into bed without taking time to find out who she really was and what she truly wanted. And they had ended up at the opposite sides of a wide, gaping chasm as a result.

A chasm that his dreams had told him was still there. Perhaps even wider than ever.

'I might not want to be married to you any more...'

Argus whined again and Zarek dragged his thoughts back to the present, opening the wardrobe to find something comfortable to run in. And once more his mind came to a sudden and jolting stop as he considered the packed interior of the cupboard.

She had kept all his clothes. Every item that he had left behind. They had all been carefully folded and replaced as if he had just set out for a simple business trip and was expected home at any minute. Would a woman who never wanted to see her husband again do anything like that?

The question nagged at him as he dressed. It burned in his thoughts as he pounded along the stony beach, Argus running ecstatically beside him. It was still there, still troubling him when he finally admitted that he could run no more and made his way back to the house, to shower in another bedroom so as not to wake Penny if she was still asleep, change into the clothes he had brought from the bedroom earlier.

And still he couldn't find any answer to the confusion of his thoughts.

He had to find some work to do. Work would distract him and focus his mind on other things. Work had always been his salvation in the past when he needed a distraction from the speed with which his marriage had gone to rack and ruin. The total change in the woman he had married.

His private office appeared just the same as when he had left it, with nothing touched, nothing moved. The computer and every other piece of equipment was in exactly the same place, unchanged. It had been kept clean and dusted so that again he had the unnerving feeling that it was as if he had just walked back in after being away for a day or so.

But it was when he unlocked one of the drawers and pulled it open that he found the first evidence of change, the first sign that someone had been in the office in his absence and had used the desk for anything more than just sitting at.

'What the…?'

Pulling the folder of papers from the drawer, Zarek opened it and spread them out over the polished top of the desk, staring in disbelief as he moved them around with his fingertips.

'I don't believe it.'

There was no doubt whatsoever who had been busy with these documents. Everywhere was the evidence of Penny's handwriting, easily recognisable even after all this time. But it seemed impossible that his wife would have anything to do with these…

And that was not the only puzzle. Once more he sorted through the papers before him, studying each one closely. There was something not quite right here. Something that didn't fully make sense. So many of the documents had been corrected, changed, with alterations made and then erased again, new ideas added all the time. And yet she could have handed over the first set and it would have been fine.

The sound of footsteps on the stairs alerted him. The study door was partly open as Penny came slowly down the wide curving staircase. He saw how she noticed the way it was standing ajar and paused, hesitating noticeably.

So if he said hello—spoke at all—would that encourage her or would it simply send her running again, heading back up the stairs or along the hallway into the big empty kitchen, away from him? He didn't have time to consider the question for long before she gave the door an uncertain push and appeared in the doorway.

'*Kalimera.*'

He kept his greeting cool and indifferent with an effort. It was impossible, unbelievable, but somehow it almost seemed as if the short time they had spent apart had actually been longer than the months they had been separated before yesterday. It was as if he was looking at her afresh, with brandnew eyes, and seeing her more clearly than ever before.

Seeing the changes he had not fully noticed in all the hours they had been together on the day before.

When he had met her she had been so young. Barely twenty-two, just a girl, working in her first job. Her face still had the softness, the faint roundness of youth, and her tall, slender figure had been almost boyish in its narrow shape. She had grown up in the past two years, her face thinning, her features refining so that she had the most devastating high, slanting cheekbones under her beautiful almond-shaped blue eyes. And her body had filled out slightly, adding gentle curves to an almost too-slender shape so that now she was no longer a girl but all woman, a woman just coming into her fully feminine prime and fulfilling all the stunning promise of her youth.

Dear heaven, but she even made the well-worn pink tee shirt and faded, shrunken jeans she wore look fantastic. No silken designer gown or elegant evening dress could look any better or flatter that glorious body any more. Briefly Zarek had to wonder if she had simply pulled on the nearest things to hand or whether the slightly shabby clothing had been chosen to distract him, disguise the sensual appeal of her body. If that was the case then she had failed dramatically. The way that the shrunken top clung to the curves of her breasts and narrow ribcage, riding up to reveal an inch or two of smooth golden skin, was pure temptation. And the denim, washed soft by repeated laundering, clung to her hips and thighs in a way that made his pulse pound, his body tightening in instant response.

'Good morning.'

Her response was cooler even than his own. And she was back to being the ice maiden again, with her face frozen into a distant mask, those blue eyes seeming to look straight through him without a flicker of emotion.

'It's a beautiful day.'

Oh, this was ridiculous, Penny told herself. They were speaking to each other as if they were near strangers. And yet she had fallen asleep, naked, in his arms.

And woken to find him gone.

'Did you get any sleep in the end?' Oh, how formally conventional could she get?

'No.'

Zarek's response brought her up short. Such honesty was the last thing she had been expecting. What she had anticipated was that the conversation was going to carry on in the way it had started, with the pair of them dancing round the reality of their situation, resorting instead to meaningless inanities.

No man should have the right to look so good this early in the morning, she thought, taking in the loose navy shirt he wore with black denim jeans, the way that his hair, still damp from the shower, curled slightly around his ears and at the nape of his neck as it began to dry in the heat. Particularly not after a sleepless night. Lying awake herself, she had heard him get up at a ridiculous hour and go downstairs, Argus pattering happily behind him.

When the front door had opened she had gone to her own bedroom window and looked out to see him setting off towards the shore, dressed only in black running shorts and a pair of battered trainers. The rising sun had gilded the jet-black hair, the olive skin of his long back, the powerful shoulders, and the lean, muscled length of his legs. All of which had featured in the heated, erotic dreams that had burned into her brain through the little sleep she had had. She had watched him hungrily as he ran down the narrow path, unable to drag her eyes away. Her throat had been dry and tight with longing; the memory of the feel of that skin under her fingers, the musky male scent of it in her nostrils made her heart clench with longing.

The long lonely hours at the beginning of night had brought home to her just how much she had lost without Zarek in her life. The physical hunger was like the bite of acid deep in her stomach, eating away at her and at her resolution to hold herself apart from him, the determination that she needed emotional love before she could give into the fury of sexual need that he awoke in her. Then when she'd slipped into his bed the feeling that had tugged at her heart had been one of perfect rightness, a sense of coming home. She had known then that if he had tried to seduce her she wouldn't have been able to resist it. She wouldn't even have tried.

But he hadn't touched her. Instead he had been intimate with her in a very different way, by opening up to her as she had never expected he would. And she had drifted asleep held close in his arms.

'But I'm glad that you made up for your earlier restlessness,' Zarek told her. 'I heard you pacing around your room. It seems that Argus was the only one who slept all night.'

He dropped a hand onto the big dog's head and rubbed it softly and, as before, Argus pushed himself against the caressing touch, his eyes closing in ecstasy. Once again Penny thought that she knew exactly how he felt, and the sight of those long, bronzed fingers ruffling the thick black and white fur had her compressing her lips tightly against the whimper of need that almost escaped her.

The thought of him lying awake listening to her prowling restlessly round her bedroom was tying her stomach into tight painful knots. Had he guessed at the yearning hunger that had kept her awake, the need that had made it impossible even to lie still in her bed? Penny's heart kicked up a gear at the thought, her pulse beating erratically at her temples and the base of her throat.

'Have you had any breakfast?'

Back on the conventionally polite track once again, she acknowledged. It was safer that way. Far less dangerous than trying any other sort of conversation that might let her foolish tongue betray her terribly.

'Should I get you something—that is unless the staff are back today? No?' she questioned as Zarek shook his dark head.

'No. I told them I would let them know when to come back. Until then they are all on paid leave.'

'So—so we're alone?' Her apprehension at the thought showed in the way that her voice quavered on the last word.

'We're alone and there is no need for this incessant desire to feed me. You don't have to keep demonstrating that you have benefited from the cookery lessons you've taken. I'm much more interested in the other skills that you seem to have acquired.'

'What other skills exactly?'

For a shocking moment, with her own thoughts still clouded by sensual hunger, she thought he actually meant some sort of skills in the bedroom and felt the hot blood rush into her cheeks as a result. But just in time she saw the plans he had in his hands and caught back the hasty words that rushed to her tongue.

'It was you who worked on these? The plans for the *Calypso*?'

She couldn't tell just what his tone meant, but there was no point in denying the truth when it was so obviously there in her handwriting, her notes.

'Yes… Yes, I worked on them.'

His response was the last thing she expected. He actually laughed. Not in mockery or even real amusement. It was a laugh of disbelief and he shook his head in obvious bemusement at the same time.

'You did all this?'

'I said I did.'

'No need to get so defensive, *glikia mou*. I'm amazed—and impressed. I never knew you had such talent or the knowledge to use it. I'm sure that you didn't when I left.'

'I listened to you, and then I studied—two years is a long time.'

'So it seems. You continue to surprise me. So what else will I discover that I never knew about my wife? What else did you learn while I wasn't here?'

When he smiled at her like that she found it impossible to think of anything else. When his mouth softened and curved, and his eyes warmed in genuine delight, there was only one thought that formed inside her head, one feeling that she recognised at all. It was the lesson she had learned with the most pain and difficulty from the day that Zarek had walked out of the house and set out for the *Troy*. The one that had been reinforced with every hour he had been absent and all the terrible days when she believed that he was dead. And it was a lesson that had been driven home again with dreadful brutality as she had lain alone last night, trying desperately to sleep and fearing that no rest would ever come.

The one thing the past two years had taught her was that

life without Zarek in it was not *living*. It was nothing more than existing, dragging herself through the days without meaning, without hope, without joy. Loving Zarek was what gave her life its purpose, its significance, its delight. She could go through her days without him and even make a reasonable go of things. She'd done that, hadn't she? She had learned new skills, discovered strengths she'd never known she had, and she had thought that she was managing well. But he had only to walk back into her life, to be part of her life once again for—what, was it really not quite twenty-four hours?—and everything became so much brighter, the world so much better simply because he was in it.

She loved him totally and completely. He was the essence of her world, the breath in her lungs, the sun coming up in the morning. And last night, lying lost and alone without him, she had learned the most painful, most powerful lesson of all.

It didn't matter whether Zarek loved her or not. He wanted her and that was enough. She wouldn't ask for anything more. She couldn't ask for it, for fear that he would tell her what she already knew deep down was the darkest truth. That he had nothing to give her but his passion.

But if she could entice him back into her bed then perhaps she could keep him with her at least.

'Penny?' Zarek's rough—voiced prompting told her that she had been standing there for too long without speaking. 'What else is there?'

'What else is there?' she echoed, looking into his face and knowing there was only one answer. If his passion was all he felt for her, all he would give her, then it would be enough. She had enough love for the both of them and she shared that blazing, burning physical passion too. Without it life was just not worth living but with it she had Zarek and the wonderful, glorious excitement they could create between them.

She was not going to give up on that very easily.

'What else? Well, to my mind there's only one thing worth bothering about. And that is—no...'

She caught herself up deliberately, tilted her head slightly to one side as she gazed deep into the darkness of his eyes. Slowly she slid her tongue out and slicked it across her bottom lip, smiling faintly as she watched his dark eyes drop down to follow the small movement.

'No, I don't think I'll tell you—I'll show you.'

Leaning forward, she pressed her mouth to Zarek's, feeling the sudden tiny start of shock, the faint gasp of his breath in between his lips.

'Show you exactly what I've learned since you were last here.'

And taking the two small steps it needed to be close up against the hard warmth of his lean body, she pressed herself to him, moulding her frame to his as she linked her arms around his neck, tangled her fingers in the dark slippery silk of his hair, and drew his head down to her so that she could deepen the embrace.

'I've learned that *this* is the only thing that matters.'

CHAPTER TWELVE

I'VE learned that this is the only thing that matters.

There was something in that sentence that jarred, sticking a mental knife in just when Zarek least expected—or wanted—it. But he didn't have time or the inclination to stop and consider just what it was that nagged at him. Penny's lips were on his, the taste of her filling his mouth. The sweet scent of her body was all around him, the warmth of her skin against his.

This was what he'd longed for since his memory had come back. Before that, he had remembered her in his subconscious, in heated, yearning flashes, in hot, erotic dreams that had him tossing and turning through the night, awakening soaked in sweat, with his heart racing as if he had run the race of his life.

And the worst part of waking had been the hunger, the craving that had filled his sleep and that still lingered long after he had woken, even after he had drenched himself in the coldest shower possible. In his sleep he had reached out to the warm and willing woman that aroused his senses, only to find that when he opened his eyes there was no one there.

That was not going to happen this time.

This time the woman he remembered was safely in his arms, her mouth taking his, the swell of her breasts pressed up against his chest. This time was no dream from which he had any fear of waking. It was real, it was hot, it was the fulfilment of his sensual fantasises and he was going to take full advantage of it.

In fact it was more than he had ever dreamed of. Because in those dreams, the woman he now knew as his wife had been warm and willing, but a little hesitant, almost softly shy as she responded to his touch, his kiss. She had been responsive but not proactive. He had been the one to initiate intimacy while she had been the giver, opening softly to him, welcoming him, but not taking the initiative.

The woman in his arms now was all forwardness and enticement, her actions coming close to demand. Her mouth took his with hunger, her tongue dancing with his in a wild, erotic provocation. Her rounded hips pressed against his hot and aching sex, making him groan aloud in barely controlled need in the same moments that her fingers tugged at the buttons on his shirt, ripping them open as if she couldn't wait to touch and taste his burning flesh. The moist pressure of her lips against his hardened nipple made him jolt sharply as if a sudden bolt of electricity had shot right through him.

'Glikia mou…' The words sounded rough and raw, coming from a throat that was tight with the tension of need. 'Not so fast. This has been a long time coming and we have all the time in the world. Slow down.'

She didn't want to slow down, Penny told herself. She didn't want to give him, or herself, any time to think. They might have all the time in the world, but only if she could show him that they were meant to be together. If she could convince him that she was the woman he needed, the woman he couldn't live without.

And the way to do that was through the blazing passion

that had always fired between them in the past. A hunger so hot she had felt it might almost melt her bones in its furnace, bringing her to her knees before it. In the past, in their marriage bed, she had always been a little shy, always allowed him to take the lead, to be the seducer and she the seduced. But that had been when she had believed that their marriage would have time and space in which to grow, and deepen. Time that she had thought she had lost completely when he had gone missing. Time she no longer had now that he was home.

And so she pressed herself even closer up against him, almost pushing him backwards until he was hard up against the wall, his shirt ripped from his back, the golden planes of his chest exposed to the hungry attentions of her mouth and tongue.

'I don't want to slow down,' she muttered, sighing, against his skin, inhaling the clean musky scent of him that sent her senses spiralling as if under the influence of some potent, intoxicating drug. 'I want you now.'

'And I…' Zarek managed before she closed his mouth again with hers, letting her hands take over from her lips, touching, stroking, teasing. She even let her nails score a delicate path down to his waist, making him jerk in wild, uncontrolled response.

'*Eisai o sizigos mou.*'

From somewhere she dragged up one of the phrases in Greek that he had taught her.

'You are my husband…you—*ise o adras mou*—you are my man. And I want my man—I want him now.'

'*Gamoto!*'

Zarek's rough curse was forced out of him as she deliberately let her wandering hands slide down to where the heat and power of his erection strained against the zip on his trousers, his choking moan making her smile with a new and very welcome sense of the power she had over him.

But as she fumbled with the buckle on his belt, tugging it free with a sense of impatience, Zarek suddenly changed the mood, the balance of the moment. No longer content to be the one who was under sensual assault, he shifted, changed position and became the one who was in control. Capturing her hands, her arms, he lifted her bodily from the floor and carried her across the room to where the long, low couch stood before the empty fireplace.

'And I want my woman,' he muttered roughly, laying her down on the cushions and coming down beside her before she even had time to snatch in a much-needed, hungry breath.

He was much more efficient at dealing with her clothes than she had been with his and it was only moments before the tee shirt and jeans were tossed aside, her underwear following them. His own trousers were dropped to the floor as Zarek came over her naked, hungry body, crushing her into the yielding cushions with the force of his weight and strength.

His skin was hot against hers, his hands rousing her to even greater heights of hunger, and she urged him on with moaning, hungry cries that seemed to drive him to the edge of distraction. When she combined them with insistent, urgent, provocative caresses that had him almost snarling her name in a wild blend of need and encouragement, he lost control completely, pushing her legs wide apart with the forceful pressure of one knee and driving himself into her body with barely a heartbeat's pause.

But Penny hadn't wanted any pause. This wonderful, this total possession was all she had wanted and she arched herself against him with a cry of delight, raising her hips to meet him, to take him fully into her where she had wanted him so long and where she had feared she would never ever feel him again.

'Zarek—yes!'

With her lips and her hands she encouraged him in the storm of sensual passion that had them both in its grip, fingers closing over the strength of his shoulders, digging into the tight hard muscles she found there, urging him on. Above her she saw his face, set in the hard, determined lines of passion, his eyes glazed with need, a sharp line of colour etched along his carved cheekbones.

'Oh, Zarek—yes. My man—my husband and my—'

Somehow still retaining the tiniest bit of rational thought, but only just in time, she caught back the betraying final word my *love*. But even if she had let it escape, she doubted if he would have heard it. And a moment later she too was incapable of speech, of thought. She was flying, soaring, reaching for the sun, the stars, losing herself completely in the wonder of the fulfilment she had hungered for for so long.

The explosion of ecstasy was so powerful that she would have sworn she actually lost consciousness for a moment or two, holding onto Zarek by pure instinct, welcoming his powerful climax into her yielding body for as long as she possibly could. Only when he collapsed against her with a cry of satisfaction did she allow herself to let go, to fall back against the couch and let herself float on the heated golden waves of the aftermath of total pleasure.

She had no idea how long she lay there, drifting in and out of consciousness. It was only when some small sense of reality began to creep back into her world that she felt Zarek sigh and lift his head. A moment later he had rolled away from her, lying on his back beside her. Drawing in his breath in a rough, uneven sound, he reached up and raked both hands roughly through his hair, cursing in dark Greek phrases as he did so.

'Zarek?' It was all that she could manage but a rush of

concern forced its way through the glowing haze that still throbbed inside her head. 'What…?'

He moved again, stirring restlessly at her side.

'We didn't use protection.'

If it was possible to freeze while her breath was still ragged and uneven, her chest still heaving, and her heart racing as if she had run the fastest marathon ever, then Penny froze. At least her thoughts did, her brain seeming to come to a complete halt as if under the effects of a powerful punch to her jaw. And in spite of the warmth of the morning, the sun that was streaming through the window, she suddenly felt as if she were sheathed in ice from head to toe, shivering violently as a result.

But it was the terrible sense of shock and horror that was making her tremble. The cold that was creeping through her body was created by a sense of horror and disbelief rather than any effect of the weather.

'What…?'

She tried to ask a question but it seemed to evaporate on her tongue, leaving her mouth opening and closing until she felt she must look like a stranded fish, gasping for breath.

'What did you say?' she managed at last, but her voice was little more than a croak and she could barely hear the words herself.

Zarek caught them though and he turned his dark head to glance at her briefly, coldly. Then almost immediately he looked away again, throwing his head back on the cushions as he stared up at the ceiling.

'I think you heard me,' he drawled coldly. 'But just to make certain—I realised that we didn't use any protection. I wasn't expecting…unless you're still on the pill?'

'No, I'm not.'

It was as she said the words that the full implications of what she had said hit home. Suddenly finding that she could move, she flung herself upright on the settee, twisted round to stare at him.

'No, I'm not!'

'Then I think we could be in trouble here.'

A cynically mocking sideways glance from those dark, dark eyes challenged her, draining all the earlier heat from her body from her and leaving her with a devastating sensation of being totally bloodless, any strength fleeing from every nerve in the space of a shaken, wretched heartbeat. She knew that her skin must have lost all colour and that her own eyes were wide and staring, their blue colour probably clouded with the brutal sense of shock and disbelief.

Zarek by contrast looked totally relaxed and at his ease. Totally unconcerned by his nudity, his long body stretched out full length on the couch, narrow feet resting on the padded arm at the far end. His hands were linked behind his neck, supporting his head, heavy lids dropping down to conceal his brilliant jet eyes from her. Lying like this, he looked like nothing so much as a sleepy, sexually replete jungle cat relaxing in the sunshine. But Penny knew only too well that the appearance was deceptive. Make the wrong move—or say the wrong thing—and the contented pussycat would turn instantly into a powerful, predatory tiger hunting down his prey and determined to deliver a brutal retribution for the disturbing of his rest.

Just for a moment those hooded lids lifted, flashed one quick, coldly assessing glance in her direction...

'One thing's for sure, there's no way you'll be able to use that desertion excuse for divorce now,' Zarek continued, the words practically a darkly dangerous purr. 'The two-year separation you accused me of yesterday is well and truly over.'

She'd thought she'd been distressed enough yesterday. Thought that she was too afraid to go through with making love with Zarek when she felt she didn't know him well enough after his long absence and all she had learned about him in that time, to risk being intimate with him. Now she had given into the yearning hunger his touch awoke in her and look where it had led her.

Feeling suddenly very grubby and tainted, shamed and terribly used, Penny couldn't bear to stay beside him any longer. Pushing herself away from him with a force that carried her across the rug, to land uncomfortably in one of the big padded armchairs opposite, she curled up into a defensive bundle, wrapping her arms around herself to hold herself together, trying to stop the shaking that racked her body.

'That's what it was all about!'

She couldn't keep the horror from her voice or disguise the disgust she felt at the way she'd been treated.

'That's all it was—a way to keep me as your wife—trap me into sleeping with you so that you could... That was what this was about.'

'Not at all,' Zarek told her calmly, easing himself into an upright position. 'I wanted to remind you of what we had between us—but I should also point out to you that you were the one who started all this. You were the one who said that *"this is the only thing that matters"*...'

He echoed her words, her voice, with such devastating accuracy that Penny couldn't control a painful shudder of reaction at hearing what she had said. And hearing just how she had said it.

Had she really sounded so huskily seductive, so provocative? She had never dared to do anything like that in all the time they had been married. She had felt the passion, adored making love with Zarek, but she had never had the real confidence to show it or take the initiative. At the beginning it had all been too new and she had felt so shy with this amazing man who seemed, unbelievably, to want her so much. And then when she had discovered that he only wanted her to provide him with an heir, shock and pain had made her withdraw from him, their lovemaking never the same again. The thought that she might have lost him for ever had changed all that. It was no wonder that Zarek believed she was different.

'I thought that was what you wanted.'

'I'd be a fool to deny that.'

Zarek's laugh was shaken, rough-edged.

'But I'm not usually this irresponsible. This stupid.'

Irresponsible. Stupid. She had wanted to make love to the man who had her heart and he thought it had been *stupid*.

'Oh, don't worry about it.'

She tried for bravado, acting as if she didn't care. She even managed to sort of shrug it off.

'It doesn't matter.'

'Even if it means that you might end up pregnant?'

The question hit her like a slap in the face. She really hadn't even considered that, hadn't spared a thought for the fact that they were not using any contraception. Or if the idea had flashed through her mind then she had pushed it away again, the need that was driving her far too powerful for caution.

Now she had to consider it. And do more than consider it. Because the look on Zarek's face had turned her blood to ice. Was it possible that just when she had resolved that her future lay with him, no matter what, *he* had decided that a child and a future with her was the last thing he wanted?

'I don't want to talk about it.'

Not like this, not sitting here stark naked, totally exposed in all possible ways, physically, emotionally. Somehow she made herself face him, schooling her expression into a total blank, revealing nothing.

'I'd like my clothes, please.'

Was that cold stiff little voice really hers?

'Your servant, ma'am…' Zarek murmured cynically, strolling over to where her jeans and tee shirt lay on the floor. Snatching them up, he tossed them in her direction, not caring that they fell several inches short and landed in a crumpled heap at her feet. She grabbed for them and scrambled into them as quickly as she could, well aware of the fact that he was pulling on his own clothes with much less haste and more efficiency. That, combined with the fact that he only pulled his shirt on, leaving it unbuttoned, meant that he was dressed well before her, giving him an unfair advantage. But with her own clothes on she at least regained some degree of confidence, ready to face whatever came.

And Zarek barely gave her time to pull the pink tee shirt over her head before he spoke again.

'Penny—if you are pregnant…' he began and the sombre expression, the dark tone, seemed to tell their own story.

'Don't!'

It was a cry of distress and she had to fight with herself not to put her hands over her ears, knowing she didn't want to hear him pronounce her fate.

'Don't tell me you don't want…won't want a baby—'

'Don't want?' Zarek cut across her in obvious consternation. 'But it was you who never wanted a child. You said—'

'I know what I said—and I lied!'

That stopped him dead. His hands that had gone to the buttons on his shirt now fell away again, leaving it gaping open over the wide expanse of his chest. Penny could see the marks on his skin where her nails had caught him in the heat of their passion and she shivered in reaction to the realisation of just how out of control she had been.

'You lied?'

She didn't think that the muscles in his face could get any tighter, or his eyes darker and more distant. But she had come this far now. There was no going back.

'I lied when I said I didn't want a child. I did—I do. Just not…'

'Just not my child,' Zarek finished for her when her tongue stumbled, unable to get the words out.

There was something in his tone that meant she couldn't leave it like that, no matter what the consequences.

'Just not your heir!' she flashed at him and saw the way a frown snapped his black brows together in confusion.

'Not my heir—my child. But they are both the same thing.'

'No, they're not! Not at all! A child would be created out of love—the start of a family. Our family. But an heir—an heir to Odysseus Shipping—to keep Hermione, your stepbrothers, from getting their hands on the company—that's what you married me for, isn't it?'

'I married you—' Zarek began but Penny couldn't let him continue. She couldn't bear it if he lied to her now. If he tried to dodge the truth. Because that was what she could see in his face. That he was actually going to try to soften the blow and, while her heart twisted with longing to hear the more gentle words from him, she knew she couldn't let it happen. That only the truth would do.

'Tell me the truth, Zarek. Give me that at least. You never loved me when you married me. You wanted me in your bed. And you wanted an heir.'

The moments before he spoke seemed to last a lifetime.

And each one of them made her heart thud so painfully against her ribcage that she felt it was impossible to catch her breath, that she might actually pass out from the stress.

But then, slowly, and strangely almost sadly, Zarek nodded his dark head.

'Yes,' he responded harshly but so clearly that there could be no doubt as to exactly what he was saying. 'Yes, that's exactly why I married you.'

CHAPTER THIRTEEN

WELL, what had she expected? Penny asked herself. She had demanded the truth—had practically forced it out of him. So how could she complain when that truth tore her heart into pieces and left her bleeding and raw?

She didn't understand why it should hurt any more this time. After all, it was only what she had lived with before, what she had decided that she couldn't go on with any longer. But the trouble was that this time around she knew she couldn't make that decision all over again. She had already admitted to herself that she would have to put up with it. She had no other choice. She would take the little Zarek had to offer her and live with it. Because the two years without him had taught her that life without the man she loved in it was no life at all.

'Thank you,' she began, icy with control. But even as she drew in a breath to complete the sentence a sudden uproar from outside broke into what she was trying to say, drowning her voice and making it impossible to continue.

The first thing was the sound of cars. Lots of cars and motor-bikes racing up to the gates at the end of the drive, screeching to a halt. Then doors slamming, feet on the stones, on the grass. A knock at the door loud and long and deafeningly persistent.

'Kyrie Michaelis—are you there? Is it true that you're home—that you're safe?'

'Just a few questions…'

'Can we have a word—an interview?'

And mingling with the demands, the questions, was Argus' low deep bark from behind the front door as he warned off the crowd who had suddenly descended on the house.

'Who is it?'

Startled, shocked, Penny could only stare round her in bewilderment, looking into Zarek's face for some explanation of what was happening.

'What's going on?'

But apart from a deep black frown that drew his brows together and the way he was shaking his head in disbelief, Zarek seemed to have no answer to give her. At least not one that could be heard above the pounding of fists on the door, the persistent, appalling, loud ringing of the doorbell.

Penny put her hands up to cover her ears, to try to drown out the battery of noise.

'What is it? What's happening?'

Unable to bear it a moment longer she dashed across to the window, pulling back a corner of the curtains to look outside.

'Penny—no!'

Zarek was right behind her, launching himself at her to grab hold of her arm, pull her away, drag her back into the middle of the room. But not before she had caught sight of what looked like a milling crowd of people outside. Men and women scrambling over each other to get near the door—or the window when they saw the curtains move. Pushing each other out of the way, elbowing them in the ribs, shoving them aside.

There were microphones and voice recorders and…

The flash of a couple of dozen or more camera bulbs made Penny jump in fright.

'What—?' she began, but as soon as she had started to speak she suddenly knew what was happening, realisation dawning in the same moment that Zarek swore darkly and confirmed what she suspected.

'The paparazzi, damn them. Someone has told them that I'm here and of course they couldn't miss out on a story like that. I can just see the headlines now—"Billionaire Returns from the Grave…"'

'And would that be so bad?'

Now that she knew what was happening, Penny was no longer quite so disturbed. Of course the press would be interested in Zarek's return. His every move had been of interest to the celebrity magazines, the social columns, before they had married and their wedding had been the event of the year with editors of glossy magazines offering small fortunes— more than small ones—for exclusive access to the event, private photographs, the whole 'whirlwind' romance story.

'You want to face them now?' Zarek questioned dryly, gesturing to their disordered clothes, the wild tangle of her hair.

And there was only one answer to that, Penny acknowledged, shuddering faintly at the thought. How could they face the press pack now, after what had just happened? How could they even consider an interview or photographs looking like this? And feeling even worse.

Twitching the curtain back again, she peeped out, then jumped back as an explosion of flashbulbs burst right in her face, or so it seemed, blinding her for a moment.

'Penny, get back! Look, it's me they want—I'll get rid of them. And then…'

The rest of what he was saying was drowned by another

storm of sound as Argus, held in check only by the door, doubled the intensity of his barking, throwing himself at the wood, roaring a challenge to all the intruders into his territory.

Zarek was gone before she could react or say anything and it was when he had left the room that Penny registered the way there had been an extra tension in his body, a raw edge to his voice. Something about his attitude brought thoughts of the night they had just spent together. The dream Zarek had had, and the memories that had shaken him so badly.

And those terrible words. 'I felt alone.'

As she watched she saw him open the door, saw the horde of reporters rush forward. And just for a split second, too brief for anyone in the crowd to notice, she saw him flinch, saw the betraying gesture of his hand lifted to fret at the scar that she had seen so many times before and knew what it meant.

Alone.

Well, she wasn't going to stand here and just watch through the window, Penny told herself. She couldn't let him go through this on his own, with no one at his side. Pushing rough hands through her hair in a vain attempt to restore it to some sort of order and straightening her clothing as best she could, she hurried after her husband.

Zarek cursed the arrival of the paparazzi. It was just what he did not need right now. What he needed was time and peace and quiet in which to get to the bottom of just what was going through Penny's mind and, hopefully, to see just where everything had started to go wrong.

Because it had gone wrong. And gone far further than he had ever dreamed.

'Kyrie Michaelis! A word!'

'Zarek—just a question—or two…'

Another explosion of flashbulbs almost blinded him,

making him pause on the threshold to blink away the coloured blotches that had formed in his eyes so that he couldn't see where he was going. Experience of being in a situation like this in the past had taught him that the only thing to do was to paint a smile on your face and keep a pleasant tone on your tongue. Anything else would be taken as an indication of a story he was trying to hide. A bigger story than the one they thought they were covering. And if they didn't find it then they would make one up. But he had had two years without this sort of exposure and somehow he seemed to have lost the knack of switching on the public image as soon as it was needed.

'What happened to you? Where have you been?'

The problem was that his mind was not fully on the situation outside the villa. His thoughts were inside the house, with Penny, seeing the look on her face, hearing the ice cold tone of her voice.

You wanted me in your bed. And you wanted an heir.

The words she had used rang inside his head, almost but not quite drowning out the persistent questions from the crowd of reporters in front of him. Somehow he supplied some answers. He knew he said Malta and amnesia and when they spotted the scar at his temple the flashbulbs went off with renewed fury. But all the time it was Penny's words, Penny's voice that nagged at his thoughts.

I lied when I said I didn't want a child. I did—I do.

Just not your heir.

'Mr Michaelis, is it true that you will now be getting a divorce?'

'What?'

That question got through all the other confusion that was buzzing in his mind. That question couldn't be answered off the top of his head, without thought. He didn't even know why they had asked it.

'We heard that you will now be getting a divorce.'

'Where did that come from?' As if he didn't know. Hermione—or Jason—was stirring up trouble again. But just the way he felt hearing the words told him what he had to do. What mattered.

But first he had to get rid of the paparazzi.

'Your stepmother told us—so is it true?' the reporter persisted.

'Is it true?' Zarek echoed coldly, dark eyes raking over the crowd in contempt. 'What do you think? Would I want to change the way things are when I have just come home to be with the woman I love?'

'But, Mr Michaelis—'

'Enough!'

He was tempted to let go of Argus' collar and let the dog clear the driveway of the reporters. But right now he had more important matters on his mind. He needed to get back into the house and talk to Penny.

'No more questions—no more photographs.'

He was moving back towards the door, taking the dog with him. A few more questions were thrown his way, a few more cameras flashed, but most of the crowd seemed to realise that they were not going to get any more out of him and already they were packing up their equipment, melting away.

Zarek didn't care what they did. He didn't pause, didn't look back until he was in the house. At one moment he glanced towards the door and saw Penny standing there, in the hallway, obviously having heard everything that had been said.

Good. The sight gave him some satisfaction. At least he would have one thing less to explain.

It was when her eyes connected with his and he saw the blank, closed-off expression in them that he felt an uncomfortable jolt. He saw her blue eyes flash just once in open

defiance and anger before she turned and walked away. There
was no warmth in her face, no hint of a smile. So perhaps she
hadn't heard.

Closing the door firmly on the departing crowd, he released
Argus and went looking for her.

'Penny—where are you?'

Penny was reluctant to answer his call. All she wanted to
do was to go upstairs, pack and get out of the house as soon
as possible. She didn't want to see Zarek's face ever again. But
even she couldn't decide if it was because she was so furious
at him for what he had done or because it would hurt so desperately to look into his eyes and know once and for all just
how ruthless and uncaring he was. How little he cared for her.

She had kept out of sight behind the half-closed door so
no one had seen her there. But she had seen everything that
happened. Heard every word.

Heard every word that had fallen from Zarek's lying, cruel
lips. The lips that such a short time before had kissed her into
a delirium of delight and that now had coldly and callously
dropped the most blatant lie into the waiting ears of the reporters, and no doubt into tomorrow's gossip column reports.

And she'd heard that appalling question.

'Mr Michaelis, is it true that you will now be getting a
divorce?'

For a moment the world had swung round her, blurring
dangerously until she felt desperately nauseous. She had
reached out to clutch at the door, holding onto its much-
needed support, forcing herself to breathe slowly and deeply
until her head cleared. Then she had made herself look again.

And that was when Zarek had opened his mouth and told
the most appalling lie she had ever heard him speak.

Or, correction, the first lie she had ever heard him speak.

Because no matter what else Zarek might have done he had never been a liar.

'Would I want to change the way things are,' he had said, 'when I have just come home to be with the woman I love?'

'Penny!'

He wasn't going to let her get away. At least not until she had faced him.

'Penny, where are you?'

Reluctantly Penny appeared in the doorway, her whole body taut, her head held stiffly upright. Once again, she tried the technique of not quite focusing her gaze so that she didn't have to look him straight in the face. There was the sound like a thousand angry bees buzzing inside her head and she couldn't concentrate on anything.

All she could think of was the way that Zarek had made love to her— Oh, dear God, no—he hadn't made love to her! He'd had sex with her, cold-blooded deliberate sex, with one intention only. That of making sure that she couldn't divorce him and—and maybe even to leave her pregnant as he had always wanted. And then—then... Her brain felt as if it would explode at just the thought of it—

Then he had had the nerve to declare to the reporters outside that he had come home to the woman he loved. The woman he *loved*. Zarek had never loved her. He had just told her so to her face.

Vaguely she became aware that Zarek was coming towards her, dark triumph in his eyes. He even smiled at her as he came close.

And she completely lost control of her temper.

'How dare you!' she exploded, stopping him dead. He hadn't expected her to come out fighting. It was written all over his face.

'How dare I what?' Zarek asked. 'Penny—what…?'

'Don't you, "Penny—what?" me! I know what was going on. I saw you, heard you… I heard you lie.'

'No, I—'

'Yes!'

She actually stamped her foot in rage, making Argus come running in from the kitchen to see what was happening.

'How dare you claim to love me in front of those reporters?'

'I didn't *claim*—I did not do it for that. Why would I?'

He actually reached out to her, almost took hold of her fingers, but she flung up her arms in a gesture of rejection, knocking his hand away.

'Because we both know that…know that…'

Her breath caught in her throat making her gasp out loud, unable to go on.

'Know what, Penny?' Zarek asked and she couldn't make out just what his tone was putting into the words.

'That you only married me because you wanted to found a Michaelis dynasty and have an heir to leave Odysseus Shipping to.'

She could only be grateful that he had stopped coming closer to her now. He had frozen completely, standing stock-still, just a metre or so away from her. But for all that the distance they were apart was so small everything about him, the expression in his eyes, the way he held his long lean body so stiffly taut, made her feel as if a huge gaping chasm had opened up between them. One so big that it would be totally impossible ever to bridge it.

'And you think that is the only reason why I married you?' The question might have been formed in ice, the words were so cold and stiff.

'I know it!' Penny cried. 'Oh—you fancied me—you made

that obvious of course! You couldn't keep your hands off me. Which must have made it all the easier for you.'

'You think?'

'I know. After all, there wasn't much else going for me. I only have to think of that carved bed head to know—'

'I had a carving made,' Zarek interrupted, 'Just for you.'

'Oh, yes.'

She couldn't erase the bitterness from her tone.

'Oh, yes—the mouse. The damn *mouse.*'

But Zarek was shaking his head, sending his dark hair flying over his forehead.

'But not just any mouse.'

'Oh, how can you say that? A mouse is a mouse—small, creeping, nervous… Insignificant.'

'But not this one. Come here…'

Penny was still trying to back away, her hands coming up defensively before her, when he reached her and lifted her from her feet, swinging her up into his arms. Holding her tightly against his chest, he carried her out into the hallway, heading for the stairs.

'Zarek, put me down!' Penny wriggled nervously in his hold.

'Keep still,' he warned as he mounted the stairs, ignoring her protests. 'And, no, I won't let you down—not until you see.'

'See what?'

He looked down at her for a moment. A searching, burning stare that seemed to flay away a much-needed protective layer of her skin.

'Until I make you see just how wrong you are.'

CHAPTER FOURTEEN

JUST how wrong?

That sounded shockingly hopeful.

Was it possible that there was something Zarek could show her, tell her, that could make this all right? In spite of herself, Penny couldn't subdue the tiny spark that suddenly lit up in her heart and made her feel so very different about the way he held her, made her stop fighting against his hold.

They were at the top of the stairs now, a couple of long strides across the landing and Zarek kicked open the door that led to their bedroom.

'In here.'

He carried her over to the bed and let her down onto the softness of the coverings. But then, when she would have jumped back up again, getting to her feet, not sure whether she needed to escape or should stay, he pushed her back into place, holding her still with the strength of just one hand. And looking up into his face, into the dark, barely focused eyes, the formidable set of his jaw, she suddenly had a rush of nervous panic.

Had she got this all wrong? Was Zarek not going to tell her what she most wanted to hear? Was his plan something else entirely?

Hadn't she played right into his hands by telling him that she'd lied about wanting a baby? Showing that she wanted to be with him, no matter what?

'Zarek—don't do this. Please.'

Tears burned the backs of her eyes. Tears of loss of the hope she had allowed herself to feel even if just for a moment. Tears of anguish and despair at the thought that he might once again be using only sex as a way of communicating with her. That still passionate desire might be all that he was feeling.

Tears of defeat at the thought that no matter how much she wanted to fight it, rationally at least, physically, she knew that she could not.

Defeat at the admission that she had settled for the sort of second best she had told herself she was never going to agree to. But she couldn't fight both Zarek and herself at the same time.

Even now just the touch of his hands on her sent excitement fizzing through her. Even now, the memory of being held close to the heat and hardness of his body as he had carried her up the stairs, the steel-hard strength of his arms supporting her, her head against his chest, made heat burn along the line of every nerve.

Even though his hands were now used to restrain her, keep her in place, she knew that she wanted them there, where they were holding her so tight that she couldn't move. Even though the powerful length of his denim-covered legs was so close to hers that she only had to move an inch or so to make them brush against each other. And his head was bent so that it was so close to her, his eyes boring into hers—but did they burn so intensely in an attempt to entice or to dominate?

'Zarek—let me go!'

She broke off as his grip tightened on her and he gave her imprisoned hand a tiny shake.

'Penny—listen. Listen—please.'

And it was that *please* and the voice in which he spoke it that stunned her, shocking her into silence and stillness, all the fight draining out of her in a rush.

'Please…' he repeated.

Suddenly it was as if the fighting had been all that had held her upright. Her spine sagged, her struggles stopped completely and she could only freeze into total stillness, staring up into the clouded darkness of his eyes.

'Zarek…' It was just a whisper. But his head was so close to hers that a whisper was all she needed. 'Just what are you doing?'

'Penny, don't fight—or talk—not yet. Just look at this…'

After that shaken, shattering *please* he'd recovered some of his self-assurance. The pleading note had gone from his voice but at the same time there was a strangely ragged sound to the words as if they—or he—were starting to fray at the edges.

He was turning her as he spoke. Practically lifting her bodily from the bed and twisting her round so that she was facing away from him and looking directly at the ornately carved wooden bed head. The one they'd been given as a traditional wedding gift and that she had seen for the very first time on their wedding night.

Recalling that night, the first night they had ever spent together, the night she had given him her virginity, Penny could only be grateful that she was sitting down. As it was she knew that her whole body was trembling in a way that Zarek, still holding her, must surely feel now.

He had been tender that night, careful and gentle as well as so ardently passionate that she had felt she were going up in flames just to be held by him, touched by him. Loved by him. At least at that time she had allowed herself to think of the word love, hope for love from him.

But that had been before Jason had warned her that the only thing that drove Zarek was the need for an heir. Hermione had commented on it too. And then she had seen it for herself, the determination to focus on the company almost to the exclusion of everything else. She hadn't realised then that Jason and his mother had their own personal agenda. In her naiveté she had listened to both of them and she hadn't turned to the one man who could tell her the truth.

But when she'd challenged him downstairs, he'd reinforced everything she'd feared.

'That's exactly why I married you,' he'd said. What else was there to say?

Swallowing hard, she looked up at Zarek's dark, intent face.

'Tell me about it,' she said, and she knew that she didn't just mean the carving on the headboard. The carving that danced before her eyes when she tried to focus on it.

But to her total shock and consternation Zarek suddenly shook his dark head. His mood seemed to have changed abruptly as he raked both his hands through his black hair, ruffling it in a way that was disturbingly appealing. The gesture took his hands away from her arms, releasing her completely, but Penny found that, although she was now free, the last thing she wanted to do was to escape. Now she was the one holding herself completely still, sitting on the edge of the bed, waiting, needing to hear what he had to say.

'I'm sorry,' he said, making her blink in shock as he dropped down beside her on the bed, sitting close but not too close. Somehow he managed to hold his long body away from hers so that he was not touching her, but at the same time she couldn't feel that he was holding himself away from her because he wanted to put distance between them. On the contrary, she had the impression that he was doing it for her sake. Because he didn't want to crowd her. Because he wanted *her* to feel separate from him until…

Until what?

'I'm going about this all wrong,' Zarek said suddenly. He was leaning forward with his arms resting on his thighs, hands clasped, staring down at the floor as if carefully considering what he had to say. 'I should have started with saying how sorry I am…'

'You just did,' Penny put in, but her response was greeted with another shake of his dark head.

'No—not for that—and that was not enough. What I mean is that I am so sorry for never understanding the reality of love.'

'I…'

Penny tried to speak but nothing would come. Had he just said *love*? And what did he mean?

'I'll admit that I never learned much about love. My mother was dead by the time I was four, and my father lost interest in life as a result. That was what left him open to Hermione and her scheming. When he became ill, I promised him I would make sure I had an heir—a member of our family to leave the company to.'

'So that was why you were so angry when you thought I was selling out to Jason. Not because you believed I had moved on to him.'

Zarek's eyes lifted briefly, burned into hers.

'You thought I was dead. You believed you were a widow. I couldn't expect you to wait for ever.'

'Oh, but…'

He hadn't heard her interjection, Penny realised. He was focused so intently on what he had to say that he talked straight through it.

'But you didn't, did you? I should have realised it from the start but it was only when I found those plans—the ones for the *Calypso*. I knew there was something wrong there but...'

'Zarek...'

She didn't know if he heard her this time, only knew that he turned to look at her, to stare deep into her eyes as if to draw the truth out of them. But at the same time what she saw in the black depths of his own gaze was that he knew the truth already. Knew it at a heart-deep, soul-deep level that needed no further explanation, no details. But he gave them anyway.

'One of the earliest plans was just right—perfect. It was everything I'd talked about, everything I wanted on that boat. But that was the one that was pushed to the back, kept at the bottom of the pile. And every other week there was a new one—one where you'd erased things, changed things, worked on the details a little more—when they didn't need it. And why...'

'I...' Penny began before she realised that he wasn't asking her why, but starting to tell her. That he had worked it out for himself and he really did understand. And because of that she knew she wanted to tell him herself. To let him hear the words from her mouth.

'I did it for you. I wanted to finish the designs on the *Calypso* because I knew how much it meant to you. I wanted the boat to be—to be...'

Remembered emotion made her stumble over the words.

'To be your memorial. But I knew that if it was finished, if *Calypso* ever went on sale, then I would really have to admit that you were gone and were never coming back. And I couldn't do that. And then Hermione—Jason—started pushing for—for a "rationalization" of the situation as far as Odysseus Shipping was concerned. But I said that I couldn't possibly think of that, not until I'd completed my memorial to you.'

'So you kept saying that it needed something new—something more. And you were erasing everything you'd worked on, showing them the incomplete version when all the time you had the perfect design hidden at the bottom of my desk drawer. You were holding them off, refusing to give in, in just the way that you kept all my clothes, when any sort of sense would say—'

'I couldn't let you go!' Penny cut in, needing to say it, to declare at least part of the truth about how she had felt even if she didn't dare to go the whole way. 'I just couldn't.'

'I know.'

There was such certainty in his tone that it made her stomach twist into tight, yearning knots. He had come so far but not quite far enough.

'I recognised what you were doing because it was how I was with my father. When I came home the only way I could win my father's attention was by being part of Odysseus Shipping—working for it—working with him. If I'd needed any proof that you'd loved me, it was there in front of me.'

'If…' Penny could only echo the word, unable to believe he'd actually used it. Had he really not needed proof?

'I realised that I was looking for "love" in all the wrong places. I saw it in the big things—like passion and hunger. I didn't know how to express myself any other way. I thought that if I gave you that you would know that I cared. And so when you started to withdraw from me I saw that as evidence that you had never loved me. Especially when you seemed to want to make sure that we never had a child.'

'The heir you wanted so much.'

'No.' Once more Zarek was shaking his head.

'No?'

'The child I wanted—or, rather, the child I didn't know I wanted until you made me so aware of the difference.'

'But you said...' Pain twisted in her heart, blurred her eyes as she remembered how he had stood before her and, calm, controlled, and totally certain, had declared, 'Yes, that's exactly why I married you.'

'I know what I said. And I had to say it because you asked for the truth. You insisted on it—and I wanted to be honest too. So I told you what it had been like. What had been in my mind in the moment that I asked you to marry me. I wanted you—*Thee mou* but I wanted you—and we both wanted a child. I thought that would be enough. It would make a great partnership. It was only later that I realised it didn't make a marriage.'

'When...?' She couldn't get the words out, the tears were so thick and heavy in her throat, almost choking her.

'When did I realise?' Zarek finished for her. 'As soon as I'd walked out on you in a rage. When I realised I was so damn furious because I was disappointed. On the *Troy* when I woke alone and missed you curled up next to me. On the pirates' boat when I thought that this might be the end—that I'd never see you again. In the black night on a black sea, when it seemed there was just one reason to hang on, to keep my head above water. I vowed that if I got out of there I would come back and tell you how I felt and ask you to start again. And this time I'd look for the smaller things, the quieter things. The things you gave when you worked on the *Calypso*—or last night when you came to my room.'

He paused, looked deep into her eyes as if searching for something and Penny could only hope that he found it in her own gaze because, even though her heart was so full of hope that she feared it might burst, she didn't dare yet actually speak what was in her thoughts.

'Just when I'd begun to realise how much brighter my life

was married to you, Fate took a hand,' Zarek continued. 'I was rescued—my life was saved but I lost my memory. I spent two long years wondering who I was—and wondering just why I always had this sense that something was missing. Something important. Something vital.'

'And when you came back…' He'd heard her saying she wanted him declared dead. Wanted to move on. 'That day at the beach…'

'I was totally off balance after seeing you with Jason. I had never known such a rage of jealousy before. Never cared enough to. But with you…'

Penny's breath caught in her throat like a small, uncontrolled sob that she couldn't hold back. She didn't know if Zarek heard it but his hands closed over hers, holding tightly but without that constraining quality they had had before. This time his touch was so much more gentle—she might almost say a lover's touch.

'It felt like I'd been given my life back only to have it—or the most important part of it—snatched away again just when I'd begun to realise how much it meant to me. I didn't know whether I'd been right all along and you were something so special I could never let you go. Or whether you had in fact been only concerned about Odysseus Shipping and all that it brought.'

His laugh was sharp, harshly ironic.

'Just when I'd realised how little the company mattered, I feared it was all that you wanted.'

'What I want…what I want is just you and me. Together. A man and a woman. Just as it was last night—'

She couldn't finish the sentence because Zarek suddenly leaned forward and stopped the words with his mouth, kissing them back down her throat. Penny stilled in shock, but not the fearful sense of being bewildered of just moments before. This was different. And it was close to something wonderful.

'I think now perhaps is the time,' he whispered against her mouth, his forehead resting against hers, dark eyes looking down into her blue ones. 'Perhaps now you could look at the carving. And before you say any more about the fact that I chose a mouse to represent you.'

Gently, with both hands on either side of her face, he turned her towards the bed head. The first thing that she noticed was that his hold on her wasn't quite steady. Something was making him shake, sending a fine tremor running down his arms, into his fingers in a way that told her just how important this was to him.

And this time her eyes were clear and focused. This time she could see what he wanted her to see.

A mouse, yes. But a mouse that was sitting upright, hanging onto something in its paw. And it was nibbling hard...

'What is that?'

'Rope.' His answer was soft but sure.

'Rope? Why rope?'

Zarek came closer, laid his head against hers, his cheek resting on her hair.

'Remember the story—a fable by Aesop where the lion let the mouse go and didn't eat her. Then one day the lion was trapped by hunters, caught in a net and the mouse came and gnawed through the ropes that held him, setting him free.'

'I remember.'

It was all that Penny could manage. Her mind was whirling with thoughts—wonderful, amazing thoughts.

'I was the lion and you were the mouse. You set me free.'

You set me free. Penny's heart jolted just once, hard and sharp against her ribs.

'But you weren't trapped.'

She spoke still with her eyes on that carving, not daring to turn, to look into his face for fear that this might all be a dream. That she might have it all wrong and he was not telling her what she thought he was saying.

'Oh, yes, I was. I was locked into a world I didn't want to live in. A world where only work and Odysseus Shipping mattered. Where I was prepared to marry solely to have an heir. A world where there was no love…'

Slowly, carefully, he turned her head until she was looking into his face. He kissed her once, softly, gently, heartbreakingly briefly.

'Not until you. After I met you. I couldn't get you out of my mind. I knew that I wanted no one else.'

'But you were so cool—so—'

'And you were so young,' Zarek told her, pressing a finger against her lips to cut off her anxious words. 'I was afraid that if I showed you the full force of my hunger for you—the way I really felt—I would frighten you too much, scare you off. But I wasn't prepared to wait. I wanted you as soon as I could have you. I had no suspicion then that fate had other plans. Plans that meant we would lose two years just when we needed them most.'

The way his eyes burned into hers told her of his answer even before he spoke.

'I should have told you before I sailed on the *Troy*, but we had rowed so badly. I was afraid. Things had been so difficult between us and I felt that if I told you, you would never believe me.'

'You might have been right.'

It was just a whisper of admission, her face sobering as she remembered how she had felt back then.

'I was feeling lost and unloved, totally unsure of my place in your life.'

'You didn't just hold the central place in my life—you *were* my life—my love—my heart. I thought that I would be back so soon that you would barely miss me. That then I could start again and show you just what you meant to me. I thought that we would have time to grow into our marriage. Instead of which—'

'No!'

Reaching up, Penny laid her fingers across his mouth to silence him.

'No more. It's time to put that all behind us. That was the past. We have the whole future to look forward to.'

'A future in which I can love you as you deserve to be loved.'

'And I can love you as a woman—a woman who loves her man. I'm not afraid or unsure any more. I've grown up. I thought I loved you when I married but it was as nothing compared to what I feel for you now. I want to be your wife and go into this wonderful future we can have together.'

She barely got the words out before Zarek had captured her mouth in a long, deeply passionate kiss. But it was also a kiss of love, of caring. A kiss that came from his heart, from the depths of his soul. And as he kissed her his hands stroked over her body, caressing, tantalising, arousing until she moaned for sheer joy of the feeling.

'And to prove that,' he whispered thickly against her mouth, holding her so close that she could not be unaware of the force of his need, his hunger for her. But this time it was a hunger that she knew was created by the passion of true love. 'Will you let me make love to you as the woman I love? The love of my heart, my life. My wife.'

'Willingly, *glike mou*,' Penny said happily, gathering him close in her arms and falling back against the pillows as she felt his warm, welcome, beloved weight come over her, his kisses on her cheek. 'I can think of nothing I'd want more—because I really believe that it's more than time I welcomed my husband home properly at last.'

POWERFUL GREEK, HOUSEKEEPER WIFE

ROBYN DONALD

Robyn Donald can't remember not being able to read and will be eternally grateful to the local farmers who carefully avoided her on a dusty country road as she read her way to and from school, transported to places and times far away from her small village in Northland, New Zealand. Growing up fed her habit. As well as training as a teacher, marrying and raising two children, she discovered the delights of romances and read them voraciously, especially enjoying the ones written by New Zealand writers. So much so that one day she decided to write one herself. Writing soon grew to be as much of a delight as reading—although infinitely more challenging—and when eventually her first book was accepted by Mills & Boon she felt she'd arrived home. She still lives in a small town in Northland, with her family close by, using the landscape as a setting for much of her work. Her life is enriched by the friends she's made among writers and readers and complicated by a determined corgi called Buster, who is convinced that blackbirds are evil entities. Her greatest hobby is still reading, with travelling a very close second.

CHAPTER ONE

IONA GUTHRIE bit back an unladylike expletive and tore off her wet smock, wrinkling her nose at the disgusting stickiness of the liquid that oozed down her front and soaked her to the skin.

'*Now* what?' she demanded of the universe, heading for the elegant little powder room close by the entrance of the penthouse. 'First the vacuum system dies, then the laundry loses the special linen, probably produced by diamond-decorated silkworms. Now this—ugh! I'm beginning to believe this penthouse is haunted by a demon. So what's next? An earthquake? A waterspout?'

She pushed back the thick strand of straight ash-blonde hair that had come adrift from her businesslike ponytail, and opened the door. Grimacing, she slung the smock over a towel rail and began to wriggle free of her bra. The scent of the roses in the exquisitely arranged vase permeated the luxurious little room, calming her down a little.

How the other half—no, make that the upper point zero zero zero one per cent—live, she thought, glancing at the flowers.

Fortunately the billionaire businessman for whom the penthouse had been prepared wasn't due to arrive for several hours yet.

And she'd almost finished the checklist. Iona made a mental note to tell the manager of the apartment complex that the maid needed supervision; one of the hand basins in the master bedroom suite had had a hair in it. She'd picked up the detergent bottle to clean it, only to discover that the lid hadn't been put on properly.

The view from the window was enough to soothe anyone, even a detergent-soaked lifestyle organiser. Relaxing into the promise of a sunny weekend, Auckland city hummed peacefully below. A warm spring sun beamed down, highlighting the white wakes of pleasure boats on the harbour and gilding islands that faded into the distance.

Iona expelled another long breath and finally managed to shrug free of the loathsomely sticky bra, glancing at her watch when a muted *ting* from the communications system warned her that the private lift was on its way up.

Good for you, Angie. Dead on time. Her cousin, who was also her boss, was collecting her for the next job, a barbecue one of her clients had suddenly decided to hold that evening.

Her bra landed on the towel rail next to her soggy smock. Pulling a face at her half-naked reflection, she extracted a handful of tissues from her bag before turning on the elegant Italian tap.

She heard the big outer doors slide back, and called out, 'Come on in,' as she began to mop the residue of the detergent from her skin.

A moment later she sensed Angie's presence. Dabbing distastefully at her bare breasts, she said, 'I won't be long.'

'You'd damned well better not be.'

Iona froze. Not Angie—*definitely* not Angie.

Deep, slightly accented, very much male—a voice chilled by a contempt that sent slivers of ice jostling down her spine.

And familiar...oh, so familiar. That voice still haunted her dreams.

Her head jerked up. In the mirror her stunned gaze met eyes like a lion's—tawny and arrogantly disdainful in a bold masculine face.

A man straight out of a Greek fable.

Or a Tahitian fantasy...

A shocked sound tore from Iona's throat when she registered the starkly classic beauty of his features. She swallowed, then croaked, *'Luke?'*

'What the hell are you doing here?' Luke Michelakis asked in a voice so cold it froze her brain.

Hot colour washed up from her naked breasts as she grabbed at the discarded smock and wrapped it around her, only to see her bra slither onto the floor. 'I was—I'm checking the place over,' she muttered. She dragged in a jagged breath and demanded, 'Why are you here?'

'I'm staying here,' he said icily.

'You are?' she blurted, heart pounding so heavily in her chest she was afraid he might hear it. Indignation sharpened her tone. 'Well, you're not due for another five hours!'

Black brows lifted. For a disturbing few seconds he let his unreadable gaze roam her face, then he stooped, picked up the bra and held it out to her, skin-coloured cotton dangling from a long-fingered olive hand.

'Th-thank you.' She snatched the offending scrap of material and tried to regain some shred of dignity. 'Please go.'

The black lashes drooping over those exotic eyes

couldn't hide a glitter that sent a shameful shiver through Iona.

Nothing of that gleam of awareness showed in his tone when he drawled, 'Gladly.'

Humiliated, she turned away. Not that there was any refuge—the mirrored walls revealed every inch of her shrinking, exposed skin to his scathing survey.

For a taut, hugely embarrassing second it seemed he was going to stand there and watch her dress.

She said harshly, 'Go now!'

'My pleasure,' he bit out, and left with the lithe, silent menace of a predator.

Weak from shock and relief, Iona slammed and locked the door behind him, then seized the wet bra and struggled back into it. Her bones felt like rubber and she had to draw several difficult breaths before the colour returned to her skin and she could think clearly.

From the moment they'd met, Lukas Michelakis had had that effect on her—he literally took her breath away.

Charisma, she thought wildly. *Presence, impact*—whatever the term, Luke possessed it in spades. Eighteen months previously it had been the first thing she'd noticed when he'd strode towards her across pristine sands in Tahiti—that, and the authority with which he'd ordered her off, telling her the beach was private.

Luke—here in New Zealand. *He* was the man she and Angie had cheerfully referred to as the unknown plutocrat.

This penthouse *had* to be possessed by a demon, and it had set her up nicely. It was probably laughing its evil head off.

She'd just scrambled back into her smock when the doorbell pealed again.

Oh, at last—Angie...

And no sign of Luke as she hurtled out and opened the door. But instead of the calm presence of her cousin, she was confronted by a harried apartment maid holding a bag.

'The linen from the laundry,' she informed Iona, eyes widening as she looked past her.

Bracing herself, Iona turned. Tall and tigerish, darkly dominating, Luke paced silently towards them.

'I'll show you the rooms to be made up,' Iona said swiftly. Holding her shoulders so stiffly they protested, she almost frog-marched the maid down the corridor towards the three bedrooms.

'Who's the guy?' the other woman hissed just before Iona left.

'A guest of the owner,' Iona said crisply.

'He can be my guest any time he likes,' the girl growled, then giggled.

Iona left the room, unconsciously walking quietly. To no avail; a grim-faced Luke appeared and said curtly, 'I need to talk to you. Come with me.'

Her spine tingled, every nerve in her body sending out a red alert. Ignoring a foolhardy impulse to announce that she didn't take orders from him, she assembled the tatters of her composure and looked up to meet his hooded, intent gaze.

A dangerous move, she thought in dismay when her body suffused with heat.

It took every scrap of control she could produce to steady her voice. 'I'm sorry the bedrooms aren't made up, but the laundry managed to lose the sheets. They've just arrived.'

A negligent shrug of broad shoulders informed her he wasn't interested. He said, 'I can still see a sticky trail of something on your skin. You'd better finish cleaning up, then I want to see you on the terrace.' He paused, his expression unreadable, before drawling, 'I can lend you a shirt if you want one.'

Once—in Tahiti—he'd slung his shirt around her when her shoulders started to burn in the sun, and its removal had led to an erotic interlude that came surging back into her mind only too vividly.

Of course he knew. Colour burned across her cheekbones, and he lifted an arrogant eyebrow, his eyes narrowing in sardonic challenge.

'That won't be necessary,' Iona said, before swinging on her heel and heading back into the powder room. She locked the door behind her, leaned back against it and bit her lip.

Arrogant? Forcing herself to move, she wiped off the detergent.

Arrogant was far too insipid a word to describe Luke Michelakis. She ran her fingers through her hair in a vain attempt to restore its sleekness, and listed words much better suited to the man—words like *cynical, dominating,* and *intimidating...*

It was a satisfying exercise, but she couldn't concentrate on it. Different, infinitely dangerous words refused to budge from her brain.

Sexy. Magnetic. Compelling.

And those words were why eighteen months previously on a hot, deserted beach in Tahiti she'd made the craziest decision in her life. One look at Luke Michelakis had told her he was just what she needed—a man vibrant with charisma, his personality vital enough to rescue her from the emotional desolation that had followed the death of her fiancé, followed soon afterwards by the car crash that took both her parents.

Instinct had whispered that this magnetic Greek would know exactly how to bring her back to life. He'd know how to make a woman scream in rapture— and in his arms, in his bed, she'd feel safe as well as pleasured.

That same perverse instinct had also been sure that because he was handsome and arrogantly sure of himself, he wouldn't want anything more than an affair.

Instinct—while perfectly correct—hadn't known the half of it, Iona thought grimly. Luke had not only introduced her to a sensual intensity she'd never imagined, he'd converted what should have been a very temporary fling into an experience that had changed her life. In his arms she'd learned just how wonderful a superb lover could make a woman feel.

And that erotic discovery had backfired big time, bringing bitter guilt. Gavin had died to save her life; she'd mourned him so deeply she'd been hovering on the edge of depression, yet somehow in ten days and nights of passion Luke took not just her body but a piece of her heart. Disgusted with herself, she'd fled Tahiti, determined to banish all memories of the time she'd spent there.

It hadn't worked, and now here Luke was in New Zealand. Of all the *wretched* coincidences!

It should comfort her that once she got out of this penthouse they wouldn't see each other again. Except that his appearance—so unexpected, so embarrassing— had lit fires she'd thought long smothered.

Iona rinsed out her bra, wrung it free of surplus water and put it back on again. Her body heat would soon have it dry. The smock still clung, and she was acutely aware of her breasts beneath it, of skin so sensitive the material seemed to drag against it, of heat burgeoning deep inside her. She took a deep breath before walking steadily out into the hall with her head held high and what felt like a herd of buffaloes rampaging through her stomach.

The hall was empty, but not for long. Silently, his handsome face grim, Luke came pacing through from the drawing room.

Luke watched Iona come towards him, the lights gilding the cool ash-blonde of her hair. Although it had been a year and half since he'd last seen her, everything about her was burnt into his brain—the warmth of her sleek body, the dark mystery of her changeable blue-green eyes, the lush promise of her mouth…

Her wild surrender.

And his searing feeling of betrayal when she'd walked out on him, the conflict that raged between his prized, iron-clad control and a primal awareness that his affair with Iona had been something rare, much more intense than mere holiday madness.

For the first time Luke admitted that one of the reasons he'd come to New Zealand was to see if he could contact her again. Just to make sure she was all right, of course.

He hadn't expected to find her within a couple of hours of landing. His over-developed sense of responsibility should be satisfied because she was obviously fine.

And certainly not filled with delight to see him again.

But she was still very, very conscious of him.

Setting aside the potent, inconvenient pleasure of that realisation, he said abruptly, 'It will be best if we talk out of earshot of the maid.'

Iona had resolved to treat him with cool detachment, and in a matching tone she managed, 'Very well.'

As he escorted her out onto the terrace she realised anew just how lithe he was. Tall, broad-shouldered, he walked with the prowling, noiseless grace of some great beast of prey.

Not the sort of man anyone would ever overlook.

Once out on the terrace, blocked from the sounds of the city by lush plantings, without ceremony he demanded, 'What are you doing here?'

'I'm making sure that the apartment is ready for you and your party,' she said with an attempt at cool detachment.

A black brow climbed. 'Your employer appears to be a little too trusting. You left the door unlocked—anyone could have come in.'

Iona suspected he was waiting for a defensive response. Well, she wasn't going to give it to him.

Crisply she replied, 'The security here is excellent. The bell sounds when the elevator is stopping at this floor, and as you were supposed to arrive much later this afternoon I assumed it was my employer—Ms Makepeace—who'd been let in by the concierge.'

He dismissed her words with another hard-eyed stare. 'I gather she is not the housekeeper.'

He couldn't possibly be interested in domestic arrangements. This wasn't even his apartment; one of Angie's clients was lending it to Luke while he was in New Zealand. Was he getting some small-minded amusement from emphasising the distance between them?

After all, in Tahiti she'd walked out on him. It had probably never happened to him before.

Or since.

But the man she'd known had not been small-minded. Repressing a rush of too-poignant memories, she replied, 'You're right, she's not the housekeeper. She owns and runs a business organising the lives of people too busy to do it themselves.'

'In other words, a housekeeper and butler service,' he observed on a note of irony.

Iona gave him her best, kindest, nursery-school-teacher smile. 'More like a manager,' she corrected. 'She's extremely successful—hugely discreet, one hundred per cent dependable, and a perfectionist. Your host asked us to make sure the apartment was ready for you, so I called in this morning to check it out. Unfortunately there were a few minor problems, which are on the way to being fixed now. If you'd arrived at the time you said you would, everything would have been perfect.'

He gave a sudden crack of laughter, and for a moment he was the man she'd known, the man she'd fallen— well, not in love with. No, *never* that.

In lust with.

Amusement didn't soften the autocratic lines and angles of Luke's face, but it did make him more approachable when he said lazily, 'It was convenient for me to arrive early. The rest of my party will be here at the given time.'

Going by the bedrooms she'd checked there were at least two other people to come. Was he planning to share that big bed with someone? A stupid pang of pain seared through Iona, as though the possibility was a kind of betrayal.

Startled and afraid, she said briskly, 'All that needs to be done now is for the beds to be made. And if you'll excuse me, I'll go and help the maid and then you'll have the apartment to yourself.'

'It is not necessary,' he said negligently, eyes intent. A slow smile curled his beautifully chiselled mouth. 'I am in no hurry to see you go. Tell me how you've been since you left Tahiti so swiftly.'

This was exactly the sort of thing ex-lovers might say to each other when they were being civilised and sensible and sophisticated about a past affair.

Well, she was just as capable as Luke of being all those things—perhaps not quite so sophisticated...

Yet it took a considerable amount of control for Iona to say as casually, 'I've been fine, thank you.'

'You didn't go back to teaching your little nursery school pupils?'

'No. I was offered this position.'

She knew she sounded stiff, but she couldn't be as relaxed as he was. Apart from Gavin he was the only man she'd ever made love to, but, more than that, his heated, generously sensual expertise had drawn her back into the world of the living, the world of emotions and joy and the ability to respond. He'd got too close to her during those passionate days and nights in Tahiti.

She flicked a glance up at him, noting the glimmer of amusement in the tawny eyes. A strange constriction of her heart took her by surprise, as though she'd spent the intervening months waiting for this moment.

It had to be his powerful physical presence. Luke was the best-looking man she'd ever seen, but that wasn't why her throat had dried. He was so much more than the strong, thrusting bone structure that framed his features, the beautiful lines of the mouth that had given her so much pleasure, the strong, elegant hands...

He interrupted her thoughts with another question. 'And you enjoy managing other people's lives for them?'

'Very much, thank you,' she said sedately.

Obviously she was only too eager to get the hell out of there. Luke fought back an unexpected spurt of temper. He wasn't foolish enough to fall in love with his mistresses; experience had taught him not to let down his guard. So Iona's calm lack of warmth should not only reassure him that she was in control of her life, but allow him to snap the tenuous bonds of an insignificant affair.

Instead he found himself resisting a wild impulse to touch her.

Alarm bells should be screaming, yet it took every shred of self-control not to reach out to her, run the tip of his forefinger around the luscious curve of her top lip, and then down the pale line of her throat, watch her changeable eyes darken into desire.

To prove she was no more immune to him than he was to her...

The doorbell rang. Iona started, then stepped back, blinking shadowed eyes. Luke felt as though he'd been poised on the edge of some dangerous precipice, and realised savagely that he'd just been about to make an idiot of himself.

She swivelled and said huskily, 'That's probably Angie—my employer.'

Luke's voice was cold and deliberate, chilling her right through. 'I'll come with you.'

It was Angie. Iona hoped Luke didn't notice the flicker of unease in the older woman's expression.

It was masked by the calm professionalism in her tone when she said, 'I'm Angela Makepeace; you must be one of the guests expected here?'

'Yes. I am Lukas Michelakis.'

Angie held out her hand. 'How do you do? I'm sorry,

Mr Michelakis, but we were told you wouldn't be here until late this afternoon.'

Somewhat to Iona's surprise Luke accepted the courtesy, long tanned fingers enveloping Angie's in a brisk shake. 'As you see, I am early,' he said, as though it were explanation enough.

Angie nodded, and went on, 'I assume you've met Iona?'

'Iona and I already knew each other,' he said without expression.

Angie's glance swivelled to Iona's still face, then back to the dark countenance of the man towering over her. 'What a coincidence,' she said uncertainly.

'An amazing one.'

Angry at being talked about as though she weren't there, Iona said abruptly, 'The beds should be made up by now—I'll just go and check.'

As she turned away she heard Luke say, 'I wish to speak to you, Ms Makepeace.'

Angie's reply was muffled as they moved towards the drawing room. Questions buzzed around Iona's mind. Why did he want to talk to her cousin?

And what had happened in that final intense moment when his gaze had dropped to her lips and tension had drummed between them, an insistent beat that drowned out every sensible thought in her mind?

Forget it, she told herself angrily, and checked the first and second bedroom. The maid had just finished making up the big king-size one in the master suite; she looked up as Iona came in and gave a swift smile. 'All done.'

'Thank you,' Iona said as she slipped into the bathroom to make sure it was free of any trace of spilt detergent.

It was clear, and she'd just emerged from the suite when she heard her cousin call her name. Angie was on her own.

'He's on the phone, and it's looking good,' Angie said softly. 'We might be put on retainer while he's staying in New Zealand. Why is your smock wet?'

Hurriedly Iona explained, ending, 'I hope you've got a spare one in the car?'

'Yep.' She handed over the keys. 'Your Lukas hoped so too.'

'He's not my Lukas!' He'd never corrected her when she'd called him Luke.

Angie grinned. 'Go down and get the smock from the back seat, then get changed here.' Reading Iona's instinctive objection she said, 'It's OK—he suggested it. I'm waiting while he runs a check on the business.'

'What?'

'He's a very rich man,' Angie said with a shrug. 'They're not into trust. Off you go.'

When Iona got back with the clean smock she heard the sound of voices in the drawing room, and hastily shot into the powder room, gratefully pulled the crisp dry garment on and, after stuffing the wet one into her bag, examined the room to make sure it was pristine.

'Good, not a rose petal out of place,' she muttered, and came through the door, stopping abruptly when she met Luke's eyes.

One eyebrow lifted, and his smile was brief as he said, 'You look much more comfortable.'

'Thanks for letting me use the room.'

That eyebrow cocked again, giving him a sardonic air. Hard eyes fixed on her face, as though he could read both her thoughts and the emotions rioting through her, he asked, 'Are you and your employer sisters?'

Iona's surprise must have shown because his broad shoulders lifted in a slight shrug. 'Your colouring is different, but the shape of your face is identical to hers. The curve of your lips also, as well as a certain silken texture to your skin.'

His sculpted mouth curled in a narrow smile, and after a deliberate pause that set her nerves jangling he said lazily, 'I have never forgotten it.'

Sensation prickled along her nerves, pooled inside her, reminding her of the bold, masculine virility that had swept her into an affair that now seemed like a dangerous fantasy.

It took all of her self-control to be able to say shortly, 'We're cousins.'

CHAPTER TWO

GOING down in the lift, Angie said, 'Where did you meet him, and why haven't I heard about it?'

Iona had been bracing herself for questions, but even so, she paused as the lift came to a halt in the basement car park. 'We met in Tahiti,' she said, keeping her tone casual and matter-of-fact. 'On the second anniversary of Gavin's death. I was walking along a deserted beach—'

'Wallowing in grief and guilt, I bet,' Angie said astringently. 'Iona, nobody knew Gavin had a heart weakness. Yes, saving you exhausted him and he drowned, but it was an unexpected, shocking tragedy, not your fault.'

Iona said quietly, 'Intellectually I knew that, but I just couldn't accept it.'

Angie unlocked the car and got in. Once they were settled she said, 'And then your parents were killed by that damned drunk driver. It's no wonder you were a mess. Then you met Lukas Michelakis in Tahiti?'

'Yes. Actually when he strode down the beach—like—like the king of the gods—to inform me I was trespassing I was actually *relieved*. He gave me something else to think about.' With a vengeance.

Once they were under way, Angie said, 'And what happened then?'

'We went around a bit together,' Iona told her in a flat voice, 'until I came home again.'

'And you haven't been in contact since?' Angie asked.

'There was no reason.'

Her cousin took the hint. 'I read somewhere that he grew up in a very wealthy family.'

'It figures,' Iona said evenly. 'His kind of confidence is bred in the genes.'

'The article was cagey, but heavy on innuendo—obviously making sure no lawyer could sue the writer or the newspaper. It implied something pretty disastrous happened when he was young—late teens, perhaps?—and he left home to strike out on his own.'

'Probably with the family's support not too far in the background.' Iona didn't try to hide the cynical note in her words.

'I doubt if he needed it. It didn't take him long to turn into an internet czar.' Angie paused before asking casually, 'If he needs to call on us, how would you feel about working with him?'

'Me?' Iona swallowed an unnecessary panic. 'A bit self-conscious, that's all. I was half-naked, mopping detergent off my breasts, when he strode in like a clap of doom just before you arrived, and I suspect he thought it was a set-up—that I'd deliberately stripped to attract his attention.'

'I suppose it's happened before,' Angie said, and gave her a thoughtful sideways glance. 'I bet he spends a fair part of his life swatting off importunate women.'

During their brief affair he'd more than met Iona halfway.

Repressing disturbing images of tropical folly, she said hastily, 'I'll be fine. He relaxed when you turned up.'

Although *relaxed* wasn't the word to describe Luke. Even on holiday she'd sensed a leashed, prowling awareness in him, an uncompromising authority that made him both formidable and intimidating.

It was still there, intensified by an ironic detachment she'd not experienced before.

Get over it, she told herself. She still resented the hard contempt of his gaze in the powder room, but that was good, because resentment was a much safer emotion than sighing lustfully after him.

The barbecue Angie had been asked to organise only the day before went on until after midnight and they were both tired when at last they left the beach house an hour's drive north of Auckland.

Covering a yawn, Iona said, 'I wish someone would persuade Mrs Parker not to throw any more impromptu parties. I suppose we should have guessed her few close friends would morph into about fifty.'

'She'll be paying heavily for springing it on us at such short notice. Besides, it's work, and we need it,' Angie said practically.

After a tentative moment Iona asked, 'How are things?'

Her cousin paused before admitting, 'You've probably guessed the recession's making inroads into the client list, but we're surviving.' Her tone changed. 'If there's an emergency in the next two days, can I call on you? The boys are going to a birthday party tomorrow—well, actually it will be today—and tomorrow we're going to the zoo.'

'Of course. Give me the work phone,' Iona said. 'If I need you I'll ring you on your personal phone. You need a break and the boys need time with you.'

It took some persuading, but at last she managed to convince Angie to agree.

Inside her tiny studio flat Iona showered and dropped into bed. Sleep came quickly, bringing with it images of a tall, dark man, images that led to dreams. Eventually she woke in a state of high excitement, blood racing through her veins, her body racked by a feverish desire.

Grim-faced and desperate, she willed her heart to settle down and her body to relax. That was how it had started. Tahiti was everything the brochures had promised—wildly, sensuously exotic, filled with beautiful people of both sexes, scented by flowers and lapped by a brilliant turquoise sea, alive with the sound of music and drums and laughter, the hush of waves on the lagoon shores. The glorious islands throbbed with life.

Iona had looked, but been unable to enjoy. Grief had dulled her senses so completely she'd felt totally disconnected from everything.

And then she'd met Luke—Lukas. She'd had no idea who—or what—he was. The moment her gaze clashed with his lion eyes, sensations she'd believed had died for ever had suddenly flared into life, introducing her to hope. A flare of conscious response had set her nerves tingling and heated her body, sharpening her senses so that the world suddenly blazed into a glory of colour and sound and sensuous delight.

Why had he pursued her? She'd asked him once, and he'd laughed.

'Perhaps the thrill of the chase,' he admitted without shame. 'You looked at me with such cool disdain, as though I was less interesting to you than the shell in your hand. I wondered what it would be like to see desire in those intriguing blue-green mermaid's eyes, as changeable and mysterious as the sea.'

For some foolish reason his words hurt. She covered the momentary stab of pain with a smile, and slid her arms around him. 'And has it lived up to your expectations?'

His gaze kindled, golden flames dancing in the depths. 'More than I ever expected; it's infinitely fascinating to watch. And even more fascinating to experience,' he said in a low growl, and kissed her.

Lost in swift passion, she'd kissed him back, welcoming the hot tide of hunger that met and matched his.

Their passionate, hedonistic affair had seemed so right in Tahiti, christened Aphrodite's Isles by the first dazzled European sailors to visit those idyllic shores.

Then one night, as the moon came up over the horizon in a splendour of silver and gold, he'd said, 'I'm leaving in three days.' He had smiled lazily at her startled face and kissed the curve of her breast, murmuring against her skin, 'Come with me.'

Each word had been a caress—a confident one. He'd had no doubt she'd do what he wanted. The fantasy world Iona had been living in crashed around her.

'I can't,' she said, shocked by a swift, aching temptation to give him what he wanted.

His eyes narrowed, focused on her face as intently as a hunter's scrutiny. 'Why?'

'Because this has been—wonderful, but we both know it's not real life.' It was surprisingly hard to say, but his words had awakened the common sense she'd abandoned the moment her eyes had met his.

He shrugged again and replied, 'It could be.' And when she remained silent, he said a little impatiently,

'I will, of course, look after you—make sure you don't lose anything by being with me.'

Knowing what he was offering, she almost flinched. For a while she'd be his lover; while she was with him she'd exist in this sensual dream.

And when it was over she'd go back to New Zealand with memories...

And the possibility of more grief. She'd had enough of that in her life. 'No,' she said.

He'd laughed deep in his throat and slid down her body, his mouth questing as he tasted her sleek skin.

Later, when she was quivering with passionate exhaustion in his arms, he murmured, 'I'm going to enjoy making you change your mind.'

But, back in her own bed at the hotel, she'd dreamed of Gavin and woke weeping. And when she slipped out early to walk along the white sands, she forced herself to face a few unpleasant facts.

Without realising it, she'd selfishly used Luke. Oh, he'd made it obvious from the start that he intended nothing more than a sexual relationship, but that didn't make her feel any better.

Her swift, reckless surrender to overwhelming passion had betrayed and tarnished the love she'd shared with Gavin. She tried to conjure up the emotions she'd felt for her fiancé, but against the blazing intensity of her relationship with Luke he seemed faded and shadowy, a lovely memory but no longer the foundation of her life.

Shocked at her shallowness, she'd managed to wangle a seat on a plane to New Zealand. Fortunately Angie had been run off her feet with work, and Iona had flung herself into it, grimly ordering her mind to forget. It hadn't been easy, but she thought she'd coped quite well.

What malevolent fate had brought Luke back into her life again?

At least, she thought just before she dropped back into a restless slumber, unless he had an emergency in the next two days Angie would be dealing with him.

Hours later the tinny, cheerful tattoo of the theme from *Bonanza* woke her. Groaning, she crawled up from beneath the sheets, blinked blearily at the morning and grabbed the work phone. 'Sorted. How can I help you?'

A deep voice said, 'You are not Ms Makepeace.'

Little chills ran down her spine. Her hand tightened on the phone and she had to swallow to ease a suddenly dry throat.

Luke.

No, not Luke. The different names somehow seemed significant. He was not the man she'd made love to in Tahiti. He was Lukas Michelakis, billionaire.

Striving to sound brisk and businesslike, she said, 'Iona Guthrie speaking. I'm afraid Ms Makepeace can't come to the telephone right now. How can I help you?'

'I need someone here, now,' Luke said evenly. 'To take care of a three-year-old girl for the day.'

'*What?*' Iona literally couldn't believe her ears. Luke Michelakis and a small child simply did not go together.

Impatience tinged his words. 'I am sure you heard correctly.'

Irked by his tone, Iona ignored her whirling thoughts and didn't hesitate. 'Yes. Yes, all right, we can do that.'

'You are sure this person will be reliable and sensible?'

'Yes.'

'I need to leave in half an hour.'

Iona's mouth thinned. 'I'll be there as soon as I can, but I'm not going to be able to make it in that time.'

'*You* will be here?'

She reacted to his incredulous words with chilly aloofness. 'L—Mr Michelakis, I'm a trained kindergarten teacher, and the only person you're likely to get during the weekend at such short notice. The child will be safe in my care.'

'Oh, call me Luke as you did in Tahiti—we know each other well, you and I,' he said derisively.

'So why are you questioning my ability to care for the child?' The moment the words escaped from her mouth she wished she could call them back.

Sure enough Luke said, 'Now you're being deliberately naïve. In Tahiti you were my lover—a very charming and sensuous lover—and nothing more.'

Of course he was right, but his casual statement hurt.

He waited, as if for a comment, and when Iona remained silent he went on brusquely, 'I have no idea what you will be like with children. And if Chloe is not safe in your care you will pay.'

'Are you expecting a kidnap attempt?' Into a taut silence, she said, 'I certainly wouldn't be much use if that's likely to occur.'

'I am *not* expecting a kidnap attempt,' he said coldly.

'I'm relieved. If all you want is a temporary nanny I can do that. I'm capable and competent when it comes to children. And I like them. I also have a current practising certificate which I'll be pleased to show you when I arrive.'

The pause seemed to drag on for ever, but finally he said, 'Very well. It seems I am forced to rely on you for this, so I will expect you here within the half hour. Give me your address. I shall send a car.'

Iona drew in a deep breath, but stifled her intemperate reply when she remembered Angie's delight at the prospect of an uninterrupted day with her sons. 'Thank you,' she snapped.

Angie had said it the night before: this was work, and the business needed the money.

Luke repeated her address after her, then warned, 'Be ready,' and hung up.

As she scurried around, assembling a kit that would keep a three-year-old girl interested, questions raced through Iona's mind. Was little Chloe his daughter? If so, she thought sickly, he must have been married or in a relationship when he'd made love to her in Tahiti.

It should have been a relief to be able to despise him. It certainly explained his antagonism; did he think she'd tell his wife he'd been unfaithful?

Never!

But it seemed unlikely that the mother of his child was with him; if she were, she'd be the one looking after her daughter.

By the time the taxi arrived Iona was ready. She'd had to forego breakfast and a much-needed cup of tea, but her large carry-all had enough in it to keep even a demanding child busy for a day. Stomach clenching, she walked out of the penthouse lift, disconcerted to find Luke in the doorway.

Like a lion lying in wait for an antelope.

Dismayed, Iona ignored the treacherous heat burning along her cheekbones while she replied to his greeting.

A narrowed tawny-gold gaze took in her clothes—cotton trousers that that reached halfway down her calves, a bright T-shirt, sandals. One black brow climbed.

'Practical,' he observed cooly, 'if a little informal.'

'New Zealanders are noted for their informality,' she returned in her most professional tone.

'I recall that very well.'

A lazily sensual note beneath the words raised the tiny hairs on the back of Iona's neck and sent a forbidden, ruthlessly exciting response shivering through her. Damn him, she thought furiously as flashbacks of the time they'd spent together surged back, drugging and potent.

Blurting the first thing that came to her mind, she asked, 'When am I going to meet my charge for the day?'

'Right now,' he said crisply, and reached out.

For a startled moment Iona thought he intended to take her arm.

A primitive, protective reaction twisted her backwards, but his hand closed around the handles of her bag and he said softly, lethally, 'You are quite safe. If you want me to touch you again you will have to ask me to do so.'

Iona stiffened. OK, so until she'd fled Tahiti probably no one had ever turned Luke Michelakis down, but she'd never promised him anything; right from the start they'd both known that what they shared was nothing stronger or more permanent than a holiday romance.

She'd just ended it a little sooner than either had expected.

Which didn't give him any right to be offended.

But then the adored only son of a powerful Greek patriarch would certainly be spoilt. Especially one who looked like some beautiful, vengeful god from ancient times.

And there was the spectre of the child's absent mother…

Choosing to ignore his terse statement, she relinquished the bag to him.

Cynically amused at her care to avoid touching his fingers, Lukas said, 'This way.'

For a moment he'd been going to ask her why she'd left him in Tahiti, but she was now his employee—and he'd overstepped the professional bounds already.

Besides, he had not allowed himself to care. He'd learned young that women were naturally treacherous—a lesson cut into his heart when his father's second wife had engineered his expulsion from the family.

He'd vowed then never to trust another woman, so it would be foolish of him to expect more from Iona.

Aristo Michelakis, his father, had expected his twenty-year-old son to fail, to fall into oblivion. Twelve years later, Lukas allowed himself a swift glance around his opulent surroundings.

He'd been coldly, furiously determined to prove both himself and his innocence of the crime he'd been accused of. That driving need had guided him into a career where his brilliant brain and passion were fully utilised. He had seized his opportunities with a zest that had led to huge success in spite of his father's attempts to ruin him.

And he had his pick of lovers from the women who'd flocked to him, drawn by his fortune and the face he'd inherited from his father.

Always he'd made sure his lovers expected nothing more from him than good sex and his protection as long as the affair lasted.

Then Chloe had been born—another outcast from the family. She'd brought a new dimension to his life, but his attitude to his lovers remained the same.

So why had Iona stuck in his mind?

Because she had been—different. He set Iona's bag beside a chair and glanced down at her, resisting an impulse to run a finger across that unsmiling, infuriatingly desirable mouth. What would she do if he kissed her? His body tightened in swift, fierce response even as he dismissed the thought.

She was not exactly beautiful, but she'd been a passionate and generous lover, and he'd enjoyed their interlude—perhaps a little too much. It irritated him to admit it, but her abrupt departure had angered him. He had missed her.

However, it was ridiculous—a stupid, unnecessary overreaction—to feel she'd betrayed him.

Acutely aware of his swift glance and his silence, Iona was glad to meet the child she was looking after. Chloe was tall for her age, as befitted the daughter of such a tall man, with large dark eyes, and a mouth that subtly echoed that of her father. It quirked in a fleeting smile for him before she transferred a solemn gaze to Iona, who introduced herself calmly.

'Hello. My name is Iona Guthrie, and we'll be spending some time together today while your father has a meeting.'

'He always goes to meetings.'

The statement, although made entirely without rancour, wrung Iona's heart.

'I'm sure he's very busy, but we'll have fun together, you and I.'

Chloe scanned Iona's large bag. 'Are you going to stay 'cos Neelie's gone?'

'Only for today,' Luke told her.

Who was Neelie? Mother? Nanny?

'I've brought some things you might like to do with me, and a few books you might not have seen before,' Iona said.

That seemed to satisfy Chloe, who obeyed immediately when her father announced, 'Take Ms Guthrie out onto the terrace, Chloe, and show her your horse.'

Horse? Surely he didn't carry around a horse as part of his ménage?

He did. A splendid rocking horse, dappled grey, with flared nostrils and flowing mane, and a saddle and bridle fit for a queen. 'His name is Pegasus,' Chloe informed her in that precise, neutral voice.

She glanced up at Iona, who asked, 'And does he fly, like the horse in the legend?'

It seemed she might have passed some subtle test, for the child smiled at her. 'Nearly. He used to be Lukas's horse when he was a little boy.' Her tone expressed a hint of disbelief, as though she simply couldn't conceive of her father ever being small enough to ride the horse.

Why did she call him by his first name?

More to the point, where the heck was her mother? Dead? Divorced? Not interested?

None of your business, Iona warned herself, and said gravely, 'You and your father are very lucky. Pegasus is a magnificent animal.'

'He's my *best* friend.'

Like her father, Chloe spoke excellent English; unlike him she had no trace of an accent. Not, Iona recalled, that Luke had much—really, only the merest hint…

Just enough to imbue every word he said with a subtle under-note of disturbing sensuality that had deepened when they'd made love.

Don't even think about that!

Iona said, 'Pegasus is lucky too—to have such a good friend as you. Would you like to show me how well you can ride him?'

After a moment Chloe hitched up her skirt and climbed onto the horse, setting it rocking with a gleeful enthusiasm that warmed Iona's heart.

'She is reserved, but not shy,' her father said from behind.

Startled, Iona swivelled. Dressed in a superbly tailored business suit that showed off his lean, powerful body, he was a formidable presence. A stab of awareness shocked Iona with its swift intensity, reminding her of all the reasons—those foolish, dangerous reasons—she'd embarked on their affair.

Moving out of earshot of the child, she asked in her most practical voice, 'Is there anything I should know about Chloe before you go?' When his black brows drew together she added briskly, 'I gather her mother is not here? No doubt Chloe will be missing her.'

'You assume too much.'

Iona lifted her head at the touch of hauteur in his words. Something odd was going on here, and if it was likely to affect Chloe she needed to know about it. 'Very well,' she said, in a tone that matched his for bluntness, 'but *is* there anything I should be aware of?'

Lukas didn't try to moderate the frown that always made his subordinates tread very carefully. It didn't seem to affect Iona. Those unusual sea-shaded eyes mirrored both the colour of whatever she wore and her emotions. Today they were a direct, cool blue with a hint of challenge.

Yesterday in the powder room when she'd been half-naked they'd been blue-green, wide and shocked, and then full of mystery.

He'd had to rein in a hunger so elemental and direct it had taken him by surprise.

Why the hell *had* she run away from him in Tahiti? Because he'd cast his suggestion she stay with him as a proposition rather than a proposal?

Surely she'd realised it was too early in their relationship for an admission of anything more than a passionate hunger? He'd wanted them to get to know each other—discover if their superb compatibility extended beyond the raptures of the bed—but clearly she hadn't reciprocated those inchoate, hardly formed feelings.

Ruthlessly repressing the sharp twist of sensation in his gut at the memory of just how good they'd been together, he forced his mind back to her question.

Discreet she might be, but he wasn't going to let her in on any family secrets. He'd had enough of seeing his private life—or fiction about it—splashed across newsprint. If the circumstances of Chloe's birth and his subsequent adoption of the child ever leaked out, some parts of the media would have a field day.

That he could cope with. What made it imperative that he keep the secret until he could trust Iona was his father's latest threat—to contest the adoption and demand custody of the daughter Aristo had refused to accept.

CHAPTER THREE

STILL, Lukas reluctantly conceded Iona had a point.

Yesterday he'd ordered his security people to check her and her cousin out; the report had arrived first thing that morning. They were clean—practically saints, he thought sardonically.

After a glance at Chloe's absorbed little face as she rocked rhythmically on the horse, Luke made up his mind, but even so, he chose his words with care.

'Her mother has never been part of Chloe's life.' She hadn't even named her. He'd called her Chloe after his maternal grandmother.

Irritated, because the silken allure of Iona's skin and the grace of her movements still had the power to stir him, he went on more curtly than he'd intended, 'I have always cared for her, and her nanny has been with her since she was a year old. Unfortunately she was called away to England last night, so it is possible Chloe will talk about Neelie. I have explained the circumstances to her—that Neelie had to go to her sick mother—and she appears to understand and accept that. I have left a contact number beside the telephone; if there is any emergency—but *only* in an emergency—ring me.'

Her eyes veiled by her lashes, Iona nodded and replied with composure, 'I don't panic easily.'

Lukas resisted another flash of hunger, deep and arousing. She didn't fit the classical standards of beauty—her face was striking rather than pretty—but something about it and her smoothly lissome body still retained a disturbing power to intrigue him.

However, he had responsibilities he couldn't neglect, and although it was some months since he'd last had a woman it would be inconvenient to embark—*re-embark*, he corrected cynically—on an affair right now with a woman who'd already caused him enough sleepless nights.

And if he'd learned anything in his life it was to control the urges of his body.

Iona resolutely turned her face away to watch Chloe, absorbed on her flying steed. Luke should mean nothing to her, and neither should the possibility that he'd been married when he'd made love to her with such blazing desire.

Yet she struggled with a foolish sense of betrayal.

Ignoring it, she asked, 'Roughly what time are you planning to be back?'

'This meeting should finish at a reasonable time— before five o'clock,' he told her, a note of austerity in his words telling her he wasn't used to being questioned. 'If it threatens to stretch further I—or my PA—will contact you. Do you have an appointment tonight?'

Iona met eyes that were unexpectedly keen. 'No.'

His expression didn't change as he turned and called, 'Chloe, I have to go now.'

The child scrambled down from the rocking horse and came running with outstretched arms. Watching him swoop down to lift her high, Iona relaxed. Luke wasn't effusive, but his love for his daughter was clear; he held her with great tenderness, and murmured something in a language Iona supposed to be Greek.

Forget the way that voice sends shivers down your spine, she warned herself. Concentrate on Chloe.

Nothing to worry about there—the child's body language proclaimed her complete faith and trust in her father. Nestled against his big frame, she looked tiny as she gave him his kiss with perfect confidence, and his hard-hewn, handsome face softened.

Somehow that touched a nerve in Iona.

Gently he put Chloe down and straightened up. 'So, be good for Miss Iona while I'm gone.' He looked at Iona. 'I have ordered a snack to arrive at ten for both of you, and lunch will be brought up at midday. Chloe has a nap after lunch for half an hour, and then a drink and some fruit when she wakes.'

'Lukas, can Miss Iona take me for a swim when I wake up?'

Smiling down at her, he replied, 'No, because she will not have brought anything to wear in the water.'

His daughter pouted, but didn't push her luck. Obviously Luke's decisions were non-negotiable.

Iona said, 'Actually, I noticed the pool yesterday so I brought my togs.' She looked at him directly, aware of a swift streak of colour along her cheekbones. In Tahiti she'd swum naked, and from the gleam beneath his lashes she suspected he was remembering. 'I have a lifesaving certificate.'

For an intimidating moment he was silent before his mouth curved in an oblique smile. 'I know you are an excellent swimmer. I see no reason why you shouldn't swim together,' he conceded to a beaming Chloe, adding, 'But only if you promise me that when Miss Iona tells you it is time to get out you do not plead to stay in for just a few minutes longer.'

Chloe's face wrinkled in earnestness. 'I won't, Lukas. I will be as good as gold, like Neelie says.'

He looked amused, but spoke directly to Iona. 'Chloe is an excellent swimmer for her age, but too much time in the water turns her lips blue and makes her shiver.'

During the morning the child's artless frankness built a picture for Iona of a man who could be stern but wasn't unfair, and whose arms held all Chloe wanted. She referred to the nanny with affection, but clearly it was her father who was the sum and substance of her life.

The situation nagged at Iona. Perhaps he hadn't known about the child when they'd had that fling in Tahiti?

But he'd said her mother had never figured in Chloe's life.

Apart from bearing her and giving birth, Iona thought ironically. Whatever, she told herself severely as she tucked the child into bed for her afternoon nap, it was absolutely *none* of her business.

While Chloe slept Iona sat out on the terrace with the book she'd been reading for the past few days, exasperated when it no longer held her attention. She got up and walked over to the edge of the terrace and leant against the railing.

Up above, the glinting waters of the harbour clouds marched in ranks across a radiant sky. After Gavin had drowned she hadn't been able to bear even looking at the sea; she'd deliberately chosen Tahiti for her holiday because the island location made it impossible for her to avoid the ocean. She'd forced herself to accept and overcome her fear.

It had worked, although not in the way she hoped. The bleak sense of responsibility for Gavin's death had been overwhelmed by the haze of sensuality Luke had woven around her—a sensuality she'd welcomed, enjoyed, basked in...

Driven by restlessness, she turned away and paced around across the terrace. Whoever had designed this garden had created a rooftop paradise, its almost tropical lushness forming a background to a carefully tended magnolia that held breathtaking, opulently rosy goblets up to the sky.

Idly, she bent to sniff a gardenia flower, wondering what it would be like to be truly rich, one of those people whose deep pockets meant that money was the least of their concerns.

People about as far removed as they could be from Angie, who had three full-time workers to worry about as well as her children, and the ever-present burden of the debts her ex-husband had left behind when he'd skipped out of the country.

Angie had admitted last night that things were tough. How tough? Was she secretly hoping Iona might return to her previous career as a nursery teacher?

If so, surely she'd have said something?

Probably not. She and Angie had no other relatives but each other. Angie could be keeping her on from some sense of family duty.

Entirely *unnecessary* family duty! Iona made up her mind; she'd ask Angie directly, because she could always find a job in a nursery school or a daycare centre. It wouldn't pay as well as working for Angie, but she'd manage.

Earlier she'd read Chloe one of the books she'd packed, delighted when the story sparked the child's imagination. They'd acted it out, with Chloe suggesting embellishments, some outrageous, some affecting—like her suggestion that a baby brother be incorporated so the heroine would have someone to play with.

'Would you like to keep that book for yourself?' Iona had surprised herself by asking at lunchtime, when she'd noted that Chloe was reluctant to put the book down.

Chloe's eyes widened. 'Oh, yes,' she breathed, adding conscientiously, 'Yes, please, Miss Iona.' She held it out. 'Can you write in it?'

Touched, Iona said, 'Of course I can.' She fished out her pen and printed on the title page: *'For Chloe, so she remembers a lovely day in Auckland. From Iona.'*

But Chloe frowned when Iona read out the dedication. 'You have to say *'With love from,'*' she said.

Iona's heart stilled a precarious second, then began to beat again. It would be very easy to become fond of this child.

She said, 'Goodness, how could I have forgotten?' And inscribed the extra words in the right place.

Chloe beamed. 'I will be careful of it,' she promised earnestly.

The book had gone to bed with her after another reading. Now, thinking of the pleasure the simple gift had given the child, Iona smiled, then turned as a voice from behind interrupted her thoughts.

'I'm awake.'

And ready for the swim she'd been promised.

Chloe's nanny had brought her up to be self-sufficient; she was already wearing a cute little two-piece, almost covered by a towel draped around her shoulders. A bright yellow cap dangled from one small hand.

Hiding a smile, Iona organised them both into the pool, relaxing a little when she discovered the child was like a small eel in the water. They splashed and played together until a cry of 'Lukas!' from Chloe whipped Iona's head around.

Luke was striding through the glass doors and into the pool enclosure, tall and extremely sophisticated in that killer suit, the sun gleaming blue-black on his arrogantly poised head.

Iona's spine melted and sharp darts of sensation shot through her. She knew what it was—desire, sweet and treacherous, hauntingly familiar...

Yet different now, deeper and more potent than the purely sensuous sensations he'd previously aroused. Somehow Luke's obvious love for the child swimming at top speed towards him had worked a change in Iona's response to him.

A *dangerous* change, she thought, nerves quivering as she stood up, only to sink back into the water. Her sleek one-piece clung to her like a second skin, tempting her to duck beneath the surface in a stupid, childish reflex.

Luke had seen her naked so often any novelty value had to be long gone, but she was relieved he wasn't looking her way; in fact, she might just as well not have been there. His whole attention was focused on Chloe, and the smile he gave when he pulled his clamorous daughter out of the pool did something very odd to Iona's heart.

He said something that lit up the little girl's face then smiled and wrapped her wet body in the towel like a small, wriggly mummy before hugging her.

Only after he'd kissed her forehead did he look over her sleek black head towards Iona. Acutely and foolishly self-conscious, she stood again, feeling the water stream from her.

'There is a problem,' he told her, eyes on her face. Without waiting for an answer he said, 'This meeting might not finish until late tonight. So you will stay until I come back.'

It was not a request.

'Very well,' Iona said, irked by his cool assumption that her time was his to command.

He set Chloe down and commanded, 'Run off and get back into your clothes. I wish to talk to Miss Iona.'

Chloe raced off, obviously eager not to miss a single precious moment of his presence.

Luke said abruptly, 'I presume your cousin can bring you clothes for an overnight stay.'

'No, she's busy today.' And when she did get back home with her two tired boys Angie certainly wouldn't want to be forced to collect clothes from across the city.

Eyes slightly narrowed, he said, 'In that case I can organise for someone on my staff to fetch them.'

The thought of some unknown person going through her clothes revolted her. 'No,' she said definitely, and hauled herself out of the water to give herself time to collect her wits.

And also because for some reason she found it demeaning to be at his feet—below his feet in fact, so that he stood looking down at her like some medieval despot with authority over life and death.

Or the power to take whatever woman he desired.

Somewhere deep inside Iona those long-repressed sensations stirred again, tantalising and decadent.

Frowning, he agreed, 'I suppose not. So what do you suggest?'

Reminding herself of Angie's shaky financial situation, Iona bit back impetuous words. 'I've brought a change of clothes,' she told him. His brows lifted and she said wryly, 'It's a sensible precaution if you're looking after children.' And her underclothes would dry overnight.

He nodded. 'Toothbrush? Toothpaste?'

'I'll use salt.' And when he looked startled she added, 'Or baking soda. It tastes vile but it does the job.'

His mouth twitched. 'It sounds appalling, but fortunately there is no need for you to suffer. I've already organised with the concierge for you to order what you want.'

The slight shrug of her shoulders reminded her she was barefoot and revealing far too much wet skin. Her hair hung in sopping confusion around her face, and water dripped off the end of her nose.

So? she thought defiantly. She didn't—*couldn't*—care what Luke was thinking while he watched her with burnished intent eyes, as opaque as gold.

'Thank you,' she said. 'I'll go and change.'

She turned away, only to be stopped in mid-stride by his crisp command. 'A moment. Stay very still.'

Iona froze, aware of the tickling of some insect on her shoulder. 'It is only a bee,' Luke said, and flicked it off, then smoothed over her skin.

The brush of his fingers sent swift needles of pleasure through her before he pulled his hand away, leaving her oddly bereft.

She didn't dare look at him, and no words would come past the lump in her throat until she'd stepped away and picked up her towel, wrapping it around her waist as though it were armour. 'Poor thing. It must have fallen into the pool.'

'Possibly. Or perhaps it thought you were another flower.'

A faint trace of cynicism in his tone made her bold enough to say, 'In that case it's got a very poor future, I'm afraid. I hope it didn't go back into the water.'

His voice sounded cool and faintly speculative when he said, 'It flew into one of the trees. You worry about a bee?'

'They sound like summer. And I like honey. Thank you.'

His expression was unreadable. 'It was nothing. Tonight you will sleep in the bedroom next to Chloe's. She goes to bed at six-thirty, and usually sleeps without waking until about the same time the next morning.'

'She sounds the perfect child,' Iona said lightly, and headed towards the little pavilion where they'd left their towels and a change of clothes. She felt shaky and light-headed, as though she'd been secretly starving for Luke's touch, missing some essential part of her life without even realising it.

She had to get a grip. The pavilion beckoned like a small haven. She was almost there when Chloe came dashing out, her clothes pulled on anyhow. If Iona had been the child's nanny she'd have caught and tidied her, but that could wait.

And so, she thought as she closed the door behind her, could Luke Michelakis.

When she emerged, fully dressed and a little more composed, father and daughter had gone inside. After a moment's hesitation she followed the sound of voices to Chloe's room; she hovered before the door, repressing a start when it opened unexpectedly.

'Chloe's in the shower,' her father said. 'She was shivering so I thought it wise. Come, I'll show you your room.'

He strode past her and opened the door, standing

aside so that she could see into the room. During her inspection of the penthouse she'd wondered who would sleep here. Clearly Chloe's nanny shared the lifestyle of her employer.

She said, 'It's charming, thank you.'

'I have to thank *you*,' he said unexpectedly. 'I am extremely grateful to you for staying with Chloe.'

How could a smile melt bones? It was totally unfair; Luke did not need his enormous wealth and position to win his reputation as a playboy. When he turned on the charm he was knee-weakeningly magnetic.

And seeing him with his daughter had added an extra depth to that stunning, sexy smile.

This is *business*, Iona thought bracingly, and so was that smile—a deliberate attempt to win her over. 'It's my job.'

'I didn't expect the discussions I'm involved in to last as long as they are, but politicians and their advisors cannot be hurried.' Wide shoulders lifted in an unapologetic Mediterranean shrug. 'Meals have been organised for you both. If you need anything at all, ask the concierge.' He turned, then stopped to say, 'I always ring Chloe to say goodnight to her, so expect a call soon after six.'

Arrogant he certainly was, but no one could doubt his love for his daughter. Iona's heart expanded. 'When I go to bed I'll leave our doors open so I can hear her if she wakes.'

'Thank you. There should be a baby monitor,' he said, his tone tinged with exasperation. 'I assume Neelie forgot to unpack it before she left. However, Chloe doesn't wake at night unless she's ill. And if that happens I wish to be told immediately.'

Iona nodded. 'As well as being a nursery school

teacher, I've had quite a bit of experience babysitting my cousin's children, so I have a fairly good idea of the difference between just a sore tummy and something more serious.'

He smiled again, and Iona felt a languorous appreciation shimmer through every nerve in her body. 'How very fortunate I am to rediscover you,' he said softly.

Struggling to resist that compelling charm, Iona said coolly, 'Good luck can come to the most unlikely people.'

Although Luke's lashes drooped, his expression remained controlled. 'Indeed it can. And a sensible person will always be grateful for what the gods offer without expecting any further favours.' Switching subjects, he finished, 'I hope to be back before midnight, but feel free to go to bed whenever you wish.'

'I shall,' she said sweetly, relieved to hear Chloe call from the bedroom. 'I'll go to her,' she told him. 'I'm sure you want to get away.'

Ignoring her, he strode back into his daughter's room. After a moment's hesitation Iona followed. He stooped to drop a kiss on his flushed, towel-draped daughter, tickled her until she collapsed into giggles, then gathered her hands in one of his own and pressed a kiss into one palm before straightening. Tall and commanding as he was, the combination of leashed male strength and tenderness touched Iona's newly vulnerable heart.

Careful, she thought warily. This was a very temporary situation—Luke and Chloe would be gone within days and she'd be stupid to let herself become emotionally involved with either the man or his child.

To Chloe he said, 'Soon we'll be staying on the island

and I shall not go to a meeting for at least seven sleeps. How does that sound?'

Judging by the radiance of her beam he'd offered his daughter a taste of paradise. Iona felt like an intruder in this picture of domestic felicity.

Innocently the child asked, 'Can Miss Iona come too?'

'Miss Iona is too busy here to take a holiday with us,' Luke said smoothly, his gaze cool and dismissive as it travelled to Iona. 'Besides, Neelie should be back by then.'

Well, that relegated her to her proper place, Iona thought on a foolish spurt of defiance. Substitute nursemaid—yet she'd loved being a nursery school teacher, so why should his words sting?

Because she was so stupidly, *violently* aware of him?

Iona followed Luke out into the hall, watching with some bemusement while he fitted a nightlight into an electric socket there. He kept startling her with small actions that seemed at odds with his intimidating character, but then, his daughter was clearly his Achilles' heel.

Iona was smiling slightly at the Greek reference when he stood up. Lord, but he was *big*, she thought involuntarily. Big in every sense of the word—tall, broadshouldered, lithely elegant, and with a presence that filled the place.

He turned and caught her watching him. Iona's heart gave a nervous leap in her chest and a traitorous anticipation stabbed her with sweet heat.

The smoky gleam in his eyes was banished by a will far stronger than hers. Coolly he said, 'If she wakes she likes to see a glow outside. We do a lot of travelling, and I think it helps her orient herself in a new place.'

'I'll make sure it's left on when she goes to bed,' Iona promised in her most professional tone.

Luke had barely gone when Angie rang. 'How are things going?' she enquired.

'Fine,' Iona said automatically.

'Do you think your gorgeous alpha boss would approve of us—you and me—taking the little girl to the zoo tomorrow? It's Children's Day, and the forecast is for gorgeous weather; I've promised the boys we'll check out the tiger babies and penguins.'

'I doubt if he'll say yes, but no harm in trying,' Iona told her.

To be fair, a man with his position and power had reason to be cautious about his daughter's security. Not in New Zealand, she thought, then frowned, because even New Zealand wasn't necessarily safe.

Half an hour after Iona had put her cell phone down there was call from the concierge. 'I have a parcel here for you,' he said. 'I'll send it up with a porter.'

It came from a very exclusive shop, one that specialised in overseas labels, and was addressed to her.

Tense for no reason, Iona let Chloe open the bag. Inside, tenderly tucked into a sheet of pastel tissue paper, was a garment in a soft rose-beige that turned out to be a nightgown.

So Luke had ignored her—just gone ahead and organised this. Warily Iona eyed another smaller parcel in the bag.

'Are you going to open that one too?' Chloe asked eagerly when she made no attempt to do so.

'You can if you like.'

Very carefully Chloe peeled back the seal and folded the paper away, first the wrapping, then the tissue beneath. Colour surged into Iona's skin. As well as the exquisite nightgown Luke had bought her a bra and a pair of panties, lace-trimmed scraps of frivolity that deepened the blush on her cheeks.

A swift glance showed her that he'd judged her size perfectly. Iona bit her lip, feeling obscurely as though she'd been bought.

'Oh, here's a toothbrush,' she said with relief. 'And some toothpaste.' With them were soap and moisturiser, cosmetics so expensive she suspected they'd cost more than her week's salary.

Her stomach contracted. Of course she wouldn't use them. Well, the toothpaste and brush would be fine, but the others smacked of some sort of pay-off.

For Tahiti? Surely not?

Of *course* not, she told herself robustly. That would be nastily petty, and the Luke she'd known wasn't petty. OK, so she'd left him in Tahiti with no explanation, nothing more than the briefest of notes, and he'd probably been astonished—possibly even angry—but they had made no promises to each other, and there were plenty of women eager to warm his bed.

While she'd been his lover she'd met several of those women.

She looked down at the exquisite fripperies. It was silly to take the contents personally; Luke was a very rich man, accustomed to giving orders. He'd probably commanded some minion to buy and despatch these pretty things. As for getting the size right—well, he was the sort of man who noticed things.

After dinner Chloe went off to bed without protest,

asking only that Iona read the book again, and then innocently holding her face up to be kissed before she was tucked in.

Much later Iona checked her soundly sleeping charge. For a few seconds she stood beside Chloe's bed, picking out her resemblance to her father, and wondering where the little girl had been when her father had holidayed in Tahiti eighteen months ago.

Like so many questions, it would never be answered, but the knowledge of the child's existence tarnished the memory of those days and nights.

She turned and went out, careful to leave the door open. And, although her bed was huge and supremely comfortable, she lay awake for what seemed a long time before dropping off.

Much later she woke with a start. Lifting herself on one elbow, she strained to hear. Nothing…no sound but the hum of distant traffic…yet something had alerted her. Chloe?

She climbed stealthily out of bed and grabbed her T-shirt and the towel she'd put close by in case her charge woke. Ears straining, she listened again, but whatever had woken her was silent. Perhaps Chloe had murmured in her sleep…

After shrugging into the shirt she peeked warily past her door. Nothing moved in the dim glow of the night-light. And then her stomach clenched when she thought she heard a sound from the child's room.

Luke. Of course it had to be him. But she needed to be sure.

She wrapped the towel around her waist, then tiptoed through the door. And stopped abruptly at the sight of the dark form standing beside the child's bed.

Intensely relieved, she recognised Luke immediately

and shot back out. She didn't hear him move, but he caught up to her before she got to her own bedroom door.

'I am sorry to have disturbed you,' he said in a voice pitched to carry to her ears only.

He'd taken off his tie and coat; in the soft yellow glow of the nightlight the fine fabric of his white shirt contrasted starkly with sleek olive skin, showing off the clean, athletic lines of his powerful body.

Inside Iona a treacherous need smouldered back into life, a forbidden, tantalising expectancy she remembered only too well. She swallowed. 'I heard something,' she said in explanation, then stopped and swallowed again because her voice sounded oddly breathless.

And she must seem a total idiot, coming out with such an obvious statement.

He nodded, eyes glinting, mouth curving in a smile that shook her defences. 'You heard me trying not to be heard.'

Quick heat burned through her. The soft T-shirt fabric felt like sacking against her acutely sensitive skin. Her breath locked in her lungs when his gaze fell to her breasts.

To her intense relief a sound from Chloe's room froze them both.

He said quietly, 'She's just turning over.'

Trying desperately to control her chaotic reactions, Iona waited until the child settled into silence again, then pushed open her own door.

Poised for flight into the refuge of her room, she said over her shoulder, 'She went to bed without any problems.'

'Good. You got the parcel?'

Thank heavens the dim nightlight couldn't reveal her scalding cheeks. She said stiffly, 'Yes. Thank you.'

'You didn't like the gown?'

CHAPTER FOUR

DAMN him, why couldn't he pretend he hadn't noticed? Tiny shivers of sensation scudded the length of Iona's spine, tightening her nerves, shortening her breath, so that her voice sounded strained when she answered, 'It's lovely, but of course I can't accept it.'

'Why not?'

'It's not—' she searched for the right word, finally settling on '—suitable.'

'I'm sorry. I must inform my personal assistant that he's losing his touch.'

The note of amusement in his tone shafted through her. She dragged enough breath into her lungs to say coolly, 'Don't do that—he has great taste.' And, rallying her thoughts into some sort of order, she added, 'I hope your meeting went well. If Chloe wakes again I'll deal with it. Goodnight.'

His assessing gaze didn't waver. 'You must be a very light sleeper—I was as quiet as I could be when I came in. But perhaps you weren't sleeping...?'

A slight uplift of tone at the end of the sentence turned it into a question. No, she realised with a jolt of outrage, *not* a question; he actually wondered if she'd been lying in wait for him.

What conceit! Yet she had to fight back a craven

desire to—what? Surrender? He seemed entirely re-laxed, but she could sense a humming energy about him, a slow, fierce lick of fire that called to something deeply subversive in her.

She didn't dare speak in case her voice gave her away. He must have taken her silence for assent because she felt his hand on her shoulder, light yet somehow pos-sessive. His touch sent shivers of anticipation coursing through her, zinging through nerves and cells like heat lightning, dazzling and dangerous and powerful.

Her mind screamed *Get the hell out of here*, but a more primal urgency consumed her, keeping her still and acquiescent as he turned her.

His eyes glittered and his voice was rough and deep. 'Perhaps you were thinking—as I have been all day—that we should not ungratefully ignore this gift of time from the gods.'

His hand slid to her back, the other lifting her chin. Excitement hammered through her. The subdued light emphasised the arrogant perfection of his features, the sensuous mouth and intent, elemental hunger in his lion eyes.

'Tell me you forgot me,' he ordered, his voice harsh.

Yes, tell him, caution insisted. Lie to him…

'No.' The admission came out like a sigh, softly lan-guorous, silken with need and longing.

At last, she thought with a relief so intense it blocked out everything but delight. *At last*.

She had been waiting for this ever since—ever since she'd looked at the mirror in the penthouse powder room and seen him standing in the doorway. Without realising it she'd been waiting for his arms to close around her and pull her against him, for his lips to touch hers in a deliciously provocative butterfly kiss on the corner of her mouth.

Waiting for the driving beat of his heart into hers, the subtle arousal of his body, the powerful seduction of being protected and desired at the same time...

Waiting for Luke.

And for the sweet, powerful hunger that leapt into life in every cell of her body, filling her with the passion only he could rouse in her.

The shock of realisation sent a rush of sensation through her, tightening her breasts and heating the pit of her stomach. For a few stunned seconds she stayed immobile, until the reality of everything hit her in an elemental, all-consuming flood, weakening her knees so that she swayed into him.

He understood the silent surrender, bending his head so that she felt the soft whisper of his words against her sensitised lips. 'Good. Because I could not forget you.'

It was like falling into an inferno, a headlong surrender to passion so intense and incandescent the primal, white-hot honesty of desire burned away common sense and caution and the cold chill of reality.

At first his lips were controlled and seeking, but the wildfire intensity of her response must have set fire to him too, because his mouth hardened and the kiss became an act of total possession, deepening into a hunger so blatant it demanded everything from her.

Iona shuddered at the exquisite sensations his touch awakened in her, and his arms tightened, bringing her into intimate juxtaposition with his hard loins. An instant rush of adrenalin stimulated her into complete arousal, recklessly whetting her appetite for him into a sensual clamour that made nonsense of all her forebodings.

She wanted him with a desperate vulnerability that terrified her, jolting her into awareness of what she was doing—what he was offering...

Gasping, she jerked her head back, rejecting the carnal impulses that rioted through every cell and clouded her mind in a haze of heady, dangerous desire.

He loosened his grip, but didn't let her go. 'So, it is still there,' he said softly. 'What is it, do you think, this incredible urge to carry you off somewhere and never let you out of my bed again?'

Iona moistened her tender lips, an effort of will almost negated when his kindling gaze followed the tiny movement of her tongue.

For a pathetic second she wondered if his comment meant he might feel something more than naked, unsatisfied lust, but he wasn't wanting her in his life, only in his bed.

'Sex,' she croaked, brutally honest. Sex for him—but so much more than that for her.

He laughed. 'Then what are we going to do about it?' he said, and bent his head again.

Iona stiffened, fighting the passionate need that roared back into life. 'I'll bite you,' she threatened.

But the words came out low and husky, intimate and too languorous to impress him. He kissed the pulse that beat wildly in her throat, his lips lingering with erotic effect against the soft skin, so that Iona shivered again, desperately resisting the tempting whisper to surrender, let him take her, lose herself again in the voluptuous enchantment of his lovemaking.

'I remember your bites,' he growled, and gently nipped the sensitive pleasure point where her neck met her shoulders. 'I soon learned that like the tigress, once you used your teeth on me your completion would soon come.'

'You were wrong,' she managed, and put paid to every instinct by pulling back, away from the taut magnetism of his body, of the mindless sex he was offering.

Been there, done that, thrown away the T-shirt, she thought wildly as she fought to repress the smouldering pangs of addictive hunger, so close to craving it almost broke through the tattered remnants of her common sense.

'If I am wrong, why are you trembling?'

She shook her head and pushed against the door. It didn't give, and she couldn't think how to open it, until Luke said something in Greek and turned the handle, pushing it back.

'Go now,' he ordered, the words low and harsh from between almost clenched teeth. 'Before I take up the offer your body is making. You want me every bit as much as I want you—at least admit that.'

Indignation at her own weakness lifted her chin, froze her voice. 'Goodnight.'

Swiftly she slipped through the door and closed it firmly on him, furious at her white-hot reaction to his potent, untrammelled masculinity. Halfway to the bed she had to stop for a few seconds and consciously relax her strained muscles, fight back a hunger that had never gone away.

Shivering, she crawled under the covers. Although she'd left Tahiti convinced she'd get over him, it had taken only one look from him to make her realise his power over her. But until that kiss of a few minutes ago she hadn't accepted that the feelings she'd stringently repressed were too potent to ignore.

Since Tahiti she hadn't been able to summon even

a flicker of interest in any other man. So why hadn't she realised that Luke had altered her in a fundamental way?

He hadn't changed. Oh, he still wanted her, but for her that was no longer enough.

A pang of deep, painful emotion tore through her.

How likely was it that he had stayed celibate? He was only too cynically aware of the charisma of his smile, the intoxicating, dangerous physical presence that backed up his formidable character. Without a cent to his name he'd still be inundated by panting women.

She'd recognised that dark male authority instantly. The impact of his personality—and the heat of his appreciative metallic survey—had overwhelmed her, melting the ice that had kept her heart and body in a frozen limbo.

Oh, stop it right now, she commanded her treacherous brain in disgust.

Go to sleep.

Easier to say that than do it, she thought wryly when she woke the next morning, eyes heavy with too little rest. Not that sleep had helped; she was still tense and wary—and oddly, *stupidly*, expectant.

The silence probably meant Chloe hadn't woken before her, thank heavens. A glance at her watch elicited a soft gasp. She'd slept through her alarm. She scrambled out of bed, showered, and got into yesterday's clothes, grimacing a little at the dampness of the underwear she'd washed the night before.

Moving quietly, she walked out of her room.

'Good morning.'

With a shocked squeak she jumped. Luke must have prowled up behind her like some predator on the hunt;

she hadn't heard a thing. She took in a jagged breath and turned, catching a black-browed frown.

'You are not afraid of me?' he demanded incredulously.

'Of course not,' she defended herself in her crispest voice.

'Something frightened you?'

She said, 'I thought everyone else was asleep.' It was a pretty lame excuse, and she didn't blame him for the ironic lift of his brows.

'You are of a nervous disposition? I don't remember that.' The words hung for a few seconds, before he said smoothly, 'Surely it is a disadvantage in someone trained to work with children?'

Admitting he was the only person who affected her so intensely was not an option. Matching his raised brows with her own, she ignored his goading tone. 'I'm not nervous—I just didn't expect to have someone come up behind me. Where is Chloe?'

'She is asleep,' he told her. 'Her body is still adjusting to the change in time zones. She will wake up when she is ready. Come and have breakfast—I have a proposition to put to you.'

A pang of shaming anticipation sizzled through her. They were almost the same words he'd used in Tahiti.

Barricades crashing into place, Iona sent him a suspicious glance. He met it with an inscrutable face and cool, dismissive eyes. Clearly the kiss they'd exchanged had had little effect on him.

Chagrined, she chided herself for overreacting so foolishly. But her tone was stiff and cautious when she asked, 'About what?'

'I spoke to Neelie—Chloe's nanny—during the night,' he said calmly. 'The news about her mother is not good, and she will have to stay in England for some time—weeks certainly, months possibly. I have more business meetings for the next couple of days, so I need someone to look after Chloe. I am offering you the job until I leave New Zealand—in about a week. Chloe is clearly enjoying your company, and you seem to have formed a bond with her.'

'I can't,' she said, automatically shaking her head. 'It's not—'

He broke in. 'I have already spoken to your cousin, who tells me she can spare you.'

'How did you contact her?' she demanded, before she could stop herself. 'I have her work phone.'

'I got someone to find her personal phone number,' he said calmly.

When Iona was angry, Lukas noted with wry amusement, her eyes frosted into a cold clear green.

Memories stirred his body into action. Hair like a waterfall against him, the long, silky strands cool and tactile, and skin as sweet and glowing as a white peach...

Yet always, no matter how passionate her surrender, there was a reserve he couldn't penetrate. Emotional closeness had never been on the cards with his previous lovers, yet from his first meeting with Iona he'd found himself challenged by her aloofness—a challenge he should have ignored.

He should certainly have been strong enough last night to resist the temptation to kiss her. Without even trying she was a threat to the foundation on which he'd built his adult life. He enjoyed women but trusted no one; bitter experience had taught him that love didn't last. He was a quick learner, and didn't need more than one lesson.

Nothing like that kiss would happen again, he promised himself. From now on he was determined to keep the situation on a professional level.

Ruthlessly he forced his mind back to the subject in hand. 'Your cousin is happy for you to do this for as long as Chloe needs you.'

The businesslike Ms Makepeace had also shown herself to be a good negotiator in organising Iona's wages and conditions.

He stated them now, watching her face closely. That steely reserve was very evident as she listened, and he couldn't help admiring her gritty dignity when she replied.

'All right.' Her tone was remote and unemotional. 'I agree.'

'You'll want to collect clothes and make arrangements. You can do that while Chloe and I go to the zoo with your cousin and her sons. I've organised a driver for you.'

Her sensuous mouth fell open, was hastily closed, and she lowered thick lashes—a second too late to conceal her surprise. Lukas realised he was enjoying himself. He might regret that kiss—because it was unprofessional—but Iona never bored him.

Did she have a lover, perhaps, waiting impatiently for her? None had shown up in her security check, so almost certainly not. Why? Surely she wasn't still holding the memory of the dead fiancé close to her heart?

Surprised and irritated by the visceral flash of possessiveness his thoughts aroused, he shrugged them off. Her fiancé had died saving her; naturally she would remember him lovingly.

Their Tahitian affair had been a magical experience,

but Chloe was more important to him than any other woman; she needed him as no one else ever had.

Even though Iona made his body sing in a way it never had with any other woman.

'That's very thoughtful of you,' she said then, in a level, aloof voice only a degree or so warmer than ice.

She was still exasperated when she arrived back at the apartment building after scrabbling together a collection of clothes and necessities. Just before she'd closed the door behind her, she had gathered up the references she'd been given when she'd left the nursery school to join Angie.

If Luke wanted proof she'd been a good teacher, she'd take great delight in waving them in his arrogantly handsome face.

The concierge hurried across the foyer to say, 'If you leave your pack and bag here I'll see they get up to the penthouse. Mr Michelakis requested that you meet him at the zoo by the elephant house.' He glanced at his watch. 'In ten minutes,' he said urgently.

Incredulously Iona said, 'Ten minutes?'

'A car is waiting for you,' he said with a little shooing motion of his hand.

Luke was autocratic—so what? It didn't need to affect her. Working for Angie had taught her to cope with everything that came her way.

Not only could she organise a party that would make the social pages for all the right reasons, but she'd turned down propositions—even insulting ones—without once losing her equanimity. She could smile with real amusement at attempts to put her in her place, and control her temper no matter what the provocation.

So why did she feel like exploding at one man's calm assumption that her life was his to organise?

Because he kissed you senseless, and you're scared.

She used the ten minutes in the car to talk herself into composure—a composure that evaporated the moment she caught sight of the small group waiting by the elephant quarters. It was impossible not to notice the way women in the vicinity looked at Luke—with a kind of delighted appreciation as though he fulfilled a set of unspoken, unrecognised conditions.

It was the whole package, Iona thought, her heart contracting; he wore his superbly cut casual clothes with a negligent grace that proclaimed a lithe, toe-curling masculinity and the kind of assets that figured in the financial pages.

That effortless impact was reinforced by the way he towered over most of the people there, with an air of authentic authority and a face like something out of a feverish female fantasy.

But what brought sympathetic smiles—and stirred a dangerous meltdown in Iona's heart—was the way he carried his daughter, as though she was the most precious thing in the universe.

Watching the curve of that dangerously compelling mouth when he set Chloe on her feet, Iona couldn't control her half-apprehensive excitement. Tossed this way and that by dynamic, perilous emotions she wasn't ready to acknowledge, she slowed down.

Luke turned his head. His eyes darkened, and he took Chloe's hand as he straightened to watch Iona come towards them, his face stern.

An apprehensive delight filled her. More perilous than desire, more disturbing than her memories, she tried to tamp it down. Luke Michelakis had no *right* to affect her like this. Losing her heart to him would be—stupid. And terrifying. And forbidden.

After all, what did she know of him apart from his prowess between the sheets?

Only what Angie had told her. And that he loved his daughter.

Don't forget he can be tender and generous when he's making love, some treacherous part of her mind reminded her.

It just wasn't enough to cover the risk, she thought desperately as she came up to them.

Hiding her emotions with a light tone and a smile, she said, 'Hello, kids. Having fun?'

Fortunately both Chloe and the boys greeted her with enthusiasm, each wanting to be the one to tell her a lion had roared at them through the huge glass window that separated the lords of the savannah from fascinated onlookers.

Above the babble of noise Angie grinned at her, but Luke's eyes were cool and measuring when she looked at him.

'All well?' he asked.

'Yes, thank you.'

Once they set off to explore more of the zoo, Iona was surprised when Chloe alternated between her and Luke. Not surprising was the way the boys also gravitated to him, unconsciously awarding him respect and attention. In turn, he was superb with them, calmly curbing their high spirits, and treating them with the same interested courtesy with which he spoke to Chloe.

Iona didn't dare glance Angie's way. Until now she'd thought the boys were getting over their father's abandonment, but the uncomplicated hero-worship in two pairs of eyes revealed just how much they missed a male presence in their lives.

On the way back to the apartment Luke lifted his gaze from his daughter's head, cradled against his upper arm as she dozed in the car seat, and said abruptly, 'I gather the boys' father does not live with them?'

With reserve, Iona said, 'No.'

He frowned. 'How often do they see him?'

Iona said stiffly, 'Not often.' Never, actually.

The arrogant features hardened and his mouth thinned. He looked down at the child beside him before saying in a voice that lifted the hair on Iona's neck, 'Does your cousin forbid any communication between them?'

She sent him a cool glance that should have warned him off. 'No.'

Contempt iced his tone, transformed his gaze into golden quartz. 'Whatever the situation between your cousin and the boy's father,' he said austerely, 'they are still his sons, and blameless. To abandon them is the act of a weakling.'

It was also affecting the boys badly, but Iona kept silent about that.

When the car drew to halt outside the apartment building Chloe woke up, crossly demanding that Luke carry her.

Iona soothed her. 'He's paying the taxi driver. We'll be at the apartment soon.'

'I don't want to walk,' Chloe said petulantly. She waited until her father joined them to say, 'Lukas, my legs are tired.'

'If they are too tired to stand while we use the elevator, they are tired enough to go straight to bed.' He smiled down at her. 'And some sleep might sweeten that temper of yours, hmm?'

Relief at his support brought a fleeting smile to Iona's face. After a pouting moment Chloe gave in with good grace, trotting alongside her father, her little hand nestled in the strength of his strong own.

When Iona came out from settling her down for her nap, Luke was out on the terrace, surveying the harbour and the islands beyond. Something in his stance stopped her just inside the huge glass doors. Big and hugely competent, a formidable, dominant man, uncompromising in his power and authority, surely he had the world at his feet?

Yet, for a quite irrational moment, she thought he looked completely and utterly alone.

But when he turned his head and beckoned her to join him, his expression showed nothing beyond lazy appreciation as she came towards him.

A secret excitement bloomed in her. Calm yourself, she commanded acerbically.

In a neutral voice he said, 'This is a beautiful city. Or perhaps I should say it has a beautiful setting.'

'We have no buildings to match the glories of Greece,' she admitted.

'In a setting like this it matters not.' He paused, and when she didn't speak said, 'I am satisfied that I need have no worries about Chloe's wellbeing when you are in charge.'

Startled and pleased, she said, 'Thank you. It's what I've been trained to do.'

'It's more than just training; you have a deft touch with children. I noticed you managed both Angie's sons and Chloe easily, sorting out any small problems before they had a chance to escalate. And the principal of the nursery school you worked at before you left to join your cousin's enterprise gave you a glowing commendation.'

Iona stared speechlessly at him. The references she'd packed that morning were still in her bedroom, waiting to be handed to him.

He lifted a brow and said a little arrogantly, 'Surely you did not expect me to accept you without a security check?'

Iona fought back a bewildering complex of responses. Of course in the world of the mega-rich everyone—especially employees—would be checked and double-checked.

Yet his action had revealed only too clearly her position in his life. Their passionate affair and last night's kiss meant nothing. They'd been lovers—surely he'd learned something about her character then?

Uncompromisingly, Luke continued, 'I trust very few people. Chloe is defenceless, and will be alone with you for long periods of time. I would be failing in my duty if I didn't make sure she'd be safe.'

Iona knew she shouldn't be hurt. Already she was forming bonds with the child, and Luke's love for his daughter was subtly altering her feelings for him. Oh, the physical attraction was as strong as ever—stronger, she thought guiltily—but it was now buttressed by emotions she didn't dare face.

CHAPTER FIVE

IONA looked up and met Luke's hard frown. He said, 'You must have had employers check your references before, especially as you taught at nursery school?'

'Well—yes,' she admitted, because of course he was right. Her objection was purely—and ridiculously—personal. She tried to lighten things with a wry smile and the comment, 'Except for Angie, of course.'

'Sometimes the ones closest to you are the ones who most need watching.' His voice was level and un-inflected, but a note in it sent a cold shiver down her spine.

She said, 'It's all right. I do understand. I was just—taken aback, I suppose.'

'You must have lived a very sheltered life. I want the same for Chloe.'

'Any father would want that for his children,' she said, relieved to get off the topic.

'I am not her father.' He spoke without emphasis, his eyes burnished an opaque gold, unreadable yet somehow ruthless when they met and held hers.

Stunned, Iona stared at him. Before she could order her thoughts words tumbled out. 'Then who...?' She shook her head. 'I don't believe you—the resemblance is so strong.'

Surely not *another* man who refused to acknowledge his child?

As though he could read that horrified thought, he twisted his mouth into a sardonic smile. 'Perhaps you should have run a check on *me*. Chloe is my half-sister.'

'Half-sister?' she said blankly.

He lifted broad shoulders in another rapid Mediterranean shrug. 'I have adopted her. The circumstances don't matter. What is important is that she be kept safe.'

She shook her head, trying to clear it. 'From whom?'

'From anyone who'd try to use her,' he said, his deep voice holding more than a touch of impatience.

'I'm afraid that's not enough information,' she told him quickly. At his frown she went on, 'Surely you understand that if she's in any danger I need to know what form it's likely to take?'

He paused a moment before saying, 'At this moment I do not expect any danger to her, but there is always the possibility her birth father might try to claim her.'

Shocked, she asked involuntarily, 'And her birth father is…?'

'The same man who sired me,' he said coldly, as though she should have known.

Angie's words drifted back into Iona's mind. Something about him leaving his family, to which Iona had replied sarcastically that they'd probably always been there for him in the background.

It seemed she'd been wrong; clearly there'd been a rift of massive proportions. As soon as she got access to a computer she was going to find out more about Luke—*Lukas*—Michelakis.

Until then the situation was beyond her comprehension, so she fixed on one thing. 'It's highly unlikely anyone would try to kidnap her here.'

His expression revealed what he thought of that. 'There is no crime in New Zealand, then?' he asked satirically. 'No families torn apart by feuds?'

'Some feud if an innocent child is endangered by it!'

He paused before saying shortly, 'Her *life* is not in danger.'

One glance at his stern face told her that was all he was prepared to let her know. She said, 'New Zealand's situation makes it difficult to smuggle people. We're a long way from anywhere else, with no land borders, so any kidnapper would have to leave by plane, and security is really tight now.'

Again that shrug, more pronounced this time. 'For some people the world is a small place.'

For the very rich, he meant. What on earth had she become caught up in? Starkly she said, 'The check you ran on me must have indicated I have no experience as a bodyguard.'

'It's not necessary—for the time you are caring for Chloe you will be protected wherever you are.'

'You won't be with us all the time.'

'I'm flattered that you think I'd be protection enough,' he said smoothly, 'but I employ security people for that.'

'Everywhere? At the zoo?'

'Of course,' he said, as though she was being naïve.

Somehow the knowledge tarnished a pleasant memory. She shivered.

He covered the distance between them in one stride and touched her bare arm.

'You are cold,' he said quietly, something in his voice alerting her.

Don't look up!

But a force stronger than her will dragged Iona's gaze to his face. Her breath stilled in her throat. Eyes dilating, she stared up at classical features saved from mere beauty by the hard stamp of intelligence and command. A sensuous awareness quivered between them, transforming his aloof tawny-gold survey into a heated, intent examination.

The light touch of his fingers ran like a caress through her, sending a feverish excitement smoking along every nerve. For a taut second she had to grit her teeth, fighting the need that urged her to sway into his arms, surrender to the potent, mind-numbing charm that would banish all her fears.

But that was no longer enough. She felt as though she were on the edge of a life-altering discovery, a step into the unknown so big and important she instinctively flinched back.

Instantly his smouldering gaze turned icy and his hand dropped away.

Random thoughts whirled dizzily around Iona's brain, and although she retained enough presence of mind to speak, her voice emerged in a husky whisper. 'I'm not cold.'

Desire rode Lukas hard, mingling with something darker and even more reckless. He was far too conscious of the texture of Iona's skin, soft and sleek, and the faint scent that owed nothing to any carefully crafted perfume. She smelt of woman, sweet and seductive; it was one of the things about her that had fascinated him.

He'd never forgotten her passion, her laughter, her quick mind and intriguing, mysterious silences. Warm and companionable, touchingly unawakened for a woman who'd spent six months living with the man she'd intended to marry, she'd kept essential parts of herself hidden behind that maddening reserve.

'Then why are you shivering?' he asked softly.

She lifted huge eyes, mysteriously shadowed a dark, deep blue-green. Eyes to lose your soul in, he thought, feeling the reins of his self-control loosening.

Iona's breath blocked her throat, set her heart drumming in a feverish tattoo.

Yes, please... Oh, please...

As though he'd heard the urgent, mute plea Luke bent his head, his mouth taking hers without mercy in a kiss that transcended the past eighteen months as though they'd never existed.

Last night he had kissed her with a purely physical hunger. This was different; it was like coming home, like following her heart into paradise, like entering a fantasy world where all things were miraculously made right. Dimly, through the surging sensations that fired every cell in her body, Iona recognised that this kiss marked a fundamental change in their relationship.

She had no idea where it was leading—and she didn't care. Ravished by Luke's expertise, she surrendered to the sweet need that clamoured through her.

Until Luke lifted his head and dropped the arms that held her against his hard body, and stepped back to say harshly, 'I am sorry—I should not have done this.'

Assailed by a dislocating awareness of where she was, Iona stared at him, her soul-deep joy fading rapidly as he re-imposed control. That formidable will chilled her right to her vulnerable core.

She stepped back and said in a thin voice, 'You're right—it wasn't sensible.'

'It won't happen again.'

Desperately clutching at the ragged shreds of her self-possession, she drew in a jagged breath. 'Is that a promise?'

Luke's dark brows drew together in a frown. 'You have my word on it,' he said shortly.

His unexpected lack of control angered him; he didn't go in for wild lusts or raging desire. For twelve years he'd disciplined his emotions, reaching into his soul to develop a granite self-sufficiency, relying only on his own strength of character. He'd deliberately chosen his lovers for their sophistication and experience and their inability to be hurt.

And then he'd met Iona, a fair trespasser. Met her, and desired her with a swiftly fierce, unexpected passion. At first he'd thought she fitted his specifications—that she was another compliant, worldly woman who wouldn't expect more than he could give—sex, luxury, and the temporary satisfaction of desire. He'd pursued her and taken her, and it had been—magical.

So magical he'd broken the rules he lived by and asked her to move in with him. Permanence was the last thing he'd thought he'd wanted, yet when she'd run away he'd felt something of the bleak sense of betrayal he'd endured when his father had believed his second wife's lies and disinherited him, cutting him off from everyone he loved and trusted.

Iona was a distraction he couldn't afford right now. He needed to concentrate on this latest effort by his father to wreck his life—one that had a fair chance of succeeding.

But that very attack meant he couldn't—yet—get rid

of Iona. He examined her face. Although his kiss had softened the outline of her lips, her wary, self-contained expression belied their temptation.

Iona looked up, meeting his eyes with heightened colour. 'Your security men must be very inconspicuous. I didn't notice anyone.'

'That's the whole point.'

'I don't think I could ever get accustomed to being watched all the time.'

How easily she could dismiss those moments in his arms! Cynically he told himself it was for the best.

'*You* won't be watched,' he said, wrenching his mind from its absorbed focus on that soft mouth and the lingering sensual impact of her slender litheness against him. 'My security men are paid very well to watch the people around Chloe.'

Stop thinking with your sex, he told himself. If he sent Iona away he'd have to find another temporary nanny to take her place. It would take time he no longer had to find someone like Neelie—middle-aged, sensible, and devoted to her charge. More importantly, someone Chloe liked as well as she clearly liked Iona.

So this leftover emotion had to be mastered. And as he'd never yet felt a passion he couldn't control, he shouldn't fail now.

Coldly he continued, 'Get used to it. You've already accepted the position—I hope you're not thinking of reneging.'

Her lashes fell, hiding those changeable eyes.

'I have power.' Simple words, spoken dispassionately. Interested, he waited for her reaction.

She stepped back, her gaze wide and clear and turbulent—but not with fear. 'Are you by any chance *threatening* me again?' she demanded incredulously.

'I did not threaten you before, and I am not doing so now.'

Iona's stomach performed a complicated manoeuvre. His nearness reached something deep inside her, scrambling her thoughts and churning her emotions. But there was a lot more to Luke Michelakis than a stunning face and a body as honed and strong as an Olympic athlete's.

This man, she thought warily, was dangerous. Dangerous in a way she couldn't put a name to, but that some instinct in her recognised.

'It sounded too close to a threat to ignore,' she said stubbornly.

He turned away and looked out across the harbour, unwittingly giving her an excellent view of a profile that could have been taken from an ancient statue.

Indignation at his dismissive action made her lose caution. 'How *dare* you?'

Luke held up a lean, tanned hand. 'Spare me the histrionics,' he said in a bored tone. 'If you're so prone to jumping to conclusions you're not the right person for Chloe.'

Iona stopped her first impetuous response. Angie needed the money, but that wasn't everything. Luke had influence. A word from him might put more work Angie's way.

Or remove it...

Slowly she said, 'And that remark skates very close to blackmail.'

'Are you always this blunt?' He sounded amused.

Chagrined, she darted a glance his way. Darn it, he was laughing at her! And she was being foolish. If she'd thought about it she'd have realised that he'd have security people; she hadn't thought about it because she'd been too overwhelmed by meeting Luke again.

She said, 'I like to know exactly where I am.'

'So do I. I am not threatening you or blackmailing you, so make up your mind. Now.'

She took a deep breath, feeling oddly unsafe, as though she were venturing into thick fog. 'I'm not planning to walk away from our agreement. I'll take care of Chloe while you're in New Zealand, bodyguards or no bodyguards.'

'Good.' Clearly tired of the discussion, he changed the subject. 'I understand this cold spell will go on for several days yet, so after I've finished what I intend to do here we'll go down to the Volcanic Plateau. I'm told the skiing is excellent there still, and Chloe wants to play in the snow. Do you have suitable gear?'

'No, but—'

'Buy some,' Luke said, adding, 'I will of course pay.'

'You don't need to,' she said shortly. 'I'll borrow from my cousin.'

He lifted an eyebrow and inspected her—a look that sent little sizzles of highly suspect anticipation through her.

Luke asked, 'Will they fit? Your cousin has a more voluptuous figure than yours.'

'She calls it matronly,' Iona said staidly. 'I can wear her clothes.' She certainly wasn't going to buy gear Luke would paid for, stuff she might never wear again.

He gave a short nod. 'Check Chloe's wardrobe, please. Neelie knew a trip to the mountains was possible, so there should be suitable garb for Chloe, but make sure. We'll be coming back here, so she won't need to take everything.'

* * *

That night, after she'd put Chloe to bed, Iona closed the door quietly behind her. She was going to miss the little girl when it came time to say goodbye.

Walking outside onto the terrace, she looked around. No sign of Luke, who'd retired to his room. Stomach tightening, she rang Angie.

'Of course you can borrow my skiing clothes, although you'll look a bit of a trick in them—I'm a size bigger than you are,' Angie confirmed.

'That doesn't matter,' Iona said before asking her bluntly, 'Angie, would it be easier for you if I found another job?'

The slight pause before her cousin responded gave her the answer. 'Why are you asking?' Angie asked cautiously. 'Has Lukas offered you a permanent job?'

'No.' She didn't say she wouldn't take the job even if Luke did offer it. His kisses had warned her it would be altogether too risky. 'I don't want to be a drag on you.'

Angie's protest was immediate. 'You could never be that.'

'I can hear the *but*,' Iona told her. 'Tell me now.'

Another pause, as meaningful as the first one. 'Well, last night Felton rang me to say he's not paying support for the boys any more. He's in Australia, so I have no way of forcing him to cough up.'

'The rat,' Iona said with venom. 'Look, as soon as this interlude with Chloe and Luke is over I'll start applying for situations. I won't have any problems getting kindergarten relief work. And while I'm doing that I could relieve at crèches and daycare centres too.'

'You'll take a big drop in income,' Angie said bluntly, but she didn't protest.

'I'll manage.'

Her cousin said, 'I won't deny that it would be—easier. But I feel a heel.'

'Rubbish!'

Her cousin's voice altered, became brisk. 'Don't worry about us—just have fun living the life of the rich while you can. I'll bet this recession hasn't affected Luke Michelakis's net worth by a cent.'

Frowning, Iona set her telephone down, jumping when Luke said from behind her, 'Who is the rat?'

'How do you do that?' she demanded, whirling around to stare at him. He'd discarded his jacket and tie, and the trousers of his business suit hugged his hips and long, heavily muscled thighs like a lover.

His brows shot up. 'Do what?'

'Sneak up on people without a sound.'

'It's not deliberate; it's just my natural gait. Who is this rat you hate so much?'

Unwilling to tell him more about Angie's situation, Iona said glibly, 'An unfaithful husband, that's all.'

It was the truth, but she felt uncomfortable under his steady glaze, and was almost glad when Chloe began to cry in her bedroom.

She'd been sick, and during that night and the next day she endured a virus that kept her in bed and stretched Iona's skills at keeping a fretful child entertained and happy. However, with the miraculous recuperative powers of children, Chloe bounced back late in the afternoon. She was sitting on the terrace under Iona's eye, intent on a picture of the lion she'd seen at the zoo, when Luke strolled out into the sun. He'd taken off his jacket and tie and rolled up his sleeves, and he looked blatantly, sensually male, the hard angles of his face softening when he saw his daughter.

Something very strange melted Iona's spine and

swirled in the pit of her stomach. And her foolish brain seized up under an urgent onrush of need, sharp and penetrating, that filled her with precarious pleasure.

The decision to stay on as Chloe's nanny had been a reckless mistake; each day that passed put her heart in more danger.

'So, you are up,' he said to Chloe, catching her in his arms when she came running towards him, little face radiant.

'I'm better,' she told him earnestly after she'd kissed him. 'I'm not sick now. When can we go to the snow?'

He set her down. 'When the doctor says you are well enough.'

She nodded and dragged him across to see her drawing. Telling her unruly pulse to calm down, Iona stood up.

After a swift glance her way, Luke asked, 'How has she been?'

'For the last two hours, as you see. No sign of a temperature, no aches, no pains, and an appetite that would do credit to a shearer.' When his brows climbed, she enlarged, 'They shear sheep, starting at dawn, and they eat six meals a day. *Large* meals.'

'We have sheep in Greece,' he said mildly. 'The doctor can check her over tomorrow morning to see if she's fit to travel.'

'I want to go to the snow,' Chloe said eagerly.

He frowned. 'Little one, you will go wherever the good doctor says is best for you.' Chloe looked pleadingly up at him, but he turned his attention back to Iona. 'I will be out tonight. However, tomorrow I'll be at home in good time, so you can take the afternoon and the evening off. You have been in constant attendance on this small tyrant here, and no doubt you have things to do.'

'Thank you,' she said automatically.

She did have things to do, and she also wanted to talk to her cousin. Angie's ex-husband's refusal to pay maintenance was upsetting but not unexpected; it had reinforced Iona's decision to find another job—a decision she spent the next evening discussing with Angie, who reluctantly accepted it.

Feeling wrung out, Iona said, 'Angie, before I go can I use your computer?'

'Of course.'

An hour later Iona closed the computer and looked up as Angie came into the small bedroom she'd converted into an office. 'You look a bit green around the gills,' her cousin said, frowning. 'What have you been doing?'

'Researching Luke.'

Angie's concern deepened into active worry. 'What have you found? Something nasty?'

'Yes. Oh, not Luke.' Angie gave her a concerned look. Hastily she explained, 'The reason for his family bust-up.' She hesitated, then said reluctantly, 'His father is Aristo Michelakis, the shipping magnate. Apparently he claims descent from Hippolytus.'

Angie looked surprised. 'Who?'

Iona shivered. 'It's a Greek myth. Or perhaps ancient history. Anyway, Hippolytus was the son of the king of Athens. His stepmother fell in love with him, but when he spurned her she claimed he raped her, and then hung herself. The king killed his son.'

'Charming,' Angie said with emphasis. 'I hope fervently this has nothing to do with Luke's departure from the family home.'

'Unfortunately it has.' Iona swallowed. 'Luke's mother died when he was seventeen, and Aristo almost immediately married his much-younger secretary—a blonde with a very hard face, judging by the photos. A year or so later she apparently told her husband that Luke had either seduced or raped her—the reports skirt around that aspect, but it was easy enough to read between the lines. The stepmother took an overdose. She didn't die, but Aristo divorced her immediately.'

'Ugh. And uncanny.'

'Horrible.' Iona still felt sick. She switched off the computer and stood up.

Angie said, 'At least Luke's father didn't kill him.'

'No, he just booted Luke out of the family—cast him adrift with no money except a legacy from his maternal grandfather.'

'Very nasty indeed,' Angie agreed.

Iona got to her feet and said abruptly, 'I rather wish I hadn't decided to pry. How could Luke's father *do* that?'

Angie looked at her with an equivocal expression. 'Perhaps it was the *old bull being tossed out of the herd by the younger one* syndrome.'

'Syndrome or not, nothing can excuse him. No wonder Luke's so—so tough,' Iona said forthrightly.

'You sound quite convinced that he didn't do whatever he was supposed to have done.'

Iona stared at her cousin, her expression stunned. 'Of course I am,' she said numbly. But why?

Angie asked curiously, 'I thought—you let me think—you didn't know him very well. What makes you so sure he's incapable of committing adultery with his stepmother? Or raping her, come to that.'

'I know he wouldn't,' Iona said, shocked by her

cousin's bluntness. 'I know it sounds silly, but he's just not the sort.' She glanced at her watch. 'I have to go now. We're off tomorrow morning. I'll keep in touch.'

'Be careful, all right?'

'I'm always careful.' But she needed to be much more than careful now.

CHAPTER SIX

LUKE opened the door to her when she arrived back. He'd changed into a short-sleeved shirt striped the same tawny colour as his eyes, and he looked slightly rumpled, an informality increased by the darkish shadow of a beard around his lean jaw. Sensation sizzled deep in the pit of Iona's stomach—desire made even more intense by what she'd just discovered.

How could his father have thrown him out? It beggared belief.

Although Aristo Michelakis did seem to make a habit of rejecting his children. Now she understood why Luke had adopted his baby half-sister, and she honoured him for it.

What was wrong with his father? Couldn't he see what he'd done to his children?

Luke stepped aside to let her in, then examined her so intently she shifted uncomfortably. Her research now seemed an intolerable intrusion into his life.

He asked, 'Have you had a good evening?'

'Yes, thank you.' And was that ever a lie!

'Good.' He waited until they had almost reached the door of her room before saying, 'I am about to make myself a drink. Would you like to join me?'

Just beyond her door stood another table, not as

opulent as the one in the foyer. During the day someone had come in to change the flowers, replacing them
with a great bowl of roses. A large mirror reflected their
elegant blooms and their scent charged the air with a
seductively heavy perfume. Several petals had fallen
from one, the matt golden forms trailing so artistically
across the polished wood it looked as though it had been
deliberately done.

Temptation warred with caution. Caution won, but
only by a whisker. Iona said, 'Actually, I'm tired. I'll go
straight to my room, thank you.'

'Perhaps that is wise,' Luke said negligently, clearly
not in the least put out.

She turned to go, then asked, 'What time do we leave
in the morning?'

'About nine.' He stooped to pick up several petals
from the floor.

Iona tore her eyes away from the slow flex and coil
of powerful muscles beneath the linen of his shirt. Her
heart was pumping blood feverishly through her, so
loudly she could hear it beating in her ears.

Luke said, 'Do you ski?'

'Yes.'

'Then you will enjoy the next few days. We'll hire
boots for you when we get there.'

She said, 'Surely I'll be looking after Chloe?'

A subtle current of communication vibrated between
them—a kind of subliminal exchange both desperately
exciting and immediate. He kept his distance, but she
felt the impact of his gaze in every cell.

'I thought the doctor told you she was perfectly all
right to holiday on the mountain?' he said.

'Yes. Yes, he did.'

He didn't even have to touch her, she thought in

confusion, to set her alight. She was so aware of him she felt adrenalin surge through her veins, a drugging anticipation preparing her for him.

'Then, although you will spend quite a bit of time with her, there will be occasions when you can ski if you want to.'

Sex with Luke had taught her that until she'd met him she'd only dabbled in love. With Gavin it had begun as friendship, deepening slowly and inevitably, sweetly and surely, into something deeper. Her only lover before Luke, he'd been gentle and patient, tenderly initiating her.

Luke had demanded a sensual energy to match his own. And she'd found it, surrendering to a sexuality that summoned something wild and unrestrained from her, a passionate yielding to the moment. He'd encouraged her to follow her impulses, to take control sometimes, to explore his body and her own with elemental, tantalising appetite until she lost all sense of self.

His generosity was part of the reason she didn't believe he'd wrecked his family. And her sweetly desperate expectation was one impulse she was not going to follow. If she did, she risked so much more—her heart and her happiness.

After dragging a sharp breath into starving lungs, she said, 'I'll go and pack now.'

She went past him, only to be stopped by a lazy hand that just grazed her forearm. Rills of sensation tightened her skin.

He dropped his hand and said lazily, 'The drink I intended to have is to celebrate a very good deal I signed today with your Prime Minister and his attendant army of civil servants and advisors. Good for me, good for

New Zealand. I don't drink alone, so I'd like you to share it with me.'

'Is that an order?' she asked, because temptation had come roaring back.

He shrugged and said indifferently, 'Of course not.'

Say no. Say no right now...

But what harm could there be in sharing a drink with him? It seemed mean to deny him the pleasure of celebrating. 'In that case, and because this deal is going to be good for New Zealand, I'll join you,' she said sedately.

In the sitting room he poured champagne, and handed a flute of the scintillating wine to her, saying with a gleam of amusement in his lion eyes, 'If you were always as blunt as you are now, you must have been an interesting child.'

Iona smiled ruefully. 'Tact and discretion did come hard. I probably embarrassed my parents until I learned the boundaries.'

'Childhood is a time for exploring life, and one for learning boundaries too.' He gave a sudden wry smile. 'And a parent both explores and learns too. It came as a considerable shock to me to find that children have a definite personality right from birth.'

Of course, he'd been an only child. 'She's a credit to you.'

'She is a credit to herself,' he corrected. 'I made every mistake possible in her first year, when I cared for her myself, yet she managed to thrive in spite of my ineptitude.'

Startled, Iona looked up. 'You looked after her yourself?' At his nod she asked, 'Why?'

He gave that slight, very Mediterranean shrug. 'I read

several books, and found that it is important for a child to bond with someone in their first year. I wanted it to be me, not a nanny who might leave in the future, so I took her to the island—my real home. Thanks to modern communications conducting business was simple enough from there.' He gave a reminiscent smile. 'Looking after a baby was not so easy, but between us—and with the help of several very experienced island grandmothers and mothers—Chloe and I managed.'

Stunned and oddly touched, Iona said, 'Well, between you all you've done a brilliant job.'

He saluted her with his glass. 'Here's to Chloe, then. And also to… Well, I shan't pre-empt the Prime Minister's announcement tomorrow, so let's call it a toast to a chance to make a difference.'

Startled, she echoed his toast and sipped wine that set her tastebuds tingling with delight. Only the very best for Luke Michelakis, she thought, trying to rein in her runaway reaction to his presence. Everything seemed stronger, more vivid, more potent—from the wine to the man who looked down at her with half-closed eyes.

He set his glass down and said, 'So…boundaries. Perhaps we should establish some too.'

No touching, she thought hurriedly, then flushed, because of course he wasn't thinking of that sort of boundary. She was his employee.

Luke went on, 'While you are in my care you will be treated like one of the family.'

'In your *care*?' she asked, stunned. She gave a wry laugh. 'That's a very old-fashioned, rather patriarchal way of looking at the situation. You're my employer.'

'I was brought up in a patriarchal society,' he told her coolly. 'It is entirely natural for me to think like that.'

'Do you consider it your duty to care for every one of your employees?'

'In a less personal fashion,' he admitted with a wry smile. 'You live in my house and care for Chloe, so it is different, but, yes, I ensure that not only do the people I employ have good working conditions, but that they are taken care of in other ways. I support an excellent pension plan and health scheme.'

She said briskly, 'Well, as this is a temporary job you won't have to enrol me. New Zealand has a good healthcare system, and of course we have universal superannuation.'

Luke thought ironically that he'd never have believed he'd drink champagne with a woman—one he wanted with a taut, driving intensity that kept him awake at nights—and talk about such dull subjects as pension plans and health schemes.

Not that he should be surprised. Iona had never fitted into any of his categories; as a lover she'd been passionate and sensuous, but she'd left him without a backwards glance.

And now, he thought, making a swift decision, was the right time to ask the reason.

'Why did you run away from Tahiti?' His tone was idly enquiring.

She gave him a shadowed glance, hesitated, then said slowly, 'I wasn't ready for anything else.'

And now? It suddenly became important to him to probe further, but he sensed that now was the wrong time. 'Because of the death of your fiancé?'

She said quietly, 'Yes, but also—my parents had died in a car accident that year. And Angie's marriage broke up around the same time. Everything I valued— everyone I loved—was either dead or in great distress.'

Her narrow brows drew together. Not quite looking at him, she said, 'I didn't dare stay. I was afraid.'

'I see.' He understood how great loss could have made her unable to trust her instincts, and stifled the urge to comfort her. She wasn't ready for that, either.

Lashes lowered, she was sipping the champagne with delicate pleasure. His whole body tightened, so that he had to lock every muscle to stop himself from going over and taking the glass from her hand, pulling her into his arms, kissing that softly lush mouth until it parted for him...

What would she do?

Respond, he thought with brutal honesty. She'd go up in flames—yet, although he could take her physically, she'd keep him shut out from her emotions and her thoughts. For reasons he wasn't prepared to explore he had an uncivilised, reckless need to shatter those barriers, compel her to see him not as a man she was unwillingly attracted to, but as a lover who meant something to her.

Was she going to hold the memory of her fiancé in her heart for the rest of her life? How could any man compete with a dead hero?

His mind went back to the conversation he'd just had with Neelie. Now was not the time to reveal the nanny's decision, he decided.

The next few days on the mountain would give him time to test his ability to resist Iona. If she proved too tempting, he'd—well, he'd face that if he was forced to.

Aloud he said, 'I hadn't realised your parents died so tragically and so soon after your fiancé's death. I'm sorry.'

She blinked, then said with difficulty, 'You gave

me something in Tahiti.' Colour burned along her cheekbones and she hurried on, 'And not just the— our relationship. I found that I could feel again, that I could enjoy things and respond to them. Thank you for that.'

It was a start.

Iona surveyed the view from the sitting room window. Clouds of pale mist rising from the base of the tall trees that surrounded the lodge gave the garden a mysterious, almost eerie air.

The man who'd showed them to their rooms said, 'That's steam from the hot springs. There are several pools, all entirely natural, and tested every day to make sure they stay pure. Soaking in the water is a wonderful way to ease out the stiffness after a day on the mountain. And there's one that's very suitable for children.'

Chloe looked hopefully up at her father, who said, 'Later, perhaps.'

Iona looked around the luxurious room. Although as casually sophisticated, the house in Tahiti had possessed a totally different ambience, tropical and beachy. Here a creative decorator had furnished the rooms with native timbers, their rich warmth set off by serene hues taken from sky and bush. Skilfully placed accents in the earthy colours of the volcanic area provided a vital contrast, as did some seriously good art.

Of course it was luxurious—a splendidly equipped lodge set up for several groups of visitors, although they were the only occupants. Their upstairs suite had its own entrance and foyer, with several bedrooms. Iona's was beside Chloe's, with one for Luke on the other side.

The bodyguard, a serious young man with a faint American accent, had been introduced as Iakobos. 'Just

Iakobos?' Iona had asked with a smile as she'd extended her hand.

After a glance at Luke he'd shaken it somewhat gingerly. 'Just Iakobos, ma'am,' he'd said.

Chloe clearly knew and liked him, and he'd crouched down to say, 'Hi, Chloe. You're growing up, young lady.'

Then he had melted into the background, something he was clearly very good at.

'What standard is your skiing?' Luke asked later, when Chloe was taking her nap.

'I used to be reasonably proficient as a schoolgirl, but I'm well out of practice.' Iona gave him a questioning look, meeting his eyes with a sharp shift of awareness that twanged along her nerves. 'It doesn't matter, surely? I'll be spending my time on the nursery slopes with Chloe.'

'Tomorrow morning, yes, that is correct. So she gets to know the instructor,' Luke said shortly. 'After that there will be times when you can ski at your level while Iakobos stays with her.'

Luke spent the rest of the afternoon in a room that functioned as an office; at one stage Iona heard him speaking in what she presumed to be Greek. A momentary gleam of compassion at his having to work on what was clearly meant to be a holiday was stifled when his tone changed, dropping into a silky quietness that sent a cold shiver down her spine.

Very glad she wasn't the person he was talking to, she took Chloe to explore the grounds of the lodge, Iakobos a silent presence with them.

Of course they made snowballs, Chloe showing a streak of mischief by tossing them at both Iona and the bodyguard. Iona could see why the child liked the young man; he entered fully into the spirit of the occasion, teasing her in a mixture of Greek and English and making her laugh.

'You know how to deal with children,' Iona said as he directed a small snowball towards Chloe.

It hit her in the stomach, exploding over in her in a flurry, and she sat down abruptly in the snow. After a moment of shock her face crinkled into laughter.

'I am the oldest in our family,' he said, hiding a smile as he watched Chloe snatch up handfuls of snow, obviously bent on retaliation. 'And she is a charming child, easy to deal with and to like.'

Indeed she was; they both pretended not to see her busily moulding a snowball, her face intent and serious.

'I think you're going to be attacked,' Iona observed.

He smiled down at her. He had a very nice smile, and he was a good-looking man, yet for some reason he didn't affect her at all. Not like Luke...

'Miss Guthrie—?'

'Call me Iona,' she said swiftly.

He didn't appear to have heard. 'When she throws, she will aim at me, which means it will almost certainly hit you,' he warned.

Iona's laughter was cut short by a level voice from behind.

Luke. In the same silkily lethal tone she'd heard before he said, 'I assume you think it's perfectly all right for Chloe to be sitting on the cold ground?'

Both Iona and the bodyguard whirled, Iona resisting an unnecessary guilt.

How could a golden gaze splinter into ice? Luke's face was like a mask, the angular features set in forbidding lines until Chloe abandoned her snowball and scrambled to her feet, hurling herself at him with a yelp of glee.

His expression softening, he picked her up and in a totally different voice he said, 'Are you cold?'

'Only my nose is,' she said cheerfully, and touched his. 'So's yours,' she said, and started to laugh before breaking into another language.

'English,' he said sternly. 'Miss Iona doesn't understand Greek.'

Obediently she switched, her words tumbling out. 'We've been playing snowballs. Iakobos threw one and it hit me in the tummy, so I was going to hit him with a big, big one.' She held out her arms to indicate just how huge it had been going to be.

'Perhaps you can try that tomorrow. For now, it's time for us to take our cold noses inside,' Luke said, and strode back towards the house with her in his arms.

Still feeling chastened, Iona fell in behind, Iakobos beside her. Within seconds Luke called the bodyguard to walk beside him.

Glowering at their backs, Iona told herself she'd done nothing that could be construed as a lack of care or duty. So why was Luke so angry? Was he still furious with the unlucky person on the other end of the telephone? Surely he wasn't one of those people who let their emotions splatter onto everyone around them?

She was obscurely disappointed. It showed a lack of self-control, something she hadn't expected of him.

And why should she care? Because she was getting too involved with him, that was why. She stumbled, righting herself rapidly as Luke turned.

'Take care,' he commanded. 'The path is slippery.'

It was, but that wasn't why she'd tripped. The sensual attraction that throbbed between them was being transformed into something new and powerful. Oh, the elemental sexual pull was still as strong as ever—no, stronger—but it was now grounded in deeper and more significant emotions. Watching him with Chloe and seeing him with Angie's boys, reading how his father had rejected him—even the conversation about taking care of his workers—had altered her perceptions.

In Tahiti it had all been about lust.

Now she wanted more. She was halfway to falling in love with Lukas Michelakis, internet tycoon, father, disgraced son, respected businessman…

She lifted her eyes, letting them linger on his broad shoulders and narrow hips, measuring the relaxed, ground-covering gait that spoke of strength and power, noting the way he held his child, the swift smile he gave her, his tenderness.

Halfway?

Panic kicked beneath her ribs and hollowed out her stomach as she reacted to a shocking flash of comprehension. Somehow, at some unknown time, ignoring any warning signs, she'd fallen the whole way in love with Luke. She wanted love and marriage and a life together.

And Lukas Michelakis was about as far out of her reach as—well, as the stars.

To him she was that most ex of all exes: an ex-lover. Oh, he still desired her, but it wasn't in the same all-consuming way she wanted him. He could control that. And soon she'd be an ex-employee, someone temporary and peripheral, only remembered because she'd been useful to him.

The emptiness in her heart expanded, cold with foreboding. She'd have to pick up the pieces of her life again—although this time, she thought as she bustled

Chloe off for a bath and to change her clothes, there would be no guilt.

That thought didn't console her, but getting the child ready for dinner and bed at least gave her something else to concentrate on.

After the nursery tea Luke came in to kiss Chloe goodnight. Apart from a short nod he ignored Iona, until they were back in the sitting room of the suite.

'I'm eating out,' he said. 'Your dinner will be brought to you here.'

'Very well, sir,' she returned, her voice expressionless.

He stopped in mid-stride. 'What did you call me?' he demanded.

Already regretting the foolish impulse, she said, 'I noticed Iakobos calls you that, so I thought perhaps it was mandatory.'

His eyes narrowed. 'You appear to have noticed a lot about him,' he said conversationally. He walked across to the door and opened it. 'I don't want to hear that again. Just remember you are here to care for Chloe, not to flirt with the bodyguard.'

'Flirt?' she sputtered, welcoming the swift rush of temper. '*Flirt?* Poor Chloe—if you think that was flirting, you're going to have a difficult time of it when she becomes interested in the opposite sex. And so is she.'

He said curtly, 'Leave Chloe out of it. You forget I have seen the way you approach a man—I have noticed the promise in your smile, the sway of your hips, the upward glance from beneath your lashes.'

His coolly dismissive words stung, yet Iona recognised a raw undernote to them. Her breath locked in her throat when she caught the hard flame of hunger in his scrutiny. Her pulses thundered and a hot surge of physical longing plunged her into confusion.

He'd never love her, but he still wanted her.

Luke smiled cynically. 'It is difficult to hide from passion—our bodies betray us all the time.' He let his gaze drift from her wide, darkening eyes to the curves of her breast and waist.

Shocked by the violence of her headstrong response—so close to craving she didn't dare say anything in case she revealed the hot tide his words had unleashed within her—Iona stared mutely at him, pulses leaping in a mixture of fear and eagerness.

No.

Any surrender now would be infinitely rash—far more reckless than those moon-dazed nights in Tahiti. The only way she could keep her self-respect was to ignore the compelling lure of passion—especially now that it was reinforced by a love that had crept upon her so slowly she hadn't realised its danger until far too late.

Yet it took every ounce of will power she possessed for her to drag in a sighing breath and shake her head.

'You disagree with me?' he asked softly, and touched the betraying little throb at the base of her throat.

Fire beat up through her, and she couldn't tear her eyes away from his, drowning in hot gold. He was judging her reactions with an expert's experience.

That thought pulled her up instantly. Swallowing hard, she managed to step back, vainly trying to armour herself against his powerful male potency. A violent yearning fogged her mind and reminded her how good—how *very* good—it had been to forget everything in the safe haven of his arms.

Her voice slow and uncertain, she said, 'I don't pretend to have your vast knowledge of sex and sexuality.' The words sounded too much like a come-on, and she stopped, took another breath and started again. 'But what's past is gone. It's over and done with.'

'Surely we've both accepted that it's not?' The hint of amusement in his words set her teeth on edge, intensifying when he added, 'This need is very much present. You can't deny that.'

Iona shook her head, trying to clear her mind from the drugging fumes of desire. 'It's a waste of time—and foolish—to let the past impinge on the present.'

'How can you stop it?' His tone was suddenly abrupt. 'The past is always there. It never leaves us. Everything we do, everything we say, every thought and emotion and sensation is directly affected by what has happened to us previously.' He looked down at her. 'You don't believe me? Then think about this—'

He bent and his lips brushed hers for a second, sending sharp darts of fire through her. Iona tensed, but he lifted his head immediately and stepped back, leaving her tingling, her lips tender and aching for more.

Luke smiled with cold irony. 'If you had never lain in my arms, never kissed me with all of that passion you're trying to conceal, you wouldn't be so defensive now, and your body wouldn't be remembering what pleasure we found in each other. We can't escape the past, Iona.'

She said harshly, 'Perhaps not, but we don't need to repeat it.'

'I agree.' His expression hardened. As a jolt of keen pain seared through her, he went on, 'You have a pretty name; in Greek it would refer to the violet—either its colour or the flower itself—valued for its modest beauty and retiring disposition.'

Something in his voice and the gleam in his lion-tawny eyes told her he didn't think the name suited her.

Feeling stupid and callow, she turned away, tense until she heard the quiet huff of the closing door. Even then she couldn't relax. The cold certainty in his voice when he'd spoken of the past made her shiver. Clearly he could never forgive his father.

She walked across to the window and stared out at the wild landscape outside—snow against black rocks, the dark, mysterious shapes of the trees silhouetted against steam formed in the heart of the earth and forced into the cold air.

She closed her eyes. Somehow she had to conquer this—this newfound love. It was embarrassing. Demeaning, even.

And scary.

Each time he'd kissed her she'd blazed up like dry tinder—like a woman who had met her one true love after long years of separation, everything forgotten in the rapturous joy of reunion.

Whereas he'd been master of the situation.

CHAPTER SEVEN

HEAT burned across Iona's cheekbones, replaced by the chill of humiliation. 'Face it,' she said aloud. 'You responded like a wanton, and he recognised it and stepped back before things got out of hand.'

She gripped the edge of the sill, knuckles whitening. Perhaps she should give in, let things take their course. Her breath quickened in time with her heartbeat. But even as temptation filled her mind with dazzling, seductive images, with memories that still had the power to corrode her will, she rejected it.

It might work—if only she hadn't fallen in love with him.

Torn between stunned joy at this unexpected love and a shadowy fear that made a coward of her, she turned away, letting the curtains fall to close out the night.

Cravenly, she made sure she went to bed well before the time Luke was likely to return. She even managed to fall asleep—although she woke when she thought she heard him go past her door, and it took her quite a while afterwards to settle.

Later—much later—she woke in a rush, her heart thudding unpleasantly, unable to place herself. The chilly grey light of dawn was sifting through the curtains, and she stared round the room, fragmented snippets of a dream playing through her thoughts.

Gavin, she thought incredulously, and shivered in the warm room, because since the last night in Tahiti the dreams had stopped. She no longer relived over and over again the moment when he'd used the last of his strength to push her up onto the safety of the rocks, then surrendered to the waves that dragged him relentlessly under.

This time it hadn't been the nightmare; he'd been sailing on a blue sea, a lazy sun washing the beloved lines of his face with soft gold, and he'd been smiling...

No, she thought with a reminiscent little smile of her own, he'd been *grinning*—the way he always had when the wind and the sea and his yacht had been in perfect tune together. He'd looked completely happy.

Wish fulfilment on her part? Or a final relinquishment brought about by her new-found love for Luke?

Restlessly she got out of bed and paced across to the window, pushing back the curtains.

The scene outside drove away the already fading images from her dream; probably the last snowfall before summer had drifted down overnight, covering the mountain in a soft white cloak and almost hiding the jagged rocks formed by old eruptions.

In the distance, high above the lodge, the irregular peak emitted a faint white plume of steam, white against the brightening sky, ethereal and gauzily sinister. Although beautiful and sacred to local Maori, Ruapehu was an active volcano. It had killed before; it would probably do so again.

Shivering, Iona checked the time; she'd better shower and get ready for the day.

They were having breakfast when Luke emerged

from the study. After dropping a kiss on Chloe's cheek, he said, 'Good morning, Iona,' as he straightened, and fixed her with a cool look. 'I trust you don't plan to wear jeans on the mountain?'

'No.' She hoped he couldn't see her inner agitation. 'They have about as much cold and wind resistance as tissue paper.'

He nodded. 'Good. I'm heli-skiing today, but I'll go with you up the chairlift to the beginners' slopes.' A glance at his watch made him frown. 'In half an hour?'

'We'll be ready,' Iona told him. Heli-skiing? Did he know the mountain well enough to go off piste?

Common sense told her it was ridiculous to worry about him. He'd have a guide.

Half an hour later one glance at him reassured her that he knew what he was doing. His clothes were weatherproof, practical, and well-worn. That they emphasised his shoulders and long legs was purely coincidental, and his masculine virility even managed to overcome the effect of heavy boots and a traditional hat.

He was dangerously, heart-shakingly sexy.

Whereas she looked odd in Angie's gear; the colours were wrong and it bunched uneasily on her.

Who cared? Luke gave her one swift glance, as though to reassure himself, before asking, 'Is Chloe ready?'

'Almost.'

Chloe had wanted to wear a bright pink all-in-one snowsuit. She'd pouted when Iona had suggested she'd be too cold out in the wind, but obediently accepted a jacket with a warm hood. She looked enchanting.

Iona's heart contracted. *Careful*, she warned herself

as they took the lift down. *In a few days you'll wave goodbye, and probably never see her again.*

Unless some time in the future she figured in a society wedding of the year, or got caught up in some scandal that made the sort of headlines Iona had read researching Luke and his family.

That didn't seem at all likely, not with a father like Luke!

He stayed with Iona and Chloe for half an hour or so, watching Chloe's progress on the beginners' slopes before kissing her goodbye. He straightened and said austerely, 'I'll see you later,' to Iona.

It felt like a rebuff, but she nodded. He looked at Iakobos, and the two of them walked some distance away and talked for a few minutes before Luke left.

It was idiotic to feel abandoned. Iona forced herself to concentrate on the peaceful, pleasant morning. Chloe showed she had good co-ordination for a three-year-old, and her beaming face shone with delight as she demonstrated her skills. Although Iakobos didn't seem to be around much, Iona had no doubt they were under surveillance.

And, no matter how hard she tried to reason it away, at the back of her mind lurked a glimmer of worry about Luke.

Once the session was over she agreed to Chloe's appeal to eat lunch at the café with Iakobos, then took the now yawning child back to the lodge and settled her for her nap.

She checked her cell phone, sent a text message to Angie telling her everything was fine and thanking her for the loan of her clothes. Then she stood at the window and looked up the mountain, wondering where Luke was.

It was utterly foolish to be flooded with relief when he returned. After greeting her coolly, he closeted himself in the room he used as an office.

Much to Chloe's disappointment, he was still in there when she woke. Once she'd gobbled a piece of fruit and a glass of milk she had to be dissuaded from knocking on the door, and by the time he finally emerged Iona had coaxed her to help put together a jigsaw.

The sound of his door opening had Chloe scrambling to her feet, her face lighting up as she ran to him, chattering in Greek.

'English, Chloe,' he said firmly, then looked across at Iona. 'What is this zoo?'

'It's a petting zoo—it has farm animals for children to stroke and learn about.'

'Can we go, Luke?' Chloe pleaded. 'There's lambs there, and little calves to suck your fingers, and some puppies and baby...' She stopped, screwed up her face, then used a Greek word.

'Rabbits,' Luke supplied. He looked at Iona. 'Where is this place?'

Iona said, 'Quite close, I believe—on the other side of the village.'

He paused a moment, then said abruptly, 'Iakobos will drive you there.'

Chloe pouted, although one look at his severe face kept her silent. However, he explained, 'I have calls to make, little one—important calls.'

In spite of his absence, the petting zoo was a success. Chloe loved the animals, and was smiling blissfully as she stroked a small black rabbit when a woman gushed from behind Iona, 'Your daughter is such a pretty child—a real charmer.'

Iona turned around, but before she could say anything

Iakobos cut in smoothly, 'Thank you. We think she is just about perfect, but of course we are biased.'

The woman was middle-aged and talkative, glancing from Iona to Iakobos. She laughed and said, 'All parents are biased. Are you on holiday?'

'Yes,' Iakobos said, and smiled down at Iona with warmth.

The friendly inquisition continued. 'Oh, you're Americans, are you? How are you enjoying New Zealand?'

'We're thoroughly enjoying your lovely country,' he told her, his American accent a little more pronounced. 'Time to go now, sweetheart.'

The words were addressed to both Iona and Chloe, who set the rabbit down carefully and scrambled to her feet, her face revealing an expression that reminded Iona very much of her half-brother when he was angry.

The woman said, 'Enjoy the rest of your holiday, then,' and beamed at them.

Iona held out her hand, but Chloe ignored it, stamping along beside her while they made their way to the car. Above her head, Iona said, 'What was that about?'

Iakobos had reverted to being a bodyguard. He opened the car door and settled them in, then got in behind the wheel. 'Nothing,' he said calmly, switching on the engine. 'Are all people so curious here?'

She lifted her brows and said with a touch of frost in her tone, 'We're noted for being friendly.'

He said no more on the trip home. And Chloe, gentle, sweet, happy Chloe, was sobbing as she got out of the car. To Iona's surprise the crying increased as they went up to their suite, turning into a tantrum that brought Luke from his office.

Iona had picked up the wildly flailing child, and was

already halfway to her room. Ignoring Luke's grim expression, she said, 'Chloe is over-tired. She'll be much happier once she's had a bath and her dinner.'

Chloe wailed, 'I'm *not* Iakobos's little girl. I belong to Lukas.'

Later, after Chloe had been soothed and reassured enough to follow the familiar routine to bed, Luke asked crisply, 'What the hell was that all about?'

'I didn't realise she'd heard.' Iona related the scene with the over-inquisitive woman. 'Just why did Iakobos feel it was necessary to do that?'

Luke was silent a moment, then said, 'You dealt with her well. It's been some time since Chloe's had a tantrum.'

She said with a wry little smile, 'I've coped with plenty of them. And she'll be growing out of them soon. I can guess why it upset her so, but you didn't answer my question.'

The silence that followed her words was oddly tense. She could feel it tighten her skin, and almost jumped when he spoke. 'I have a proposition to put to you.'

'Another one?'

Her attempt at lightening the atmosphere failed miserably. His shoulders lifted an inch or so, then fell.

'Another one,' he agreed shortly. 'I want you to marry me.'

Shock sent Iona's head spinning. She blinked, tamped down a wild hope, and opened her eyes again. The angular set of Luke's face convinced her that he'd actually said those words. *I want you to marry me...*

But she could read nothing except grim determination in the strong features and flinty eyes.

Something splintered inside her. It might have been

her heart. Still too dizzy to think clearly, she asked baldly, 'Why?'

He turned away and poured a couple of drinks—a glass of the white wine he must have remembered she liked from that holiday in Tahiti, and something considerably stronger for him.

'Here,' he said brusquely, and handed her the glass. 'There are several reasons. Neelie is not going to be able to come back to Chloe in the foreseeable future. Her mother will be an invalid for the rest of her life, and Neelie wishes to care for her.'

Iona took a gulp of her drink, then set the glass down with a sharp clink. 'You don't have to get married for that reason. Good nannies are reasonably easy to find,' she managed to croak. 'For heaven's sake, Angie knows a couple of really top-class ones.'

There had to be more to it than that. Hell, he could simply ask her to take on the job. He didn't have to offer marriage.

Well, *offer* wasn't exactly the right word. It had sounded more like an order than an offer.

With a real effort she reined in her chaotic thoughts.

He too drank from his glass before putting it down. Eyes shielded by his thick lashes, he said, 'I have just received confirmation that my father—who as you know is also Chloe's birth father—is about to sue for custody.'

Appalled, Iona reached for her glass, decided against it and dragged air into her famished lungs. Right now, more than anything, she needed a clear head. 'Why would he do that?'

In a steely, expressionless voice that made his reluctance palpable, Luke told her, 'Until now he has been convinced that I was fooled by his greedy, unfaithful mistress into adopting a child of unknown parentage. He has just found out she is truly his daughter, so he wishes to take her from me.'

And that's enough information, his tone indicated.

No, it wasn't. Outraged, Iona said, 'Just like that—as though she's a discarded plaything? You must be able to arrange a mutually satisfactory solution so that both of you—?'

'No.'

The stark, flat denial cut her composure to shreds. Silenced, she met implacable eyes above a mouth set in an inflexible line.

'He does not want that,' he said. 'And neither do I.'

Iona shook her head, trying to clear it. 'I thought you said he rejected her?'

'He was convinced his mistress had been unfaithful, so he refused to consider the possibility of her child being his.'

And that, his level, emotionless tone told her, was all she'd learn about that. But beneath the words she sensed an anger that sent a shiver scudding the length of her spine.

Nevertheless, she couldn't allow herself to be intimidated into taking such a step—even though some abject part of her was rashly trying to persuade her to accept his proposal.

Marshalling her thoughts, she said, 'Luke, a custody dispute is always better for the child if it is negotiated by both parties. Surely your father and you can come—?'

'This is not simply a custody dispute,' he interrupted, and for a moment she caught a glimpse of deep weariness. It was rapidly replaced by a ruthless lack of compromise.

'So tell me what it is,' she said steadily.

He turned away and stared out of the window. In a voice she'd never heard him use before he said, 'For my father, Chloe is nothing more than a weapon he can use in the ongoing war between us—a war that started when he believed my stepmother's lies and cast me out of the family for ever.'

Whatever his emotions, they were so rigidly controlled she couldn't recognise them. 'I can understand that you're bitter about her lies—'

He turned and fixed her with a stone-hard gaze. 'She accused me of trying to seduce her.'

Iona refused to pretend she didn't know about the old scandal. 'Your father should have known better than to believe her.'

His gaze pierced through her as though he could read the thoughts in her brain, the emotions in her heart. 'My father believes he is a direct descendant of Theseus, king of Athens, who had his son killed for supposedly raping his stepmother. I think he probably believed—still believes—it is a case of history repeating itself.'

'Why?'

He said reluctantly, 'We had been quarrelling—he wanted to control my future, and I was determined to make my own way. He scorned my hopes, my plans, and my ambitions.' He shrugged. 'I was stupidly hot-headed and defiant. And I suspect he was jealous. I was young—he was not. It seems you believe that I didn't do it.'

'Of course I do.' Iona stopped, astounded by the thought of him doubting her. When she'd read the story on Angie's computer screen she'd had no question whatever about Luke's integrity.

Big and dominating and forceful, eyes narrow and

penetrating, Luke said, 'There's no *of course* about it. Why?' His voice was almost indifferent.

'Because I just can't imagine you behaving like that,' she said after several taut seconds had ticked by. It sounded lame, and she added, 'I think it's probably because you're so good with Chloe.'

When his brows lifted sardonically she flushed, trying to explain the inexplicable. 'OK, so it's not much of a reason, but that and sheer gut instinct are the only ones I've got. And the fact that for as long as I've known you, you've been completely honest with me.'

Before their brief, torrid affair he'd made it clear there would be no future for them, and she'd welcomed that unsparing honesty because it had eased her conscience.

Heat curled her toes as memories flooded back—not ones she wanted to relive now.

She stumbled over her next words before saying, 'To put it in simplistic terms, you just don't seem to be the sort.' And she held her head high and finished, 'But I still think you're overreacting. You don't need to be married to prove that Chloe is better off with you, whom she knows and loves, than a man she's never met.'

Luke looked at her intent face, the fathomless eyes a mysterious mixture of blue and green, and wondered whether she was telling the truth.

Not that it could be allowed to matter.

Resolution hardened within him. Chloe was too important, too vulnerable for him to allow Iona's natural fears to change his mind. His legal advisor had stressed that the best way of making sure his father didn't get his hands on the child would be for Lukas to front up with a wife—one who adored Chloe.

If he were superstitious he'd be tempted to believe

that the gods had been kind to him, sending Iona his way for just this reason. As it was, he was prepared to use whatever bait he could find to persuade her to marry him.

'Probably plenty of seducers have been good with children,' he said cynically. 'However, I am honoured by your trust.'

'Exactly how did you come to adopt Chloe?' she asked quietly.

He paused, then shrugged. 'I was contacted by my father's discarded mistress, frantic because she was pregnant. She told me my father refused to believe it was his child, and although she didn't want the baby, some scruple forbade her to take the obvious way out.' Also, she had seen the child as a bargaining chip, an asset that could be cashed in. 'When I offered her enough money she happily signed the papers for me to adopt the baby.'

Iona said blankly, 'You mean she *sold* Chloe to you?'

'Yes.'

Her face revealed her shock and dismay, and then she asked a question that reinforced his conviction she'd make Chloe an excellent mother. 'Why did you buy her?'

'Because she is my sister,' he said honestly. 'I had her DNA tested when she was born, of course.'

'Of course,' she said on a spurt of irritation.

Luke almost smiled, but this was too important. The fact that he'd had her investigated clearly still stung. Besides, she'd done her own checking; she certainly already knew of the sordid reason for his father's disinheritance. 'I am Greek, Iona, the only son. I was brought up to believe that the family was my responsibility—and that means everyone in it.'

'What about your father?'

He shrugged. 'I am no longer his son.'

'How did he find out Chloe was his daughter?'

She had the right to know.

Concisely, Lukas replied, 'The woman who gave birth to Chloe has run through the money I paid her. She approached me for more and I refused to give her any. My initial payment to her should have been enough to support her for the rest of her life, but she has wasted it away. So out of spite she went to my father and told him what she'd done. Possibly he paid her well for the information—I neither know nor care.'

Iona glanced at him, her mysterious mermaid's eyes troubled. 'Why does he believe her now?'

'I don't know whether he did believe her,' Luke said curtly. His father simply hadn't been prepared to pass up a possible opportunity to attack him. 'However, she must have been convincing enough for him to obtain a sample of Chloe's DNA—bribe a chambermaid at a hotel we've stayed at, possibly—and have it tested.' He glanced at the documents he'd unpacked, and then back at Iona. 'The results show conclusively that she is his true daughter.'

Her brow wrinkled. 'But you adopted her—legally *you* are her father, not him. He has no claim to her.'

'Not all countries have legal systems as impeccably lacking in corruption as yours in New Zealand, and the fact that he is her birth father is strong support to his case. My father has power and connections, and the will to use both. It is important to him to take from me what he believes is rightfully his.'

Iona felt sick. Scandalised, she blurted, 'She's not a

thing—to be bought and sold with no concern for her feelings. I wouldn't do that to a pet, let alone a child.'

'Good,' Luke said calmly. 'I thought as much. I'll set the wheels in motion for a quick wedding. I believe Tahiti has just established a residency period of three days, so we'll go back there.'

Her shock chilling into an unbearable mixture of panic and betraying anticipation, Iona scanned his uncompromising face.

She was being torn in two, her new-found love warring with a profound caution warning of heart-wrenching danger. To live unloved—to marry a man who saw her as someone who'd help him win a legal case... 'I haven't agreed to that! Why is it so necessary for you to marry someone?'

'Not *someone*—you.' He paused deliberately. 'If you were making a decision about the welfare of a three-year-old, which father would you choose—a bachelor who travels a lot, or a man happily married to a wife who is fond of the child?'

Chilled, she said stubbornly, 'If they loved her either would be better than a total stranger like your father.'

'I will do whatever I have to retain custody,' he said inflexibly, 'and I have a much better chance of achieving that if I show that Chloe is happy in a stable family situation. She loves Neelie, and her nanny loves her, but Neelie is old school and not comfortable with displays of affection. Even in these few short days you have given Chloe something Neelie never could—fun and vitality and youth. She already relies on you, and is learning to love you. You might not love her yet, but it won't take long.'

Iona opened her mouth, then closed it again. She

didn't dare admit that leaving Chloe would be a huge wrench.

His brows lifted, but when she remained resolutely silent he went on, 'If I can prove I'm giving Chloe a settled home life, with two people she loves and who love her—as opposed to life with an old man who has never seen her and a nanny who will also be a total stranger—my legal team tell me it will make an important difference.'

But what about me? Iona thought cravenly. Torn by a mixture of temptation and stark fear at his cold-blooded summation of the situation, she chewed on her lip, only stopping when his gaze came to rest on her maltreated mouth and a spark lit the tawny depths of his eyes.

'Don't do that,' he said imperiously.

His intent gaze set need smouldering into life, tightening her skin and setting her nerves alight.

Only to be quenched when he went on, 'And, as the only man in the family, I will, of course, make sure your cousin and her sons are cared for.'

'Don't try that—you can't buy Angie,' she flashed. 'Or me, if it comes to that.'

'I'm not trying to buy either of you,' he said evenly, but his eyes narrowed. Holding her gaze, he drawled, 'And if I were to *try* anything with you, it would be seduction.'

His smile sent hot little rills of anticipation through Iona. Colour swept up, heating her skin, only to fade, leaving her cold and uncertain when he spoke again.

'But that is not my intention. This is too important for cheap tricks. Chloe's future depends on integrity from both of us.'

Relief swept over Iona—followed almost immediately by aching disappointment. Some weak part of her wished he'd dazzle her into taking this step into the unknown instead of logically—honestly—setting out his reasons for needing a wife.

A temporary wife at that, she suspected. And the stark chill of that thought numbed her into silence.

CHAPTER EIGHT

'As I told you before,' Luke said, 'I was bred to take my place as head of the family—it is part of what I am. By marrying me you will become my responsibility, and so will your cousin and her boys.' His expression iced into contempt. 'Especially since their father doesn't take an interest in them, and they apparently have no other relatives except you.'

Iona felt the jaws of a trap closing around her. A trap made of her love for both the man and the child. Panic tightened her nerves. 'I suppose you found that out when you had me investigated?' she snapped.

'Relatives have to be taken into consideration when I'm choosing a nanny for Chloe,' he said, equally blunt. 'Now, give me an answer.'

Thoughts jostling chaotically, feeling herself backed into a corner, Iona put off a reply by asking, 'If I refuse, what will you do?'

'Persuade you,' he said promptly, and smiled at her.

He didn't move, but she felt the power and intensity of his will, fierce and compelling, backed by the force of his personality.

His voice deepened into a lazy caress. 'Would it be so difficult, Iona? We are good together—you can't deny

that. For me there has never been another woman like
you. Is it the same for you?'

'Yes,' she said, dazzled into foolishness, then could
have cut her tongue out. She'd handed him an overwhelming advantage.

Ruthlessly he used it. 'So would it be so difficult to
become my wife? We could have a good life together,
you and I.'

Temptation clouded her mind with honeyed urging;
she didn't dare look at him because she could feel her
defiance seeping away. She should be angry for even
considering his outrageous proposal—no, not a proposal,
she reminded herself, he'd called it a proposition.

Thoughts jostled feverishly in her mind. Denied of
his family, Luke had built himself another. If his father
succeeded in destroying that, she would always feel responsible. Luke loved the child he'd adopted; if he lost
her something hugely important would be taken from
him.

It would be a measure of Iona's love if she did this
for him.

When she spoke her voice sounded oddly disconnected. 'And how long do you expect this marriage to
last?'

'For as long as you want it.'

She said desperately, 'Luke, it wouldn't work. We
don't even know each other—not really.'

His lashes drooped, hiding his thoughts as he covered
the floor between them in several strides. He stopped,
close enough to tease her nostrils with the faint, fresh
tang that was his alone. A surge of white-hot sensation—
raw and sinfully enticing—locked Iona's breath in her
throat and sent her thoughts stumbling into confusion
again.

His textured voice warm with amusement, backed by something more primal—a distinctly territorial note—he said, 'Now you're scraping the bottom of the barrel. We have slept in each other's arms night after night, made love with unconfined passion, laughed together, played together. I know you make love like some ancient goddess, and that your delicious sensuality is reinforced by genuine honesty, a warm heart and a good mind. Of course we know each other. I know you are growing fond of Chloe. And you did not doubt that I was innocent of the accusations of my father's wife.'

Every nerve quivering with the restraint she enforced, she said unevenly, 'But it wasn't anything more than a holiday romance. You made no attempt to get in touch with me afterwards.'

'You hoped I would?'

'No.' It was almost the truth; her guilt over what she'd seen as the betrayal of her love for Gavin had made her feel she didn't want anything to do with Luke. But the time she'd spent with him had laid the foundations for her to think more clearly, and the guilt had dissipated.

Now she wondered what she'd have done if he had contacted her.

She saw his chest lift as he took in a breath. 'The day you left my father took another step in the never-ending war he conducts with me. I had to fight on several fronts; it took me some time to block him. And then Chloe got meningitis.'

She gasped, and he nodded. 'It was a difficult time. And I didn't know if you had got over your love for your fiancé. But I never thought it was simply a holiday fling—surely you understood that when I asked you to go with me?'

'You didn't intend permanence,' she said slowly,

her body insensibly warming. His closeness was a threat, undermining the part of her brain that warned her no joy could possibly come of a marriage based on practicality.

And sex, she thought practically. Marvellous sex. Surely as their lives knitted together her love would be enough to make a success of any marriage?

'I didn't,' he admitted. 'But I did intend us to get to know each other—out of bed,' he said on a low laugh, and took her in his arms, pulling her so close she could feel the taut strength in his body.

'This is not going to help,' she managed to mutter, before his grip tightened even further so that every honed sense leapt into full awareness.

His mouth found hers and took it in a kiss so disturbingly sensual she forgot everything in the wonder of it.

Until he lifted his head and looked down at her with intent, gleaming eyes.

Unbearably stimulated, she shakily blurted the first thought that came to her from the maelstrom of her mind. 'I thought you said you weren't going to try seduction.'

His lashes drooped, hiding his satisfaction. 'That can wait. But I intend this to be a real marriage,' he said calmly as he released her and stepped back. 'I am not of the temperament to stay celibate, and when I remember how it was for us both in Tahiti I think that you'll agree it would be unnecessarily foolish of us to even consider such a thing. Besides, I would like more children; Chloe needs brothers and sisters.'

Iona's heart jumped in her breast. The sensations still churning through her blocked any coherent thought process; she wanted to tell him that the whole situation was outrageously impossible, but some treacherous part of her kept reminding her of new-found love, of the passionate eroticism of those nights and days in Tahiti.

Mingled with the memories were fears for Chloe, possibly to be taken from the man she considered to be her father and handed over to an old, bitter, angry stranger who viewed her as a weapon. It would be a devastating blow for the child.

A knock on the door made her start. Luke frowned and said, 'Leave it.'

'I'll go to my room. I need time to think,' she said swiftly.

He fixed her with a keen glance, but didn't object. However, when she turned to go he commanded, 'Stay a moment. If this is what I suspect it is, you should know about it.'

Puzzled, she watched him take delivery of a courier parcel. He signed a receipt, waited until the courier had gone, then slit open the package.

The contents were documents. Luke flicked through them, his face impassive, and then dropped them onto the nearest table as though they contaminated him.

'My father,' he said shortly. 'To tell me he is sending a nanny to pick up his daughter.'

Appalled, Iona stared at him. 'Surely he doesn't expect you to just hand her over? She's lived with you for three years...'

Her voice trailed away at the smile that hardened his face. Cold and satirical, it chilled her blood.

'He knows I will not do that without a fight,' he stated. 'Apparently Chloe's mother is now willing to state on oath that I forced her to allow me to adopt. That almost guarantees a very nasty legal case that could drag on for years.'

'How could they do that?' Iona asked numbly. 'Can't they see what such a case would do to Chloe? Don't they care about her at all?'

Luke said cynically, 'Chloe's mother wants money so that she can indulge herself; my father wants only to assert power over me. Chloe means nothing to them except a way of achieving what they want.'

Closing her eyes, Iona fought back a deep sense of foreboding. There was no longer a choice; she could not do that to the child. She'd seen the damage done to Angie's children by a father who'd abandoned them, and there had been others in the nursery school—children without roots, already showing signs of disturbance.

If it was possible to save Chloe from such a fate, she had to do what she could. But first she had to face the final hurdle—one even her love wouldn't be able to overcome.

She took a deep breath and said thinly, 'All right. I'll marry you. But *I* want something too.'

'I understand,' Luke said cynically. 'What is it?'

Holding her head high, she met eyes of burnished gold, searching and unreadable. 'Your promise that you'll be faithful.'

When he said nothing she braced herself. If he wouldn't give on this, she wouldn't—*couldn't*—agree to marry him. A union of one-sided love was bad enough; one where she'd be faced with his adultery was impossible. It would kill her.

No muscle moved in his face. 'Of course.'

'I don't think there's any *of course* about it,' she said, her tone matching his expression. 'I happen to despise people who break their vows.'

Luke said quietly, 'I too. I will do my best to make sure that you never regret your decision.'

His grave, oddly formal statement wasn't what she wanted, but she trusted him to keep his promise, and her hopeful heart dreamed that the attraction he felt might some day turn to love.

So she ignored the pang of useless disappointment to ask, 'In that case, what happens now?'

In an oddly taut voice he said, 'We will fly to Tahiti as soon as possible. Knowledge of our previous affair there will establish a history for us. It might help convince a judge that our marriage is not a deliberate attempt to forestall my father's claim to Chloe.'

No sentimentality there. Feeling empty, as though he'd dashed some forbidden hope, she said, 'I'm still finding it almost impossible to believe he has any chance of success.'

Luke shrugged. 'I hope you are right. However I don't want her life overshadowed by years of legal wrangling. It is possible that when he realises he is fighting a good marriage and a devoted pair of parents with a happy child he might give this up without going so far as taking us to court.'

'Possible, but not probable?' she guessed.

He gave a sardonic smile. 'I see you understand. Do you have a ring that fits you?'

Iona glanced down at her hands. 'Not here.'

Gavin's engagement ring still nestled in a drawer at home, but it was hardly appropriate.

Luke said crisply, 'Then we need string to measure the size of your ring finger.'

Iona's fingers curled into her palms. She forced herself to relax, unclenching both fists at her sides. Gavin's memory had faded into the past, relinquished without pain, but a residual guilt hurt her for a moment. So many times she'd said goodbye to him; this would be the last.

Uncannily, Luke said, 'He is dead, Iona.'

She went white. 'How…how did you know what I was thinking?' she whispered.

'A certain look—a shadow across your face.' He shrugged, a typical brief lift of his shoulders. 'He was a good man, and you would have been happy with him, but he is long dead. Let him go in peace.'

'I have. It's just that the last time my finger size was taken was for his engagement ring,' she said quietly, and gave him the measurement, adding, 'He's gone from my life, Luke.' And, because it had to be said, she added with a shaky smile, 'He left when I met you.'

'Good.' He held out his hand, and reluctantly she put hers into it.

In a strange way that simple handclasp was more intimate than the kiss they'd just exchanged. Lean, long fingers closed around hers so firmly she tensed, but before the grip tightened into pain they eased. Yet it felt as though Luke was establishing some sort of claim on her—a claim he reinforced by lifting her hand to kiss the back of her fingers, then turned it and kissed her wrist.

With the touch of his mouth lingering on her skin, she thought he was gentling her into acceptance, forging a connection between them that transformed their purely physical previous one.

He looked down and said, 'You have lovely hands, as graceful as they are capable. We'll fly back to Auckland tonight and I'll organise a ring fitting for you at the apartment. If there's nothing you like we can wait until we reach Tahiti—they have an excellent selection of pearls there, some of which are as changeable as your eyes.'

But that evening she picked a tourmaline so blazingly blue it reminded her of the lagoon in Tahiti. On either side of the stone diamonds blazed in platinum.

Approvingly, the jeweller said, 'A superb choice. The stone comes from Brazil, and this colour is so valued that a perfect gem like this is more precious than a diamond of the same quality.' She glanced up at Iona and added, 'It matches your eyes.'

'Just now, perhaps.' Iona smiled. 'They tend to change shades when I wear different coloured clothes.'

'They are beautiful,' Luke said. He nodded at the ring. 'And so is that. Leave it here, thank you.'

He saw the jeweller out and came silently back. Iona hadn't moved. She was still standing a few feet away from the window, staring at the ring as if it were a snake. For a moment compunction struck him; he banished it. He would make her a good husband, and he couldn't allow himself to feel anything but relief that Chloe now had a much better chance of a happy childhood and adolescence.

He picked up the ring. 'Come here,' he said softly.

Shadowed eyes shifting between a deep blue and a fathomless green, she said huskily, 'Why?'

'Because I want to give you this ring.'

All expression vanished from her face. 'Nothing's stopping you.'

He wondered just what was going on behind that calm face, that mysterious gaze. She was a challenge; the only things he really knew about her was that she didn't want to marry him, and that she made love like a siren.

No, he knew much more; she was also tender-hearted

enough to be manipulated by affection for a child. He started towards her and saw a quick flush heat the skin along her cheekbones. Hunger tore at him like a whirl-wind, eating at the control he'd been forced to exercise since he'd received the first parcel of legal papers from his lawyers.

It would be easy enough to forget his cold anger at his father in wild sex, but now was not the time. Iona was prepared to sacrifice her life for Chloe; he would give her the knowledge that he respected her as well as wanted her. He could wait until their marriage to take her to bed.

He stopped in front of her, saw the colour come and go in her skin, and lifted her left hand. Frowning a little, he slid the ring onto her finger. It slipped easily enough at first, but had to be eased past the second knuckle.

Iona stiffened, then watched lean tanned fingers settle it into place. The silvery circle felt cold and heavy, but it was swiftly warmed by the blood pumping through her body, the burgeoning heat of her response to Luke's closeness.

Kiss me, her mind pleaded, so importunately she wondered if she'd actually said the words out loud.

No, thank heavens.

And Luke didn't kiss her. In a gesture that made her shiver, he raised her hand and kissed the ring, then pressed his mouth into her palm, before folding her fingers over his kiss.

Her breath came short through her lips.

He said quietly, 'I shall never be able to thank you enough for this.'

Don't thank me, she thought frantically, unable to read anything in the arrogantly handsome face, the steady golden glint of his eyes.

Don't thank me, love me...

Words she couldn't say.

No, that was defeatist; perhaps one day she could whisper them to him.

One day, when she was confident he'd say them back.

Luke dropped her hand. 'Because of the international dateline we will arrive in Tahiti only an hour or so behind New Zealand time, so neither Chloe nor you should have too much difficulty adjusting your body clocks.'

'I hope not,' Iona said. 'It's only a few days since she went through the process in Auckland.'

He said calmly, 'She is remarkably adaptable.'

Because she'd had to be, travelling with him. Iona realised she had no idea of the sort of life he intended for them. She asked, 'Do you plan to have us travel with you when...from now on?'

'Once we are married?' he said, his voice hard. 'You can say it, Iona; it is not a death sentence or a deed so foul it can't be mentioned.'

She flushed, but said spiritedly, 'I'm still getting used to the idea! If you insist on bulldozing your way into people's lives you have to expect them to be shell-shocked for a few days!'

Brows drawing together, he stared at her—and then to her astonishment he threw his head back and laughed.

'I see all of us will have adjustments to make,' he said dryly, 'and not just to various time zones. Yes, whenever it's possible—certainly while Chloe is not at school—you will travel with me.'

She looked up to find his eyes on her, unexpectedly keen. 'It's good for a child to have a settled base.'

Luke said, 'So people have said. I don't think she's missing anything.'

'That's because to Chloe you are her home.'

He said sombrely, 'Yes. However, until we know her future, it will be politic to lead a less peripatetic life. I have a house in London, and apartments in New York and Athens as well as the beach house in Tahiti, but the place I call home is an island south of Greece. Once we are married I intend to spend more time there. Will you be bored on a Greek island?'

Not when you're there, she thought with an inward tremor. 'I doubt it. I usually find plenty to do. I'll want to learn Greek, and I have a degree to finish.'

'A degree? In what?'

'Early childhood education,' she told him.

His expression softened into a smile. 'Excellent—I learn new things about you all the time. Will you be able to finish it from half the world away?'

'I'll find out. Don't worry about me, Luke. I'm adaptable.'

The next few days passed in a blur. When Luke made up his mind, Iona realised, things happened—fast. He even managed to dazzle Angie into acceptance of the situation. It took a considerable expenditure of his effortless charm, but nowhere near as much as Iona had expected.

After a very early start Luke's private jet landed in Tahiti in the heat of a tropical noon, to the scent of flowers and the mingled sound of singing and the sea, and the stunning physical beauty of the people.

Even in that hothouse atmosphere Luke garnered more than his share of attention, with women eyeing him with open appreciation before transferring envious gazes to Iona. Aware of her chainstore clothes, she felt an unusual sense of inferiority; she couldn't compete with these women in the brilliantly hued swathes of cloth they called a *pareu*, women who wore flowers in their long, glossily dark tresses with an insouciance she'd never be able to match.

And that she was even thinking in terms of competition made her angry with herself. Somehow being with Luke had turned her into a different woman, one with a disheartening lack of confidence.

They took a boat across the lagoon to the palm-fringed beach where they'd met, walking beneath the palms and through a garden perfumed by more flowers. Vivid and gaudy, they looked exquisitely at home.

'Pretty,' Chloe said with satisfaction, touching the silken petals of a scarlet hibiscus. However, when she sniffed the long pollen-laden centre stamen she quickly released it and looked disappointed.

'Try this,' Iona suggested, snapping off a bloom from the native gardenia.

Chloe sniffed the fragrant white flower, and beamed. 'Nice,' she announced, and held it out to Luke, who stopped and inhaled the scent.

'Better than any perfume in a bottle,' he pronounced, and tucked it behind the child's ear, smiling down at her. 'It is called *tiare tahiti*,' he told her, 'and the Tahitians use it for garlands. When Iona and I get married we will both wear a garland made of *tiare* flowers, because they are the wedding flowers for Tahiti.'

Her face crinkled against the sun. 'Will I have one too?' she asked.

Luke glanced across at Iona, who nodded, for the first time feeling she had a part to play in the arrangements.

'Of course, if you wish to wear one,' he said.

'I do,' Chloe said fervently, transferring her wide beam from him to Iona.

Cradling the blossom in place in her long dark hair, she tucked her other little paw into Luke's big hand as they walked the rest of the way, ending at the house Iona remembered so well. There they were enthusiastically welcomed by the caretaker, a short man of French extraction, and his tall, serious-faced wife who acted as housekeeper.

'Moana and Jacques you remember, I'm sure,' Luke said.

'Of course I do.' She smiled at them both, and went off with the housekeeper to settle Chloe in.

For Iona the day was clouded by a pang of…not envy, not even regret, an emotion more shadowy and fragile than either.

Last time she'd been here it had been as Luke's temporary lover.

CHAPTER NINE

THINGS were so different now, although the sun still beamed down in a languorous caress. Desire uncoiled in supplication, summoning heated, erotic memories that tightened every nerve in delicious anticipation.

Cut that out, Iona ordered her body. Face facts—especially when they're terrifying.

This time she loved Luke. And she'd promised to marry him. Her stomach hollowed out as though in anticipation of a blow. How was she going to cope with marriage to a man who saw her as nothing more than a necessary evil?

Don't overdramatise, she commanded, trying to ignore a swift flash of desolation. Emotions were all very well, but they needed to be reined in by logic and reason. She didn't really believe Luke thought of her as an evil.

A frisson of sensation sizzled through her when she recalled the glint of heat in his eyes whenever he looked at her. But a lot of men found it quite easy to have sex with a woman they didn't necessarily like much. Did Luke see her as a pawn to be manipulated for his own—and Chloe's—ends?

Possibly. If she were in his position she'd probably feel the same—the welfare of her child taking paramount place. Whereas she felt much, much more than that for him—and not just because of his potent physical presence, either, or memories of his superb talent as a lover.

She stood on the terrace, eyeing Luke's powerful back, the lean strength of his torso set above long, muscled legs, the purposeful grace of his movements as he moderated his steps to fit Chloe's little trot.

How had his father's rejection affected him? Had he been a spoilt young man, taking his position as the adored only son and heir for granted? Aristo Michelakis's refusal to accept his word had bitten deep, and being thrown out of his family must have scarred some essential part of his soul.

He'd certainly set out to prove himself, and succeeded brilliantly. His reputation as a businessman was legendary and the speed of his rise in that cut-throat world had taken it by surprise.

He'd even made a new family for himself. And succeeded there too; Chloe bore all the hallmarks of a child secure in the knowledge she was loved.

Discovering he'd spent the first year of Chloe's life caring for her himself might have been the tipping point, the hidden moment when Iona had crossed the border from desire to love. His affection for the child had touched an unknown hunger in her, and before she'd realised it—with no effort on his part—she'd let down her barricades. Somehow that unrecognised surrender had helped transform a powerful physical desire into love.

She was certainly nothing like the woman who'd once walked along this beach convinced she'd never feel again, that she was doomed to a grey existence of no emotion, separated from the rest of life by a veil of despair.

Luke, with his open and genuine appreciation of her as a sensual, desirable woman, had torn that veil into shreds, reuniting her with the world.

Would she have agreed to marry him if she hadn't loved him?

It was a question she couldn't answer.

But the decision was irrevocable. Not only did she love Luke, but in this short time Chloe too had wound her way into her heart; it wasn't just for Luke's sake that she'd do whatever had to be done to keep the little girl secure.

'Look, Miss Iona,' Chloe said importantly, running up to her, a shell in one little hand. 'I found it on the beach.'

Without looking at Luke, Iona said, 'Chloe, how would you like to call me Iona?'

'Can I really?' Chloe beamed, then lifted her face to Luke, seeking confirmation.

He nodded. 'A good idea,' he said, his gaze warm as he smiled at Iona.

Whose heart somersaulted in her chest. 'Let's go and wash it in our bathroom,' she said.

Again her room was right beside Chloe's—something that startled and disappointed her, because presumably Moana had followed Luke's orders. The placement made a definite statement about the reason she was there—to take care of Chloe.

As she unpacked she indulged in a gloomy vision of being left behind on some Greek island while Luke zoomed around the world, of loveless sex for the sole attempt to conceive those children Luke said he wanted, of his eventual terminal boredom with her...

Too late now, she thought wearily as tension closed its claws on her. And she was overdramatising again—a habit that seemed to have crept up on her since Luke had re-entered her life.

She glanced out of the glass doors with their shutters pushed back. The small terrace outside served the two bedrooms; furniture beckoned, and the scent of the sea mingled with that of the flowering shrubs. Sunlight sifted down through the fronds of palms, casting shifting shadows that looked like a pattern of textiles. Through curving grey trunks the lagoon glimmered, an intense colour that echoed the sky.

At least she'd have a variety of beautiful places to be miserable in…

Snap out of it, she told herself abruptly. Luke wanted her—he couldn't hide that. She'd have to learn to be content with what she had, and hope that his desire would one day grow into real love. Setting her jaw, she went into Chloe's room and her unpacked her clothes, the child's chattering lifting her mood.

Luke was called away to the telephone, so she took Chloe down to the lagoon and splashed in the warm, silken water, overseen by a Tahitian man with the same watchful, silent air of competence as Iakobos, who'd left them at Auckland airport.

They ate lunch together with no sign of Luke, and then Iona settled Chloe down for a nap. She saw nothing more of Luke until it was time for him to read to Chloe before she went to sleep.

Over dinner Luke said, 'I am sorry I had to spend the day working. Something came up that needed my attention.'

A note in his voice warned her the *something* hadn't been welcome. 'All well now?'

He shrugged. 'I have done what I could,' he said briefly before abruptly changing the subject. 'Our wedding will be held on the beach here; it will be a ceremony with traditional Tahitian features. I hope you do not mind that?'

The already familiar mixture of excitement and apprehension roiled through Iona. 'What exactly will it entail?'

'First we will be given Tahitian names, then we will exchange leis of *tiare tahiti* as a symbol of our unity. After that a priest will bless us, and we will be married. There will be singing and dancing, of course. Like Greeks, the Tahitians accompany all of life's great moments and most of its lesser ones with both.'

'It sounds lovely and informal,' she said cautiously.

His smile held more than a hint of irony. 'I hope you will enjoy it. Angie and the boys certainly should.'

Iona said, 'Thank you for flying them over.'

'Naturally you will want them here,' he said dismissively. He paused, then said, 'Did Chloe speak to you about being a flower girl?'

'No,' she said, with a glance towards Chloe's room. 'I told her I'd ask.'

Remorsefully she said, 'I should have thought of that myself. I'd love to have her as a flower girl, but where can we get her a frock?'

She'd chosen her own wedding dress in a boutique in Auckland, taking far too long selecting a creation that virtually emptied her bank account. Fortunately she already owned a pair of sandals that would look great with it, and for flowers she wanted nothing more than a wreath of gardenias for her hair and a small posy to carry, both of which had been organised.

When she'd arrived back at the penthouse Luke had

looked up from the game he was playing with Chloe, and casually asked for the details of her bank account.

'Why?' she'd responded, a little curtly.

He'd sighed heavily as Chloe gleefully shouted, 'Go Fish!'

'I think you can see through the cards,' he complained, widening Chloe's grin. He picked up the card and went on in the tone he used to indicate to Chloe that there was no negotiation. 'I shall make you a monthly allowance.'

Iona stiffened, but he said reasonably, 'It is either that or you'll have to come running to me whenever you want to buy a packet of chewing gum.'

'I don't chew gum,' she pointed out.

'Toothpaste, then.' His smile summoned a reluctant one from her. 'You'll want a reasonably large sum at first for clothes and other things. Afterwards we can discuss a monthly amount.'

Of course it was sensible. She thought now of the indecently large amount that had appeared in her account and told herself it was ridiculously missish to feel as though she'd been bought.

Luke said, 'Tomorrow morning a woman from Papeete will come across with a selection of suitable outfits for Chloe. And perhaps I should warn you that our daughter has very definite ideas about her clothes.'

Our daughter... His words kindled a warmth in Iona's heart.

While they'd been eating dusk had swooped in from the sea, turning the island into a magical place of moonlight and shadows, of scents that became more potent and evocative after the sun went down. The thickening atmosphere almost silenced the ever-present whispering of the trade winds in the coconut palms, and far out to

sea a bird called—a faint, solitary sound that echoed
Iona's fey mood exactly.

She wanted—oh, she wanted Luke...

Couldn't he sense she longed for him to sweep her
off her feet, to banish every doubt and fear with passion,
convince her with fierce lovemaking that she'd made the
right decision?

Instead he seemed determined to stay detached and
practical. The splendid moulding of his face revealed
no emotion; he looked at her with cool golden eyes,
and all through the day he'd treated her with the sort of
neutral, impersonal courtesy that forbade any emotional
response.

They could be entering on a business partnership,
she thought dismally.

Actually, that's almost certainly how he saw it.

Unless he too was wondering if he'd made the wrong
decision—if tying himself to a woman he didn't love
would doom him to a life of barren emotions and sex.

Somehow she knew he'd keep the promises he'd made
to her, but here in lush Tahiti that knowledge was no
consolation. She didn't want him chained to her by his
sense of honour.

Coolly, he said, 'I hope you're not considering a
change of mind, Iona.'

Startled, she looked across the table to him. His relentless gaze roamed her face, and then he smiled, a
humourless movement of his lips.

'I thought as much,' he said, and got to his feet.

Eyes widening, she watched him stride around the
table. Even in a casual shirt with a lavalava swathed
around his narrow hips, he projected an air of effortless
intimidation.

A reckless hope surged through her, sweeping away common sense in a few wild, nerve-racking seconds.

He said objectively, 'It's called pre-wedding nerves, and I have been best man at enough weddings to know that it affects both sexes.'

How could he be so *reasonable*?

Coming to a stop behind her, he rested his hands on her bare shoulders. Only a few moments before she'd been longing for him to touch her; now it was not enough. The sensation of those long, tanned fingers against her pale skin dried her mouth and smoked through her brain, rendering her almost witless.

'It would have been better if we could have had a week or so by ourselves, so that we could get reacquainted,' he said, still in that pleasant, level tone. 'At least by marrying here we won't be faced with a media circus. No one knows we are here, and even if they do they certainly won't know our plans.'

Iona blinked. 'I doubt that very much,' she said trying to match his level tone. 'News travels very fast in the Pacific. By the time we've established residency I imagine everyone who's interested will know exactly why we're here.'

The tension within her was spiralling out of control, but she managed to stay still, soaking up pleasure from his nearness and the steady warmth of his hands.

Yearning softened her mouth, brought a flush to her skin. Surely he could feel it heating beneath his fingers?

And then he said, 'You must be tired. And I unfortunately have this—situation to deal with. So I shall say goodnight.'

But before he moved away he stooped and brushed his lips across the nape of her neck. Every tiny invisible hair on her skin stood upright at that lightest of touches and she stopped breathing as a tide of delight filled her.

Without volition she turned and lifted her face. Stone-faced, he looked down at her and she held her breath, and then he said in a harsh voice, 'I cannot stay.'

'I know.'

Tension wound between them. His eyes kindled and he muttered, 'You are too tempting, and I must go...'

His mouth came down on hers in a kiss that ended far too soon. He lifted his head and put her from him, and without a backwards look strode from the room.

It was little enough to dream on, that swift kiss, but it comforted her as much as it frustrated her.

The next morning Luke was closeted with a telephone until after lunch. From her seat beneath the big tree that shaded the terrace, Iona looked up from her book. His face was drawn, the strong framework emphasised.

'Everything all right?' she asked tentatively.

He shrugged, as though easing out kinks in his shoulders. 'As far as it can be.' He paused, then said, 'A family matter.'

She frowned. 'I thought—I thought you had no contact with your family.'

'That is so. A young cousin rang me—we have not met since I left home, but she was distraught and I was her last hope. Her parents have been trying to push her into a marriage she does not want—her father's business is going under, and the groom-to-be is prepared to help. My father thinks it will be a good alliance, so she has no help there. To be fair to Aristo he has bailed them out several times before—my uncle is not a good businessman. So my cousin was reduced to calling on me.'

'What did you do?'

He gave a brief, mirthless smile. 'It took a little time, but I managed to persuade her parents that saving the family business was not worth their daughter's happiness.'

Indignation burnt through her. This was the family who'd accepted his father's version of events and cut him out of their lives. Without thinking she got up and went to him, putting a hand on his arm. Every muscle was flexed and taut. 'In other words, you bailed them out?'

He looked down with hard, unreadable eyes. 'Of course. She was a charming child, and she has always wanted to become a doctor.'

Iona said quietly, 'They don't deserve your help.'

He smiled, and cupped a cheek with one hand, eyes warming as he looked down at her. Anticipation soared, but almost immediately he stepped back and said, 'My uncle did not enjoy the conditions, but his desperate situation means he has no option. Enough of them—they are not important. It's unlikely we'll hear from them again. I have some unsettling news about our wedding.'

A cold pool of foreboding opened up under Iona's ribs. She said, 'You've discovered that you haven't quite divorced your fifth wife?'

His brows shot up, followed by a shout of laughter. 'I'm not so careless,' he said dryly. 'You need have no fear that any discarded woman will cast a shadow over our union. No, it is just that before we have our charming beach wedding we need to marry in a civil ceremony at the office of the local mayor, in what passes for the city hall here.'

'Of course—Tahiti is a French territory. So why is that unsettling?'

'Because the media are already gathering.'

Frowning, Iona chewed at her lip.

He said, 'Don't *do* that! It pains me to see you mal-treating your soft mouth.'

Thrilling at his hot, thick voice, she said, 'You sound like my mother.'

'I doubt it,' he said roughly, and the air between them was suddenly charged with an intensity that tightened every nerve in Iona's body.

'I'll try to stop myself, but apparently it's always been a habit of mine.' Her voice emerged oddly off-key, and she went on hurriedly, 'I'm not...I've never had to deal with the media.'

'You will not deal with it,' he said instantly. 'I shall put out a press release as soon as we are married, but it wouldn't surprise me if we have to run some sort of gauntlet. It seems word has somehow got out that my father is suing for custody.' He ignored Iona's shocked dismay. 'Which means we will leave Chloe here when we go for that first ceremony; I will not have her worried by any questions. And the security will have to be increased.'

Iona didn't blame him for being thoroughly fed up; this new development, combined with the pressure of the family situation, was enough to erode the control of any man, even one as accustomed to pressure as Luke.

She turned as he said something in Greek. Eyes narrowed, he was looking across the silken, empty sands of the beach to the aquamarine depths of the lagoon, placid and devoid of any activity except for a canoe edging in towards the beach.

Following his gaze, Iona saw two men appear briefly

from the coconut palms that bordered the sand. One spoke into some sort of communications device while the other strode down to meet the craft and the three men in it.

'Journalists?' she ventured.

'Probably,' he returned austerely, switching his gaze to her face. 'I will make sure this fuss affects you as little as possible, even if I have to blanket the island with security men.'

A couple of expert swishes of the paddle from the oarsman in the canoe had it backing away from the beach, but Iona saw a man in a loud Hawaiian shirt lift a camera and take several shots of the house.

The downside of power and privilege, she thought, the chill hollow beneath her ribs expanding. And this would be her life…

'Don't look so worried,' Luke said crisply. He came towards her and took her hands, lifting them to his lips for a lingering second.

His heavy-lidded eyes gleamed with a golden promise—a promise extinguished too soon when he said, 'That should provide them with a photograph romantic enough to show we're lovers.'

Although the last thing Iona wanted was an embrace then, she had to fight a bitter spasm of disappointment when he released her.

Almost offhandedly he said, 'Most of the time the only media interested in me are reporters for the financial columns. If it weren't for the custody case our wedding would have been the quiet affair we both want.'

'Do you think your father released the information to the press?' she asked, appalled.

Thin-lipped, he said, 'It seems likely. Forget about him. On my island in Greece we will have complete freedom; everyone has known me since I was born, and while they are interested, as everyone there is in all their neighbours, they would not dream of intruding—just as I would not intrude in their lives.'

Iona wondered if *his* island, as he so tellingly described it, was the one place where he felt truly at home.

She said, 'I can cope with journalists, however intrusive, but I hope your heavies can keep them away from the beach ceremony. I'd hate Chloe to be frightened by any sort of media pack.'

Luke said grimly, 'My men will have it under control.'

'That canoe got close enough a few minutes ago.' When he lifted a brow at her, she said, 'Ah—of course. They were allowed to.'

'You see too much,' he said, with a brief unamused smile. 'No one else will get that close. And we may be overreacting. We are not film stars marrying for the third time, or royalty with jewels to display.'

And I am a complete nobody, she thought wearily, then turned her head when he said, 'Is that Chloe I hear?'

'I don't think so.' But she went to look, only to find her charge slumbering, cheeks flushed, her toy lion hugged to her chest.

Wondering if he'd deliberately changed the subject, Iona turned to slip out again, but, as if realising that someone was watching her, Chloe woke, and smiled sleepily at her before holding out her arms.

Iona's heart expanded. 'Hello, darling,' she said softly, and went across to lift the small warm bundle from the bed. 'Good sleep?'

Chloe buried her face in Iona's shoulder and snuggled,

before yawning prodigiously and rubbing her eyes. 'Can I have a drink?' she asked, before adding seriously, 'Please?'

'Of course you can.' And, because Chloe seemed perfectly content to stay in her arms, Iona carried her through to the kitchen.

Halfway there she met Luke. 'She is too heavy for you,' he said, and took her from Iona's arms, kissing Chloe's cheek before he set her on her feet. 'You must not let Iona carry you,' he told her firmly. 'You are a big girl now, and Iona is not strong enough. See, she is slim like a princess.'

Chloe nodded, but when her mouth trembled Iona interposed, 'Truly, carrying you for short distances won't hurt me at all.'

Luke straightened. 'For short distances only,' he said sternly, adding, 'And Chloe must jump.' He smiled down at his daughter. 'Let's show Iona how we lift you up. One, two, three, *jump*!'

Chloe leapt into the air, was caught by his strong arms, and laughed joyously, holding her face up to be kissed again. Iona watched them with something like envy. Whatever happened she'd never regret adding to this child's security. She already loved her, and to take her away from Luke would cause him as much pain as it would the child.

CHAPTER TEN

THAT evening before dinner Iona changed into a pair of soft aqua trousers, topping them with a camisole the same colour. After a moment's frowning pause in front of the mirror she shook her head.

Nobody could call the camisole tight, but the fabric clung to every soft curve. It was stupid, but she felt self-conscious. She pulled on a floaty polyester tunic in mingled shades of blue and green and critically inspected her reflection again.

'Yes,' she said aloud. She loved that tunic, because it gave her skin a glow and turned her eyes into deep pools the same turquoise as the lagoon.

Of course, she thought with a hint of wistful irony, Luke was accustomed to women who wore designer clothes in exquisite fabrics.

She slid her feet into cork-soled green sandals that gave her an extra inch or so of height, and set her shoulders. Two-year-old chainstore clothes or not, if she wanted to eat she had to leave her room.

The meal was served outside on the long terrace, romantically lit by candles. The food was superb, but afterwards Iona couldn't remember it, only the conversation—she remembered every word of that.

And the way the candlelight flickered on Luke's dark,

arrogant features, playing over the angles and planes so that sometimes he looked like an avenging Zeus, sometimes like a magnificent Apollo, sometimes distant, periodically amused.

And always stimulating—in every sense of the word, she thought wildly, thoughts zooming randomly around her head as her body responded to his vital male physicality.

'Chloe tells me she has the prettiest dress in the whole world,' he said. 'I did suggest she model it for me, but she said I wasn't allowed to see it until the wedding.'

Iona laughed softly. 'She loves it. And she's looking forward so much to Angie's arrival with the boys. I had to explain to her how Angie and I are related.'

'She will enjoy having cousins,' he said calmly, but his eyes had turned cold. 'When my father decided to disinherit me, he made it very clear to both my mother's family and his that anyone who so much as recognised me in the street from then on would immediately suffer the same fate.'

Scandalised anew, she said, 'I don't understand how they could do that—believe the lies and turn their backs on you.'

The chill in his eyes was intensified by a flash of bitter amusement. 'It was convenient for them to do so. At that time he was the one with the power and the money.'

Iona said indignantly, 'And apart from your desperate cousin *no one* has made any effort to get in touch with you since then?'

He laughed, a cynical sound that lifted the hairs on her neck. 'Some have made approaches.'

'And?'

'I ignored them,' he told her crisply. 'I do not

subscribe to the notion of revenge, but I learn—and learn well—each lesson that comes along in my life. I trust only those who earn my trust.'

'Or those whose CVs convince your security men that they're decent citizens,' she teased.

His smile returned, the humour plain. 'I can see that will be cast up at me for ever,' he said with mock resignation. 'Perhaps I have something that will help you forgive me.'

She leaned back in her chair as he got to his feet, and watched him walk away, his effortless masculine grace and power working its usual response in her.

What now?

He went into the house, emerging a few seconds later with a small parcel in his hand. Iona eyed it apprehensively, and that smile curved his lips again.

'It is quite harmless,' he said, and handed it to her. 'Consider it a wedding gift.'

She took it, but a thought caused her to lift a dismayed face to him. 'I haven't got you anything,' she said, appalled.

'You have,' he said calmly, golden eyes warming. 'You are giving me yourself—that is all I want.'

If only he wanted her for herself, not for her usefulness... Iona bent her head to the parcel, fumbling to undo it.

It contained a jeweller's case, sleek and expensively branded in gold. Iona didn't dare look at him; her fingers trembled as she opened it.

A sighing gasp escaped her lips. Inside were pearls, exquisitely matched, perfectly graded, their soft silvery-white sheen draping across her fingers like sensuous drops of moonlight. They made a necklace, and beneath them hung a pendant, a heart-shaped pearl framed in diamonds and platinum.

She said quietly, 'Thank you. It's utterly exquisite.'

'Would you like me to help you put it on?' And when she hesitated he said dryly, 'Perhaps not.'

Iona hesitated only a moment before making up her mind. The hunger that gnawed constantly at her had become a driven thing, demanding, insistent, compelling. In silent answer she handed him the pearls and slid the tunic over her head, dropping it over the back of her chair to stand before him in the camisole and trousers.

His eyes kindled, and that involuntary reaction gave her the courage to say, 'Perhaps you could fasten it for me.'

Her voice sounded oddly throaty. Swept by an unexpected attack of shyness, she turned around and presented the tender nape of her neck to him, her breath catching in her throat while she waited for what seemed an eternity.

But it probably only took a few seconds before she felt the silky glide of the gems from the sea against her skin and heard him say, 'So, turn around and let me see.'

She turned, half hiding her eyes with her lashes.

In a voice that sent little shivers of anticipation through her he murmured, 'Ah, I thought that skin like yours, delicate and translucent, would match the pearls for beauty.'

When she coloured his smile turned feral, almost wolfish, but to her mounting—and bewildered—frustration he took a step back, so he could survey her with half-closed eyes.

From a safer distance, she thought, tantalised

beyond endurance. He wanted her—she could see that he wanted her—so what was preventing him from following through?

Short of blurting, *Take me, I'm yours,* like an ingénue in a melodrama, she couldn't make her need any plainer without humiliating herself. All her fears rushed back, pooling in a cold mass beneath her ribs.

'I'm glad you like it,' he said.

'It's lovely.' Her voice was wooden and before he could see her disappointment she turned and said stiffly, 'Can you undo it, please? I'll wear it when we get married.'

She waited, and felt her skin prickle at the light touch of his fingers as he unclasped the necklace.

And then he said in a tense, goaded voice, 'I shall look forward to that. But at the moment all I can think of is making love to you while you are wearing it—and nothing else.'

So what's stopping you?

She turned her head to look up into a face drawn and dark with hunger. Her breath came quick and fierce, her temperature soared into the stratosphere, and the keen desire became a torrent, a force she couldn't deny.

'Iona,' he said, on a hard, fast note.

At long last he bent his black head and kissed her, plunging deep into her mouth with no finesse, a driving imperative that swept her into something perilously close to ecstasy. Like a conqueror, he took what he wanted in a kiss so ravishing she moaned into his mouth.

His head jerked up; he scanned her face, then gave a long jagged sigh and swivelled her around, his arms closing about her in a grip that revealed his arousal. Iona shuddered, and his grip relaxed, but she tightened the arms around his shoulders, shamelessly pressing against him and rotating her hips in slight, seductive movements.

His thick, impeded voice muttered something in Greek before he demanded, 'How the hell can I withstand such temptation?'

'Why do you want to?' she flung back at him.

He moved lightning fast, pinning her hips against his loins so she could feel their strength and the urgent hunger that possessed him. Her pulses rocketed even higher and her lashes drooped in sultry, involuntary invitation.

Luke slid his hands into her hair and tilted her head so he could stare into her eyes. Almost formally he said, 'I want two different things, and the wanting is tearing me apart. I wish to show you respect—that I value you, and am not merely using you to fulfil my own purposes. Perhaps I misjudged, but I thought making love should wait until after our wedding.'

Joy ricocheted through her, setting off small explosions of pleasure and delight. She said huskily, 'You *did* misjudge! I hope you're not one of those men who believe a bride is somehow too pure to want or enjoy sex?'

'No!' he said explosively, and laughed, his eyes glittering with appreciation. 'How is it that I never know what you're going to say next?'

'Because you don't understand women very well?'

Something hard moved in the tawny depths of his eyes, and his tone had a ring of aloofness to it. 'I have no problems with most women—it's just you who continually surprises me.' He bent a little further, so that his lips just grazed hers. Against them he said, 'I want you so very, very much. But if we make love now I will be cheating you of the wedding night you deserve...'

She shook her head. 'I won't feel cheated whatever we do,' she said shakily, adding with a hint of bite in her words, 'But if you come over all noble on me now I'm going to be seriously frustrated.'

His laughter came from deep in his throat, and he startled her by sweeping her up in his arms. 'I like it that you are so honest about your need for me,' he said, looking down into her face. His arms tightened around her as he headed towards the bedroom wing.

He carried her along the wide, shady terrace, through the scents of the night, the silvery light of the moon, into his room.

'Do you mind?' he asked, setting her down on her feet.

She looked around, remembering other nights here in this tropical ambience, all cool wood and white paint with touches of blue. 'What about Chloe?'

'I have another baby monitor in here, just in case she wakes—which she rarely does.' And then he set her down on her feet and said in a voice that came close to a growl, 'I want to ravish you, and you make the most erotic soft cries when that happens. Possibly that might wake her if we go to your room.'

Colour burned up through her skin as her blood leapt at the need that smouldered in his eyes, the dangerous note in his words. Fighting a desperate desire, she slid her hands up beneath his shirt. His skin was hot and smooth against her seeking palms, his heart thundering into her palms with a rapid, primal beat that echoed within her.

She said huskily, 'Do I?'

'Don't you remember?' he purred, and eased away so he could strip off his shirt.

It was amazing to realise what details had imprinted

themselves on her mind. Powerfully muscled, with the dusting of dark hair across his wide chest adding to his virile impact, he was all male.

Next to him she felt small and fragile, yet unafraid. 'I remember,' she whispered, and leaned up to kiss his shoulder, allowing her tongue to drift sensuously over the smooth, taut skin.

He tasted slightly salty, a flavour that was dark and delicious and entirely his own. And that simple caress made him shiver, contracted the lean muscles against her into hard, heady potency.

Excitement thrilled through Iona, voluptuous and addictive, setting her alight with a fire that had never been truly extinguished. Her breasts tightened in ardent anticipation, the nipples pressing against the fabric of her camisole, urgent and pleading.

Luke looked down. 'Yes,' he drawled wickedly, 'I can see that you do.'

He caught her close and kissed her again, mouth exploring as he tried to remove the only barrier between them.

After a few shattering seconds he tore his mouth loose and demanded, 'Is this some sort of corset? Don't tell me they're coming back into fashion?'

'No.' It was all she could think of to say; waves of shattering pleasure were tossing her higher and higher.

'Hmm, perhaps it's a pity. This is hard enough to take off and a corset would be worse, but I can imagine you in something ribboned and laced, alluring as hell and damned dangerous...'

His fingers eased the reluctant fabric upwards. 'When I saw you again in the apartment, all alabaster skin and sweet curves, I wondered why the hell I'd let you go.'

'You didn't let me go,' she managed, holding up her arms so that the garment could come over her head. 'I left.'

His hands closed for a sensuous second around her breasts before she was free of the camisole. And this time he kissed her without interruption, slowly backing her across the room until her legs met the side of the bed, and only his arms held her up. His mouth travelled the length of her throat, stopping at the intensely sensitive junction of shoulder and neck. Gently, carnally, he bit the skin there.

Adrenalin rushed through Iona, so mingled with eagerness and anticipation that she gasped and turned her head into his shoulder. Those tiny nibbling kisses gave no quarter; he had remembered the exact location of each hidden pleasure point, and set them on fire with his deliberately tormenting lips.

Astonishingly, before that too-knowing mouth had journeyed anywhere near her breasts, the preliminary signs of ecstasy sent a molten tension zinging across every nerve and cell in her body.

'What is it?' he asked against her skin, and when she shivered under an inrush of clamouring pleasure, he murmured in a voice that held both amusement and passion, 'Ah, I remember this also...' and resumed his ruthless seduction.

The ravishing tension became too much; resist as she did, she felt it ride her like a whirlwind, until the climax hit her and she collapsed, still locked in his arms.

He laughed softly and said, 'Do you know how that makes me feel?'

'Ch-cheated?' she muttered, her bones refusing to hold her upright.

'Far from it. I like…no, I *revel* in the knowledge that I can do that to you. It makes me feel ten feet tall…'

He kissed her hard then, without finesse, a fiery kiss that let her know more than any words could just how much he wanted her, then tumbled her backwards onto the bed, skilfully removing her trousers, and with them the briefs she wore beneath, so that she lay fully exposed to his heated, desirous gaze.

In a thickened voice he said, 'I suspect I am not going to be able to last long enough to give you the second round of pleasure you deserve for making me feel like that.'

'It won't matter,' she whispered, adoring him with her gaze, her lashes drooping so heavily at the stunning impact of all that untrammelled masculinity that she had to blink several times before she could lift them.

He tore off the rest of his clothes, revealing his muscled elegance, sleekly powerful, as he came down beside her. Tanned skin gleaming in the shafts of moonlight across the floor, he bent his head and kissed the peak of one flushed breast, his mouth closing over the tight, pleading nipple.

Iona's back arched off the bed, and the delicious sensations that had ebbed slightly surged back, pulsating through her as he gave his full attention to the other breast.

'You taste like honey and roses,' he said, and turned his head so that his roughened cheek swept across one over-sensitive nipple.

Iona shuddered, and he said urgently, 'I'm sorry—'

'No,' she breathed, and opened her eyes, meeting his gaze. 'It felt wonderful. Don't stop…'

'Your skin is so delicate,' he said, and kissed the track

his cheek had taken, then moved down to loop a chain of kisses around her waist.

Iona tensed, her senses tuned so exquisitely she shuddered. He took her throat, then lifted one hand, tracing from her mouth down the centre line of her body, delicately caressing the tiny hollow beneath her waist, and edging further until those knowledgeable fingers found the most sensitive part of her body.

That acute awareness gave way to a flood of heated anticipation, wine-sweet with promise; holding her breath, taut with desire, she waited.

Instead he lifted his head and said, 'You're sure?'

'So sure I might just do something drastic if you don't keep going.' Her voice was hoarse, the words coming in short gasps as her spine arched again, pushing into his hand in a silent plea.

'One of these days,' he said, wicked glints in his eyes, 'I shall find out just what you threaten me with, but for now I cannot...cannot...'

His voice died away as his fingers slid inside her. Iona stiffened at the enormous surge of molten pleasure his touch summoned, her lashes fluttering down to shut out his dark intent face.

'It's too much,' she said hoarsely.

'Look at me,' he said in a thick, goaded voice. '*Look at me.*'

His thumb brushed across her, and she arced at the bursting sweetness from the slight pressure while tiny shivers chased each other through her, each more reckless than the last.

Eyes suddenly dark, he said, 'No—not yet, Iona. Not yet. Wait for me.' And he settled his lean body over her, supporting himself on his elbows so she wasn't crushed by his weight.

Tormented by erotic craving, she felt every nerve in her body tense under a rushing overload of voluptuous sensation.

'Take me now,' Luke said on a raw, dangerous note, and thrust, making himself master of her reactions in one strong movement.

Voluptuous sensation rocketed through her, piercing her with a delight so powerful she almost fainted. Locking her arms around his powerful, sweat-slicked back, she met his fierce sexual drive as fiercely, tightening around him with demanding internal muscles.

Easily, naturally, they established a soaring rhythm, blocking out everything but the desperate, sensuous craving in each that fed off the other. Deep within Iona a divine anticipation built and built, pushing her ever closer to the mindlessness of rapture.

And then it came, a starburst of ecstasy in every cell, banishing everything but an addictive intoxication that sang through her. Luke flung back his head and she forced open her eyes, watching the starkly drawn contours of his face as he joined her in their private sensual paradise.

Slowly, slowly, she came down, his beloved weight anchoring her, safe as she hadn't been since the last time she'd been in Luke's bed, in his arms.

Without realising it she'd longed for this, and not just the torrid surrender to desire, but the comfort and security of his arms. Eighteen months ago in this bed she'd returned to the world of the senses, able to enjoy the taste of food, the scents she'd ignored, the colours and hues of life, the feel of the sea on her skin, the sounds of laughter and music and birdsong.

Now she ached to yield herself entirely to him, yet didn't dare. The sex had been mind-blowing before, but recognising her love had added an extra richness to it. She opened her eyes a slit. Luke was watching her, his mouth oddly grim, although it softened when he caught her peeping at him.

'Stop looking so guilty,' he said.

Colour burned along her cheeks. 'I've just broken the first commandment of all employees,' she replied, trying to sound bright and in control.

'Don't sleep with the boss?'

'That's the one.'

His brows lifted. 'If sleeping with the boss is forbidden, what's the commandment about marrying him?'

'I don't think that's covered in the lexicon,' she said primly, tensing as his hand drifted down to curve around one breast. Trying to ignore the little tingles of response, she went on, 'Luke, I'd better get back to my own bed. Chloe—'

'We'll hear her.' He nodded at the baby monitor. As if in answer a small snuffle emerged from it, dying into silence.

Iona said, 'I want to go back to my own room.' When he frowned she said, 'It's all been a bit too much. I need time.'

'What for?' He didn't sound angry, but he wasn't letting her go, either.

She took a deep breath. 'To regroup, I suppose,' she said honestly. 'I don't really know. Everything's happened so quickly. You overwhelm me. I'll probably get used to it, but right now I feel as though I've been dragged into a raging torrent, and although what's happened was magnificent, I need—well, to use a cliché, I need a bit of space.'

'Magnificent?' His golden eyes narrowed. 'I'm flattered.' Unembarrassed, he dropped his hand, sat up on the side of the big bed and switched on the lamp before stretching, lean muscles coiling and flexing beneath the sleek satin skin she'd marked, she noticed with another onrush of colour, with both her nails and her teeth.

He followed the direction of her shocked gaze, and drawled, 'Don't look shocked. These are honourable scars.'

She laughed and picked up a pillow, only to put it down again when the gleam in his eyes turned distinctly predatory.

Back in her room, she showered and slipped into pyjamas before checking Chloe.

She felt pleasantly exhausted, but once she'd got into her own bed she lay awake for a while, listening to the low rumble of ocean combers on the distant reef, and wished she'd stayed with Luke.

Her skin heated as she recalled his frank, sensuous appreciation of their lovemaking. He'd made her feel she was beautiful, that he found infinite pleasure in her body—but he hadn't told her he loved her.

Whereas she'd had to bite the words back several times.

So although he had been honest with her she'd not been—entirely—honest with him. And even though it hurt fiercely she had to bear the consequences of loving without having it reciprocated.

She could do it, she thought. She *could*. She'd keep her forbidden love hidden, and she'd make Chloe happy and bear his children, giving him what he wanted from her without counting the cost.

Yet as she finally slid into sleep she wondered if the price might perhaps prove too high…

That fear came back to her the next morning, when she watched Chloe on the beach, face intent and serious, while she built a magnificent sandcastle and decorated it with tiny bright shells and some long drifts of seaweed.

'Iona, who is that man?' Chloe asked, looking past her to the coconut palms behind.

Iona turned around, and one glance at the man who stood a few paces behind them told her immediately who he was. Once he too would have been as sinfully good-looking as his son, but the years had blurred his features, and he leaned heavily on a stick.

Aristo Michelakis—Luke's father.

And half an hour ago Luke had gone into the nearest town to make the final arrangements for their wedding...

Where, Iona thought as she stood up and tried to control the sick panic that kicked her in her stomach, is the bodyguard?

CHAPTER ELEVEN

IONA'S first instinct was one of sheer terror—she had to stop herself from snatching up Chloe and running. That lasted only a moment, because Luke's father was alone.

Heart still pounding in her ears, she fought for control. How had he got there?

She'd have seen him much sooner if he'd walked along the beach, and to reach them from the road meant negotiating a perimeter with a sophisticated security system.

She could worry about that later; right now she needed to speak first, so she could take control of the situation.

'Hello, Mr Michelakis,' she said smoothly. 'Luke isn't here, I'm afraid.'

Chloe left her sandcastle and came up to her, slipping her hand into Iona's, her gaze fixed on the man who had fathered her.

Iona bent down and said to her, 'Chloe, I can see Moana up by the house. Run up to her and tell her I said you need to stay with her until Luke comes back.'

Aristo Michelakis made no attempt to detain the child, not even noticing that she carefully steered well clear of him on her way up the beach. Silently Iona kept her eyes on her, until the housekeeper took Chloe's hand and drew her inside.

'You need not be so concerned,' he said abruptly. 'I have no need to steal her—I prefer to do things legally.' He waited a moment and added, 'Unlike my son. You can tell him this fake marriage isn't going to win him anything but everyone's mockery.'

To Iona's huge relief one of the bodyguards appeared in a silent rush through the wavering shadows of the palms and headed purposefully towards them.

Thank heavens the housekeeper had warned him. She said, 'I'm sorry you've come all this way to no avail. I must ask you to go now.'

'And if I do not want to go?'

Calmly, in the voice she'd use to a child having a tantrum, Iona said, 'The bodyguard will see that you do. I imagine you'd rather leave with dignity.'

He made a gesture that hinted at disdain and frustration before turning and limping away towards the palms. Iona watched him out of sight, and then drew in an uneven breath, filling starved lungs with the fresh sea air. She blinked, and set off swiftly for the house.

A kind of worried relief flooded her when she found Chloe ensconced in the kitchen, a glass of coconut milk in front of her, chattering away in what sounded like a mixture of English and French to the housekeeper.

Her face lit up when she saw Iona, but she looked past her to the doorway and asked apprehensively, 'Did the bad man go away?'

'He's not a bad man,' Iona corrected, because there was just a chance that some terrible lack in the justice system would see Chloe eventually delivered to Aristo Michelakis's custody. 'He's a grumpy man, because his leg hurts.'

Then Chloe bounced to her feet, announcing, 'Lukas is home,' and ran through the door.

After thanking Moana for caring for the child, Iona followed, catching the moment when Luke put Chloe down after her exuberant greeting.

He said to her, 'Go back to Moana now and help her make us some coffee. Iona and I want to talk to each other.' When she'd gone he transferred his gaze, hard and clear as topaz, to Iona. 'We'll go to my office.'

No tenderness in his tone, nothing but cool authority. Chilled, Iona asked sweetly, 'Is that an order?'

His brows drew together for a taut moment, then relaxed as he gave a reluctant smile. 'A request, of course.'

Iona walked into the office, trying to bolster her spirits with sturdy common sense. For heaven's sake, what had she expected—that one night of passion would turn Luke into the lover she so desperately wanted?

It wasn't going to happen. The sex was a bonus, one enjoyed by both her and Luke, but their marriage was for strictly practical reasons—and, having now met Aristo Michelakis, she fully understood why Luke had taken such a step. After that first glance he hadn't bothered to look at Chloe, much less acknowledge her.

Lukas glanced downwards. As always, Iona seemed calm and self-possessed. Except when she was in his arms. Then the wildly passionate woman was revealed, sensual and erotically charged, while she gave him everything he wanted from her—more than any other woman ever had.

'What did you think of my father?' he asked.

She said, 'I was sorry for him.'

Sorry for him? 'What do you mean by that?'

Unabashed, she shrugged, the fine cotton of her shirt

tightening around her breasts. Lukas dragged his mind away from the sudden urgent pressure in his groin and back to the matter of his father's unexpected and extremely unwelcome arrival.

'Just that,' she said, meeting his gaze without a tremor. 'He's alone, and lonely, and he hates it.'

'It is his own fault.'

She said, 'I don't suppose that ancient Greek king was particularly happy after he'd ordered his son killed and then found he was innocent.'

Surprised, Lukas let his brows shoot up, but she went on. 'When I watched your father limp away he looked old and defeated and sad.'

Lukas said abruptly, 'Ironic, isn't it? My father calls the story the doom of his house. Of course it doesn't necessarily play out the same down the years. Hippolytus's stepmother killed herself after he'd rejected her. My father's second wife only pretended to commit suicide— her overdose was carefully calculated so it would scare the hell out of everyone but not actually kill her.'

'What happened to her?'

Without attempting to hide his scorn he told her, 'She sank into deserved obscurity after he divorced her.'

Iona said, 'If your father calls the myth the doom of your house, why didn't he take in the lesson it taught?'

'Presumably for the same reason Theseus believed Phaedra, his wife—because he resented his son.' He shrugged, watching her absorb that.

'He should have been proud of you.'

Lukas said, 'He was, until about a year before he accused me. Then we quarrelled, and continued quarrelling until he had an excuse to send me away.'

'One alpha male feeling his potency diminish while

his son's increases,' she said dryly, meeting his gaze
with rueful sympathy. 'You men!'

Lukas returned coolly, 'I've seen it happen with
women too; a beauty who resents her daughter's growing loveliness while hers is fading.'

'Even if it is part of the human condition, that doesn't
excuse your father's lack of faith.' Iona knew she wasn't
getting anywhere, but she wanted to know as much about
the rift as she could persuade Luke to tell her.

'Nothing would have given him greater pleasure than
to see me sink into contemptible mediocrity. In fact, he
banked on it,' Luke said, his tone bored. 'He was quite
certain that without his backing I'd go under—and he
did his best to make sure I did just that.'

'He doesn't know you very well.'

Luke showed his teeth. 'He learned. I set myself
against him—and I won.' He paused. 'And by now he
should understand me well enough to know that nothing
and nobody will take Chloe from me if I can possibly
prevent it.'

'He knows you well enough to be convinced that our
marriage is a fake,' Iona said bleakly.

He smiled at her and came across the room.
'Then we'll just have to show him—and anyone else
who's watching—that it's not, won't we.' It was not a
question.

Iona angled her chin, met gleaming tawny eyes, and
hid an odd chill in the region of her heart with a gallant
smile. 'Yes,' she said quietly, and let herself be drawn
into his arms.

And then all thought stopped as Luke's hard, possessive kiss submerged her in a tide of erotic promise.

Eventually, when he lifted his head and surveyed

her face with a fiercely kindling gaze, she gazed up at him.

'I'm going to enjoy being married to you very much,' he said, his voice unexpectedly raw.

She said, 'Remember how the myth ended? Theseus was reconciled to Hippolytus as he lay dying.'

Releasing her, Luke said with cold finality, 'That will not happen. And if there was ever any truth in that legend, the sentimental deathbed scene probably didn't happen either. Now, I have things to tell you.'

The civil ceremony had been organised and would take place early in the morning before the traditional wedding. 'It will be informally formal,' he said. 'This afternoon a woman will bring a selection of clothes for you to choose from.'

She blinked, but saw the point. Her wedding dress had been chosen for a romantic beach ceremony, not for one in a mayor's office.

'What on earth does one wear to an informally formal legal ceremony in the town hall?' she asked.

'I'm wearing a grey silk suit.' He gave her a swift, reassuring smile. 'Don't worry—you'll look good no matter what you wear, and the boutique owner will be able to guide you in your choice.' His tone altered. 'From the moment of signing in the mayor's office we will be legally married, but the traditional ceremony will still be held here. The gazebo will be a suitable setting, but if you want a different place tell Moana so they can decorate it.'

'I thought it was to be on the beach?'

He said curtly, 'The media have arrived. I have done what I can to make sure we are not interrupted, and have the local authorities' full co-operation, but there is a chance we could be overlooked.' He glanced at her. 'Do you want to take it?'

'No,' she exclaimed, horrified at the prospect of flashing paparazzi cameras. 'Of course not.'

He nodded. 'Is there anything you need? Any arrangements? Anything I have neglected to take into consideration?'

In spite of the passion in that kiss he had retreated into a cool aloofness that set her teeth on edge. 'I can't think of anything.'

'I would like us to feel that we can be completely honest with each other,' he said, still watching her.

How could she be honest when she was holding back the biggest truth in her life—that she loved him?

Taking a tangent, she said, 'Somehow I thought that a wedding here would be easier to organise.'

One black brow lifted. 'Marriage is too important an occasion not to be hedged about with formalities and ceremony in all societies. The wellbeing of the next generation is paramount.'

The reminder of the reason for their wedding flicked her on the raw. Foolishly, she felt like demanding, *But what about this generation?*

It was too late for second thoughts, for asking for the stars. She'd already decided that if this was all she had, it would have to be enough.

And if she didn't stop worrying the situation like a dog with a bone, she'd wreck any chance of happiness and possibly jeopardise Chloe's future.

Besides, meeting Aristo Michelakis had only reinforced Luke's decision for her; lonely and self-absorbed and spiky with bitterness, Chloe's birth father was no fit person to be guardian of any child.

'You must agree with that,' Luke said, his voice

hardening, 'or you would not have consented to marry me.'

'Of course I agree with you,' she said briskly, hoping he couldn't hear the thin, forlorn undernote to the words.

He did, but fortunately he attributed it to the wrong reason. 'Yet you still feel sorry for my father?'

'I'm afraid I do.'

He caught her hand and lifted it to his lips. 'You have a tender heart,' he said with satisfaction.

Then he said, in an entirely different voice, one so flinty and uncompromising it made her flinch, 'My father chose his own path. Possibly he regrets it now, but it is too late—he has said too many harsh things, shown too much rage, connived too long to destroy me. There will never be a reconciliation.'

When she said nothing, he finished curtly, 'It is better that way.'

'How did he get onto the beach?'

Luke frowned. 'Easily enough—he told the gate-keeper he was expected. I had given no orders that he was to be denied, and my resemblance to him meant he was given access as of right. It won't happen again.'

'Did you know he'd had you watched?'

'Of course,' he said indifferently.

Struck by another thought, Iona felt her skin crawl.

Had Aristo Michelakis learned that she and Luke had made love last night and come to see if he could frighten—or buy—her off?

Luke guessed what she was thinking. 'It's all right. I trust my staff, and he has no chance of finding out what happens here. And you needn't fear that we'll be under constant scrutiny from him. He keeps a distant eye on what I'm doing. This is the first time he's ever come onto my property or anywhere near me.'

Unconsciously she bit her lip, stopping guiltily when he said, 'Each time you do that I shall have to kiss it better.' He followed suit, pulling away far too soon, and said with a glinting smile, 'So from now on remember that whenever you chew on your lip you're asking for a kiss.'

She laughed and left it at that, but the knowledge that Aristo was having them watched was like a cold hand on her shoulder. Until it occurred to her that perhaps it was the lonely old man's way of having some connection with the son and daughter he'd abandoned.

Somewhat comforted by that, later Iona chose a sleek silk dress to wear to the mayor's office, glad that no prices were mentioned. Tahiti might be on the opposite side of the world from Paris, but the clothes she was shown were pure designer chic with a twist of tropical bravura. And had prices, no doubt, that would make her gasp.

The slim garment, pale blue and ethereal as a summer dawn, draped her body without being blatantly sexy, and high heels in the same colour meant she wouldn't look quite so short beside Luke's tall frame. The matching fascinator added a touch of frivolity and fantasy.

'You know how to pull your hair back into a chignon?' the boutique owner asked, touching her own sleekly sophisticated hair. She gave a wide smile. 'It will show off the hat better. And your beautiful skin.'

Iona nodded, and, after practising in her bathroom with both style and fascinator, decided she agreed with the owner and would wear it like that on her wedding day.

She didn't sleep much that night. The words *wedding*

day kept echoing in her head, locking her into thoughts of a different wedding, which had been planned for New Zealand amongst family and close friends.

Gavin was now a loved memory, he and her parents no longer a source of anguish, yet she felt an aching emptiness as she lay in the luxurious room listening to the trade wind rustle through the leafy crowns of the coconut palms.

The arrival of Luke's father had upset her. She couldn't stop herself from feeling an immense sorrow for both the old man and the son he'd rejected.

Her eyes were hot and heavy, and she had a disconcerting urge to let the tears flow. Too late now, she told herself, and determinedly counted her blessings. In two days' time she'd marry the man she loved, become mother to the child she loved too. She was certain from seeing Luke with Chloe that beneath that authoritative, dominant and very Mediterranean exterior was a man who could be trusted to keep his word.

Surely that was enough? she asked herself, knowing it wasn't...

Then you're greedy, she scolded, and to escape her thoughts got up and walked across to the doors, pulling back the drapes to look out onto a tropical fantasy, softly silver-gilt and black, the full moon's rays shafting down between the palms and skimming the tiny waves as they creamed onto the milky sand.

Why hadn't Luke come to her tonight? She needed the reassurance of his passion.

From the corner of her eye she caught a movement and froze, her breath blocking her throat. Only for a second, but she didn't relax when she recognised Luke walking up from the beach, his head bent as though he was thinking deeply.

Or regretting deeply?

Iona let the drapes fall and stepped back into the darkness of her room, listening to the sound of her heart thudding unevenly against the ceaseless murmur of the waves on the reef.

The following day was so busy she and Luke barely exchanged a private word together. Early in the morning Luke drove in to pick up Angie and her children, and from then it was all noise and laughter as the two boys explored the house and beach, Chloe trotting along with them, Luke in charge.

In the afternoon more people arrived; Luke introduced her to a gorgeous Spaniard who turned out to have a name several pages long and an ancestry even longer. He was to be best man at the wedding, and although he greeted her with charming courtesy she suspected he was probably wondering how on earth someone as entirely lacking in glamour had caught Luke's eye.

A little later two couples—close friends of Luke's—flew in to celebrate the wedding with him.

People came and went; she had almost no time to talk to Luke, and in the late afternoon he left with all the guests except Angie and the children—because, of course, the bride and groom could not be allowed to see each other until they met at the wedding ceremony.

Feeling oddly abandoned, Iona showered and changed, and walked across to the bed. She'd got into it when she saw a parcel deposited on the table.

Carefully wrapped, it had her name on the outside, with 'Delivery By Hand' written beneath in strong handwriting.

Luke? She opened the parcel with an eagerness she didn't try to restrain.

She couldn't control the shock of disappointment

when she realised it was just a magazine—one that seemed to combine gossip with interviews, and mostly featured celebrities. Titles were scattered through the pages, alongside photographs of impossibly elegant people posing gracefully in superb clothes.

'Who on earth would send me this?' she muttered, flicking through the pages. Not Luke, that was for sure; she couldn't believe he'd be interested in anything like this—

Her gaze stopped on a photograph. Luke. And a woman.

With an odd detachment Iona realised her hand was trembling. She glanced back to the cover and saw the same woman, smiling with mystery and sultry, slightly mocking invitation.

Iona dragged in a jagged breath and turned to the page. Luke's companion was utterly gorgeous, in an ethereal, fine-boned way, and she was very familiar— the newest and most beautiful Hollywood star, with a string of hit films behind her, plus rave reviews for her acting, poised on the verge of a dazzling future.

Slowly, a dark dread coalescing around her heart, Iona braced herself, turned back to the cover of the magazine and found the date. It was the latest issue.

All she wanted to do was ignore this poisoned gift from Aristo Michelakis—because of course that was who'd sent it—yet she couldn't put the magazine down. Something inside her crumpled and died as she examined the picture, noting the way Susan Mainwaring looked up at Luke, the care with which he was helping her down a step.

The caption told her they were at the opening of a new theatre in London. In what could only be called gushing prose it detailed the dress the film star was wearing, and referred readers to the next pages for an in-depth interview with her.

Summoning every bit of will she possessed, Iona forced herself to read it, and finally closed the magazine. Nausea gripped her, and a dark despair.

Not only had Susan Mainwaring made it obvious— without exactly saying so—that she expected to marry Luke, but when asked about combining a family with her glittering career she'd laughed and asserted, 'Oh, plenty of time for that in the future—if it happens. There's no room for children in my life right now, and I'm not hearing any clock ticking.'

Thereby neatly underlining that she was years younger than her nearest and greatest acting rivals.

And, from the schedule she gave, she wasn't going to have time for anything much—not even Luke—for several years yet. Certainly if she'd married Luke there would have been no place in her heart or her life for Chloe.

Although she'd been discreet, only letting a few words escape about the man in her life escape, it was clear she and Luke were lovers.

A fierce jealousy almost tore Iona apart. She had to pace around her room, her mind seething, her heart contracting into a painful lump in her chest. She could not marry Luke without knowing what promises—if any—he'd made to the film star.

Her first impulse—to call him—was dashed when she realised she didn't know how to contact him. He'd not given her a number for his cell phone. Moana had gone home for the night, and Iona didn't know the hotel phone number—wasn't even sure of the name of the place or where it was. It could be in the next bay, or halfway around the main island.

She could look it up—but would they know who she was? They might think she was a journalist. Still, she could try.

A couple of minutes later she put the telephone down. The receptionist had said politely that there was no answer from Luke's room.

She had to talk to Luke.

For a few seconds she hated his father for doing this to her; he'd gauged her well, rightly guessing she'd know she couldn't compete with Susan Mainwaring.

She said angrily, 'Horrible old man! I wish—' and stopped, because of course she didn't wish him dead.

Just out of her life—and Luke's. And Chloe's.

Driven to her feet, she unlatched the door and walked outside into the moonlight. Where was Luke when she desperately needed him?

A lovers' moon shone down, all traces of gold vanished so that the light was a pure, hard-edged white.

She stood on the edge of the terrace and shivered in spite of the warmth. Because it hurt less to think of a tragedy more than two thousand years old than to face what she'd read, she mulled over the story of doomed Hippolytus and his stepmother, Phaedra, who had wanted him and then betrayed him.

Perhaps Aristo was right when he called the story of Theseus his family's doom. Luke would do anything to safeguard Chloe, even marry a woman he didn't— perhaps could never—love.

She turned and went back inside, turning the magazine over, hopefully scanning the article to see if she could work out when the film star had been interviewed.

No clue; she didn't know anything about magazine production, but surely this interview must have occurred before Luke knew Neelie had to care for her mother?

In which case he could have been planning to marry the film star, feeling that with the constant presence of her father and Neelie an absent stepmother wouldn't harm Chloe.

She dropped the magazine as though it poisoned her.

'Think,' she said aloud, her voice fierce. '*Think*, instead of wallowing in angst.'

So how had Aristo seen the interview? Her mind worried with that question until she dismissed it. It didn't matter—someone could have told him, or he could have had a press clipping service so that anything about Luke was sent to him. What *did* matter was that this very interview could have persuaded Aristo that he had a chance of wresting Chloe away from his son. Any lawyer conducting Aristo's case would consider those airy comments on Susan Mainwaring's lack of interest in children a godsend.

Aristo Michelakis must be pretty sure Iona would be convinced. Not just convinced, but shattered enough to jilt his son.

She collapsed limply onto the side of the bed. Even to her it seemed ridiculous and irrational, but she had to know whether or not he'd made any promise to Susan Mainwaring.

And if he had…?

She set her jaw. She'd face that when she came to it. First she had to find out.

CHAPTER TWELVE

IONA finally got through to Luke late at night.

'What is it?' he demanded, his voice hard with concern. 'What is wrong?'

'I need to see you,' she told him baldly. 'It's all right—Chloe's fine.'

The pause that followed her words screwed her nerves to a point of pain, until he said in a matter-of-fact tone, 'I'll be there in ten minutes.'

Setting the phone down, she glanced across at the curtains billowing softly in the breeze and thought wildly, *He's going to think I'm mad. And this business with the magazine can only make things worse between him and his father.*

Too late now.

It didn't occur to her to pull on a dressing gown. It wasn't until Luke came noiselessly through the curtains, big and dark and dominant, that she realised she was wearing a pair of pyjamas that had seen much better days.

He said coolly, 'Is this a seduction scene, Iona?'

But his eyes had kindled and a raw note ran through the words, and she suddenly felt a little less tense. 'No,' she said raggedly, and gestured at the magazine, open on the bed. 'Read that.'

Black brows drawing together over his blade of a nose, he picked up the magazine, glanced at the cover and looked up sharply. 'Where did you get this?'

'Never mind that,' she said calmly. 'Please read it.'

Frown deepening, he scrutinised it, then dropped the magazine onto the floor. 'I suppose you want to know whether or not we were lovers.'

'Not that,' she said, muscles contracting as though she faced a blow. 'I want to know whether or not she had any right to hint at a marriage between you.'

'No.'

Just one word—so easy to say, so simple—but a word that meant more than anything else he'd ever said to her. Their eyes locked; his were dark and unsparing, and for a moment Iona wavered, and then at a purely instinctual level she understood he was telling the truth.

'That's fine, then,' she said quietly.

He stared at her. 'Is that all you need?'

'Yes.'

After a pause he said in a level voice, 'I don't know why she said that—or even if she did. Journalists have been known to get things wrong. But Susan made it obvious from the start of our affair that she wasn't looking for marriage. She certainly wanted nothing to do with Chloe while we were lovers.'

That hurt like a blow struck at her heart, but she steadied herself enough to say, 'Go on.'

He said, 'I finished our affair when I discovered my father was planning to sue for custody of Chloe. Just before we arrived in New Zealand.'

'Did you love her?' No sooner had she said the words than she longed desperately to be able to call them back. She sounded so needy. Love had no part in their bargain; she had no right to quiz him about his feelings.

He shrugged. 'No.' He paused, then said with taut irony, 'It was a very convenient affair—for us both. But Chloe comes first.'

'Of course.'

On a note of exasperation he said, 'You forget how I was brought up—to be the one to look after the family. It was always part of the deal—to behave as my father did, and his father before him.'

'Except that your father didn't,' she said in swift anger. 'He tore the family apart because he didn't believe you. He rejected you.'

Luke looked bored. 'I'm not interested in him now—or only in as much as he affects Chloe.' He glanced at the magazine and said on a steely note, 'And you.'

Iona's breath clogged into a painful lump in her chest. 'He doesn't affect me at all. No, that's not quite true—I still feel a bit sorry for him. But not sorry enough to feel you shouldn't fight him in this.'

His smile made her shiver. 'To the death. Now, why was it so important for you to hear from my lips that I had no intention of marrying Susan?'

She didn't dare confess her love for him. He waited, and when she didn't speak his brows rose. In a dry, deliberate voice he said, 'Very well. Tell me why you chose me for an affair eighteen months ago.'

A cautious glimmer of hope smouldered into life. She took a jagged breath, then with a rashness that startled her, risked everything. 'You're so alive, so much in control of your life, and so strong. That's what drew me to you at first. And when you made it obvious that for you it would only be a holiday affair—nothing serious, just fun and pleasure and brilliant sex—I thought it was perfect. But I only wanted to be healed, not to fall in love.'

Still he didn't turn. It was like talking to a statue. Heart in her mouth, she heard him speak.

'I was a fool.'

She could gain nothing from his tone—cool, flat, without expression. She said, 'No, I was the fool. When you suggested we keep up the affair, that I live with you, I was afraid of being hurt all over again.'

At last he turned, his face set and frowning like one of the old gods of his country. 'Why, for heaven's sake?'

'I refused to admit it, but I was falling in love all over again, and this time it wasn't the sweet boy-girl thing I'd had with Gavin. It was powerful and frightening and heart-wrenching. And I knew...'

Her voice trailed away into a silence that held her still.

'You knew what?' he rasped.

Inwardly quivering, she forced the words out. 'That last night, after you'd asked me to live with you, I dreamed that I was married to Gavin, and you arrived and said, "Come," and I left him, running towards you with such joy, such happiness.'

'You left me because of a *dream*?' he demanded incredulously.

'No, not that, but because it showed me something I hadn't faced until then.'

'And that was?' When she didn't answer immediately he commanded ruthlessly, 'Tell me, Iona.'

She was horrified to find she was wringing her hands. Hastily putting them behind her, she whispered, 'Oh, it sounds so *stupid*. I left you because I was a coward.'

Luke came towards her, stopping a mere pace away.

She didn't dare lift her eyes further than the small pulse of a muscle in his jaw.

In a deep, quiet voice he said, 'Like me, you had learned in a hard school that love can be followed by disaster. Why did you believe me when I told you I had not slept with my father's wife?'

Iona stared at him. 'I…I told you before. I can't give you an exact reason beyond sheer gut instinct,' she said unevenly. 'I just *know* you wouldn't do that.'

'You must also know that I have had several lovers— none of whom I've married—and been credited with many more. Such a man could be one who takes women lightly, uses them, then discards them. Why didn't you believe that of me?'

'Because it isn't in you to behave like that,' she said instantly.

'I forced you into looking after Chloe, bulldozed you into this marriage.' His gaze raked her face, intent, compelling. 'What makes you think I would not force my father's wife into my bed?'

'You never call her your stepmother.'

'She was an insult to the word *mother*. Why do you not believe the lies she told? Because I can make you weep with ecstasy in bed? Because I am far richer than my father?'

'No,' she told him quietly. 'Because I've seen you with Chloe. And…' She stumbled, searching for words.

'Tell me, Iona.'

'I just *know*,' she repeated in confusion, because she couldn't give him the reason he seemed to want.

'Just as you knew that with me you'd find life and rapture again?'

'Yes.' And then, more bravely, 'Yes. I'm sorry I can't be more explicit than that. You wear your honour, your integrity, your strength like a banner.' Still he said nothing, and she finished in a tired voice. 'Which sounds stupid, I know—'

'It sounds magnificent,' he interrupted swiftly, and smiled, and she realised with a soaring heart that he believed her.

Oh, they hadn't solved everything—he hadn't even mentioned the word she longed to hear—but perhaps, in time, he would learn to love her...

Thoughtfully he said, 'The ancient Greeks had the right idea when they ascribed love to Eros, a wayward child who shot arrows into people's hearts for the sheer mischief of it. I think there is a little more logic to it than that, but I have to admit I fell in love with you when I first saw you walking along the beach out there, your long hair blowing in the trade wind. You looked like a Botticelli angel come down to earth—a wistful angel who wanted nothing more than oblivion.'

Speechless, hardly able to believe her ears, she lifted her gaze, saw a warmth in his tawny eyes that held something of passion, but even more of love.

'I'd like you to say that again,' she whispered.

He laughed deep in his throat. 'Only if you reciprocate. I am too Greek to take any pleasure in vowing love if you don't feel the same way.'

'Oh, Luke,' she said on a broken sigh, 'you must know I do.'

'Do what?'

His voice was amused, but the dark heat in his eyes had flared into fire and she said fiercely, 'Do *love* you, you idiot. Of *course* I love you—I think it must have happened that first day too, when you ordered me off your beach and then made me sit down and drink something before driving me back to my hotel. You've been part of me ever since.'

'Which is why you fled from me as soon as I asked you to stay with me?' he said austerely, and as she opened her mouth he held up his hand. 'No, I understand. I *do* understand. To love someone and then lose him is a tragedy, and your parents' deaths so soon afterwards...' He made a quick gesture. 'My own mother's death was tragedy enough for me.' He paused, then said sombrely, 'And for my father.'

After a quick glance at his watch, he looked at her, his expression stripped of everything except naked longing. 'A declaration of love should be sealed with a kiss—but I don't dare touch you, let alone kiss you.'

For the first time Iona let herself believe that what he felt for her was all that she'd ever wanted—no, she thought with breaking joy, *more* than she'd ever wanted. He couldn't look at her with such intensity, such open hunger and tenderness, and not mean it.

'Why?' she asked.

'It is too close to midnight for what I want to do— ravish you for hours—and Angie is convinced we're wooing the very worst of bad luck if we set eyes on each other before our wedding tomorrow.'

Iona choked back a laugh. 'I'm prepared to risk it if you are.'

He took a half-step towards her, then stopped. 'I can wait,' he said heroically. 'The first time after we have declared our love should not be hurried. Tomorrow will be our wedding night and we can make love all night long—if I can stand it.'

Frustration drummed through her in a driving crescendo. 'I love you,' she said.

He stiffened, and for a moment she thought he was

coming towards her. However, he stepped back and said roughly, 'I am only too human where you are concerned! I'll go now. But tomorrow—this time tomorrow...'

Although he left the sentence unfinished, his smile and the swift golden glitter in his eyes sent a shiver of sheer delight and need through her.

'Luke...'

Luke slid a questing hand from her hip to the soft curve of her breast. 'What is it, my dear one?'

'Earlier today, just as we were all getting ready for the garden wedding, Chloe asked if she could call me Mama.'

The slow sensuous movement of his hand stilled. 'And you said...?'

'I said she could.'

He lifted her chin and kissed her, long and tender and passionate, then tucked her head into his shoulder.

'I hadn't realised she felt the need for a mother.' He kissed her and said, 'You have given her something Neelie was never quite able to be for her.'

'I've been thinking about Neelie,' she said. 'She might not be openly motherly, but I'm sure she learned to love Chloe.'

'Of course.' He sounded slightly surprised.

'Do you think she'd like to be a grandmother?' When he said nothing she went on, 'Chloe has no grandmothers. And I'm sure she'd like to see Neelie whenever we're in the UK, just as Neelie must want to keep in touch with her.'

He said quietly, 'You fill my heart with your sweetness. Yes, of course we must make sure Neelie is part of our family.' He paused, then went on, 'And now I have something to tell you. Two things, in fact. This morning—before the official ceremony—my father came to see me.'

She stiffened in his arms, then tilted her head back so she could see his face against the pillow, dark and saturnine. She could read nothing from his expression. 'Why?' she breathed.

'To tell me he'd sent a letter to his lawyers instructing them he no longer planned to sue for custody of Chloe.'

Dumbfounded, she stared at him.

He watched her with a lurking smile, then said, 'I think this is the first time I've ever seen you without a word to say.'

'Why—what...? What made him change his mind?'

'He had never seen her before. She looks like my mother. And he loved my mother deeply; he was desolated when she died.'

He stretched, but when she moved to give him room he pulled her back into his arms, leaning his head on top of hers as her body curved against the hard contours of his. 'I like the way your hair falls in a curtain across me,' he murmured lazily. 'Such warm, living silk. As he had sent the magazine to you, it did occur to me his unexpected surrender was made so that I could pull out of the wedding if I wanted to—which would prove I was only marrying to safeguard Chloe.'

She asked hesitantly, 'Do you think that is the reason?'

'Strangely enough, no. Apparently you—although you do *not* look like my mother—also reminded him of her.'

Stunned, she demanded, 'How?'

'My mother was forthright, loving, and not afraid

to speak her mind.' He finished a little roughly, 'He said that she would have liked you. And he's right—she would have.'

Iona curved her hand around his jaw, relishing the soft abrasion, the warmth that beat from his skin. 'I feel as though some heavy weight has been lifted off my shoulders. Is this the end, do you think?'

'Perhaps the beginning of the end,' he said.

She twisted up onto her elbow and looked down at him, her gaze caressing the beloved contours of his face. 'How do you feel about that?'

His shoulders moved in the nearest approach to a shrug he could manage in bed. 'I didn't start it,' he said evenly. 'I never attacked him; I merely blocked his moves to bring me down. If at any time he'd come to me and told me he was ready to make an end to it, I'd have welcomed it.'

'And now?'

Luke thought for a moment, then said slowly, 'It will take time, but I hope we can build on the ruins of our old relationship. I think he has realised that he is the only one being hurt by his refusal to accept me.'

She nodded. 'You said you had something else to tell me?'

He frowned, then gave a sardonic smile. 'I was jealous of Iakobos.'

'What?'

He laughed wryly. 'Yes. You and he seemed to like each other, and I was so jealous I sent him away.'

'You had no reason,' she protested, still dazed at such a confession.

'I know,' he admitted cheerfully. 'And it will not affect his career. I did not believe myself to be a jealous man, but I realised that I have it in me. It was a shock—a salutary one.'

His arm tightened and effortlessly he brought her down to lie on his chest. Iona shivered as his body stirred, hardened beneath her. In a thickened voice he said, 'I will not make your life miserable with jealousy, and I will always protect you and cherish you and tell you the truth. And always, dear heart, *always* I will love you—with all that I am, everything I have.'

Her tears fell onto his chest, and he said in a shaken voice, 'What have I said to make you cry?'

'I'm crying because I'm so happy.' She wiped the tears away and bent to kiss him. 'I will always love you, and tell you the truth too—even when you don't want me to,' she added.

He laughed. 'I know that,' he said with satisfaction and kissed her again, and once more she felt the sweet hunger, the passionate love she was at last free to express.

She lifted her head and kissed him again, lips lingering on a swell of muscle, the sound of his increasing heartbeat music in her ears.

'Mmm, you taste good,' she whispered against his skin.

'So do you.'

Luke would always fire out orders, organise lives, rule his empire with formidable authority, but she had known from the moment she'd seen him that he was so much more than a dominant male. She and Chloe and any children they might have would be safe in his love.

As his hand traced the curve of her breasts, the narrow indentation of her waist, the flare of her hips, she sighed and whispered, 'You'll have to teach me how to say *I love you* in Greek.'

'Later,' he said, laughter catching in his throat. 'Much, much later...'

And then, locked together in passion that had been transformed so stealthily into love, they found the heaven that would always be theirs in each other's arms.

GREEK TYCOON, WAYWARD WIFE

SABRINA PHILIPS

Sabrina Philips first discovered Mills & Boon one Saturday afternoon in her early teens at her first job. Sorting through a stack of books, she came across a cover which featured a glamorous heroine and a tall, dark, handsome hero. She started reading under the counter that instant— and has never looked back!

A lover of both reading and writing since childhood, Sabrina went on to study English with Classics at Reading University. She adores all literature, but finds there's nothing else *quite* like the indulgent thrill of a Modern™ romance— preferably whilst lying in a hot bath with no distractions!

She grew up in Guildford, Surrey, where she now lives with her husband—who swept her off her feet when they were both just sixteen. When Sabrina isn't spending time with her family or writing, she works as a co-ordinator of civil marriages, which she describes as a fantastic source of romantic inspiration and a great deal of fun. A decade after reading her very first Mills & Boon® novel, Sabrina is delighted to join as an author herself, and have the opportunity to create infuriatingly sexy heroes of her own, whom she defies both her heroines—and her readers—to resist! Visit Sabrina's website: www.sabrinaphilips.com.

To Phil
For planting the seed of an idea in my mind
and for keeping me sane whilst it grew

CHAPTER ONE

'I'M AFRAID, Mr Delikaris, that you are still behind Spyros in the opinion polls.'

Orion glared at the bar chart projected on the wall, and then at the pessimistic expression of his campaign manager, who sat beside him at the long, highly polished table. A nerve spasmed at his jaw in disapproval. Orion never allowed himself to contemplate failure. He expected the members of his team to think the same way. That was what he paid them for.

'We have made progress,' the man continued anxiously, sensing Orion's displeasure, 'Especially since the campaign has focussed on how much you are willing to invest in both affordable housing and the new hospital. It's just not quite as *much* progress as we had estimated.'

He clicked the button in his hand and the image on the wall changed to a far more positively weighted graph, which only served to irritate Orion further, since it proved that his team's predictions had been wholly inaccurate.

Orion pinched the bridge of his nose. 'So, despite the fact that our policies are exactly what Metameikos needs, a man who is as corrupt as his father was before him is *still* the most popular candidate?' He looked down the table at the rest of his team. 'Would anyone care to volunteer a reason why?'

A long, uneasy silence followed.

Finally a voice came from the opposite end of the table. 'Perhaps people are wary about voting for you.'

There was a collective intake of breath. Rion slowly raised his head to see who had spoken. It was Stephanos, an assistant press officer and the newest member of his team. He was also the youngest. 'Go on.'

'People see you as a billionaire bachelor who has decided overnight, or so it seems to them, that you want to be their leader.' Stephanos paused, awaiting Rion's condemnation, but it didn't come. It gave him the courage to elaborate. 'Your promises may be what people want to hear, but these results show they clearly don't trust you'll deliver them. Perhaps they think you're simply running on a whim—to try and prove that you can succeed at anything you choose—or perhaps they think that if you do get elected you'll be too tied up with your business in Athens to devote the necessary time to the role. It's not true, of course, but they don't know that. People would rather vote for the devil they know.'

Orion studied Stephanos thoughtfully. The boy had guts. He liked that. It reminded him of himself. He also understood that politics was different from business, that people voted with their hearts, not necessarily in conjunction with their heads. Orion had always understood that too, but it hadn't occurred to him that people would instinctively stick with what they had rather than take an outside chance. He would always have taken the chance.

'So, what would *you* have me do?'

The rest of the men around the table exchanged astonished looks. His campaign manager looked affronted.

Stephanos took a deep breath and continued. 'For people to trust you they need to be able to relate to you, to see that your concerns, your values, are the same as theirs—good old-fashioned Greek values.'

Orion grimaced. His values *were* good old-fashioned Greek values—always had been. 'I grew up in Metameikos,' he said gravely. What had happened there had made him who he was.

'Then convince them you still think of it as home,' Stephanos replied animatedly. 'That the house you've bought there isn't just another property, but that you plan to settle down there.'

'And how do you suggest I do that?'

'Honestly?' Stephanos paused, a note of hesitancy entering his voice for the first time, 'In my opinion, the best solution would be to return to Metameikos with a wife.'

The receptive look on Rion's face immediately vanished and his expression grew dark, 'Then I hope you have an alternative solution,' he ground out, 'because that is not an option.'

Libby stared at the huge three-dimensional Delikaris logo rotating hubristically in its own fountain, at the enormous revolving glass doors which formed the en-

trance of his state-of-the-art office, and told herself
again that this was the right thing to do. It was the same
thing she'd been telling herself ever since she'd discovered that she'd be required to cover the Greek tours for
the duration of Zoe's maternity leave.

But she'd been finding excuses not to ever since
arriving in Athens a week ago, and even now she still
had the urge to run in the opposite direction. Which was
completely and utterly ridiculous, because of *course* it
was the right thing to do. It was time they both moved
on for good. How could it be anything else when she
and Rion hadn't spoken in five years?

It was just that being back in Athens, having to pass
the city hall, the old apartment block, had brought her
memories to the surface—that was all. But that was all
they were: memories. She just felt this way because they
hadn't seen each other since back then, and she was remembering the man she'd once been in love with, when
the reality was she'd probably barely recognise him now.

If the exterior of his office was anything to go by,
he'd be much changed. And so was she. Whilst she'd
been off leading low-cost tours around the globe, with
only a guidebook and a battered rucksack on her back,
he mustn't have spent a single day out of his suit, must
have worked every hour since to achieve all this.

Was that why he'd never got his lawyers onto it,
then? Libby wondered for the umpteenth time. Had he
been so focussed on his work that the legalities had
simply slipped his mind? As she finally forced herself
to take on the revolving doors, and found herself depos-

ited in a vast, gleaming reception area, she could well believe he had.

'Can I help you?' the glossy-haired receptionist ventured, shooting a condescending glance over her tie-dyed dress and comfy leather sandals. Libby grew suddenly conscious that she was the only woman in the busy entrance hall who wasn't wearing a pair of impossibly high, pointy stilettos and a designer business suit, but she didn't let it faze her.

'I was hoping to see Orion Delikaris—'

'Have you an appointment?'

Libby knew that trying to speak to him at his office was hardly ideal, but without his address, or any means of obtaining it, she had no other alternative. 'No, but as it's lunchtime I thought—'

The receptionist tossed her head and gave a snort of laughter. 'Then you thought wrong. Mr Delikaris does not have time for a *lunch break*. He is an exceptionally busy man.'

Libby didn't need to be reminded. Didn't doubt that he'd only got busier. But surely after five years he could spare her ten minutes?

'Maybe you will be so kind as to call Mr Delikaris and let *him* decide whether he wishes to see me,' she said, with emphatic sweetness. She'd once negotiated borrowing twenty-two camels to take an entire tour group across the desert at night, when a coach hadn't turned up, so she'd be dammed if she was going to be frightened off by a woman whose deadliest weapon was immaculate grooming and an over-inflated sense of self-importance.

The woman exhaled through her teeth, wearily lifted the receiver of her phone and tapped a button with one perfectly manicured talon. 'Electra, darling, so sorry to disturb you. I have a woman here who insists that we notify Mr Delikaris that she is in Reception. Mmm. Yes, another one. She seems to think if he knows she's here he'll agree to see her.'

She turned back to Libby. 'Your name, please?'

Libby took a deep breath. 'My name is Libby Delikaris,' she replied. 'I'm his wife.'

The office was silent.

'I'm afraid there's no alternative solution as far as I can see,' Stephanos answered. 'You can continue to spend as much time in Metameikos as possible; support local businesses, attend local events and keep trying to get the Mayor on side, but I don't think anything but getting married is going to truly convince people you plan to settle down there.'

Rion grimaced. 'I repeat. Marriage is out of the question.'

Stephanos was surprised that the man who'd sworn he would stop at nothing to win this election wouldn't even consider his suggestion, but decided it would be wise to drop it. 'Oh, well, even that would have been no guarantee. Without a long-term girlfriend it might have looked a little too much like a publicity stunt—especially so close to the election.'

The intercom on the desk behind Rion suddenly burst into life.

He swooped across to it, his voice curt. 'Yes?'

'I'm very sorry to interrupt you, Mr Delikaris, but there's a woman in Reception who is demanding we inform you that she's here.'

'Who is it?'

There was a loaded pause. 'She says her name is Libby Delikaris and that…she's your wife.'

Rion didn't move—couldn't. The instantaneous flood of pleasure that ran over him was so profound it rendered him motionless.

At last she had returned. At last she deemed him worthy enough.

It was the moment he'd been waiting for—far, far too long. Not because he gave a damn about her opinion any longer, he qualified quickly. But because now, finally, he could take his revenge.

He straightened victoriously. As he did, he caught sight of his team out of the corner of his eye, and suddenly the fortuity of her timing struck him. She had chosen to come crawling back *now*, just when he needed to convince the world he was all about good old-fashioned Greek values. His eyes glittered, and his mouth curved into a sardonic smile. How convenient.

He pressed the button on the intercom and replied with perfect composure, 'Thank you. Send her up.'

Rion sensed every eye in the room widen. It was understandable; he'd never mentioned her. But then he never spoke about failed ventures or the past. Since she fell into both categories, he did his best not to even think about her. Sometimes he even succeeded.

'Apologies, gentlemen. I'm afraid we will need to continue this meeting at another time.'

The men cleared the room without another word. Only Stephanos lingered.

'You know, an alternative way of convincing people you are the settling kind *has* just this minute occurred to me,' he said wryly, looking Rion straight in the eye and walking backwards towards the door. 'Nothing melts hearts like a reunion story.'

Libby hadn't used his surname for five years; hadn't called herself his wife for just as long. If the look of shock on the receptionist's face was anything to go by, Rion hadn't mentioned her existence either. Yet it seemed his instruction to send her up immediately was proof enough that she was telling the truth, for within seconds the receptionist had become politeness personified—even explaining in detail how Libby could get to his office on the top floor via the stairs when she mentioned she'd rather not use the lift.

As she ascended the stairs, Libby ignored the doubts churning in her stomach and told herself to get a grip. What they'd had once was already lost, the emotional side of it dealt with long ago. This was just a formality, bound to be nothing more than a slightly awkward but amicable exchange between two people who were virtual strangers to one another now, she tried to convince herself. Maybe when it was over she'd even feel the complete sense of freedom she'd always been searching for but had never quite found. She clung to that thought as she arrived on the top floor, passed through a landing area, and then proceeded along a corridor to knock on a large mahogany door emblazoned with his name.

'Come in.'

Yes, in theory the emotional side *should* have been dealt with long ago, but the instant she saw him Libby knew that she had been seriously mistaken.

Of course she was well aware that Orion Delikaris was the most desirable man on the planet. She hadn't expected that to have changed. But she had expected that age and wealth would have altered him at least fractionally. Instead, to her horror, save for the fact that his suit now looked ludicrously expensive, everything was exactly as she remembered. His strong, proud jaw, his resplendent dark hair, those liquid brown eyes that had fuelled her teenage fantasies and shaped her adult ones. Which had gazed right back at her on their wedding day, their wedding night.

She blinked, blocking out the memories, blocking out the urge to run again—away from feelings she shouldn't be feeling any more. 'Hello, Rion,' she managed, somehow.

Rion ran his eyes over her, frustrated to find that the action induced the most powerful kick of arousal he'd felt in years. But he knew it was only because his body still saw her as the woman who'd rejected him, was just responding the way it did to any challenge. The second she started begging him to take her back his desire would evaporate. And yet it annoyed him that she should still get to him that way—especially when she looked so…different. The thick blond hair which had once hung in a silken curtain down her back was gone, now cut short in the kind of style he usually considered unfeminine, but which somehow made her features look even more delicate. Her petite, pale figure, which had once driven him to distraction, had also disappeared, but in its place was an even more enticing mass of toned, sensual curves tanned to a beguiling shade of golden-brown.

He gritted his teeth. Which suggested she spent her life on holiday. That would be about right: Caribbean beaches and designer shops, no doubt funded by her parents. Though somehow that image didn't seem to fit with the clothes she was dressed in. Perhaps Ashworth Motors had fallen on hard times. A perverse part of him hoped that it had. It would make telling her no—after she'd been of use to him, of course—all the sweeter.

'So tell me,' he said, unable to fathom her delay if that was the case, 'what took you so long?'

Libby was taken aback by his question, by his implacable expression that bordered on hostile, but she told herself it was understandable. She, for all the good it had done her, had at least been able to prepare herself mentally for seeing him again. He'd had no such luxury.

'I took the stairs,' she answered, looking up at the clock on the wall and noting that she'd only been five minutes. She was about to shoot out *You know I don't do lifts,* but then she remembered that he didn't know, that he'd really known so little about her, and she about him.

And they knew even less about each other now,

which was why not doing this was ludicrous. 'I apologise if this isn't a good time.'

He gave a wry smile. 'On the contrary, now is the perfect time—but that wasn't what I meant. I've been expecting you for years, Liberty.'

Libby wanted to correct him, to tell him she never let anyone call her that any more, but the revelation that he'd been expecting her, that he obviously agreed this was the right thing to be doing, was so welcome that she let it pass.

'You mean you *have* been trying to contact me? I'm sorry. I did wonder if you had, but I've been overseas almost permanently. Bank statements from three years ago are only just starting to catch up with me.'

'If I had wanted to find you I would not have failed.'

But he hadn't wanted to find her. What would have been the sense, when he'd always known she would come crawling back once he'd made it, that he would have his chance to turn the tables—make the humiliation hers instead of his? Yes, it had been far too long coming, but he wouldn't have denied himself this moment for anything—would have waited fifty years if that was what it had taken.

Libby frowned.

'I rather expected you to come back the first time my name appeared on the International Rich List. Or have you been waiting for me to reach the top ten?'

Her relief evaporated. He thought her coming here had to do with money? She stared back at him in disbelief, and in that instant she realised her initial appraisal had been wrong. He had changed. Grown harder, more cynical. Perhaps she ought to be relieved that he was the stranger to her she'd imagined after all. Instead she just felt sad. 'I don't read things like that. I never did.'

He gestured around his enormous office, to the roof-top garden adjacent and the incredible view of the Acropolis, and raised his eyebrow cynically. 'You mean you weren't aware that my circumstances have changed?'

'Of course. But that has nothing to do with why I'm here.'

Rion gave a disparaging laugh. So in many ways she was the same old Liberty Ashworth. Still intent on denying that money mattered to her. That explained her nomadic-looking clothes, at least. They were obviously just part of her plan to convince him she didn't care about material things any more.

'So, if not because of my change of circumstances, why *have* you returned?' he drawled, deciding to humour her.

Libby took a deep breath, aware that the moment had come. 'I'm here because it's been five years, and we should have sorted this out a long time ago,' she said softly, opening her bag and sliding a sheaf of papers across the table.

Rion didn't register what she was saying at first. He was too busy watching her face, the flush of colour that had risen in her cheeks at the sight of him, guessing how long she was going to keep up the act. But when he realised she was waiting for him to respond he dropped his eyes to the table—and that was when he saw it.

Libby felt a plunging sense of guilt as she watched his eyes widen in horror, guilt, and disbelief in equal measure. Surely he couldn't really be that surprised?

Petition for Divorce.

Rion stared down at the words, reeling inwardly in both shock and fury. But the shock was only momentary. It was obvious, really. Despite all he'd achieved, the millions he'd earned, he still lacked the right pedigree for the daughter of Lord and Lady Ashworth, didn't he?

'Of course,' he said bitterly.

Libby swallowed down the lump in her throat. 'Then you agree that getting this paperwork sorted is long overdue?'

He closed his eyes and drew in a deep breath, anger and agony warring in his chest. When he'd imagined the moment of her return it had never been like this.

But the second he realised that anger was starting to win out he forced his eyes open. He would *not* allow himself to feel that pain—not a second time. So she wanted a divorce? So what? He wanted one too. The only reason he hadn't had it finalised already was because he'd been waiting for the chance to savour his revenge. And who was to say this wasn't that chance anyway? Fate, he'd come to understand, worked in mysterious ways.

He looked up at her face. The flush of colour in her cheeks was bordering on crimson. She might not want to return as his wife, but it was obvious she did want his body as much as she always had, as much as he still wanted hers—whether he liked it or not. Maybe reminding her that she would never stop desiring him, however low her opinion of him remained, would be even more satisfying. Not to mention useful.

A slow smile spread across his lips. He didn't need her good opinion. He needed his wife by his side for the duration of his campaign, and he wanted her back in his bed one final time. *Then* he could discard her, exactly as she had discarded him—with a bit of luck at the exact moment he'd proved to her that her physical desire for him went deeper than any class divide.

'No, *gineka mou,*' he said deliberately, curling his tongue deliberately around the Greek for *my wife.* 'I'm sorry to disappoint you, but I don't agree.'

The hint of menace in his voice started a pulse of trepidation behind her ribcage, but she refused to accept that its presence was justified. He was just worried about getting stung financially. 'Please, have it checked out by your lawyers, if you wish. They'll confirm I'm not asking you for anything.'

'Nor would you get anything if you were,' he replied, his tone so cold that it felt as if someone had dropped an ice cube down her back, demolishing every last hope of being able to discuss this amicably as it fell.

'So enlighten me,' he continued, wondering if she actually possessed the gall to come out and say it. 'If not for money, why *do* you want to get divorced from me so badly?'

'Because it's ridiculous not to,' she justified. 'Legally we're each other's next of kin, but we don't even know each other's phone numbers any more. When I fill in a form I still have to tick the "married" box, even though I haven't seen you for half a decade. It's a lie.'

Rion looked at her intensely. 'It wasn't once.'

No, Libby thought bleakly, shocked that he'd brought emotions into it, and had managed to do so with just three small words. *It wasn't once.* A montage of images flashed through her mind: Athens under an unexpected foot of February snow, falling like nature's cold confetti. Tucking her hired wedding dress into her Wellington boots. Coercing two frozen passers-by to witness their simple ceremony in the town hall in exchange for the promise of hot chocolate. Their wedding day had been the first day in her life which *hadn't* felt like a lie.

'No,' she admitted, trying to keep her voice level, 'it wasn't once. But it is now. It's been five years.'

'Indeed it has. Five years in which you could have come asking for this, but didn't. So why now?'

She shrugged self-consciously, his words forcing her to ask herself the same question. Why *had* she waited so long? Because all this time she'd been hoping…? *No,* she'd always known they could never go back.

'I always supposed you'd get in touch about it. Then I was too busy abroad to worry, but when my job required me to come to Athens it seemed crazy not to take the opportunity to sort things out amicably, in person.'

'You think that there is an *amicable* way of divorcing your Greek husband?' He shook his head. 'Then you do not know very much about Greek men, *gineka mou.*'

'I presumed that as a Greek you were a man of

logic—able to see that there is no sense in remaining married when what was once between us has been over for half a decade.'

'If that was the case, then I would,' he breathed, and to Libby it felt as though the temperature in the room had dropped to sub-zero. 'But it's not. You still want me. I can see it. You always have, from the moment you laid eyes on me.' He took a step towards her. 'And even though you ran thousands of miles away from me, you still want me—don't you?'

Libby felt her face flush instantly crimson. 'Even if that were true, sexual attraction is no reason to stay married.' Especially sexual attraction which had been one-sided from the moment they'd said their vows, she thought wretchedly, knowing he was just trying to find ways to talk her out of it because he thought he needed to protect his bank balance.

'It's a reason that's a hell of a lot more substantial than the ones you've given me for getting divorced.'

Libby frantically searched her mind. 'That's not true. There are plenty of other reasons why getting a divorce is the most logical thing to do. I mean… maybe…maybe you'll want to marry someone else in the future.' The thought made her feel physically sick, but she ploughed on. 'Maybe I'll want to marry someone else too.' She couldn't imagine it ever being true right now, but at least it might convince him it was time they both moved on, that she had no financial motive.

'So finally we get to why you are really here,' he

breathed. 'Who is it? Let me guess. An earl perhaps? A duke?'

Libby took a sharp breath, not anticipating that he'd jump to the conclusion that she meant she was with someone *now,* but at the same time noticing the way his hand had moved back towards the divorce papers, as if he was finally starting to see sense.

'Does it matter?' she goaded.

Rion gritted his teeth in frustration, imagining some effeminate member of the English aristocracy with his hands all over her perfect body. He'd always forbidden himself to think about it in the intervening years, but he'd known her sexual betrayal was likely, for she'd been the most responsive lover he'd ever had. So responsive that at times he'd found it near impossible to show her the kind of restraint he'd thought she'd deserved. Which she never had, he thought grimly, his desire doubling at the thought of taking her with the full force of his need, proving that, even though he'd never be good enough in her eyes, no one else would ever turn her on the way he did.

'Since *I'm* your husband, I don't suppose it does matter who he is,' he said, moving his hand away from the table again.

Libby shook her head despairingly. When had he got so cold?

'But what possible advantage is there to remaining married? For the last five years I've been on the other side of the world.'

'You're not on the other side of the world any more.'

She shook her head exasperatedly, deciding to call his bluff. 'So what are you saying, that instead of signing this divorce paper you want me to back as your wife for real?'

'Yes, *gineka mou*. That's precisely what I'm saying.'

CHAPTER TWO

'YOU can't be serious,' she stammered.

'I'm perfectly serious.'

Libby stared at him in disbelief. How many times had she dreamed of hearing him say that? Dreamed that all this time he'd never forgotten her the way she'd never forgotten him, that now that they were both older, had had the time to find themselves, they could find one another again? More times than she wanted to admit.

It was the deeply buried part of her heart responsible for those dreams which wanted to believe they were coming true now, but her head knew that was not what was happening. Because she didn't see before her a man who wanted to get to know her again, who was looking at her with hope. She saw a man who was afraid that she was after his fortune, who was prepared to do anything to protect it.

She took a shaky step in the direction of the door. 'I shouldn't have come here. I'll instruct my solicitor to be in touch. Perhaps when *he* tells you that I want nothing from you, you'll believe it.'

He took a step towards her. 'You aren't curious to find out whether the sex between us is as good now as it was then?'

Libby's breath caught in her throat. She could smell the distinctive scent of him, which she'd always thought would sell by the ton if it could be bottled. But there was no way it could be, because it didn't contain any tangible ingredients. It was the smell of pure male heat, energy, virility, as potent as the first taste of mint on the tongue. It was overlaid with some expensive aftershave now, but she felt in danger of bursting into flames before she even got a whiff of that. And maybe she would have, if not for the cold douse of remembrance that she had never made him feel anything other than lukewarm in return.

'Come on, Rion, don't pretend I satisfied you in the bedroom any more than I satisfied you in any other area once we were married.'

He stared at her, almost unsure that he'd heard her correctly. Didn't she know that even now he was fighting to stop himself from lying her back against the desk and making her his in the most basic way there was? That, despite how far he'd come, she alone seemed to possess the unwelcome ability to remind him how unrefined he truly was?

'You think I'm *pretending*? Then stay. I can assure you I will take great pleasure in convincing you that I'm not.'

Libby shook her head. He was just trying to use her weakness for him against her. 'You can drop the act, Rion. I know you're only afraid that I'm after your money.'

'Oh, I am, am I?' He raised his eyebrows. 'Or do I just want to give our marriage a second chance?'

Libby swallowed hard, felt her heart begin to pound, felt it echo at her temples, 'No…I know you don't.'

'Well, if you're so sure then I guess this is it,' he said, his eyes never leaving hers as he swiftly slid the divorce papers back across the table towards her. 'But I don't doubt we'll be seeing plenty of each other in court. If you still intend to proceed, that is?'

'I—'

'You really ought to think very carefully about exactly what you want,' he cautioned, as he reached for a slip of paper from the inside drawer of his desk and scribbled down an address. 'I'm travelling to Metameikos on business tomorrow afternoon. Should you wish to join me, we leave from this airstrip at four.'

She did a double-take. 'Sorry?'

'I'm travelling to Metameikos tomorrow,' he repeated, handing her the slip of paper. 'Come with me and let me spend the next two weeks showing you why getting divorced isn't in the least bit logical. If I fail, then at the end I will sign.'

Libby's mouth dropped open in shock.

She'd been sure he'd only suggested trying again to protect his bank balance. But now…

'Even if… I can't—I'm supposed to be working out some potential new tours for next season before my first group arrives,' she stuttered.

Rion frowned. 'Tours?'

'It's my job,' she said, realising she'd never explained

what had brought her to Athens in the first place. 'I work for a company called Kate's Escapes.'

So she was working, he thought in surprise. In the tourist industry. That explained the tan, but not why. Surely Ashworth Motors *had* to have fallen on hard times. 'So come to Metameikos.' He shrugged. 'Work out a potential tour there. The scenery is the most beautiful in all of Greece.'

Libby's eyes widened even further.

'I...I—'

'Shouldn't make an impetuous decision, *gineka mou,*' he finished for her, striding forward and pinning back the door. 'Think about it. You have until tomorrow to decide.'

And with that he ushered her out of the door and closed it behind her.

Outside his office, Libby stood rooted to the spot, not sure she was capable of the neurological function required to make it down the stairs.

He'd said he wanted to see whether they could make their marriage work. Even more astounding than that, he'd asked her to go away with him, to work alongside him, in Metameikos.

They weren't the kind of statements that sounded particularly momentous. They didn't offer an answer to world peace or hint at a cure for some deadly disease. But to Libby they stopped her world on its axis and started it rotating in the opposite direction from the one in which it had been spinning for the last five years.

Because it showed her that he might be ready for

marriage now, in a way that neither of them had been before.

For never, in the three months they had spent together as husband and wife, had he seemed to want to spend time with her or share his work with her, and he'd only ever discouraged her from working. Nor had he ever really spoken of Metameikos, never mind suggested he had attachment enough to return to the place where he'd grown up.

Libby leaned back against the door, her memories surfacing like lava in a volcano disturbed.

No, from the day they'd arrived in Athens, his focus had always been on leaving the past behind him and making it on his own. And whilst she'd been delighted to escape her tyrannical father and leave her past behind too, she'd arrived with a head full of dreams. Dreams about living a life which didn't revolve around money and status, but love and freedom. But they'd barely finished saying their vows when he'd thrown himself into working eighteen-hour days. She'd virtually never seen him, and on the rare occasions when she had, all he'd done was talk about moving to a bigger apartment, putting money down on a house, finding an investor in his business idea.

At first Libby had admired his diligence. She knew very little about his childhood, but what she did know was that, unlike her, he'd grown up with nothing, on the poor side of Metameikos. It was understandable that getting another decent job was important to him— especially after the way her father had treated him— and she knew they couldn't survive on their wits alone.

But as he'd come home later and later every day, she'd found his obsession harder and harder and harder to cope with. Because she had known that simply working eight-hour days earned him enough to cover the rent and the bills, so why did he feel the need to work any more? If he loved her, wasn't spending his evenings and his weekends with her worth more than overtime pay?

It hadn't seemed to be. And as the weeks had passed she'd begun to wonder if he had ever really loved her at all. Because not only had it appeared to fail to cross his mind that a life spent isolated and alone, wondering if and when he was going to come home from work, was nothing like the life she'd imagined when she'd married him, but he hadn't even really talked to her about his job either—hadn't involved her in the very thing that had determined the course of her days. The same way it had been with her father and Ashworth Motors. Perhaps she could have dealt with that if they'd shared other things, but he'd never seemed to have time for anything else—save for lovemaking, late at night, when he came home. But he'd only ever seemed disappointed in that.

And eventually she'd had to admit to herself that she was disappointed with their marriage too. Yes, in marrying him she'd escaped the physical restrictions her father had placed on her, avoided marrying a suitor of his choosing, but being Mrs Delikaris hadn't really felt much different from being Miss Ashworth. She'd felt no more in control of her own life than she had before. What had happened to her chance to just be Libby?

It had disappeared, she had finally admitted to herself one day, three months after their wedding. And unless she did something about it, their marriage was going to destroy her.

He had been tying his tie in the bedroom the following morning, when she'd finally plucked up the courage. 'Rion, before you leave for work again there's something I want to talk to you about.'

'Oh?'

She took a deep breath. 'I've decided to apply for a job at the language school down the road.'

It wasn't going to solve all her problems, but it might be a start. She'd wanted to get a job ever since they'd arrived, for herself as well as to help out with paying the bills, but he'd told her it wasn't necessary. She realised now she should have fought harder.

'They're looking for native English-speakers to help with classes,' she continued, 'and I thought an extra bit of cash coming in might mean you needn't spend so much time working.'

He shook his head. 'I told you before, it's not necessary for you to get a job.'

She sucked in a frustrated breath. Couldn't he see that she *needed* a life of her own? 'But I want to. I'll be able to learn Greek whilst I'm there and—'

'I promised you a private tutor.' He looked pained. 'And you will have one—just as soon as I secure an investment.'

'But I don't want to wait that long. I can't even greet the neighbours!'

Rion's face contorted. 'I can assure you it won't be *that* long.'

She shook her head. 'Even so, it isn't just that. I want to go to a class, to meet other people.' Her shoulders dropped. 'When you're at work I just feel so…lonely.'

Rion blinked up at her. 'I am more than willing to have a child, if that is what you mean.'

Libby's eyes widened in disbelief. She'd always dreamed of having a family of her own one day, but not before she'd had the chance to really live herself, and certainly not now, when he was only suggesting having a baby as a solution to a problem.

A problem he didn't even understand. And was it really any wonder? No, she realised, feeling her heart rupture, he couldn't, because the truth was he didn't even know her. They'd married so hastily that she'd hadn't even had the time and space to get to know herself.

And in that instant Libby suddenly saw, as if a bolt of lightning had forked down from the sky and illuminated everything, that as long as she remained here she never would. That even if she stayed and fought and fought she would never really gain control of her own life. No, there was only one way to do that.

She shook her head. 'No, Rion, a child isn't what I want. I want—' She dropped her eyelids and took a deep breath. 'I don't know exactly what I want, but I know it isn't this. I…I don't want to stay here.'

And that was the moment she discovered for sure that she *was* just as big a disappointment to him as he had been to her.

Rion grimaced. 'Then go. I think we both know it's been on the cards from the start.'

Libby drew in a ragged breath, forcing her eyes open and blinking under the bright artificial lights of the corridor outside his office, remembering the twin feelings of both heartbreak and release as she'd walked away. She couldn't have gone on living that way. She had needed time to find herself, to take control of her life.

But now she had. And he was implying that he had too.

What was more, though it seemed so much *had* changed, her physical reaction to him most definitely hadn't. She breathed out deeply, listening to the sound of her heart, still racing. In a way that shocked her most of all, and to her shame it was undoubtedly the hardest thing to fight. Because she'd been convinced she'd never felt anything like it in the intervening years for the simple reason that she was no longer a young girl in the throes of her first love affair. The reality, it seemed, was that there was just no other man on earth who could make her whole body go into meltdown quite the same way that he did. Just by looking at her.

And, whilst she knew that instructing a solicitor to proceed with the divorce the hard way was the logical thing to do, she couldn't help it—her body longed for her to say yes. And so did her heart, because, no, they didn't know each other now, but what if they got to know one another and rediscovered what they'd once had before all that? Then divorcing him would be a huge mistake. So shouldn't she seize the chance to find out whether they could recapture it, even if the odds were minuscule and—?

Suddenly the ground gave way from under her, and she felt herself stumble backwards into hard, compacted muscle. As her mind played catch-up amongst the shock of lost footing and the treacherous thrill of arousal, she realised that to her enormous embarrassment Rion had just opened his office door. The one she'd been leaning against, with all of her weight. She leapt out of his arms, cheeks burning.

'I was just…' Libby exhaled, her mind completely blank. But then what excuse *was* there for being so utterly stupid as to remain leaning up against his door?

'Oh, no need to explain,' he said, his mouth quirking into a smile as he walked past her, his hands briefly brushing her sides as if to steady her. 'Happens all the time.'

He hit the button for the lift and the doors opened immediately. He gestured for her to join him, but she shook her head frantically.

'Until tomorrow, then,' he said with a grin.

And before Libby had time to protest that she still had twenty-four hours in which to decide, and that taking a breather before going downstairs didn't mean anything, the doors of the lift had already closed.

Which wouldn't have been half so frustrating if they hadn't both known he was right.

CHAPTER THREE

SHE'D had a whole sleepless night and the clarity of a morning in which to talk herself out if of it, but at three-thirty the following afternoon Libby found herself and her well-worn suitcase in a taxi on her way to the airstrip.

And she even seemed to be managing to sit still. For, although there was a part of her that *was* tempted to tell the driver to turn around and go as fast as he could in the opposite direction—the part which believed Rion had been far too cold in his office for this to end in anything other than heartache—over the course of the last twenty-four hours the rest of her had decided that going with Rion wasn't just following her heart and her hormones, it was logical.

Because unless she went with him she'd never fully be able to move on, and that had been half the point of her seeking to finalise their separation in the first place. The logic was the same as if she'd been handed a lottery ticket. She'd know the chances of it containing the winning numbers were tiny, but until she checked she'd never know, and every day she'd wake up with a voice whispering *what if?* in her ear.

Not that if they had an actual lottery ticket it would matter to Rion whether it bore the lucky numbers or not, Libby thought ruefully as they drove alongside a hangar and a sparkling white plane bearing the striking Delikaris Experiences logo taxied round in a semi-circle and stopped in front of them. Because she was fast coming to realise that in their years apart his obsession with personal success had taken on gargantuan proportions.

Which suggested that the more she got to know him, the more she'd discover that they were incompatible. It was obvious that he cared about nothing other than money if he had earned so much in five years, and, what was more, he'd clearly chosen to spend it on flashy possessions like his own private jet. If *she* had that volume of cash she'd head straight back out to Africa and do some good with it. She shook her head as she stepped out onto the tarmac. She'd once thought Rion was the antithesis of her father, but now she had to wonder if they'd been two sides of the same coin all along.

But it seemed owning a plane was not enough for Rion, Libby acknowledged ruefully as she looked up and saw that he was also piloting it. She watched with a dry mouth as he disappeared from the cockpit and re-appeared at the top of the steps, looking devastatingly sexy in a pair of dark aviator glasses and a casual white shirt with the cuffs rolled back, revealing his tanned forearms. Instinctively she reached up to undo the top button of her cotton blouse, feeling constricted.

'The thought of being back in my company making you hot under the collar already, *gineka mou*?' he asked dryly as he descended the steps to the satisfying sight of her waiting for him.

For a second inside his office—when she'd implied she had a titled lover waiting in the wings to marry her—there had been a small part of him which had wondered whether the combination of her desire for him, the promise of a private jet and the threat of lengthy court proceedings was enough to persuade her. But then he'd found her lingering outside, had felt her whole body ignite when she'd fallen against him, and he'd known for sure.

'I'm glad,' he added, 'but I'm afraid you will have to hold that thought. Although my autopilot mode is exceptionally sophisticated, I'm not sure it would be wise to join you in the cabin for the length of time I intend to spend making love to you.'

A shiver of pleasure rippled through her, but as soon as Libby clocked her automatic response she stopped it in its tracks, suddenly afraid. Daring to hope that he was serious about giving their marriage a second chance was one thing, but starting to believe he felt anything other than lukewarm in her presence was a different delusion altogether—a dangerous one. And suddenly she foresaw how easily he could trample all over her heart if she went into this with rose-tinted glasses on.

No, she was safest going into this from the standpoint that remaining married was irrational and that he was no more excited by her now than he had been during the months of their marriage. If he presented her with actual evidence to the contrary—well, that would be the time to re-evaluate her views.

'What's wrong with the cockpit?' she challenged audaciously.

Rion's eyes flared in shock. So, the innocent young girl he'd married was long gone, and in her place was an experienced adulteress, who only yesterday had been claiming she needed the divorce to move on with another man, and was now suggesting they make love at the earliest opportunity. To his infinite frustration his disgust was accompanied by the overwhelming urge to take her right here on the tarmac, and an erection so hard it was painful.

And it made him furious—because it seemed that no matter how *she* behaved, she still reminded him of *his* lack of refinement. She always had. He drew in a ragged breath. But at least he'd feel no shame taking her back to his house in Metameikos, no shame in flying her there on his plane. Unlike five years ago, after their pitiful wedding, when he'd been forced to take her on the bus back to that shabby rented apartment. He smarted in distaste. From the second he'd opened the front door of that place—the only one in Athens he'd been able to afford—all the self-belief that maybe he could be good enough for her had evaporated. He'd never felt more ashamed of who he was in his life.

And he knew she'd never felt more ashamed of him—she'd been so desperate to escape it, her lack of faith in him so unequivocal, that she'd even volunteered to work. But even though he'd done everything he could so that she didn't have to, even though he'd avoided involving her in the sordid details of his pathetic day job, worked every hour there was to try and save for their own place—a place she could be proud of—it had never been enough.

And it never will be, a voice inside him taunted, *even though you fought so hard for all this because you believed if you succeeded she'd come crawling back.*

No—that was a lie. That hadn't been the reason. His determination might have doubled the day she left, but he'd succeeded for himself, and for Jason, his brother.

He turned away from her, his voice terse. 'You will be travelling in the cabin.'

There wasn't any evidence to the contrary then, Libby acknowledged with ridiculous disappointment. She really didn't excite him. And the sooner he admitted it, the sooner she could silence the *what ifs*? She ducked down, pretending to look for another pair of legs on the opposite side of the plane. 'Because you have a co-pilot joining you up front?'

'No. I fly alone.'

She walked towards the steps defiantly. 'Then there is no reason why I shouldn't join you, is there?'

It was only when he'd followed her in and sat down beside her that she realised in fighting so hard to prove that he didn't really want her she'd just inadvertently guaranteed their close proximity for the duration of the flight.

'How long will it take us to get to Metameikos?' she asked hesitantly.

'Just under an hour.'

No time at all, she thought, trying to feel relieved as he hit the starter switch and took the controls. But they hadn't even taken off yet, and she was already transfixed by the sight of his long-fingered hands manoeuvring the complex equipment, unable to prevent herself remembering how they had once felt against her bare skin.

God, why did looking at him keep making her think about sex?

She moved awkwardly in her seat and tried to think of a logical answer. Maybe it was because he'd been the object of her first teenage crush, and somehow that made him the blueprint for the kind of man she found attractive. But, whilst his dark Mediterranean looks had been a novelty to her at fifteen, she'd met plenty of men since who fitted that description. The language teacher at the night classes she'd enrolled in as her first act of freedom once she'd arrived back in England; one or two of the other tour guides that Kate—whom she'd met at those language classes—had introduced her to when she'd expressed her enthusiasm for travel; the multitude of men she'd inevitably met the world over once she'd started filling in. But none of them had made her feel this irrepressible physical *hunger*.

Or maybe it was just that he was the only man she'd ever made love with, and like Pavlov's dogs, who had salivated when they heard bells ringing because they had come to associate that sound with food, her body had connected the sight of him and the smell of him with sex. Yes, that was probably it. She just needed to uncondition her response, to associate him with something negative instead—the way he'd become so obsessed with money, perhaps. She took a deep breath, relieved to have alighted on a course of action that would bring about an end to it.

'So, when did you learn to fly?' she asked, deciding to lead the conversation down the 'needless luxury' route.

'Years ago, for research. Flying lessons were one of the first gift experiences I decided to market, along with luxury driving days,' he answered, handing her some headphones as they approached the runway.

It was genius, Libby realised, for the first time contemplating *how* he'd made his money. He'd recognised other people's dreams and found a way of offering them neatly packaged in a box. But then that had always been what he did best—it was what had once persuaded her father to promote him from valet to salesman to showroom manager. He'd always known exactly which element of an Ashworth motor to push, depending on the customer and their body language. Speed and performance for men on the brink of a mid-life crisis; style and sex-appeal for the computer geek who'd just earned his first million; an investment opportunity for the retired banker and safety features for his anxious wife.

But did his customers ever really get everything they'd dreamed of? Or was the reality quite different? Libby thought bleakly, unable to help making a comparison with their marriage as they took off.

Marrying Rion had been her dream from the very first day she'd seen him—when she'd taken her father some papers he'd forgotten and caught Rion looking up at her from the 1964 Ashworth Elite he'd been polishing with those devastating liquid brown eyes. She'd been so infatuated that it hadn't occurred to her that neither of them were ready for marriage, full-stop.

And it was no wonder she had felt that way really, she thought as they soared above Athens, the Parthenon shrinking to the size of a hotel on a Monopoly board below them. Because not only had he looked so different from the suitors her father had kept forcing her to meet, but when the furtive looks between them had eventually turned to snatched conversation on the days when her father was off-site, she'd discovered he *was* different. So unpretentious, and so exciting. He hadn't spent their conversations praising her father or calculating the acreage of the Ashworth estate; he'd talked to her about the travel books she liked to read, about the customs in Greece—which had seemed the most exotic place in the world to Libby, who'd never left Surrey, and whose long, monotonous days had been spent walled up inside Ashworth Manor and its grounds.

Libby felt a tightness around her wrists and her ankles at the memory of how her father had deemed even a walk to the village shops too much autonomy, even in her late teens. How her mother, plagued by the guilt her husband had made her feel for never producing a son, had enforced every rule he created.

And so her conversations with Rion had become a ritual, however infrequent, which she'd survived on for the duration of her teenage years. And though the details they'd actually shared with one another during those conversations had been sparse—he'd rarely spoken about his childhood, and never mentioned any family other than his mother, who'd brought him to England when he was in his early teens—at the time she'd only seen that lack of information as a positive. He'd obviously had no wish to discuss what must have been a difficult period in his life, and she had understood that, because she'd had no wish to talk about her childhood either.

The whole appeal of their conversations had been that they'd offered an escape from that—a freshly created world where nothing that had gone before mattered. And, although she'd never really been able to see a way in which marriage to him might be possible, nor imagine exactly how it might be if it was, she hadn't stopped dreaming about living in that world all the time.

Until one January day, not long after her nineteenth birthday, when she'd passed the showroom accidentally-on-purpose and found him actually waiting for her. He'd had a smile on his face so uncontainable that remembering it made her heart flip over even now.

'Rion, what is it?'

'Your father—he's promoted me. I'm going to be the showroom manager.'

'That's fantastic!' She beamed and threw her arms out, but just stopped short of embracing him, suddenly afraid that she might have imagined the significance of their conversations. Until he reached out and took her hands in his for the first time, and looked her straight in the eye.

'It means that I'm going to be on a really decent salary.'

She nodded enthusiastically, her hands shaking.

He took a deep breath. 'There's something I want to ask you. That I've wanted to ask you for a long time. Before I didn't think…but now…'

Libby's heart rose ten inches in her chest.

She heard his breath come thick and fast, his voice shaky. 'Would you consider marrying me, Liberty Ashworth?'

Her arms didn't hesitate this time. She threw them round him, and then he kissed her. The first and most magical kiss of her entire life.

'I know that technically I'm supposed to ask your father first, but—'

'No…this is perfect,' she breathed—because it was. The choice of who she married was hers, not anybody else's, and it meant the world to her that he understood that.

But her father didn't agree. When they went to ask for his blessing Thomas Ashworth fired Rion on the spot for his impudence.

'I have promoted you from valet to showroom manager in four short years and that is still not enough for you? How dare you consider yourself worthy enough to even *look* at my daughter? I try to nurture your talent for selling and this is how you repay me?' he spat. And then he made it clear to Libby that if she even tried to contact Orion again, he would banish her from the Ashworth family completely.

Her father had meant is as a threat, of course, but to Libby it had simply acted as an incentive. To swap her life of oppression for one of freedom. But it hadn't been until she and Rion had eloped to Athens that she'd realised she'd been utterly naïve to suppose they could go on living in that imaginary world, that marriage to anyone could have given her the autonomy she'd so desperately needed.

Libby drew in a ragged breath as the view from the aircraft window became more rural, and ran her hand through the short length of her hair, frustrated that she'd recalled the past in such damned fine detail again. But then she'd always had remarkable powers of recollection. It was a blessing in her job—that she remembered every travel guide she'd ever read was what had convinced Kate to take her on in the first place, when her practical experience had been non-existent—but it felt like a curse now.

'So, what business do you have in Metameikos?' she said loudly above the noise of the plane, determined to distract herself from remembering any more.

She saw the edge of his lip curl in amusement. 'For a minute there I thought the cat had got your tongue.' He paused over the English phrase, as if it amused him to remember one so fitting. 'What were you thinking about?'

'Nothing in particular.'

'No? I could have sworn you were looking at my hands, remembering how it felt to have them touch you.'

Colour flooded her cheeks. 'So you're a mind-reader *and* a pilot? Is there no end to the talents you've acquired in the last five years?'

'I wasn't reading your mind, *gineka mou*, I was reading your body.'

All too aware that he was an expert at that, Libby reverted to her original choice of subject. 'So, what business *do* you have in Metameikos?'

'I have some meetings to attend, some functions at which I need to make an appearance. Plus there are some things I need to sort out at my property before I settle there permanently.'

Libby was so surprised by this information that she let the frankly detailless description of his business go unchallenged. He'd barely mentioned Metameikos in the past, let alone expressed any desire to return there permanently.

'You are making Metameikos your home? I always presumed it didn't mean that much to you.'

Rion's lips barely moved. 'It's a business decision.'

'But your main offices are in Athens, aren't they?'

'Indeed.'

Libby frowned. That he'd as good as stated he had no emotional attachment to the place came as no surprise to her—especially now that it appeared he had no emotional attachment to anything other than money—but then why move there? She didn't know a great deal about Metameikos, compared with her detailed knowledge of many other parts of the world, but she did know that it was no Athens when it came to its business credentials. What she *could* recall was that it was Greece's only independent province and that it was pretty much divided in two—one half being one of the poorest areas of the whole country, where she knew Rion had grown up, whilst the other was full of luxury holiday homes belonging to the very wealthy. If she remembered correctly, it was best known for a well-preserved ancient amphitheatre somewhere in the middle. There were no prizes for guessing which side they were heading to now, but why he planned on staying there permanently was a mystery.

'I hope to have an office in Metameikos too, soon.'

Libby nodded, but remained unconvinced. She supposed if he was branching out into all aspects of the leisure industry then the location was a desirable one for watersports and the like, but it still puzzled her. Maybe it was some kind of tax haven. 'Your meetings these next couple of weeks are related to that, then?'

'Indirectly,' he replied vaguely. 'This evening we will attend a play at the amphitheatre there.'

'A play?' she repeated back at him in astonishment, surprised not only that his time would be spent on something other than crunching numbers, but also that he wanted her to join him.

Rion gritted his teeth. So, she thought a man like him wasn't capable of enjoying a little culture. 'How is it that you are so adamant we lay the past to rest, when it is perfectly obvious you will never forget mine?'

She frowned. 'What do you mean by that?'

'I mean that much has changed.'

'Has it?' she asked, a flicker of hope igniting in her heart as the plane touched down, his landing utterly flawless.

'Why don't you see for yourself?' he asked, inclining his head towards the extensive property spanning the horizon. 'We're here.'

CHAPTER FOUR

OF COURSE, he only meant much had changed in terms
of the kind of house he now owned and the kind of car
he now drove, Libby thought dejectedly as they headed
away from the airstrip towards the property in the
distance, in his top-of-the-range Bugatti—the only car
on the planet, if her memory served her correctly, that
was worth more than the 1958 Ashworth Liberty. The
car her father had named her after in the single greatest
irony of her life.

But, although all signs pointed towards Rion's home
being some equally extravagant and overstated villa on
the more affluent side of Metameikos, when he rolled
the car to a halt outside, she discovered to her surprise
that it was not.

It was a period house built of stone, and had two different levels with steps running between them that were
covered in terracotta pots overflowing with flowers.
There were charming wooden shutters at the windows,
and although the grounds were extensive, the house
itself wasn't oppressively huge or ostentatious in any

way. It looked like the perfect family home. What was more, if she'd ascertained things correctly during the drive here, it was situated pretty much *in between* the affluent side and the less privileged side of the province, just in front of the impressively preserved amphitheatre—which must have been the structure she had seen from the runway.

'What made you choose here?' she breathed, running her hand over the stonework, convinced he'd say he hadn't picked it out himself at all, but that when the need to relocate had arisen he'd left the selection of his accommodation up to an employee.

Rion paused for a moment, remembering how he and Jason had sat at the top of the amphitheatre, looking down at the house and the well-off family who had called it home. Owning it one day had been his only life goal then. Until Jason's death. Until she'd left him. He answered gruffly, 'As a kid, it was the house I always swore I'd own one day.'

He indicated for her to follow him in but Libby stalled on the threshold, astonished not only to discover that he *did* seem to have some attachment to Metameikos, but that for one of the first times ever he'd just given her a glimpse into his childhood.

Rion looked back over his shoulder to find her hovering on the doorstep. 'It's a little late to be having second thoughts about our arrangement now, *gineka mou.*'

'I'm not,' she said quickly, and then wished she hadn't sounded so sure about it. 'I was just admiring the house.'

And having second thoughts of a different nature, no

doubt, Rion thought cynically as she admired the décor of the hall. Like why she hadn't demanded half of everything he owned in her precious petition for divorce.

'I never expected it to be so…I don't know…'

But before she could find the right word to complete her sentence they both heard footsteps.

Rion turned and walked to the bottom of the staircase. 'Eurycleia.' He smiled warmly.

Libby looked up to see a woman who must have been in her mid-sixties descending the stairs, duster in hand.

Rion tilted his head upwards and switched into Greek. 'The house looks fantastic.' He shook his head ruefully. 'I hope you have not been working here all day.'

The old woman's eyes twinkled as she reached the second to last step, which put her on a level height with Rion. She placed her hands on the sides of his head in a motherly gesture and kissed him on the forehead. 'You know it's my pleasure. Welcome back.'

She raised her eyes then, and caught sight of Libby for the first time. 'Orion Delikaris,' she said, swiping him with the duster. 'Are you so rude that you are going to leave your guest just standing there, without even introducing us?'

Rion sighed and shook his head in an affectionate gesture which said *Well, I would have if you'd given me the chance.* 'Libby,' he said, beckoning her over, 'this is Eurycleia, my housekeeper and a dear old friend. Eurycleia, I'd like you to meet Libby…' He paused. 'My wife.'

Eurycleia's eyes widened, and then she gasped in

delight, clapped her hands together and rushed over to greet Libby with a kiss on both cheeks.

It took Libby completely by surprise. Not Eurycleia's benevolent welcome, but the way Rion had introduced her. It had been perfectly obvious in Athens that he'd never mentioned he had a wife, and she hadn't supposed he'd planned on changing that now. Because surely if word got out that he was married it would be unpleasantly public for him if it didn't work out? Unless… unless he was really that certain that it would?

Libby ignored the blood pounding in her ears at the thought. If Eurycleia was an old friend whose confidence could be trusted, it didn't count. She switched into Greek herself. 'It's a pleasure to meet you, Eurycleia.'

Rion's head shot up in surprise, but he didn't say a word.

'Beautiful *and* clever.' Eurycleia gave another delighted gasp, but before Libby could deny any such thing, Rion interrupted.

'Thank you, Eurycleia, for all you hard work. But I'm afraid Libby and I do not have long to refresh ourselves before we must attend the play this evening. Will you leave us now?'

Eurycleia looked inexplicably serious, as if he'd just announced he had to prepare to go to war. 'Of course you must. I will just collect my things and then I'll be gone.' She touched Rion's arm on her way past. 'There are some fresh honey and walnut biscuits in the kitchen, if either of you are peckish.'

'Thank you,' Rion said gratefully. 'And perhaps if

you wouldn't mind taking the next couple of weeks off—paid, of course. You'll understand, I'm sure, that Libby and I would like some time alone.'

Eurycleia looked momentarily hurt, but then nodded respectfully and began to scuttle back upstairs.

'Spend some extra time with that toy-boy of yours,' Rion chuckled after her, lightening the mood.

Eurycleia threw her hands exasperatedly in the air and turned back to Libby. 'He is three years younger than me—sixty-two!' She clicked her tongue at Rion. 'You make it sound as if he is twenty!'

Libby smiled after her, but the second Eurycleia had turned the corner at the top of the stairs she followed Rion into the open plan kitchen/living room and her face became solemn. 'I hardly think dismissing her altogether was necessary.'

Rion scowled, completely misinterpreting her meaning. 'No? You mean so long as you have someone to wait on you hand and foot you don't care whose sensibilities you might offend?'

She blinked, baffled. 'You mean if Eurycleia realises our marriage isn't what it seems?'

'No, Libby. I mean if Eurycleia walks in and finds us making love in the shower, or on the kitchen table, or sprawled out on the rug—'

Libby's heart-rate rocketed, and she fought to stop her mind from filling with all the erotic images he'd just conjured. 'Just because you are technically my husband it doesn't mean you *have* to make love to me, Rion.'

Rion searched her eyes for proof that she was just

feigning naïveté again. But he couldn't see it. He stood back and regarded her thoughtfully. Was it possible that she *really* believed he didn't want her? Yes, he realised suddenly, maybe it was. Because a man who possessed any integrity *wouldn't* want a wife who didn't think him good enough, who'd run away, who was guilty of infidelity. He gave a bitter snort of laughter. It had to be the only time she'd ever over-estimated him.

'No,' he growled, 'I *shouldn't* want you. But my body doesn't give a damn about that.'

Libby eyed him doubtfully, but before she had time to wonder if there was a strand of truth in his words he showed her, placing his hands around the small of her waist and drawing her so close to his body that she could feel the hard shaft of his erection against her belly.

'Now are you convinced?' he murmured.

Liquid heat began to pump through her veins. She forced herself to step backwards, but he hauled her against his body again, placed one long finger under her chin and tilted it upwards, forcing her to look into his eyes.

'I want you.'

No, it wasn't possible. She knew it wasn't because— Libby searched his face for the look of indifference she'd read on his face every day of their marriage, every time they'd made love.

But she couldn't see it now.

She blinked hard and searched again.

She still couldn't see it, because unless she was mistaken it wasn't there. All she could see was what looked like red-hot need.

'And I know you don't want to, but you do still want me, don't you, Libby?' he whispered raggedly, lowering his head so that his mouth was so agonisingly close she could feel the heat of his breath against her lips.

'I…' Her breath caught in her throat as he stroked the finger he had been resting beneath her chin across her shoulderblade and down the side of her body, so that the backs of his knuckles grazed the side of her breast. Her nipples tightened to unbearable peaks. 'I—'

'I'll be off, then—oh, I'm sorry.'

Libby and Rion sprung apart as Eurycleia stuck her head around the door of the living room and then beat a hasty retreat.

Rion left Libby reeling in the middle of the room and strode towards the door, utterly shameless. 'Thank you, Eurycleia. Enjoy your time off.'

'I'm sure I will.' She nodded, hurrying towards the front door with an embarrassed wave goodbye.

Rion closed the door behind her and turned back to Libby. 'Now do you see why dismissing Eurycleia is a good idea, *gineka mou?*'

Libby could feel her chest rising and falling, but her mind was too hazy with desire and disbelief to speak. Was it possible that he did really want her? She had sworn she wouldn't let herself even imagine it until she had evidence, but what had that been, if not solid proof?

Rion flicked a look down at his watch. 'Much as I would gladly finish *proving* why, I'm afraid it will have to keep another few hours,' he drawled. 'The play starts in forty-five minutes. I presume you wish to change?'

Libby looked down at her crumpled blouse, her mind racing. The play. His desire. How many other things had changed too? She nodded.

'The bathroom is the second door on the right at the top of the stairs. Be ready to leave in twenty-five minutes.'

She'd showered, changed into a gypsy-style dress, and been ready to go in even less time that that, but three-quarters of an hour later, as they settled down on the cushions and blankets which had been laid out to make the stone seats of the *theatron* more comfortable, she only wished her mind was as settled. Because now Eurycleia wasn't the only one he'd told about her. He'd just introduced her as his wife to the man who'd shown them to their seats, and to the elderly couple next to them too.

Once the play had started—an adaptation of Homer's *Odyssey* by the local drama group—and the hubbub of the audience had been replaced with tranquillity, she couldn't go on denying what that meant. She'd wanted evidence that he was for real, that he *did* want to give their marriage another shot, that recapturing what they'd once had before everything had changed might be possible. And, even though she'd thought the chances of that were minuscule, he'd given it to her. He'd given her hope.

And it was both exhilarating and terrifying. Because she wanted to open her heart to it, to revel in it, but there was still so much they didn't know about each other, so many ways they might not be compatible, and deep down she knew it was too soon, too dangerous, too easy to be seduced by the romance of it all. The sky growing dark, the stars beginning to twinkle above them. The stars of Orion's belt, which always reminded her of him no matter where in the world she was, even though until yesterday she'd been convinced that looking up at the constellation which bore his name was the closest she'd ever get to him again.

Just as it was too easy to be seduced by the way he'd placed a blanket around her shoulders and left his hand lingering there as the players re-enacted the moment at the end of Odysseus's adventures when he and his wife Penelope were reunited after many years apart.

But not until they had each tested one another and banished their doubts, Libby thought, the play's pertinence far from lost on her. If she hadn't known better, she would have sworn that it was no accident. But hadn't he been planning on coming here alone before she'd even arrived in his office yesterday? Yes, Eurycleia's reaction when he'd mentioned the play tonight had proved that he had.

It had to be a coincidence, then, or simply that the ancient epic was full of such universal truths that it resonated in one way or another with everyone, as stories that stood the test of time always did. Yes, Rion was probably sitting beside her identifying with a totally different part. Like Odysseus's need to make his journey alone, or something.

Like Odysseus's need to make his journey alone? she repeated in her mind. *Before being reunited with his wife?*

Libby stole a sideways glance at his profile. Could it be possible that *was* what he was thinking? That when they'd married he'd been too young, that what he'd needed then was the space to make his own way in the world first, just as she had? And could he be thinking that he was ready for marriage now, and that the feelings which had drawn them together in the first place had never really gone away?

Suddenly the audience broke into rapturous applause. Libby's mind had been so far away that the sound made her jump, but she quickly recomposed herself and joined in enthusiastically, afraid that if he noticed her distractedness he might start asking questions she wasn't ready to answer. Not yet.

As the actors took their bows and filed off the stage, Rion stood and led the way down the stone steps. The street outside, which had contained just a few people carrying tables when they'd arrived, was now full of stalls, selling every kind of food and drink imaginable.

'The performance is just the first part of the local *panigiria*,' he explained. 'The rest of the celebrations will go on into the early hours of the morning.' He walked up to one of the stalls, exchanged pleasantries with the old man serving, and then ordered them two small glasses of golden liquid. 'This is the local liquor, sweetened with honey. Try it.'

'Thank you.' Libby accepted the glass and took a sip. Trying local food and drink had always been one of her favourite parts of travelling. Guidebooks filled with photos had given her an idea about the way different places looked ever since she'd begun devouring them in

her childhood, but discovering how a place tasted was
something you could never know until you'd been.

'It's delicious.'

He nodded. 'Come, I'd very much like to introduce
you to someone.'

Would he? Her heart blossomed ridiculously in her
chest.

'His name is Georgios,' he said, surveying the crowd.
'He's the Mayor.'

For a moment Libby felt staggered that he should know
someone so prominent—until it occurred to her that
he was now probably the most famous resident of
Metameikos himself. But just as Rion appeared to spot
Georgios in the crowd, and moved his hand to her elbow
to guide her forward, a loud voice thundered behind them.

'Ah, Delikaris. I might have known you wouldn't
pass up *this* opportunity.'

Libby turned round to see that the voice belonged to
a large man with a balding head and an incongruously
thick moustache.

'Spyros.' Rion inclined his head civilly, but Libby
could hear the hostility in his voice. If Spyros heard it
too, he didn't take the hint.

'I'm glad to see you're making use of the stalls *I*
granted permission for this evening.' He dropped his
eyes to their glasses.

'You mean the stalls belonging to men who have traded
here every year for decades, but who now have to line *your*
pockets for the privilege?' Rion ground out bitterly.

Spyros gave an unpleasant laugh. 'For the good of the

community at large. I only grant permission to those whose produce meets health and safety standards.'

'Which all of them did before, because they don't sell anything they wouldn't feed to their own families.'

'Well, we'd all like that to be the case, but you can never be too careful these days. It's important to know exactly who you're dealing with. Talking of which…' Spyros ran his eyes lecherously over Libby. 'I don't believe we've been introduced.'

The tops of Libby's arms broke out into goose pimples and she stroked her hands over them, wishing she hadn't had to leave the blanket that Rion had placed around her shoulders in the amphitheatre.

'This is Libby,' Rion said reluctantly.

'Libby,' Spyros repeated, so lewdly that for the first time in her life she hated the shortened form of her name even more than the extended version.

He turned back to Rion. 'Decided on a change of tack, eh? Why keep your lovers behind closed doors when everyone knows you have a different one for every day of the week? Your honesty is gutsy, I'll give you that. Or is it just a sign that you've already accepted defeat?'

Libby frowned, wondering what the hell he was talking about, but her mind was too full of the nauseating image of seven scantily clad women labelled Monday through to Sunday to even hazard a guess.

'I'm afraid not—for your sake,' Rion said between gritted teeth. 'As it happens, Libby is my wife.'

To Libby's surprise, Spyros looked from her to Rion and then let out a guffaw of laughter. 'It's imaginative,

I'll give you that. But surely you don't think even this lot will fall for it?' He signalled to the crowds of people enjoying the festivities and then turned to Libby. 'So, tell me, how much does it pay, playing the part of his wife? Handsomely, I hope. Sex and politics *are* the two oldest professions in the world, after all.'

The cords in Rion's neck went taut, and he raised himself to his full height, but before he could take another step forward Libby cut in front of him. She didn't know what the hell was going on, but Spyros's condescension and disrespect was such an unpleasantly vivid reminder of her father that she couldn't remain silent.

'I'm not sure what business it is of yours, but I can assure you that we *are* married.'

Rion looked at her, and she saw something flare in his eyes. She wasn't sure whether it was pride or horror.

'Don't tell me he actually convinced you to go through with it? Do you *really* think people are stupid enough to believe that he's capable of some whirlwind romance, that overnight he's become a family man? All it screams is rashness and irresponsibility.'

'You think so?' Rion said, pretending to ponder the concept. 'Lucky, then, that Libby and I married five years ago.'

He paused to watch Spyros's face drop before continuing, 'We have been apart for a period of time, yes, but what marriage doesn't go through bad patches?' He looked critically at him. 'I'd say those that seem *not* to are the ones which invite suspicion.'

Spyros's conceited expression turned to one of pure

malevolence. 'You will not win this, Delikaris—' he twisted his head and glowered at the crowd '— You're no better than they are.'

'No, I don't believe I am,' Rion replied. 'And that's the difference between us.'

Rion fought the urge to show Spyros that wasn't the only difference between them, that if he ever insulted his wife again he would pay, but he knew that would only be living up to the creep's preconceptions. Instead he placed his hand on Libby's arm, momentarily wished he could repress his rudimentary urges with such ease when it came to her, then encouraged her forward and smiled with intentionally nauseating civility. 'Now, if you'll excuse us, we were just off to see Georgios.'

Libby watched as Spyros angrily pushed his way back through the crowd to a small, grubby-looking man and a large woman in a gaudy peacock-print dress whom she presumed must be his wife. Her nose was turned up at two young boys acting out the fight between Odysseus and the Cyclops, one with one eye tightly shut, the other brandishing a rolled-up theatre programme, creating clouds of dust.

Libby would have cheered them on if she hadn't felt as if she'd just been engulfed by a dust cloud herself. A dust cloud which, once settled, she had a horrible feeling might reveal a truth she didn't want to see. She turned her head back to face Rion, who had the audacity to be scanning the crowd for the Mayor again.

'Would you care to tell me what just happened?'

'Sorry?'

'That man—Spyros, or whatever his name is—who is he?' *And who are you?*

'He's the current leader of Metameikos,' Rion replied through gritted teeth.

As he spoke she pieced together the bits of information she'd gleaned from their conversation. 'And what? You're standing against him in some sort of election?'

As she said the words aloud, she knew she'd hit the nail on the head before he even had the chance to nod. *That* was why Eurycleia had been so reverential when he'd mentioned coming here tonight—*that* was why he wanted her to meet the Mayor—that was why—

Libby felt as if the fragile threads keeping her heart suspended in her chest had just been cut.

That was the real reason why he'd refused to sign the divorce petition and invited her here. Not because he wanted to give their marriage another shot. But because he thought that playing the family man in the local community for a couple of weeks might win him a few extra votes.

'And you just didn't think you'd bother mentioning it?' Libby exploded, almost as angry at herself for thinking he might have changed as at the concrete proof that he didn't give a damn about anyone but himself.

'Do you mind if we don't do this in front of the whole of Metameikos?' he said under his breath, steering her away from the throng of people who had started to turn around.

Libby shook him off angrily. 'Oh, no, it wouldn't do for your wife to make a scene, would it?'

'Not over nothing, no,' he said matter-of-factly, as if *she* was the one who was being unreasonable. 'This isn't a secret, it's a public election, *gineka mou*. I'm sorry if you didn't realise I was running but, given that you've been gone for five years, unfortunately there will be some things we don't know about each other.'

She raised her head to look at him, standing so righteously with the amphitheatre behind him. He looked like Alexander the Great, and in that instant she hated him. 'I don't care if there are a million things I don't know about you, Rion. I care about being lied to, about being used as an accomplice to deceive others without even knowing about it.'

He gave a sceptical laugh. 'Are you protesting for the innocent people of Metameikos, or for yourself?'

'Both.'

'Spyros is corruption personified, as his father was before him. He runs this province on lies. I hardly think I'm doing the people of Metameikos a disservice by turning up to a play with my wife.'

'You still deceived *me*. You told me you didn't want to sign the divorce papers because you wanted to see whether now there could be a second chance for us.'

He shook his head. 'Indeed—and I do. That this fortnight happens to coincide with the election is irrelevant.'

Fury almost choked her. 'Then it won't affect your plans if I leave, will it?'

'Affect my plans? Not in the least.' He smiled disparagingly. 'But I'm afraid it may affect yours, since I won't be signing the divorce papers unless you stay.'

CHAPTER FIVE

'You blackmailing bastard,' she breathed, flinging out her arms in disgust and walking back along the dusty road which led to the house.

Much as she would have liked to lead him back to the growing frivolity of the *panigiria*, so that the whole of Metameikos could hear how emotionally backward he was, she needed the open space.

'There's no need to be upset, *gineka mou*,' he said, catching up with her in two easy strides. 'The agreement was that we would spend two weeks finding out whether our marriage could work, and I still have every intention of proving to you that it can.'

Good God, the lies tripped off his tongue so easily. 'So you're just going to go on pretending that you want me because keeping me here is beneficial to your campaign?'

'Don't lecture *me* about pretending,' he growled, catching her wrist in his hand and spinning her round to face him. 'You can tell yourself whatever you want— that I don't want you, that you don't want me, that you're being faithful to this lover you've got waiting in

the wings—but we both know what's happening between us…that if we hadn't been interrupted it would
have happened already.'

He gave her no time to assemble her defences. The
instant she realised what was happening his lips were
already on hers, hungry, demanding, urgent. And, before
she could even think about whether it was wise or not,
her body had already kicked into its natural response:
to kiss him with the same intensity right back.

It *wasn't* the least bit wise, of course, but by the time
she'd reached that conclusion the voice of reason in her
mind was inaudible, obscured by the heady release of
five years of deeply buried need. Desire exploded in her
belly as he crushed her to him, as he tangled his hand
in her hair and angled her face upwards so that he could
explore her mouth even more thoroughly. And she let
it, because just for one moment she wanted to believe
that at least something about the last twenty-four hours
had been real.

For a nanosecond, as she compared the force of his
passion now with that of her memories, she actually
gave headroom to the possibility that it could be—that,
yes, he did want to rule half the world as well as owning
it, but maybe he wanted *her* too.

Yet just as that thought echoed through her mind, so
too did his words: *you can tell yourself whatever you
want…that you're being faithful to this lover you've got
waiting in the wings…* And immediately the bubble burst.

Oh, Rion wanted her, all right, but not because he'd
suddenly realised she was what he wanted. He'd carried

on believing she wanted this divorce in order to marry another man, and the thought of someone else having her was like a red rag to a bull. Not out of genuine jealousy, but because the chance to prove he could turn her on more than any other man turned *him* on. It was a challenge, another contest to be won.

Libby wrenched herself out of his embrace, the realisation like being doused with cold water.

'I have no lover,' she shot out suddenly.

She knew it was bound to invite a thousand questions, but it was the only way to eradicate this danger.

Rion eyed her skeptically, and looked down at the space she'd created between them. 'Do you think that if you start pretending he doesn't exist now, you can avoid the possibility of him finding out about this?'

Libby shook her head in vain. 'Do *you* think that if I did have a lover I'd betray him by coming here in the first place?'

Rion didn't know what the hell to think, but he did know her use of the word *betray* was the admission he had been waiting for. 'So you're confessing that your thoughts about me *have* been lustful ever since you walked into my office, *gineka mou*?'

'The only thing I'm confessing is that I would never have allowed myself to be seen in public as your wife if doing so humiliated anyone other than me.'

Rage flared in his eyes. 'Oh, yes, if only you'd married someone less *humiliating*, someone as refined and morally seamless as you are—oh, no, wait a minute. Haven't you, who has just spent the last ten minutes accusing me of omitting the truth, been lying about this other man all along?'

Libby's cheeks started to burn. 'You assumed—'

'In the same way that you *assumed* my business here had to do with Delikaris Experiences. Only you went one step further by perpetuating your lie.' His eyes narrowed. 'Why?'

She dropped her head. 'I thought it would make you see the logic in signing the divorce papers. You seemed sure that all I wanted was money, and I needed you to see that it wasn't.'

'Even though all the time it *was*?' he bellowed.

'No, I told you—'

'Oh, yes, you told me—getting a divorce now is *logical*. But you've already lived with the *humiliation* of being my wife for five years, so why did remaining married suddenly become *illogical*? Has Ashworth Motors folded? Is that it?' he went on. 'Are you here because you hope a hefty divorce pay-out will restore your family's fortunes, prevent you from having to work a day more?'

Libby drew in a ragged breath and began walking back in the direction of the house. How had she spent even a minute believing he was capable of understanding a single thing about her? He wasn't the Rion she'd once known. He'd grown so cynical. She glanced at him as he came alongside her. Why was that, when in the years since she'd been gone it appeared that so much had gone his way?

'I love my work,' she said tonelessly. 'And I've

already told you I don't want your money. After all this
time I just thought it was the right thing to do. As for
Ashworth Motors, I honestly have no idea. The last time
I saw my parents was the day we left for Athens together, so your guess is as good as mine.'

'Your father refused to have you back?' He looked
appalled.

'I didn't *go* back.' Didn't Rion realise she'd had
nothing to go back to?

'So where did you go?'

'The first flight back to the UK from Athens landed
in Manchester.' She shrugged. 'It seemed as good a
place as any.'

It had been two hundred miles away from her parents
for a start. Not that that had stopped her father getting
hold of her phone number three years later, when he'd
read about Rion's success in the paper and thought it
was in his interest to call her and repent.

'So living alone in a strange city was preferable to
being married to me?'

Libby's expression grew taut. 'It was what I needed
to do, Rion. In the same way that I knew you were
happier working, making it on your own.'

Rion turned sharply to look at her as they reached the
front door. 'Happier? The only reason I was always
working was to earn enough to get us out of that hovel
we were living in!'

Libby felt as if someone had just removed the ground
from beneath her feet. Working so hard had been his
dream, hadn't it? After the excitement of getting married

had gone, when she'd realised that she wanted to take control of her life, *he'd* discovered that what he really wanted was to make a success of himself alone. Hadn't he?

'It made you happier than I could, Rion. Our marriage wasn't what either of us was expecting. You said yourself the day I left it had been on the cards from the start.'

'Only because you never believed in me.'

Libby clung on to the front wall of the house for support, guilt washing over her in a wave. Was that true? *Had* she been the only one who'd been disappointed in their marriage? Her mind traced back over those three short months. No, whatever he said, she knew he had been too. But the reality was she was the one who'd given up on it altogether, who'd left her proud Greek husband. And suddenly she saw with hideous clarity the answer to her question. *Why* had he become the dark, jaded man stood before her now when so much had gone his way in the intervening years? Because she'd walked away from him.

Hot tears pricked behind Libby's eyes. 'I always believed in you, Rion, that's why I married you.'

Rion gritted his teeth. Yes, when she'd accepted his proposal she'd *believed* in him, believed her father would give them his blessing. And maybe she'd desired him so much that even after her father had given them the opposite she'd allowed herself to believe he was still *someone* back in Greece. She'd gone through with the wedding, after all. But once he'd taken her back to that god-awful apartment he'd known she must realise that he was really no one at all.

And, though he'd tried to convince himself that she didn't think like that, deep down he'd been half expecting her to bolt from the minute he'd carried her over the threshold.

He grimaced. God knew why he'd persisted in hoping she was immune to the same prejudices as her father even at that point. Or why, before that, he'd believed Thomas Ashworth was any different from Spyros and his father. He supposed he'd been blinded by gratitude because he'd given him his first proper job, because he'd been on the first step of the ladder to becoming the kind of man he'd sworn he'd become: a man whose life *was* worth something. A man whose family—mother, wife, child one day—would never have to suffer what Jason had.

But even so he shouldn't have been blind, should have recognised that the only reason her father had promoted him was because he made him more money than all his other Ashworth Motors employees put together. Should have realised it wasn't the mark of respect he'd taken it to be, that there was no way on earth Thomas Ashworth would even consider accepting someone like him as his son-in-law and successor to his company.

Not that Rion had ever wanted the latter. He'd always planned to build his own company the second he'd earned enough to go solo. But Libby—from the first time she'd looked at him with those wide blue eyes which hadn't seemed to see any difference between them at all, he'd never been able to help wanting her. Even though they'd really known so little about one another, even though he'd always felt like a boy from the slums compared to her elegance and beauty, even though he should have known she was out of his league. He'd wanted her regardless—more than he'd ever wanted anything else in his life.

His eyes roamed over her. He hated the feeling of weakness. Wished that now he knew the look in her eyes was a lie, that she *was* just the same as her father, the wanting would disappear. It never had. Maybe it would when he took her again, one final time, with the full force of his need. Maybe it never would. But at least he was not in any danger of ever being so gullible again, of falling for her lies—so carefully engineered to absolve herself of blame.

'Well, if you've always believed in me so unfalteringly, and now you've had the time to *find yourself*, what could be better than two weeks discovering whether our marriage can work, just as we agreed?'

Libby shook her head desolately. 'Because you only want me for the good of your campaign!'

'I've already told you. The fact that your return happens to coincide with this election is just a fortunate coincidence. Allow me to spend two weeks convincing you this marriage can work, just as we agreed. If I fail, then I will sign the divorce papers.'

Her voice choked. 'I already know this marriage can't work. You've changed too much.'

She missed his wince. 'But we agreed that I had two weeks.' He looked at his watch patronisingly, knowing she was only so outraged at the prospect of staying now that she knew about the election because it meant there'd be no chance of her keeping their marriage—so shameful in her eyes—a secret.

'I'm afraid it's only been a matter of hours.'

Libby pressed the heels of her hands into the sockets of her eyes. She wanted to run away as far as possible, so she didn't have to face being blackmailed by the only man she'd ever loved, so she could forget this whole sorry episode had ever happened. She wanted to shake him until the old Rion rose to the surface, understood her, saw what he was doing was wrong, told her she wasn't the one who had done this to him. But she knew that was like wishing for sunshine at midnight. That even if she ran she'd never forget. He'd never let her, because he'd drag her through the courts indefinitely.

Which left only one option. She dropped her hands and raised defiant eyes to meet his.

'Then it seems you leave me with little choice. But I can assure you you'll live to regret not agreeing to this divorce while you had the chance.'

She turned quickly, to deny him the satisfaction of looking her in the eye and giving some gloating response. But as she picked up her small suitcase, which she'd dumped in the hallway earlier, and began walking up the stairs, she felt his gaze rake over her rear view and decided a snide comment would have been preferable. Because she knew it wasn't real, and that hurt most of all.

Rion sensed her telling hesitation and smiled, enjoying the sight of her bottom and her shapely legs. 'I doubt that either of us is going to regret being back in one another's company for two weeks, Liberty. The master bedroom is the third on the right, if you'd rather just cut to the chase and admit it.'

Libby swung round at the top of the stairs, her eyes blazing furiously. 'Libby,' she ground out. 'And the divorce petition is right here,' she replied, whipping it out of the front pocket of her suitcase and tossing it down the stairs, 'if *you'd* rather just rediscover your conscience.' And with that she stormed into the first room at the top of the stairs and slammed the door behind her.

Rion gathered up the papers and smirked to himself. She'd just shut herself in his storage room, and something told him that bedding down for the night amongst a heap of clutter he hadn't got round to sorting yet wasn't exactly the alternative to the master bedroom she'd had in mind.

Not that he had any idea what was really going on in her mind, he thought, turning at the foot of the stairs and trying to get his head around her revelation that she had no duke or earl waiting in the wings to marry her after all.

He walked into his study, tossed the papers into the bottom drawer of his desk, slammed it shut, and poured himself a generous measure of Scotch. It made little difference, of course; he was under no illusion about that. She'd still no doubt had other lovers, still found the idea of being married to *him* abhorrent, no matter how hard she tried to absolve herself of guilt by arguing that she'd simply needed time to 'find herself'.

He swilled the amber liquid around his glass. But what it did mean was that if she'd been pursued by men she deemed suitable husband material—and he had no doubt that she had been—in one way at least they hadn't matched up to him.

Was that why she'd never gone back to her parents?

Discovering that she hadn't had shocked the hell out of him at first, but then maybe she'd known that her father would require appeasement in the form of a second, more appropriate match. And maybe she hadn't been able to bear that thought, because she understood that, ironically, the kind of man she wanted fathering her children was not the kind of man who turned her on.

Rion lifted the glass to his lips and knocked back the measure in one go. It appalled him that his wife had been out there alone, that her father was such an unforgiving man that she'd felt unable to go back home. He'd gathered that Thomas Ashworth was a strict father even before they'd naïvely gone to seek his blessing to marry, but he'd always imagined he'd forgive Libby just as soon as she'd dumped him. For once, his own father's abandonment seemed almost tame.

But most of all he was appalled that he empathised with Libby whatsoever, when by definition empathy meant feeling on the same page as another person and she thought of him as a whole other book, on a different shelf altogether. The bottom shelf.

Rion put the glass down on the table with a bang. Well, maybe they would always be on different shelves in her eyes, but their bodies spoke the same language, and this time around he wasn't going to let her forget it. He was going to make her beg, and only then would he let her go.

Libby hadn't expected to turn on the light and find a room full of his photos and personal possessions, but it seemed fate had made up its mind to just keep dishing out the pain tonight.

Although she could have opened the door and asked him if she could sleep elsewhere, or gone and tried to find another room herself, the last thing she needed was to run into him and receive another insincere invitation to his bed.

Besides, she needed to train herself to look at his face and feel nothing, instead of remembering the man she'd fallen in love with. That man no longer existed. Her heart ached at the realisation, at the thought that her actions might be partly responsible—actions he couldn't or wouldn't understand. She wanted to believe there must have been some mistake, that he hadn't become a ruthless, blackmailing brute, that it was just a nightmare—but she knew it was the part before they'd met Spyros which had all been a dream.

So maybe finding herself in such close proximity to all his possessions was the best thing that could have happened. Maybe she could uncondition those old feelings and build up her resistance ready to confront the real thing again tomorrow? Like presenting images of a spider to an arachnophobe, she thought, remembering something she'd once read in an in-flight magazine about the way cognitive behavioural therapies worked.

But hadn't it also said something about the dangers of presenting the phobic with too much too quickly? She shook her head, wishing for the second time that day that she didn't recall everything in such categorical detail, before deciding that the analogy was pointless anyway. Because she wasn't *afraid* of Rion, she reasoned with herself, ignoring the voice which said *no, but you're afraid of the way he still makes you feel.*

But at least she had discovered the truth early— wouldn't have to go through the pain of slowly coming to realise that he only had space in his heart for money and power. And now she knew that making their separation official was one hundred per cent the right thing to be doing. That the way forward was to refuse to comply with his blackmail until he couldn't bear her remaining as his wife a moment longer. Yes, she was actually grateful for tonight, because it had banished all the doubts she'd started to have about whether getting divorced was the right thing to do. It was. Unequivocally.

At least she was sure she would feel that way once she'd slept on it.

CHAPTER SIX

LIBBY woke at six, after a surprisingly easy night's sleep. She put it down to emotional exhaustion, and the relief of having settled on a course of action. Six was actually relatively late by her standards; she'd been an early bird since her childhood, reading voraciously in the early hours of morning when her father wasn't around to forbid her on the grounds that no man wanted a wife more intelligent than he was. Now, getting up at the crack of dawn to lead an excursion, catch a flight, or meet a new tour group was part of her job description, and ordinarily she adored it.

So why did just the thought of returning to that life, even if she successfully got Rion to sign the divorce petition, fill her with such depression this morning? Because all these years she'd thought that if she saw him again she wouldn't feel anything any more, she supposed, and yesterday she'd realised she was wrong. Because he'd made her realise that the life she'd carved out for herself didn't make her as happy as she'd told herself it did. And because, just when she'd allowed herself to believe she had a shot at *real* happiness, she'd discovered the man who'd once made her so happy had been replaced by a man who wanted to control her for his own gain.

Well, today he was going to discover that she would not be controlled by anything or anyone, Libby thought defiantly, rifling through her suitcase and digging out a sleeveless top and skirt. She got up and pressed her ear to the door to see if she could hear any sounds of movement on the landing. Nothing. She was thankful that in giving her the co-ordinates of his bedroom, and having directed her to the bathroom to freshen up yesterday, he'd prevented her from having to embark on a Russian-Roulette-style door-opening session this morning, which would most certainly have resulted in waking him, and probably stumbling across him in bed too.

Appalled to catch herself lingering outside his door, wondering whether he still slept naked, Libby rushed to the bathroom and jumped straight in the shower. But she was frustrated to find jets of water shooting out from the walls to massage her body from every angle, and, despite the fact that she had to contend with different shower mechanisms all the time, she couldn't work out how to turn them off. Defeated, but adamant that she would not be subjected to such a sensual assault, she turned the temperature unarousingly low, soaped, rinsed, and then dried herself off briskly in record quick time before flinging on her clothes and leaving the house.

It was a gloriously sunny morning, with a light breeze rising off the ocean that caught the scent of wild thyme as it blew inland. To her relief, it blew her melancholy aside and immediately put her in the mood to explore.

She decided to turn right and begin in Metameikos's old town first, taking photos along the way and sketching out a rough map in her notebook. She told herself the old town was the most logical place to start, but if she was honest she was too curious about the place where he'd grown up not to start there. Especially when he'd always been so reluctant to talk about it, and tried to argue that there was nothing remotely sentimental about his decision to come back here. He'd admitted that he'd bought the house because as a child he'd sworn he'd own it one day, so surely there *was* more to his decision to come back to Metameikos than he was willing to reveal? After all, the place where you grew up always shaped the person you became, didn't it? Even if only in the sense that it made you want to escape it.

But as Libby began to wander through the streets she couldn't imagine Metameikos could have that effect on anyone, and knew almost instantly that it would go down well with the clientele who booked with Kate's Escapes. Yes, some parts were in need of serious rejuvenation, but at the same time she couldn't recall anywhere else she'd visited that was quite so charming: the rows of washing strung out across the narrow streets, the small gardens lovingly planted and teeming with butterflies, the natural stream of water that trickled down through the mountains to the village square, where locals gathered to collect water and exchange gossip.

But, she thought, stopping at a small café for a cup

of lemon tea and a delicious pastry, she didn't suppose stopping the rat race and enjoying life's simple pleasures would appeal to Rion. Yet he'd still chosen to return to that house—even though there were newer, far more luxurious and impressive properties that must have sprung up since his childhood.

So surely that meant he didn't want to escape the simple charm of the place where he'd grown up completely?

Or maybe it just conveniently happens to be the most politically neutral location in Metameikos, the voice of reason piped up in the back of her mind as she walked along the promenade towards the new town, the boats changing from small fishing vessels coming in from a morning's work to enormous yachts with last night's empty champagne bottles strewn across the deck, their curtains drawn tight. For if Metameikos did mean something else to him, then surely the few times he'd spoken about it he wouldn't have done so reluctantly. *And maybe he knows that having been raised here gives his bid for power an added credibility?* Yes, now she thought about it, it was obvious that that was the reason why he'd chosen to run for office in his home town—it increased his chances of winning. That, and the fact that, as Metameikos was the only independent province in Greece, if he *did* win his power would be far greater than if he'd simply become a member of the *vouli* in Athens. She cursed herself for wanting so desperately to believe she'd been mistaken about him when she knew it was so futile, and carried on.

After only half an hour of wandering between the

enormous, characterless, whitewashed villas that comprised the new town, Libby came to the decision that it was far too generic to warrant inclusion on any tour, and went back in the direction from which she'd come. She spent the rest of the morning in and out of a tiny museum that had been set up by a few of the locals who were keen to profit in a small way from the few tourists who ventured down the coast. The lady working there, who turned out to be a dear friend of Eurycleia's, was a mine of information, pointing out all the local sites of historical interest and keenly offering ideas when Libby suggested she might be interested in securing accommodation for small groups.

After taking lunch at the taverna across the street, where she sampled some delicious sea bream that had been caught by the local fishermen that morning, Libby decided to head back to the house, filled with enthusiasm for plotting out a potential itinerary based on what she'd discovered so far. Until she passed the amphitheatre, and was reminded that running any such tour would involve being virtually on his doorstep. It made her stomach roll so unpleasantly that she was almost tempted to report back to Kate that the whole of Metameikos was unsuitable for tours.

But that feeling will pass once you're divorced— once you've forced him to regret trying to control you like this, she reassured herself as she reached the house and let herself in through the back door, ignoring the army of doubts that sprang up in response.

'Where have you been?' He was hunched forward on

a stool at the breakfast bar when she entered the kitchen, eating bruschetta with one hand whilst tapping away on his laptop with the other, but he stopped both and fixed condemning eyes on her the second she entered.

'Oh, you know—here and there,' she said waspishly, wanting to feel glad that his anger meant she'd success-fully pushed him one step closer to signing the divorce papers, but feeling the opposite.

'You don't think I deserve to know your whereabouts?'

'You haven't cared about my whereabouts for the last five years.'

'Things are different now.'

No, they weren't. He hadn't suddenly started caring. All he meant was that now where she was and what she did reflected on him. 'Perhaps you should have checked that I agree with you on that.'

'I rather thought a basic code of conduct was implicit.'

'Did you?' she said scathingly, sucking air between her teeth and tapping her forefinger against her chin. 'Oh, dear. So you mean that you were gambling on my code of conduct coinciding with yours? I really think we ought to have compared notes first. But if we must do it retrospectively, let's see… There was that gorgeous young waiter this morning, and I just presumed that it was okay to—'

'Don't play games with me, Libby,' he growled, in-stantly reaching out his hand to encircle her wrist.

The sheer eroticism of his thumb on her pulse-point made her bravado falter. 'I only popped out to do some research for work.'

The tension in Rion's shoulders eased marginally. When he'd woken up and found her gone he'd thought—he didn't know what he'd thought. That she'd left him again, he supposed, or that she was out making plans to. 'Then perhaps if you're going to be *popping out* in future it would be courteous if you could let me know where you're going—or at the very least how I can contact you if I needed to find out.'

'You're asking me for my phone number?'

'Do you usually reserve it for men you're not married to?'

Libby was ready with a curt response and a fake number, but his words stopped her in her tracks. No, she didn't usually give out her number full-stop, because she didn't like the thought of anyone keeping tabs on her the way her parents always had. But for the first time ever Libby suddenly considered how sad that was. Yes, in the intervening years she had achieved the independence she'd always craved, but the result was that no one ever knew where she was going unless it was detailed in an itinerary. And, whilst there was a sense of freedom in that, it also screamed loneliness. If she went missing, who would notice? A tour group of people she'd never met before?

'Okay,' she mumbled. 'Seems reasonable.'

As he whipped out his mobile and she began to list the digits, Libby tried not to think about the *we're each other's next of kin,* but *we don't even know each other's phone numbers* argument she'd levelled at him as a reason why they should get a divorce two days ago. If she did, she'd be forced to admit that, even though she had every reason to be certain that excluding him from her life completely was the right thing to do, she seemed to be encouraging him to waltz back into it.

When he'd finished punching in her number he swiftly replaced his phone in his pocket, took his plate to the draining board and shut down his laptop.

'I have a meeting this afternoon,' he said, flicking a glance at his watch. 'I'll be back around five.'

'Oh? What kind of meeting?'

The corner of his mouth lifted in amusement as he slid on his dark suit jacket and ran a hand down his tie— far, far too sexily. 'For someone who considers it an intrusion for her husband to question *her* whereabouts, you have an awful lot of interest.' He raised one eyebrow provocatively.

'I'm just a little surprised. I presumed you'd demand my presence at every event even remotely connected to your campaign.'

'Well, you'll be pleased to know that, save for the Mayor's pre-election party next week, I don't require you to do anything other than remain here, gracing the marital home.' He nodded to the sun terrace, slipped on his shoes and opened the front door. 'I dare say you won't find it too much of a hardship. See you later.'

In a moment of impulsive anger, Libby grabbed one of Eurycleia's biscuits from the plate on the side and threw it after him, but he shut the door so quickly behind himself that it didn't connect with anything other than the wood, breaking into a trillion pieces and falling in a shower of crumbs to the floor.

So, she thought acrimoniously as she stomped over to sweep up the mess, full of guilt that Eurycleia's baking had taken the brunt of her anger, not only was he using her, but he'd become a blatant misogynist as well. He didn't want a woman with a brain who might actually aid his campaign. He just wanted a walking, talking cliché. No wonder he'd sent Eurycleia away— after all, why did he need a housekeeper when he had a wife 'gracing the marital home'?

Well, she thought, her eyes scanning the kitchen and finding his laptop, if this morning hadn't convinced him that she wasn't prepared to play any such role, then this afternoon would. Quickly she turned it on and ran a search for 'public meeting, Orion Delikaris, Metameikos'. The results immediately threw up the details of the town hall she'd passed that morning, and a start time of two-thirty. Perfect.

It was two thirty-three when Libby turned the corner of the street and saw Rion's Bugatti parked outside the town hall. Which was pretty good going, considering she'd only left the house at ten past, and had been on foot during the hottest part of the day. She pinched her top at the neck and fanned it to create a cool column of air down her body, took a moment to catch her breath, then stepped inside.

The hall was filled with a large cross-section of people. There were fishermen who must have finished the early-morning trawl and come up from the docks, elderly men with backgammon boards tucked under their arms, women with babies strapped to their chests, and a group of students she presumed must be from the somewhat dilapidated college she'd spotted on the other side of the old town that morning. Perceptive, Libby thought as more people filed in behind her, to choose the time just before siesta, when everyone was walking past on their way home.

'Welcome, and thank you for coming.'

Libby heard his voice at the front of the room and stood up on tiptoes, trying to find a gap between the heads.

'The aim of this meeting is to explain the main improvements we plan to make to Metameikos if we're successful in the forthcoming elections. However, first and foremost, we want this afternoon to be a no-holds-barred opportunity for you to ask questions of us.'

There was a murmur of surprise from the crowd, as if such an invitation was unheard of, but, as Libby finally found a direct eyeline to the low stage, she was almost too mesmerised to notice. Because all of a sudden she realised that her husband was the embodiment of the phrase 'natural-born leader'. She'd never really thought of him that way before, but now he was up there he looked so commanding, so confident and so capable, that even *she* felt an instinctive need to follow him.

She silenced her inner floozy, which whispered, *Yes, straight to bed.* Because, whilst she couldn't go on pretending that she wasn't attracted to him, when had she ever been turned on by what boiled down to a display of power, arrogance and control? Since it was accompanied by a look which said he was willing to do anything for the good of these people, she supposed. But then *looking* that way was what politicians were best at, wasn't it?

'I didn't realise you were coming,' a voice behind her whispered, suddenly interrupting her thoughts. She turned to see a stylishly dressed young man, hand outstretched. 'I'm Stephanos, one of Rion's press officers.'

Libby shook his hand warily, wondering how on earth he knew who she was.

'You were snapped together outside the theatre last night,' he said, reading her puzzled expression. 'It made the front page of the *Metameikos Tribune* this morning.'

Libby sighed. 'Then I guess today is a good day for you.'

He raised his eyebrows towards the stage. 'It has the potential to get even better. Come with me?'

For a ridiculous moment she wondered whether Rion had spotted her in the crowd and sent him down to get her. Until it occurred to her that not only was it unfeasible that he'd seen her, or had the chance to do anything about it, but that if he had he probably would have dispatched someone to send her home.

Stephanos had obviously just noticed her and recognised an opportunity to make use of her. And, although part of the reason why she was here was to protest against being used, the opportunity to defy Rion's instructions and prove that his colleague clearly didn't share his chauvinistic opinion that she should be 'gracing the marital home' was too tempting to resist.

She nodded. 'Sure.'

Stephanos led her to the side of the crowd and along

the edge of the room, whilst Rion launched into an explanation of his plans for a new hospital. His speech was flawless—or at least it was until they were a few metres away from the stage, when she heard him hesitate mid-sentence.

Libby knew instantly that their movements had caught his attention. She raised her head, and was met by a look of horrified disapproval which momentarily rooted her to the spot. But then, just as quickly, he looked away and continued speaking, his composure seemingly unaffected after all. Blinking to check she hadn't imagined it, Libby saw that Stephanos had forged ahead and was beckoning for her to follow him up some discreet steps at the edge of the stage. Still dazed, she caught up with him at the top, where he quickly grabbed an extra chair out of nowhere, added it the semi-circle of people seated behind Rion, and signalled for her to join them.

As Rion began the second half of his speech he sensed her sit down behind him, and felt the tendrils of dread begin to snake around his heart. He'd worked so hard for this: the one remaining goal he was yet to fulfil. Now, thanks to his fixation on proving to her that he had become a success, that she was still as hot for him as he was for her, she was about to condemn him to failure. To lose him the one chance he had to put right everything that was still so wrong here. How foolish he'd been to suppose that two weeks of luxury and a shot at what she wanted would be enough to keep her mouth shut. Now he thought about it, it was obvious; of *course* she'd seize the opportunity to ruin him. The prospect of a man like him holding any position of power was bound to appall her.

Rion gritted his teeth, praying he could transmit a telepathic command to Stephanos to get her off the stage. *Now.* He understood why he'd brought her up here: since she'd turned up of her own accord it would avoid any negative speculation as to why she was in the crowd and not by his side. But what Stephanos didn't realise was that they'd have more than just speculation to worry about if someone directed a question at her or if she decided to open her mouth.

But Rion, it seemed, was not capable of telepathy, because, whilst he could see Stephanos at the very edge of the stage, the only movement he was making was with his mouth, silently repeating *Start the questions.*

Reluctantly, Rion wrapped up his explanation of how the affordable housing scheme would work. 'So now it's over to you. Who has a question for me?'

'Or for one of us,' his recently demoted campaign manager, who'd always been keen to push the team approach, chipped in.

Rion pasted on a smile which didn't reach his eyes. 'Of course—or for the team.'

'I have a question.' A middle-aged man at the front of the crowd raised his hand, and Rion signalled for him to go on. 'You say there'll be a new hospital, and five hundred new houses that the likes of us'll be able to afford, but after that how do we know that the rest of Metameikos won't become like it is up there?' He motioned in the general direction of the new town amidst murmurs of agreement.

'How *indeed*?' another male voice—sly and deeply unpleasant—piped up from further back in the crowd.

Libby leaned slightly to the right and saw immediately that the owner of the voice was the grubby-looking man who had been standing with Spyros and his wife last night.

'For wasn't Delikaris Experiences' last project an exclusive block of apartments?'

There were renewed mutterings from the crowd, this time of concern.

'Indeed it was,' Rion said with calm assurance. 'And, whilst I consider my business endeavours entirely separate from what I hope to achieve in Metameikos, since you have asked I will gladly explain why that was.'

Spyros's man looked triumphant, but only for a second. Rion continued. 'Athens is the best location from which to run Delikaris Experiences. A capital city is always best for business, and,' he said with a proud curl of his lips, 'why would I choose anywhere other than the capital of *Greece*? However, it's also a very expensive place to live. In order that I might help my employees I bought a block of apartments which had fallen into disrepair and had the whole building renovated— far more cheaply than if each apartment had been bought and refurbished individually. It allowed me to offer them to my staff to buy or to rent at a very reasonable price, if they so chose.'

Spyros's man looked incensed that his question had backfired—until he seized upon a counter-argument. 'Because you do not pay your staff enough for them to be able to afford a home on the open market, Mr Delikaris?'

'No, Stamos, because I believe people deserve a break. So to answer your question, sir—' he returned his attention to the man at the front '—I believe luxury has its place, but I'm no fonder of the idea of Metameikos becoming a sea of over-priced holiday homes than you are. Once I've built five hundred affordable homes, I promise you I will endeavour to build five hundred more. After all, I'm sure your children would like to be able to buy homes of their own one day too.'

The man nodded earnestly, and the murmurs of the crowd became more approving, until Stamos interrupted once again.

'Oh, yes, we learned yesterday that, contrary to wide-spread opinion, you're the ultimate family man. This is your wife, is it not?' He pointed at Libby.

There was no gasp of surprise. It seemed the news had travelled fast. Instead there was a sea of awkward yet curious glances, as though Stamos had asked an inappropriate question, but one to which everyone wanted to know the answer.

She took a deep breath, wishing she could see the expression on Rion's face instead of the back of his head. But the composure in his voice suggested it would be giving no more away than it ever did.

'Indeed. My wife and I have been apart for some time, but I'm delighted to say that's no longer the case.' He turned to look at her fleetingly, before nodding as if to invite more questions. Preferably *not* about the woman he hadn't wanted at this meeting in the first place, she thought glibly.

'And was it your husband's heart-warming policies that drew you back to him just in time for his election campaign?' Stamos said archly, directing his question at her.

Rion's head turned sharply towards the edge of the stage, anger flaring in his eyes, but Stephanos shot him a warning look which said *It will do more harm than good if we throw him out.* When he turned to face the front again he saw to his horror that Libby had stepped forward to take the microphone.

'No,' she said, and heard him draw in a sharp breath behind her.

It was tempting to blurt out the truth, but the thought of it made her lungs fill with the guilt that had been rising ever since last night. And suddenly she wondered whether if she bit her tongue at this moment, when she had the chance to ruin him, he might see that she was sorry for the pain she had caused him, whether it might make him reconsider whether she really deserved to be used in this way.

'No. Actually, I wasn't aware of my husband's de-cision to run in this election until…very recently. It was my career which led me back to Athens, where we were reunited.'

'But you are undoubtedly in full support of your husband's policies now?'

'From what I have just heard, yes.' She paused, drawing the line at actually lying. They *did* sound good, but so did a lot of things which came out of his mouth. 'But they are as new to me as I am sure they are to many of you. So, since I'm afraid I have never believed in adopting the opinions of those close to me simply because of the ties of marriage or blood, ask me again when I have had time to mull over the facts.'

To Libby's surprise the whole room suddenly filled with delighted applause—from the women in the crowd, who seemed to be bowled over that she had spoken her mind, and from the men, who nudged each other knowingly, as if it was heartening to know that even Orion Delikaris had a headstrong wife to contend with. From everyone except Stamos, who slipped out of the back door with a face like thunder.

Libby resumed her seat as new questions about healthcare and schooling began to pour in thick and fast, the crowd's tongues apparently loosened by the moment.

'You're a genius,' Stephanos whispered from the edge of the stage.

But something about the look on Rion's face told her that was not going to be an opinion he shared.

CHAPTER SEVEN

As LIBBY sank down into the low leather seat of the Bugatti, Rion removed his tie, loosened his collar, and turned the key in the ignition. The car roared into life.

He had maintained his flawless composure during the remainder of the meeting, effortlessly answering each new question from the floor with just the right blend of consideration, substance and wit, but she'd known that inwardly he was seething. And if she'd been in any doubt, then the firm hand at her back and his frosty silence as he'd escorted her to the car afterwards had made it explicitly clear.

Well, Libby was positively seething herself. Yes, she'd gone to the meeting with the intention of riling him, but surely he could see that in the end she'd decided to try and breed a little common decency? It seemed she'd made a serious error of judgement. He didn't have an ounce of common decency left.

'Has it escaped your notice that I actually did you a favour in there?' she shot out suddenly, convinced that if she didn't say something then the car's windows would implode under the tension, 'That the people of Metameikos got to see you as a human being instead of a billionaire who flies around the sky in his own plane and whirls around the streets in his Bugatti?' She made a disparaging spinning gesture with her forefinger.

'Hark at you, "Lady" Ashworth, lecturing *me* about keeping in touch with the common people.'

'I'm not the one swanning around in the fancy transport.'

'No, you're the one who—in the absence of your parents' wealth to wallow in—has come to wallow in mine.'

She seethed at the accusation. 'Being forced to do so has only reminded me that money counts for nothing. Doesn't it occur to you that the people of Metameikos might feel the same?'

Rion's knuckles went white against the steering wheel, and for a moment his fury was so acute he couldn't speak. 'You think that money *counts for nothing*? Here, of all places? But of course—why *would* you think anything else when you've never known what it is to have none?'

'That's not what I meant. Just because my parents have money it doesn't mean I have no idea—'

'How it feels to live in squalor? Oh, yes, I'm forgetting the slum of an apartment *I* made you live in.'

She shook her head, wondering how it was possible that he always got her so wrong.

'Just because my parents have money it doesn't mean I have no idea about poverty, Rion. I've been all over the world—*all* over it, not just to the places with bright city lights.'

'And what did you do when you saw it? Put away your digital camera and thank God you were born lucky?'

'I did what I could,' she said solemnly, turning to look out of the window. Which hadn't been much when she'd been living on her wits herself. But the fund at Kate's Escape she'd set up, to encourage staff and clients to donate to the areas they visited which were most in need, was now really starting to make a difference.

'What I meant…' She took a deep breath, steering her thoughts back to their original argument as they approached the house. 'What I meant is that I doubt your display of excess is doing anything to endear you to your electorate.'

'You don't think so?' He raised his eyebrows patronisingly. 'Surely I don't need to remind you that I was a boy in that crowd once?'

'No, you don't need to remind me.' That was why they were here, instead of in Athens or anywhere else. He wanted power to go with his wealth and success, and the added authenticity of doing it here gave him the best chance of getting it. She missed his grimace.

'Then—tricky as this may be for you—try for a moment to think yourself into the mindset of someone living in the old town. Wouldn't you be inspired to see a man who started in the same place as you are now returning home a success?'

Libby thought about it, and about the announcement that he intended to plough his own wealth into hospi-

tals and houses too. She had to admit that if she didn't
know he was only in this for the power and the thrill of
winning then she probably would. In fact, she didn't
know why for a minute she'd supposed the people
would think anything else; he'd painstakingly considered *every* aspect of his image and made sure it was
tailored towards gaining maximum support, hadn't he?
That was why she was here. But what was wrong with
showing people that he was a human being as well as a
success story?

'So, if you're so keen for the people of Metameikos
to feel an affinity with you, how can you possibly be
angry about what happened back there?'

Rion pulled onto the driveway and killed the engine.
How could he be angry about what happened back there?
Oh, there were of plenty of ways: he could be angry that
he'd allowed his desire for her to weaken his faculties;
that for a moment she of all people had held his fate in
her hands whilst he'd looked on powerlessly; that he
hadn't even slaked his goddamned desire for her yet!

He flung open the car door. 'I am needed in a conference call with Delikaris headquarters.' He looked
down at his watch. 'Now.'

Libby scrambled after him as he unlocked the front
door, desperate to force him to see how unreasonable
he was being. 'If you can't think of an answer then why
not consider the fact that maybe there isn't a reason? I
could have told everyone exactly how you're capitalis-
ing on my return, but I chose to help you, and yet you
still look like you're about to explode.'

The second the words were out of her mouth Rion turned so sharply back on himself that she almost crashed straight into him. 'You're right,' he breathed, stretching out his arm and pushing the front door shut behind her head. For a second she froze, her eyes wide with hope that he was about to announce that he'd been wrong to try and use her in this way, to reveal that he was still the old Rion she'd fallen in love with. But then he continued. 'I *am* about to explode. And so are you.' He reached down for her hand and then raised it to his chest, placing it at the exact point where the fabric of his shirt gave way to flesh.

It was so unexpected that for a second she just stood there, feeling the heat of his hair-roughened chest, the pounding of his heart which began to reverberate through her body so she couldn't tell which was her rhythm and which was his, almost as if they were—

'No!' she gasped, wrenching her hand away and drawing in a fast, deep breath, hoping the rush of oxygen would kick her brain into gear, remind her that he didn't really want her, that he wasn't the same man any more, that it would only lead to heartache. She tried to take a step backwards, but she was already up against the front door, and when she took a side-step to the right he mirrored it, keeping her hemmed in.

'No?' he said huskily. 'That *isn't* what you want? Then why is your body temperature soaring? And why tear your hand away as though you're terrified of what you might do next?'

'I'm not terrified—'

'Good—then there's no reason to remove it, is there?' He reached for her hand again and placed it back inside his shirt, his eyes never leaving hers.

Libby's breath caught in her throat. So now she was damned if she removed her hand and damned if she didn't? She lowered her eyes, desperate to reduce the effect that touching him was having on her by blocking out the sight of him, knowing her only hope was to try and convince him she felt nothing whatsoever.

Gently he ran his forefinger along her outstretched right arm and softly up her neck. Libby closed her eyes and shook her head, so that the short length of her hair fell forwards. For the first time since she'd had it cut, in a bid to start afresh upon arriving in Manchester five years ago, she wished she hadn't—just so she had some-thing more substantial to hide behind.

'Don't you know that trying to look away says even more than if you just drank me in with your eyes, as I know you're longing to do?' he murmured. 'Do you think I don't remember how you always hid behind your hair…' he smoothed the wisps away from her face now, tucking them behind her ear in a gesture which made Libby's stomach lurch in painful remembrance '…when you wanted me most?'

She opened her eyes wide and looked directly into the depths of his, hoping he didn't notice the increased pressure of her hand against his chest as she fought to steady herself. 'The meaning of things can change, Rion. Just because I lacked self-confidence then it does not mean I avert my gaze out of coyness now.'

'Coyness?' He laughed nastily. 'No, I'm well aware that's not the reason.'

Wounded at his insinuation, Libby dropped her lashes again. 'Then why can't you just accept that I don't want to look at you or to...touch you?' She removed her hand from his chest a second time, and stared down at her palm as if it had betrayed her.

'I don't know,' he answered, marching his fingertips against his lower lip in feigned deliberation. 'Maybe it's because you can't say that and look me in the eye. Maybe it's because ever since you turned up in my office you've been looking at me the way a man who is starving might look at a banquet. So why don't you just come and taste it?'

She heard her breathing grow heavy, felt the exaggerated rise and fall of her chest. Why had she bothered even *trying* to fool him? He could read the subtle body language of people he'd only just met, for goodness' sake, never mind the unsubtleties of hers.

And he's been using that against you from the start, a voice reminded her from deep within the lust-filled labyrinth of her mind. *Not because he desires you, but for the benefit of his political career.*

Which meant that if she looked hard enough she'd catch the look of reluctance in his eyes, she thought with both pain and relief. For surely if she could *see* that his desire was nothing but a mask he wore, as a means to an end, she'd have the strength and the self-respect to walk away?

But as she flicked her eyes up to his face again there

wasn't even a hint of disinclination. And although it had been missing yesterday too, then she'd been sure that he'd just been turned on by the challenge of proving he was better than her 'other man'. Now he knew that there was no other man. So could it really be possible that… *she* was turning him on?

'Stuck for an answer yourself now, *gineka mou*?'

'No, I'm—'

'Still here,' he finished, stepping back and sweeping his arm across the gap between them, to emphasise the fact that he was no longer blocking her escape.

'Yes,' she whispered, willing the words *I'm just leaving* to come out of her mouth. But they didn't. Because how could she leave when he was looking at her the way he had that very first day when she'd walked into her father's showroom, as if no amount of her would ever be enough?

'Yes,' she repeated, 'I'm still here, and I…don't want to go anywhere.'

Triumph and arousal surged through Rion's veins. He'd never been in any doubt that her body craved this as much as his did, but for a minute there he'd wondered whether the shame she felt at that was going to win out all over again. But it hadn't, and that made *him* the winner. Because this time around there would be no holding back.

'Good,' he growled, lowering his head. 'Because right here is perfect with me.'

Libby's stomach did a part-fearful, part-excited somersault as she realised he'd interpreted her words literally. He'd made it clear that he suspected she'd had other lovers, and thanks to her failure to correct him he probably presumed that she was now some experienced seductress who was used to making love in the middle of the day, wherever the urge took her. And if that was the kind of woman he was used to making love to, she was bound to disappoint him.

An arrow of pain shot through her at the thought, but as his mouth descended to feast on hers with such hot, hedonistic pleasure that she wouldn't have been surprised if she'd actually caught alight, her fears didn't just diminish, they were eclipsed by sensation completely.

Of course he'd always known exactly how to turn her on—he'd *introduced* her to the pleasures her own body was capable of—but he'd always rebuffed her attempts to learn what turned *him* on. She'd always supposed it was because once he'd taken her to bed she hadn't excited him half as much as he'd expected, but now he was showing her that just exploring her mouth was driving him wild, and, to Libby, that was the most powerful aphrodisiac she'd ever experienced.

Desperate to learn what else he liked, she used his earlier action as a guide and hurriedly unbuttoned his shirt. He sucked in a deliciously impatient breath as she encouraged it over his shoulders and began to explore the hard planes of his chest, skimming her fingers over the sensitive area of his nipple without restriction.

In the next instant he returned the favour, his fingers moving quickly to the buttons of her top. But rather than discarding it immediately he placed his hands flat against her tummy and slowly began to move them upwards beneath the thin fabric.

Libby closed her eyes and arched her back against the wall, imagining the symmetrical pattern his hands were making on her body as they skimmed upwards until they reached her bra, where they changed shape in order to cup her breasts. It sent a dart of need between her legs so acute that it was painful.

'Rion!'

Aroused, but frustrated by the material obstructions, she scrambled to discard both offending items herself. She rid herself of her top, but as it hit the floor his hands came behind her to work the fastening of her bra. Slowly he peeled it away from her body. Like a gift to be unwrapped, she thought glowingly, *and enjoyed.* Because, whilst he clearly hadn't forgotten the way she liked to be touched, now he was revelling in the way *he* liked to touch her, stroking, kneading, tasting.

Libby groaned, and he smiled in delight, his hands going in search of more pleasure, trailing lower, finding the globes of her bottom beneath her skirt, reaching for the hook, the zip. She kicked off her sandals, the marble floor cold beneath her feet, and in seconds she was completely naked before him.

Desperate for him to join her, she began to feather kisses down his chest whilst her hands moved to unbutton his trousers. He moaned in encouragement, but it excited her so much that her fingers lost their way.

He came to her aid, discarding the rest of his clothes at speed—only stopping to slip his leather wallet out of his trouser pocket before they hit the ground. But Libby didn't even notice. She was too transfixed by the smooth beauty of his erection.

She'd had the instinctive desire to touch him in all his glory since the very first time she'd seen him naked, but in the past he'd always steered her hand away. Now, encouraged by his pleasure at her exploration of his chest, she pushed those memories aside and took his tip between her fingers, running her thumb around its head.

She felt his whole body go still, his breathing become loud and fast and irregular. She looked up, excitement rippling through her at the effect she was having on him. His eyes were wide and black with desire. She moved her hand to stroke the whole length of him. His eyes grew darker still. This time he did not stop her.

At least not until it was obvious to both of them that unless she stopped now, this was going to be over too soon.

Instantly he turned his attention back to his wallet. He'd already torn open the silver foil before it occurred to Libby that his protecting himself was actually unnecessary, given that she was on the pill. She'd only gone on it for the convenience of knowing when to expect her previously irregular periods whilst travelling, had never had reason to consider its other function before. But she sensed it would rather shatter the mood if she suddenly tried to explain that now, when his hands were already sweeping purposefully up thighs, beneath her bottom...

Deftly, his upper body taut with strength, Rion lifted her up and took a step forward, so that her back was supported by the wall. Libby gasped at the sheer eroticism of what his body was proposing, but as she wrapped her legs around his waist, her body accepted it instinctively.

The feeling as he drove into her was exquisite. Maybe it was sinful, a crime against her sex to be glad that he'd made no attempt to tenderly touch her, to check that she was ready for him first. But to her it was proof that they'd never been closer. That he understood he could toss the rulebook out of the window because she couldn't wait a moment longer. Any more than he could.

His thrusts were urgent, primitive, perfect. She looked down at his thick dark hair, ran her hands through it, over the hard muscles of his arms that held her there so effortlessly, loving the incongruent looks of both power and powerlessness she saw intermittently on his face, heard in the shameless, guttural sounds that he mouthed into the hollow of her shoulder.

She leaned her head against the wall, the movement arching her back so that she could feel her nipples graze the taut plane of his chest. Every nerve-ending in her body was tight—no, loose—no, a whole mixture of sensations. As if her body had given up trying to work out which ones it was supposed to be possible to feel at the same time and was just making her feel *everything*.

'Oh!'

Her internal muscles began to contract around his hardness, but she wanted him to go first. Taking a risk that she could hold on, she wrapped her legs around his back even more tightly and drew him in deeper.

It was a risk worth taking, because at the exact

moment that her muscles clamped around him totally she felt Rion give one final, colossal thrust and cry out his own release.

And for one single moment there was just stillness. Perfect, silent stillness, accompanied by the most unexpected feeling of liberation.

Until he spoke.

'Now do you see that we're driven by exactly the same urges, *gineka mou*?' he drawled, depositing her back down on the cold marble floor, the look of unwavering power back on his face.

But Libby was not about to forget that only moments before it had been none so steady.

'No,' she said boldly, 'now I see that my defiance actually turns you on.'

CHAPTER EIGHT

'YOUR defiance?' Rion's mouth twitched in amusement.

It had occurred to her the second she'd seen that look of powerlessness on his face. He'd said he wanted her to simply remain in the marital home, implied that all he needed was any woman to play the role of his wife for the duration of his campaign, but when she'd defied him, showed him the kind of independent woman she'd become, it had turned him on. He'd made love to her like never before, as though deep down maybe he *did* want something from life that had nothing to do with this election, with power or success. And it felt as if she might have just seen the first glimmer of light at the end of a black, black tunnel.

'You don't think it a little coincidental that your desire just happened to arise at the exact moment I made it clear that I will not allow you to control me?'

He gave a loud, disparaging laugh. 'No, *gineka mou*. I think it was just a question of how long you could go on fighting it.'

'So making love to me right then was all part of your

nicely controlled plan, was it? I don't think so, Rion. I disobeyed you, and even though it frustrated the hell out of you, it aroused you so much…' She hesitated, still having to remind herself it was true. The sight of his manhood still standing proud just a few feet away from her helped. 'It aroused you so much that you even missed your precious conference call.'

He flicked a glance at his watch. 'So I did.' He shrugged nonchalantly. 'But I dare say it will do no harm if word gets about that I missed it because I was busy devoting time to my wife.'

Libby bit down so hard on her lower lip that she could taste blood. So, even though their lovemaking was the one thing which hadn't had anything to do with his campaign, he was still going to use it for that purpose rather than admit otherwise.

Furiously she swiped her skirt and top from the floor and wrenched them on. 'Well, if that was really what this was all about, why didn't you say? We could have gone to your office and set up the webcam, so your colleagues could have photographic evidence of just how attentive you are.'

Rion's mouth twisted in disgust. 'Don't be depraved.'

'No? You think you prefer it when I'm the submissive little wife, do you? Fine, let's see.'

She could have done better given half an hour in a charity shop, but fifteen minutes later, as Libby heard him descend the stairs, she was pretty sure she would have the desired effect. On her lower half she was wearing a faded old ankle-length skirt—the one she always kept in the bottom of her suitcase for slipping over her shorts in case an excursion involved going inside a temple or a church where it was necessary to cover her legs—and on her top half she had a brown and orange paisley tunic, which looked quite funky when she wore it with a belt and boots, but was an absolute fashion disaster with the long skirt. Coupled with Eurycleia's apron, and a strategic splattering of flour on her face, she was pretty sure she had un-sexy subservience written all over her.

He was talking rapidly in Greek when he entered the living room, head down, phone pressed to his ear. Libby translated. He was apologising for missing the conference call. Quickly she put down the rolling pin she'd just extracted from one of the kitchen drawers and strained to hear whether he really did have the nerve to cite quality time with her as his excuse.

But just as she was about to find out the rolling pin slid off the edge of the surface and hit the marble floor with an almighty crash.

Rion's eyes flew to her instantly, and she abandoned the curse that had been on her lips, morphing it into a polite, whispered apology, which she swiftly replaced with the blithe smile she'd made up her mind to keep plastered to her face for as long as it took her to discover whether that really had been a glimmer of light at the end of the tunnel, or just a mirage.

He looked her up and down as if she was insane, swiftly moved in the opposite direction so that she couldn't hear a damned thing he was saying, and only turned round to face her again once he'd cut the call.

'What the hell are you doing?'

Libby eased the honey off the spoon and into the mixing bowl with her finger. 'Oh, you know, the biscuits Eurycleia made were running low, so I thought I'd better make us some more.' She pretended to scrutinise the recipe she'd found. 'How about you? Off out?'

Rion looked down at his fresh white shirt and nodded warily, as if he needed to be careful about what details he gave away in case she followed him again. 'I have an evening meeting with my team.'

'Well, good luck,' she said, suppressing the urge to vomit at her own sickly-sweet tone. 'I'll still be here when you get home, just the way you like it.'

'Not *exactly* the way I like it,' he drawled.

'No?' she asked hopefully.

'No,' he breathed, and suddenly he came up behind her, removed her right hand from the mixing bowl, placed her finger in his mouth and then slowly began to suck off the honey. 'I'd prefer it a little more like this.'

Libby's whole body was still on fire ten minutes later, long after he'd returned her hand to the bowl with a lingering look and left for his meeting. She shook her head and began stirring the biscuit mixture far more violently than was necessary. This was going to take time, that was all. It was overly optimistic to suppose that the results would be instantaneous if she just acted a little domesticated and looked as if she'd got dressed in the dark. But she had no doubt that he'd soon cease to show any interest in her whatsoever, and be forced to admit that her defiance alone turned him on.

And then declare that he didn't want her acting as a caricature of his wife, but to be his wife for real? *Oh, don't be ridiculous, Libby,* she remonstrated as she dropped the biscuit rounds haphazardly onto a baking sheet. The best she could hope for was that he'd realise that blackmailing her wasn't worth the effort, and just sign the divorce papers.

But as she closed the door of the oven, leaned her back against its warmth and remembered the limitless joy she'd felt back in his arms, she couldn't stop herself from hoping.

In the days which followed, almost all of Rion's time was taken up with the campaign. When he wasn't attending meetings, or trawling the rest of the province to drum up support, he was on the phone to Delikaris headquarters, checking everything was running smoothly in his absence.

It gave Libby the perfect opportunity play the bland wife to the letter. She didn't ask too many questions, nor express too many opinions. She didn't attempt to accompany him anywhere, and although she quietly continued with her work during the day, she always made sure she was home before he was. She left the fridge well-stocked, the house clean and tidy, and continued to wear the drabbest clothes she could find.

And it worked.

Over a week had now passed, and Rion had not made love to her again.

Yes, on the rare occasions that they'd found themselves in the same room he'd still looked at her as though he wanted to lick honey off more than her finger, but she put it down to a half-hearted effort to continue with the pretence that she was wrong. Admittedly, the ultimate test would have been her waiting in his bed every night, rather than opting for the room next door— out of fear that she wouldn't be able to help *herself*— but she'd always passed off her decision as the action of a considerate wife who knew her busy husband needed uninterrupted sleep, whilst leaving her door ajar should he wish to prove her wrong.

But he hadn't. Not once. So, whilst he hadn't yet admitted that she actually left him cold this way, she remained certain that it would only be a matter of time before he did. And, God, she prayed it would be sooner rather than later.

Because acting this way all the time made her feel as if her wings had been clipped, she justified quickly, *not* because she was yearning for a repeat performance of that afternoon. Except, to her surprise, she didn't *actually* feel as if her wings had been clipped at all. Even though he was out almost as frequently as he had been in the early days of their marriage, it didn't bother her in the same way that it had done before she'd had her own focus in her work. In fact, she actually quite enjoyed the domesticity, the being in one place rather than finding herself in a different hotel room every night.

In short, her time here had proved that in the last five years she had successfully taken control of her life to such a degree that she did now feel properly ready to share her life with someone, and she wanted to. Which, she decided, might have just knocked her father naming her Liberty off the top spot of the list of greatest ironies of her life. Because, aside from some amazing sex, everything pointed to the fact that the only thing her husband wanted was world domination.

She drew in a deep breath, the memory of his lovemaking scorching across her mind *again.* She needed a distraction. It was too late to go back to work on another potential itinerary, Rion would be home soon, and cleaning would be pointless—the house was already spotless. She looked out of the window. The garden it was, then.

So she was still playing at it, Rion thought as he stepped out of the back door and spotted her picking figs from the tree behind the old swing seat. For a minute there he thought she'd gone out, given up this ridiculous pretence.

Didn't she know he was hot for her whatever she did? If she wanted to try and repel him she could at least try something a bit more drastic, like listing every one of their wedding vows she'd broken. Not that it would have had any greater effect, he thought grimly as he watched her reach up, the loose-fitting top she'd no doubt purposely chosen for its modesty paradoxically exposing her flat stomach, making him hard.

But it wasn't *his* desire she was really trying to deny, was it? Rion clenched his teeth, frustrated that she'd managed to convince herself that it was for so long. If it went on much longer—even though he'd sworn to himself that he'd wait for her to come to him—he might just have to show her it wasn't. His body—no, *her* body—was driving him too damned crazy.

And that frustrated him even more. He was supposed to be taking pleasure in wreaking his revenge, preparing to let her go with her desire half but never fully satiated. But the truth was that intention was slowly slinking away, because he didn't want to let her go. Coming home to her felt too good, and he was beginning to wonder whether her wistful looks meant she was beginning to feel the same way. He gritted his teeth. No, he knew that was impossible, that it was probably just a plot to win his sympathy, get him to sign sooner or something. Was he forgetting what he'd promised himself? He would never be so gullible again.

'Ripe?' he said huskily, coming up behind her.

Libby jumped and let go of the branch, which sprang back, creating a shower of purple which dropped to the floor and exploded red around their feet.

'I didn't hear you get back,' she said, almost crossly, then checked herself and sweetened her tone. 'Yes, they're ripe. Would you like one?'

'Tempting, but it will keep for now,' he drawled. 'I have a meeting with the Mayor this evening, but before I left I just wanted to remind you that it's his pre-election party tomorrow night.'

Of course. She'd been so focussed on counting down to the election itself—and the end of their fortnight,

which loomed in her mind like an approaching storm—
that she'd forgotten. 'The one you wish me to attend?'

The one that Stephanos would have a blue fit if she
didn't attend, Rion thought. People had been asking for
her at every event since the meeting. And if she could
have been trusted there was no doubt that her presence
would have had a positive impact. But the fact that the
words *blackmail* or *divorce* could have dropped from her
lips at any time had been too much of a risk. Besides
which, just the knowledge that she was waiting at home
had been distraction enough, never mind having her by
his side all day long. But tomorrow night he had no
choice. *Not* having her there was out of the question. He
was just going to have to keep an eye on her. And himself.

'That's the one. We're also required to stay at the
mayoral residence whilst the election takes place the following day. You will join me?'

For the first time ever her submissive answer came
naturally. A whole evening in which to play meek and
mindless, followed by the night spent together? It would
be the final test.

'Certainly,' she said in that sickly sweet voice.
'Nothing would please me more.'

CHAPTER NINE

WHAT to wear had caused her something of a dilemma. The cobbled together, little-woman-at-home look she'd been sporting for the last week had successfully failed to attract his interest. But tonight he wanted her to be the little woman on his arm, and that demanded an evening dress.

She'd only brought one. In fact, since evenings on Kate's Escapes tours were invariably smart-casual—save for the rare occasions when she covered the Austrian trip, which took in the opera in Vienna—it was also the only one she owned. It was made of a soft, floaty fabric in an ethereal sort of blue. It was perfectly appropriate for the occasion, but it fitted every inch of her body so closely, had always felt so distinctively 'her', that wearing it when she was supposed to be aiming for clichéd felt distinctly inappropriate.

But it was how you acted, not how you looked, which aroused him that afternoon, she reassured herself as she walked down the stairs, eyes deferentially downcast. But not so downcast that she failed to notice the incredible sight of him in his tux, which sent a powerful ripple of longing beneath her skin.

'So is the Mayor at this pre-election party the same Mayor you wanted me to meet at the theatre that night?' she asked, swallowing hard as he led the way to the Bugatti.

Her words interrupted Rion's thoughts—thoughts which involved rucking up her sexy little dress and arriving very late to meet the Mayor indeed. He forced them from his mind. Tonight, of all nights, he needed to stay focussed.

He nodded as he held open the car door for her. 'His name is Georgios Tsamis. Here in Metameikos the role of Mayor is an honorary one rather than one that carries any political power—deservedly bestowed upon Georgios for fighting for his country in the past, and his subsequent work in the local community.'

Libby threw all her efforts into listening, and *not* looking at his powerful hands on the steering wheel as he turned the key in the ignition.

'It has always been the tradition that prior to a new election the Mayor holds a party at his residence, for both the candidates and the voters, as a celebration of democracy and to show that he supports whoever the people elect.'

She nodded her head thoughtfully as they began to zip through the streets towards the new part of Metameikos, daylight just clinging around the edges of the whitewashed villas as the sun began to set. 'But presumably there is always speculation as to which candidate he favours?'

Rion was surprised by her political astuteness. 'Indeed.'

'And he has supported Spyros in previous years?'

'Georgios is a good man, with very traditional values. Unfortunately he is also an extremely poor judge of character and has been oblivious to Spyros's underhand dealings for years.'

Libby wanted to retort that maybe he shouldn't be so quick to complain about a mayor unable to see through people's guises, but she kept her lips tightly locked together and simply nodded.

Rion added nothing further, and a tension similar to the one she'd felt the last time they were in the car together seemed to return as the silence stretched out. Which had to be the product of her imagination, Libby decided, because that had been sexual tension, and even if he *did* keep shooting her sideways glances that looked far from chaste, it couldn't be that, because she hadn't been insubordinate in the least.

Out of the corner of his eye Rion caught her gnawing at her bottom lip with the same frustration that had been eating away at him for days. She wasn't going to hold out much longer. He could feel it. Could feel her trying to convince herself that the atmosphere between them was in her imagination, and the slow dawning realisation that it was not.

He smiled as he rolled the car to a halt outside the mayoral residence and gently ran the back of his hand down her bare arm.

'We're here,' he breathed, feeling her melt beneath his touch.

Instantly, a valet came to open the doors of the Bugatti, and Rion went round to her side of the car ready to escort her in.

She couldn't fail to notice the irony as Rion handed his keys and a hefty tip to the young man in the red-and-grey uniform. Couldn't fail to be reminded of back then, when *he* had been the valet. She dropped her head, the memory of a simpler time, when she'd been convinced that he cared for her, tearing at her heart.

Rion instantly saw the change in her body language. She'd been on the verge of sinking into him, raising her lips to his and giving in. Then she'd caught sight of the valet and her whole demeanour had changed.

Anger coursed through his veins. Red-hot. Relentless. And too instinctive to realise that it was also ill-advised.

He grabbed her wrist and spun her round to face him.

'It doesn't matter how often you remind yourself of what I am, or how hard you try to convince yourself that I'm the one whose desire is an inconvenient truth, it's *never* going to go away.'

Libby's head shot up and her heart began to pound in her ears. 'What are you talking about?'

'This.'

His arm came around her back to hold her steady, encouraging her to arch slightly, so that the whole column of her throat was exposed and her head lay back at the perfect angle for him to take her mouth.

It was hard, punishing, and sexy as hell.

And Libby didn't have a clue what it meant. She

tried to unravel what he'd said, but her mind was too fuzzy with desire—the desire she'd kept locked up for days, but which was now spilling out and into their kiss. It made no sense. He wasn't supposed to desire her when she was being compliant—unless he was so frustrated that she was repressing the woman she'd been that afternoon and he wanted to let her out.

But then he broke away from her, and when the world stopped spinning she realised in horror where they were. Surrounded by the people of Metameikos, all heading towards the soaring mayoral residence before them, all witnessing their public display of affection. She blushed furiously, but it wasn't the dent to her modesty which hurt. It was the realisation that *they* were the reason he'd kissed her. It stung so badly that she forgot she was supposed to be being demure.

'Oh, of course,' she said acidly. 'We're in public again.'

Rion's mouth hardened. 'And what? You think you can use that as an excuse to keep pretending that what's between us isn't real?

'No. I think I've spent the last week being exactly the kind of wife you thought you wanted me to be, but it hasn't appealed to you in the slightest.'

He looked her in the eye, knowing his comeback could be a dire mistake, but too incensed to let it go. 'Or maybe that's just what I let you think.'

Libby stared at him, fresh horror crashing through her, demolishing everything.

He'd *known* what she was trying to do, and he'd spotted that so long as he left her to it he would get exactly what he wanted—a wife 'gracing the marital home' for the duration of his campaign. She felt sick. How had she spent the last week failing to see that he was using her *again*? That light at the end of the tunnel—that glimpse of the Rion she remembered—had been a mirage after all. He *did* just want to control her.

'Ah! Mr Delikaris.' Libby spun round to see an old man who looked a bit like Father Christmas in black tie approaching them. 'And this beautiful young woman must be your wife.' He smiled at her benevolently.

Rion nodded. 'This is Libby. Libby, it's my great pleasure to introduce Georgios Tsamis.'

For the first time in her life Libby was grateful that social niceties had been so drummed into her as a child that they came naturally, even now, when her mind was in complete disarray. She held out her hand. 'It's a pleasure to meet you.'

'And mine to meet you,' Georgios said sincerely. 'And may I say—if you don't mind—how pleased I am to hear that the two of you have recently been reunited.' He leaned towards them with a wink. 'What a joy it is to see two people so in love.'

Libby's nausea rose with a vengeance. Oh, of course—Rion wouldn't have put himself through kissing her just for the benefit of a few citizens. He must have seen the Mayor approaching from a distance and timed his move exactly.

'The staff here will see that your bags are taken to your room,' Georgios explained, looking over to where the valets were carefully parking cars and loading luggage onto trolleys. 'And if you make your way through the main atrium you will see that food and drinks are being served in the Rose Garden. Anything else you need, please just ask. For the next twenty-four hours I want you to think of this as your home.'

'Thank you.' Rion smiled, pressing his hand stiffly into the small of Libby's back. 'I'm sure we will.'

'Wonderful.' Georgios beamed. 'Now, if you'll excuse me…' He looked a little sheepish. 'Mr and Mrs Spyros have just arrived.'

Rion's face was the picture of civility. 'Of course.' He nodded, motioning for him to go ahead and take his leave.

'How convenient that Georgios is such a poor judge of character,' Libby hissed as they walked through the main house towards the garden. 'Else it would have been obvious that I'm only here because you're black-mailing me.'

Rion's whole body tensed. He glanced around to check whether anyone else was in earshot, but thankfully no one seemed to have heard. Yet. *Gamoto!* Thanks to his damned pride, he'd tripled the risk of having her here—and for what?

He swooped on two glasses of rosé from the tray of a passing waitress, handed one to Libby, and took a large gulp of his own. But just as he was about to attempt some serious damage control, Eurycleia came bounding towards them.

'Oh, how delightful to see you both!' She kissed them both affectionately on each cheek. 'Now, I know you've probably got a hundred important people to see this evening, but I just *had* to come over and see that you're well.' She furrowed her brow in motherly concern. 'Is there anything you need? I can bring round some more biscuits if you're short. I'd only need to pop in for a minute—'

'Thank you for the kind offer,' Rion interrupted, 'but Libby's been keeping us fully stocked in the biscuit department.'

Eurycleia clapped her hands together in delight. 'Oh, but of course—just as it should be.' She turned back to Rion. 'Though you mustn't let her spend too much time in the kitchen. A woman must have her own life too, you know.'

'My thoughts exactly,' Libby replied gravely. 'And I have no doubt that Rion will soon have every reason to beg for your return.'

Rion scowled at her as Eurycleia's face lit up.

'You just enjoy your time off,' he said gruffly, then tilted his head to look at the man watching her from across the lawn with a twinkle in his eye. 'I don't doubt Petros is keeping you busy.'

Eurycleia looked back at him and rolled her eyes affectionately. 'I dare say he is.'

'He looks as though he really dotes on you,' Libby added. She'd meant it to come out jovially, but she could hear the wistfulness in her own voice. Thankfully, neither Eurycleia nor Rion seemed to notice.

'Oh, he's just come over all protective because I've been talking to that charming young man who works for you,' Eurycleia said to Rion. 'Now, what's his name…?

Stephanos? Yes, that's it. He was telling me how you and he-who-I-shan't-even-name are now neck and neck in the opinion polls. I mean, really, as if a young man like that is going to be interested in me!'

She threw her hands in the air in exasperation, and then clapped them back together again.

'Oh, listen to me—waffling on. I've already taken up too much of your precious time.' She reached out to squeeze their hands in turn. 'If you need anything, you know where to find me.' She winked, held up two sets of crossed fingers, and then scuttled back across the lawn.

Libby watched her go, taking in the garden's swirling mix of fairylights and flowers for the first time. It reminded her of some of the parties her parents had held in the grounds of Ashworth Manor—the ones where they'd invited every wealthy family in the south of England with sons about her age. But here there was no such discrimination; the designer-clad of the new town were mixed with the home-made Sunday best of the old town, exactly the way she would have preferred those other parties to have been. Yes, she recognised that some people didn't look a hundred per cent comfortable in their surroundings, but save for a few of Spyros's clan everyone seemed to be making the effort to mingle.

In fact, it looked exactly what it was supposed to be: a celebration of democracy. Except it wasn't, was it? she thought miserably. Democracy was about the freedom to choose, but the people of Metameikos had no choice. This election was between one deceptive, power-hungry fat cat and another; she had no doubt about that now. And she couldn't bear the thought of being a part of it.

She took a swig of wine from the glass in her hand and turned back to face him. 'I told you from the start, Rion, I'm not prepared to lie for you. Especially when as far as I can see you're no better than Spyros.'

Rion gritted his teeth. 'I'm not asking you to lie for me.'

'You're asking me to stand by your side and look like I want to be there. That's a lie.'

'Is it?' he murmured scathingly. 'It didn't feel like you ever wanted to be anywhere else when you were making love to me.'

Libby shook her head wretchedly. 'And that became a lie the second you used it as nothing more than an aid to your campaign.'

Rion's anger turned to puzzlement, and then his face stilled. 'When I rang the office I told them I'd missed the call because the meeting overran, that was all.'

Her cheeks flushed. God, she wanted to believe him. But how could she? He'd say whatever it took to stop her from leaving, from ruining his chances of success. He had done so from the start.

'No.' She shook her head again, more fiercely, and felt her whole body begin to sway from side to side. She took a step backwards, but he grabbed onto her wrist and pressed his lips to her ear.

'You want honesty, Libby? The truth is this isn't about the election, or what it says about our marriage on paper. This is about you and me. It always has been—'

'No!' She wrenched herself away from him so

fiercely that a sharp pain shot through her shoulder. She'd believed that for so long, but tonight just proved that was the biggest lie of all. 'I can't do this, Rion!'

She had to go. If she didn't, her poor battered heart might never recover.

She was surprised he didn't haul her back and physically bar her escape, but as she began to dart through the crowds, clattering her half-empty wine glass onto a passing silver tray, she supposed it made sense. Holding his wife by force would do even more damage to his precious reputation than her absence altogether.

She didn't know where she was going, except to somewhere wide and free and as far from him as possible—which meant away from here. But, just as she was about to run into the main house and back through the door they'd used to come in, she spotted a side passage by a laurel tree, to the far left of the building, which had initially been obscured as she'd crossed the garden. From this angle, it looked as if it would lead back to the road a lot more quickly, and cut out the possibility of her running into anyone she knew.

She quickly made her way towards it, but just as she was about to turn into the passageway she heard hushed voices and stopped dead in her tracks.

'Come on—I hardly think pocket money is going to cut it. I'll have to close their precious museum and turf at least fifty of them out of their homes.'

It took her a few moments to place it, but as she concealed herself alongside the tree she realised that the sly, unpleasant voice belonged to Spyros.

Ever so slowly, clutching on to the trunk so that she could lean forward without making a sound, Libby peered down the passageway. She could just make out a lanky man she didn't recognise removing a roll of notes from the inside of his jacket pocket and adding it to the bulge already in his hand.

'That's more like it,' Spyros declared lustily.

The man continued to cling onto the cash, despite Spyros's outstretched palm. 'And the planning permission?' he said expectantly.

'Will be on your desk by the end of the week.'

The man looked annoyed. 'And what if you are no longer in charge of Metameikos by the end of this week?'

Libby saw Spyros flinch and run his chubby forefinger around the back of his collar.

'You think I'm worried about Delikaris?' He forced a laid-back laugh. 'A boy from the slums who thinks a new hospital will bring back his brother?'

Libby's eyes widened in disbelief. Brother? What brother?

'But even Stamos said he was beginning to think that—'

'Do you want to build your luxury apartments or not?

Libby strained to hear, strained not to cough.

And then suddenly a hand grasped her waist from behind.

CHAPTER TEN

LIBBY gave a yelp as she was lifted off the ground, limbs thrashing helplessly. But as her assailant dragged her past the laurel tree and through a gate in the wall an unmistakable scent filled her nostrils. Rion's.

'Put me down!' She struggled out of his grip, her relief swiftly turning to anger. 'I just saw something!'

She tried to dart back through the gate of the smaller walled garden they now found themselves in, but Rion placed his hands on her upper arms, easily restraining her. 'I guessed.'

'Spyros,' she said breathlessly, 'taking a bribe…to pass planning permission for some luxury apartments…in the old town.'

His face remained unmoved. 'Like I said, he's corruption personified.'

'If we go back now I can tell everyone what I've seen!'

Rion said nothing, simply continued to hold her there. She found it so maddening that she tried to push past him a second time. But when he held her firm again she forced herself to question why, and suddenly it was obvious.

Running back into the main garden screaming treason at the eleventh hour would do more harm to Rion's reputation than to Spyros's. The fastest, most effective way of putting an end to his corruption wasn't to slander him, it was to beat him in the polls.

Libby's eyes remained on Rion's face, dimly illuminated in the pale moonlight. Ten minutes ago she hadn't been able to bear the thought of staying here a second longer, had believed it would make no difference who won. But now she had unequivocal proof that Spyros was everything Rion said he was. And Rion?

She took a deep breath, hating that she had to ask such a basic question of the man she'd been married to for five years. 'Spyros said something else too…something about you having a brother.'

'What about my brother?' he shot out, his voice loaded with venom.

So it was true. Part of her heart soared at the possibility that he was driven by something other than just power and success. The other part wished it *had* been a lie, because it proved that even now there was still so much they didn't know about one another. But most of all she wished it wasn't true because she could see the pain in his eyes and it tore at her heart.

She chose her words carefully. 'He said you wanted to build the new hospital because of him.'

Rion said nothing, simply continued to stare out into the darkness.

'It's true, then?' she ventured after several moments.

He gritted his teeth. Thanks to that creep Spyros it

looked as if he had no choice but to tell her, did he? Not
that it mattered. It wasn't as if he could fall any lower
in her estimation. Besides, she'd already made up her
mind that she was leaving.

He nodded sharply. 'His name was Jason. We were
twins.'

Twins? They'd been even more than brothers, then.
Libby looked up into his face. It felt as if she was seeing
him for the first time. 'What happened?'

'He caught pneumonia the winter we both turned
twelve.' He mistook her frown of sorrow for one of incomprehension. 'Mum, Jason and I—my father left
before we were even born—shared a place with another
family. Eurycleia's,' he explained abruptly. 'It was
damp, freezing cold, and a wonder any of us survived.'

Libby's eyes fluttered down to meet her cheeks.
*Whilst you grew up in the log-fire warmth of Ashworth
Manor,* she added to herself, knowing that was what he
was thinking and suddenly racked with guilt for ever be-
moaning her upbringing. Was that why he'd always
coveted the house where he lived now? Not because it
was the most luxurious in Metameikos but because it
was the perfect family home?

'We took him to hospital, where we were told to
wait,' Rion continued, his voice loaded with bitterness.
'And we waited. Whilst every other patient, no matter
how trivial their condition, nor what time they'd arrived,
was seen before us. On the third day Jason was the only
one left in the waiting room. But the doctors still refused
to see him.'

Libby winced as the grossly inappropriate sound of laughter from the party drifted over the wall.

'They wanted their palms greased. Believed, I suppose, that my mother would find the money.' He shook his head. 'She worked day and night for a pittance, just to be able to feed and clothe us. She had nothing to give but a few coins and a mother's love, and no friends or relatives with anything more.' A look of pain began to cloud Rion's eyes. 'In her desperation she did the only thing she could think of. She went to Spyros's father—the leader of Metameikos at the time—to beg for help.' The look of torment was instantly replaced by one of loathing. 'He told her that life, like everything else, had a price. He was right. Jason died right there in the waiting room.'

Libby's heart twisted in empathy. She wanted to go to him and wrap her arms around him, but he was looking at her as if there was no way she could ever understand. And in a way maybe she couldn't.

'My mother almost died of grief,' he went on. 'I believe that was what killed her in the end, but it would have happened ten years earlier if we'd stayed here. Eurycleia's husband worked on the docks; he helped us stow away to England.'

'I'm sorry,' Libby whispered, but the words had never seemed more inadequate. She was sorry for so much: that he'd been through all that; that her assumptions about why he was doing this had been so far off the mark; that she hadn't given him her support when his motives were so admirable.

Rion looked at her resentfully. 'I don't want your pity, Libby.'

No, she could tell he didn't want her to know, full-stop. Yet wasn't it obvious that if he had explained the real reason he wanted to win this election from the start she would have automatically wanted to help him succeed?

Yes, she thought, it probably was, but he clearly found the prospect of her staying because she felt sorry for him abhorrent. Just like the prospect of winning this election for the same reason, she realised suddenly. Spyros knew about Jason because of his father, but no one else did, did they? If they did, Rion would have no need to convince them of his commitment to family values, to Metameikos—but he'd chosen to avoid the sympathy vote.

'You don't have my pity,' she whispered, needing him to believe that her support had nothing to do with that and everything to do with believing in justice, believing in him. The corners of her mouth turned downwards. 'Are you telling me this kind of thing is still happening here now?'

He spoke through gritted teeth. 'Spyros Junior has had to get more subtle about it, but the divide between rich and poor is as wide as it ever was.'

'I had no idea.' How naïve her idealistic view of the old town had been, how small-minded to think that indifference was responsible for his reticence. She shook her head, ashamed. 'I thought that you just wanted the power…the success.'

'And now you know it's about the street urchin wanting his revenge?'

Libby stared at him. But it wasn't that, was it? He could have exacted his vengeance on the doctors or on the Spyros family in any number of ways, but he'd decided to take the high road, to make things better for the next generation.

Suddenly they were interrupted by the sound of something metal being chinked against something glass on the other side of the wall, then a hushed silence, which was followed by a loud voice.

'Ladies and gentlemen, Mayor Tsamis will be giving the traditional toast to the candidates in the main hall in five minutes.'

Immediately the shutters came up on Rion's face. 'I need to go.'

Of course he did. As Libby watched him turn on his heel, without even glancing back to see whether she had any intention of joining him, she knew she needed to go too. Not away from here, but inside, with him. Because the freedom he stood for was the very thing she'd spent *her* whole life fighting for.

And because she finally had the proof that he *was* the inherently good man she'd fallen in love with after all.

Rion stood at the front of the main hall beside Stephanos and stared bleakly into the glass of champagne he'd just been handed.

Libby was gone, long gone, he had no doubt about that. She'd known he was poor, that he had no connections, but the horror in her eyes when he'd told her the sordid details of his past had been palpable. If her plan earlier had been to walk away, she'd probably sprinted halfway back to Athens by now.

Anger burned in his throat. Anger at her—for leaving him. Twice. Anger at himself for believing deep down he might be able to seduce her into staying, for even wanting to try. Most of all for jeopardising everything by supposing this could ever have worked.

Stephanos stood beside him, anxiously leaning back to look for her through the crowd as Georgios ascended the podium. Out of the corner of his eye Rion could see Spyros's fat stomach protruding from either side of his scarlet cummerbund as he did the same, only the expression he wore was one of glee.

Georgios tapped a fork against his wine glass and the room fell silent.

'Good evening, ladies and gentleman, and thank you all for coming. It's a great pleasure to see so many of you here on the eve of what is set to be the closest and without a doubt the most exciting election we have seen in Metameikos for many years.'

'Hear, hear,' Rion heard a female voice which sounded a lot like Eurycleia's call out from the crowd. Spyros's face turned to thunder.

'Over the course of their campaigns both candidates and their teams have worked tirelessly in new and innovative ways to listen to your views and broadcast their policies, and I'm delighted to be able to say that when I stand before you tomorrow with the results I am sure that, no matter what the outcome, you will be guaranteed a leader who will give his all to Metameikos.'

But all of what? That was the question, Rion thought grimly.

'Which leaves me, without further ado, to raise a toast to the candidates, and to their wive—'

Georgios looked down to pick them out in the crowd, and spotted immediately that Libby was missing. Rion's heart stopped beating in his chest. Excuses hovered on his tongue—she'd been taken suddenly ill, there'd been a family emergency—but he couldn't bring himself to utter any of them. Because he couldn't stop recalling the accusation of dishonesty that Libby had levelled at him earlier. Wanting her by his side *hadn't* been a lie, but saying any one of those excuses aloud, however well-intentioned, would be. And if he won the election based on deceit, *wouldn't* that make him just as reprehensible as Spyros?

But just as Rion was about to open his mouth and declare the truth he noticed that the heads of the crowd were all turning towards the door. And then they parted.

Libby.

She looked so nymph-like as she floated in in her pale blue dress that for a moment Rion was convinced that what he was seeing was actually an apparition.

But then she spoke. 'My apologies, Mr Tsamis. For a moment the events of this evening were a little overwhelming.'

'Completely understandable, my dear.' Georgios smiled as she went to stand beside her husband. 'No need to apologise.'

Georgios turned his focus back to the crowd. 'And

now that we are all present and correct, it gives me great pleasure to raise a—'

'You were busy forming an opinion on your husband's policies, perhaps?' Spyros suddenly interrupted, turning viciously on Libby. 'For I hear that the last time you were asked you declared you needed more time to make up your mind. I'm sure I'm not the only one here who thinks you should be given a fresh opportunity to express your views.'

Libby was so startled by his breach of etiquette that it took a few seconds for his hypocrisy to hit home. But no longer than that. She took a deep breath, suppressed the urge to share with the crowd what she'd witnessed in the passageway earlier, and turned on her well-pefected, sickly-sweet voice instead.

'Why, thank you, Spyros. Whilst I'm not sure that now is the time—' she lowered her head respectfully towards Georgios '—I'm pleased you feel so strongly about people's views being heard.' She caught the eye of Eurycleia a few rows back. She clearly hadn't missed the note of sarcasm in her voice and was grinning jubilantly.

'You are correct that when I arrived just under two weeks ago I'd had little time to consider my feelings on any policies. What was more, I believed that no one could know what Metameikos needed better than its people themselves. I still believe that. But now I'm certain of one thing. Orion Delikaris is not the man you think he is.' She paused, and heard him suck in a breath beside her. 'Orion is *one* of the people. He hasn't just flown in from Athens with a bunch of policies he's plucked out of thin air because he thinks they're the ones that will gain him the most votes; this is his home. His policies are born out of the same desire for a better, fairer Metameikos that everyone here—' She stopped and looked directly at Spyros. 'That *almost* everyone here shares. They're more than just policies; they're the promises he's already made to himself.'

There weren't the whoops and cheers she'd got at the meeting this time. Instead there was a kind of silent awe, a collective hope.

Georgios smiled at her and gently bowed his head. 'Thank you, Mrs Delikaris. Now, lest we should all be quizzed—' he glared at Spyros, whose expression was one of complete and utter horror '—I should like to finally raise that toast: to the candidates of this year's election, and their wives.'

'The candidates and their wives,' the crowd repeated, raising their glasses.

'And may the best man win.'

As Georgios descended from the podium amidst a round of applause, Rion stared at Libby, dumbfounded. Yes, he knew precisely what she'd meant when she'd described him as *one of the people,* but she'd nevertheless done everything in her power to help him.

It was the last thing he'd expected, but now he thought about it—about her reaction when she'd overheard Spyros, the things she'd said before about witnessing injustice around the world—he supposed it did add up. *She* might not want to be married to a man of his background, but it seemed she had compassion for those who could hope for nothing more.

'Thank you,' he whispered stiltedly in her ear as the crowd began to disperse.

Libby inclined her head in gratitude as they headed back towards the garden, but she didn't allow herself to *feel* glad until Stephanos and the other members of his team came over to rejoice in the good fortune of Spyros's outburst and the quick-wittedness of her response. Not because she wanted their thanks—Rion's meant far more—but because she knew that unless she kept her guard up when she was alone with him she was in serious danger of telling him that she was in love with him.

Which, she told herself as the party continued in a blur of introductions, small talk and sipped champagne, would be an exceptionally foolish thing to do. Because she might have proof that all along he had been motivated by good, but she had no evidence that he'd retained any of the feelings that had once prompted him to propose all those years ago, or that he was capable of understanding why she'd left and moved forward. On the contrary, if their original agreement still stood—and he'd given her no indication that it didn't—then tomorrow he would sign the divorce papers and be done with her.

By the time the crowds began to thin, and Libby found herself alone with him again, she'd almost built her defences back up.

'Come on,' he whispered, inclining his head towards the house. 'We've done everything we can.'

Libby was glad. Her feet were sore and the muscles in her cheeks had begun to ache. Whilst she'd genuinely enjoyed talking to many of the local people, the awareness that she was being scrutinised had induced a kind of facial fatigue she hadn't experienced since those parties at Ashworth Manor.

Yet her relief was accompanied by trepidation. Georgios was bound to have reserved them a double room, and unless she wanted to undo all their hard work tonight she had no choice but to stay in it—with Rion. And, whilst she'd spent the evening schooling her heart against him, she knew that would do her about as much good as a map of Metameikos in Malaga if he came anywhere near her.

'Ah, Mr and Mrs Delikaris.' She heard Georgios's voice behind them as they walked through the atrium. 'You're off to bed? Not a moment too soon. Tomorrow is going to be a long day for you both.' He lowered his voice and came in between them, placing his arms around their shoulders. 'Come. I would prefer it if you kept this to yourselves, but I have reserved you the best room in the house.'

So good it had two beds? Libby wondered optimistically.

Georgios pressed a key into Rion's hand and guided them down the main corridor that led off of the hallway, and then along a narrower one to the right, where the high walls were covered from floor to ceiling in beautiful neoclassical paintings.

Libby spun around, her concerns temporarily forgotten as she looked up in awe. 'Is this part of the residence open to the public?' she asked, wondering if she'd reached her conclusion that the new part of the town had nothing worth visiting too quickly.

'Yes, of course,' Georgios answered. 'The mayoral residence really *belongs* to the people of Metameikos. The Mayor has permission to add to it—this wing was built by a mayor named Leander back in the eighteenth century, whilst the one we are headed to now was constructed by my predecessor—but really we're just its guardians.'

She nodded in appreciation. 'I'm a tour guide,' she explained. 'I run excursions for small groups. I'd love to add a trip here to the itinerary I'm currently working on.'

Georgios looked delighted, but at the same time perplexed. 'And you enjoy your work?'

'Yes,' Libby said sincerely. 'I love it.'

He turned to Rion, rolled his eyes and threw his hands in the air. 'Just like my wife! All my life I do the honourable thing—work hard so that she doesn't have to—and then she insists on getting a job! I never understood it.'

His words forced Libby to do a double-take. What had he just said?

That he'd always tried to do the honourable thing and support his wife, and that he'd never been able to understand her desire to work?

Rapidly, Georgios's words seeped into her mind, changing the colour of the past. After she and Rion had married she'd thought that he wanted to make his own way in the world, buy a better house, without any contribution from her. When he'd refused to admit that, she'd been convinced he was in denial, but suddenly she thought she understood. It hadn't been a question of

ambition, it had been a question of honour. And what
had she done? Walked away.

As a whole new wave of guilt washed over her, Libby
failed to notice that they'd slowed right down and that
Georgios had just hit a square gold button in the wall.
Because it had just occurred to her where that code of
honour came from. It wasn't just that he was Greek, it
was that he'd had to watch helplessly as his mother had
had to work day and night to support him and his brother.

And suddenly she saw why he had never compre-
hended that working and living alone was what she
needed to feel free. Because freedom to his mother
would have been a home, a husband to support her. Her
heart turned over. Everything he'd given *her.*

Suddenly a loud *ping* broke through her thoughts.
'Here we are. It's on the top floor, straight in front of
you as you exit the lift.'

Lift? Libby felt her pulse-rate rocket.

'Um, I'd really rather take the stairs, if you don't
mind,' she shot out abruptly, desperately flicking her
eyes past Georgios and around the new wing, looking for
a stairwell. 'Walk off all those delicious hors d'oeuvres.'

Rion eyed her quizzically, unable to fathom her expression. She was probably just worried about what
she might do if she found herself in an enclosed space
with him. Good.

Georgios shook his head and tutted. 'My son married an English girl too—barely eats a lettuce leaf!
Hasn't Rion told you that Greek men don't like their
women too skinny? Particularly if it means a longer

journey to the bedroom.' He chuckled softly, ushering her forward as the doors opened and Rion thanked him for his hospitality.

She wanted to back away from the lift, to have Rion look at her, automatically understand, and endorse her suggestion that they take the stairs—but then he still didn't know some fundamental things about her, did he? And what would it say about their marriage to Georgios if she suddenly blurted out something like that now?

'Sleep well,' Georgios called after them as the doors slowly closed.

The second they shut Libby's heart began to thunder in her chest and her breaths became short, sharp and raspy.

'Are you okay?'

'I don't do lifts,' she choked, pushing her hand up against the doors, leaning her head into the crook of her elbow and focussing on the crack, willing it to open.

Instantly Rion saw her words were an understatement and put his hands on her shoulders. He spun her round. 'You're claustrophobic?'

She nodded.

Gamoto! He hit every button on the lift's panel to try and make it stop—at any floor he could. Why hadn't she told him downstairs? He bent his knees slightly, so that his eyes were level with hers. Because if she had Georgios would have known something was amiss, he realised suddenly. A wave of guilt coursed through him.

They both quickly realised it was one of those lifts which obeyed commands in order and was going all the way up to the top floor first.

Visions of the walls closing in around her began to flood Libby's mind, her temperature soared, and then the muscles in her neck went so weak that her chin lolled against her chest.

'No,' he said, firmly but gently. 'I need you to keep looking at me.'

He placed his hands on either side of her face and guided her head upwards, so that her eyes were level with his again.

'We're not here,' he said, very definitely, searching her face for inspiration, needing a memory he could use to transport her mind away from there. Somewhere open, out-of-doors, where they'd both been together. He was momentarily struck by how tragic it was that there was such a lack of options, even from the months of their marriage they'd spent together, but he didn't have time to dwell on what that meant.

'We're in Athens,' he said suddenly. 'We're in Athens and it's snowing.' *All right, the options are limited, Delikaris, but surely you could have thought of something other than that?*

The tension in Libby's chest, the growing movement towards the black hole was immediately immobilised. Had he just said Athens? In the snow?

Rion couldn't miss the way her whole body seemed to pull back from the brink just a fraction. Oh, what the hell? If it took her mind off this… Reminding her that even their wedding day had been a let-down was hardly going to make any difference after all that he'd been forced to reveal tonight.

'We're slowly making our way to the town hall—on foot, through the National Gardens, because the taxi can't make it up the road.'

'They haven't got round to clearing it yet,' she whispered, her words slurring into each other a little at first. 'But a few people are just starting to come outside with shovels.' The memories seemed to form a dam in her mind, holding back the rising panic.

'And we manage to talk an old man and woman into coming with us to witness the ceremony—'

'In exchange for the promise of hot chocolate.'

To Rion's astonishment she smiled—and it wasn't tinged with any of the distaste he would have expected. Only because she'd temporarily lost control of her faculties, he was sure, but for a second he allowed himself to forget that.

'They thought we were crazy.' He smiled too.

We were hung in the air. But neither of them said it.

Suddenly the lift made that pinging sound again and the doors opened.

But Libby barely even registered it, because she was looking at him with tears in her eyes and she couldn't look away.

CHAPTER ELEVEN

'WE'RE here.'

His words broke the spell. Libby blinked hard, forced the tears back behind her eyes, and looked down at her feet. To her astonishment she realised they were still firmly planted inside the lift. Even though the doors were wide open. *How was that even possible?*

'Are you okay to walk?'

She nodded, not entirely sure that she was.

Rion looped his arm through hers and encouraged her out onto the landing, but she couldn't focus forward. She kept looking back over her shoulder, trying to work out what the hell had just happened. How could she have felt less restricted in a small space with another person than she would have done alone?

'You're okay,' he whispered, mistaking her backward glance for a look of trepidation. 'I promise we'll take the stairs from now on.'

Oh, she was scared, all right, but she didn't think the kind of fear she was feeling now could be eradicated by avoiding enclosed spaces.

He delved into his jacket pocket for the key as they reached a large wooden door. 'At least our room is bound to be spacious.'

Her vision was still a little blurry, but when he unlocked the door there was no mistaking that it was. Nor was there any mistaking that, despite its gargantuan dimensions, there was only the one bed. An enormous four-poster bed, bedecked with crisp cream sheets and decadent aubergine drapes. It stood in the middle of the room, staring back at them like an enormous question mark. Or at least that was how it seemed to Libby.

'You should sit down,' he said, his voice raspy. She had a feeling the bed seemed that way to him too.

He strode across to the windows, which stretched the length of the opposite wall, and opened a couple to let in the cool evening breeze. Then he disappeared through a doorway at the far end of the room.

Libby was still standing dazedly in the same spot when he returned, carrying a glass of water.

'Here.' He swapped the glass for the handbag she was still clutching in her right hand, and dipped his head in the direction of the bed, his voice more insistent this time. 'Sit.'

Libby did as he commanded whilst he pulled up a chair, shrugged off his jacket and sat down facing her.

'When did it start?'

She tried to sound breezy, raising the glass to her lips to take a sip of water. 'Oh, you know—when do all these things start? When I was a kid.'

'When you were *a child*?' She felt him strain not to

raise his voice. 'How did I not know about this?' He shook his head as if her answer wouldn't compute. 'We lived on the fourth floor!'

'We didn't exactly enter or leave the apartment together very frequently,' she said quietly. 'Besides, the lift was usually out of order.'

Rion smarted, but let it go. 'Do you know what started it in the first place?'

Libby drew in a short, sharp breath, not wanting to make a big deal out of it. Especially now that she knew it was nothing compared to what he'd gone through in *his* childhood. 'I think being locked in the cupboard below the stairs for hours at a time if I displeased my father had something to do with it.'

Rion balled his hand into a fist and fought the urge to take out his anger on an inanimate object in the absence of Thomas Ashworth himself. *Gamoto!* Ever since he'd learned that her father had kept her cut off, even after their separation, he'd known he was more than just a bigot. But this was something else. 'You should have told me.'

She exhaled deeply. 'I did try—in my own way.'

But maybe she should have tried harder, Libby thought for the first time as she registered the look of shock on his face. Because she'd never sat him down and made him understand what was at the root of her need to feel free and in control, any more than he'd told *her* about where his drive to provide for them really came from. They'd just both thought the other should understand instinctively, and she'd bolted when they hadn't.

She shook her head, the tragedy of it piercing her heart as she realised how different things might have been if they'd known. But then again, maybe not. Because how could they have fought each other's demons when they hadn't been done fighting their own?

'*When* did you try and tell me?' he demanded.

He knew there was no way he'd forget a detail like that. She'd never once mentioned any fear of— Libby looked up at him with wide eyes, and suddenly the bottom dropped out of his stomach. Her expression took him right back to the day she'd walked away. No, she hadn't mentioned a fear of enclosed spaces specifically, but she had always been desperate not to be left alone in that apartment, to go out and get a job and—

Rion squeezed his eyes tightly shut. But that had been because she couldn't bear living in that hovel, hadn't it? Suddenly the memory mixed with what Georgios had said downstairs, about his wife *wanting* to get a job. Libby *had* only ever spoken of working with pleasure. And, come to think of it, she'd never complained about the apartment itself. So had he been wrong? And, if he had been, what the hell else had he got wrong about her?

Nothing, a voice in the back of his mind ground out, refusing to let him go any further down that path and lay himself open to that level of pain all over again. Yes, maybe he *had* been wrong about the reason why she'd wanted to get a job, why she hadn't wanted to be alone in the apartment, but it didn't change the underlying reason why she'd gone. Why she was here now, demanding a divorce. That night after they'd been to the theatre she'd admitted it—she found being his wife *humiliating*. Because in her eyes he'd never, ever be good enough.

He forced his eyes open and stood up. 'I'll get you some more water.'

'No—' She reached out her hand and placed it on his forearm. 'I'm fine, honestly.'

Rion clenched his teeth, just the feel of her fingertips on his skin causing a tightening in his groin. 'Nevertheless, you should get some rest.'

He walked round to the opposite side of the room and Libby heard him turn on the bedside lamp. Her eyes remained fixed on the chair where he'd been sitting. She recognised that last look on his face. It was the one he'd worn that afternoon. He wanted her. He actually wanted her. And it wasn't about control or defiance or the election. She knew it wasn't. It was about those memories. Her heart blossomed. He wanted her, but he was fighting it because he thought she was still unwell, that it wasn't what she wanted.

She drew in a deep breath, his thoughtfulness seeping into her heart, mixing with everything else that she'd discovered about him tonight. And even if she hadn't left all her defences in the lift, then the remainder slid off the bed and slunk out of sight at that moment.

'Rion, I don't want…' She heard him go still behind her, heard the nervous quiver in her own voice. 'I don't want you to fight this. I know I can't. Not tonight.'

The tightness in Rion's groin instantly intensified, but he didn't move, simply carried on staring at the back of her head. Had that moment in the lift weakened her faculties *and* taken her defences with them, then? Or had thinking about her father simply reawakened her desire to rebel by having it off with the boy from nowhere?

It was the admission he'd been waiting for—another chance to wear her down, remind her that they were driven by just the same urges. But tonight he had to wonder whether the only thing he was really wearing down was his self-respect.

'And what about tomorrow, Libby? Your defences will return with the sunrise?'

She turned to face him, her voice barely a whisper. 'No, I doubt I'll be able to fight it then either. Or the next day.'

Triumph flooded through Rion's chest as he realised the depth of her capitulation. She was saying she wouldn't *ever* be able to fight it.

Instantly, what was left of his plot to take revenge went up in smoke. It would never have been satisfying enough anyway. The only thing that could satisfy him was her, returning as his wife, for good. 'Then you'll stay?' he growled. 'After tomorrow?'

Libby stared at him and felt her heart swell to double its normal size.

He was asking her to stay. After the election. When the reason he needed her here would be gone. And the only reason remaining would be because he wanted her to.

Hours ago she'd been sure that leaving was the only sane thing to do. That he would never love her... Now she still had no guarantees, knew they had a mountain to climb, but he had just given her every reason to hope that it *was* possible.

She stood up and walked towards him, emotions washing over her. 'Yes, Rion, I'll stay.'

Rion stared at her in amazement. He'd done it. He'd actually broken her, made her realise that their desire for one another did transcend all else. And he didn't hesitate. Suddenly, definitively, he dropped his head and found her mouth.

Libby revelled in it, roving her hands up his back, hungrily raking her fingers through his hair, then sliding his tie from beneath his collar. She tossed it to the floor while Rion's hands stroked up her arms and then straight back down again, taking the straps of her dress with him and exposing her to the waist.

He let out a growl of pleasure at the discovery that she was not wearing a bra, and stilled for just a moment to watch as her nipples peaked under his gaze. God, she wanted him to look at her like that for ever.

She let out a moan as he lowered his head and began to slick his tongue over her nipples, nuzzling her, caressing her. But the aching need between her thighs made her impatient for more. She ran her hand up his leg, towards the waistband of his trousers, feeling his arousal jump as she skimmed over it, and then encouraged him back towards the bed.

'Wait,' he said, placing his hands on hers and returning them to her. 'Just a second.'

He moved quickly to their bags, which had been neatly placed in the corner of the room, and swiftly unzipped a pocket to extract a condom.

The second Libby realised what he was doing she

knew she had to stop him this time. Yes, it might result in a few moments of awkward explanation, but she understood now that honesty was essential if their marriage was ever going to work. 'No.' She shook her head, gnawing on her lower lip and praying that it wouldn't destroy the moment completely. 'That's not necessary.'

Rion stared down at the foil packet between his fingers, then looked up at her face in astonishment. No, he thought, as the full extent of her capitulation truly sank in. Now she'd agreed to return as his wife permanently, he supposed it *wasn't* necessary, was it?

But the soaring triumph that accompanied the realisation that she'd just suggested the one thing he'd always wanted was curtailed by the look of resignation on her face. Because it was perfectly clear that she didn't deem him any more worthy to be the father of her children now than she had done then. The only difference was that now she understood she was never going to want another man the way she wanted him, and that, unless she was prepared to live without desire like that, his lack of breeding was something she was just going to have to try and forget.

And, whilst his instinct was to pull down the remainder of her dress, spill his seed inside her, and prove that class was irrelevant to Mother Nature, the thought of doing so in such a way that would remind her of his uncivilised roots, of the concession she was having to make, was utterly repugnant to him.

Instead he dropped the condom, inwardly vowed to

keep his philistine urges on a tightly coiled leash, and slowly stalked back to the bed to focus on her pleasure.

'Lie down.'

Libby felt her desire rocket at his husky command and stepped back, slid off the remainder of her dress, and stretched out on the bed in answer. She was surprised that he asked no questions, levelled no accusation of infidelity, but she was glad. She took it as proof that his feelings mirrored hers, that he saw whatever had happened in the intervening years—not that anything *had* happened on her part—as history.

He quickly came to join her on the bed, and Libby felt him run his eyes downwards, over her breasts, across her scrap of underwear and down her legs. But as she looked up into his face to savour his appreciation she was surprised to see that his expression wasn't the one of urgent need she'd expected, instead he looked— detached. *The way he did when your marriage was on its last legs,* a voice taunted in the back of her mind.

But as his mouth homed in on hers once more, she told herself she'd imagined it. He'd just asked her to stay, for goodness' sake, admitted he couldn't fight this any more than she could. Determined to prove it, she rolled over on to her side, splayed her hand across his chest and began butterflying kisses down towards his belly button. But just as she was about to curl her fingers around his length he caught her wrist and shook his head.

She felt an arrow of disappointment fire up inside her chest, but it never got the chance to land. For Rion instantly took his tongue on a sensuous journey of its own, lower and lower, to the point of aching need, until he was tasting her, filling her with such delicious heat that she could do nothing but throw her head back helplessly against the pillows and surrender to a pleasure so agonisingly intense that she wasn't sure whether she wanted to scream for it to stop or for it never to end.

But if she'd supposed she had time to do either, she was mistaken. Because, as she gripped the back of his head in one hand and the sheets with the other, she was already there.

Dizzy with pleasure, but desperate to bring him the same, Libby threw her arm across his middle and encouraged him to move on top of her. Rion's body jolted eagerly, but instead of following her lead he placed his hands around her waist and moved *her* on top of *him*.

Libby didn't complain, convinced his way would be equally effective. She straddled his body and sank down onto him, angling herself forward so that she could move up and down on just the tip of him.

Rion let out an anguished moan and she smiled, taking the whole length of him inside her. He closed his eyes and let his head roll to one side momentarily, but seconds later he snapped his eyes open again, smoothed his hands up her sides, and grazed her nipples with his thumbs. Combined with the feel of their bodies moving together, it created a pleasure so intense that she didn't have the strength to lower her mouth and kiss the sensitive hollow beneath his ear, or to tease him by slowing down the rhythm as she'd planned to, because her body was already tightening again.

And, before she could help herself, suddenly she was drenched in another flood of sensation.

Only when she had finished, and cried out for a second time, did she feel Rion give one final upward thrust and hear a primitive growl tear from his lips. But just as she was revelling in the sound of it he cut it short.

Libby lay down by his side, the arrow of disappointment finally landing in her heart. She tried to stop it, but she couldn't. Because until then she'd been sure that lovemaking was the one area of their marriage which needed no further work. She told herself it still didn't, that he'd just climaxed for heaven's sake, but she knew his passion had been nowhere near as unchecked as it had been that day in the hallway.

She propped herself up on one elbow and looked down into his face, praying for the courage to ask him what the problem was—or, more to the point, the courage to stick around for the answer. But his eyes were closed, and she could hear his breathing growing slower and deeper, verging on the edge of sleep.

And no wonder. Suddenly she felt racked with guilt for being so self-absorbed—especially after an evening in which she'd realised how important it was for them to really try and support and understand one another. Of course he was going to be a little detached tonight. If he wasn't completely exhausted after two tireless weeks of campaigning, then he was probably worrying about the election tomorrow.

After that, everything would be different. She looked over at the bedside clock, realising the polls would be opening in a few hours. Yes, she thought, as the reality of what she had agreed to began to sink in, after that everything would be very different indeed.

CHAPTER TWELVE

LIBBY had never seen a man look so calm and collected. Or a man so impossibly handsome, either, but that went without saying. Everyone else in the main hall seemed unable to keep still: Stephanos had almost worn a hole in the polished wood floor with his pacing; Georgios must have gone to check that everything was still running smoothly in the counting room at least a dozen times; and Spyros—despite his proclamation of confidence in the passageway last night—seemed to have developed a sudden predilection for hand-wringing. Even *she* didn't seem to be able to stop fiddling with one earring, glancing behind her as the main hall of the mayoral residence filled up with more and more people.

But not Rion. He was perfectly still, hands pressed together, forefingers resting just under his chin. Waiting with the same supreme composure that he'd exhibited from the minute he'd woken up and gone to cast his own vote to the moment he'd returned here to assemble his team for the result. It wasn't the stillness of lethargy— she could see every muscle in his body was pumped with anticipation—instead he seemed to possess the unique ability of being able to keep his body's natural responses under control. A week ago she wouldn't have been particularly surprised about that—nobody got to be the owner of a billion-dollar company without the ability to remain cool at the operative moment—but now that she knew how much this result meant to him personally, she found it incredible.

Almost as incredible as the fact that she would still be here tomorrow, she thought, looking at the dashing figure he cut in his suit, impatient to prove to herself how good the lovemaking would be between them again once the stress of this election was over.

'Ladies and gentlemen.' Georgios's words cut through her errant thoughts and the room fell silent. 'Good evening, and thank you for your patience.' He craned his neck to look at the clock on the right-hand side of the wall behind him, which read just before ten p.m. 'The turnout at the polls this year has been unprecedented, but I can now confirm that all votes have been collected, counted, and verified.' He raised the sealed envelope in his hand. 'People of Metameikos. Your results are in.'

It felt as if the whole room simultaneously stopped breathing and blinking; all energy was focussed on the sound of the envelope being slowly torn open, on the sight of Georgios carefully extracting the slip of paper that held the answer to everyone's future.

He took a deep breath. 'Taking sixty-four per cent of the vote…ladies and gentleman, you have elected a new leader: Orion Delikaris.'

The room erupted in a cheer; Stephanos gave a whoop so loud it was only surpassed by a woman's delighted high-pitched squeal from the back of the room. Libby instantly recognised it as belonging to Eurycleia.

But before the round of applause had reached its natural conclusion there was another loud noise that sounded a lot like a blow being struck. As Libby turned her head, she realised to her astonishment that it had been a blow being struck. Spyros had placed his fist through one of the ornate panels of the eighteenth-century wall.

He swore obscenely, muttered something she couldn't fully discern about a lower class mutiny, then pushed his way through the crowd of smirks and frowns, belatedly followed by his wife, who reluctantly shuffled after him.

But Libby only spared them a single glance, because her eyes were fixed on Rion. She liked to think that if she hadn't already known, then at that moment she would have guessed his motivation for running in this election *was* noble. Because he didn't lord it over Spyros, even though he had every right to do so. His chest wasn't puffed out; he was not self-righteous in his success and newly won power.

No, he looked…supremely humble. Victorious, yes, but as if his victory transcended personal success and belonged to everyone in the room. And, whilst she had seen the tension in every sinew of his body ease slightly as Georgios had read out his name, she also saw a man who was aware that he might have been handed the crown, but it was what he did from this moment onwards which would determine whether he deserved to wear it.

The way all politicians *ought* to look, Libby philoso-
phised, thinking how unfortunate it was that they rarely
did. Yet it made her even prouder to be standing there
beside him.

'Congratulations,' she whispered, squeezing his hand.
'The people of Metameikos made the right choice.'

For a second Rion felt such an acute sense of fulfilment at her words that it even surpassed the moment
Georgios had read out his name. But then he remembered. All she meant was that the other candidate had
been a corrupt pig, and in the absence of anyone else
the people of the old town had been best off choosing
one of their own. Abruptly he let go of her hand.

'I would like to invite the new leader of Metameikos
to the podium, please.' Georgios beamed, gesturing for
Rion to step forward as the disturbance died down. 'A
man who—' he looked at the empty space Spyros had
left behind '—I'm in no doubt whatsoever *is* the best
man for the job.'

Libby felt the uneasiness she'd experienced last night
rise again as Rion dropped her hand without a backward
glance. But as she watched him make his way to the microphone she gave herself a stern talking-to. He was
about to deliver the most important speech of his life, and
all she could worry about was that he hadn't squeezed her
hand and smiled at her in return? Good God! She should
be ashamed of herself. If they were going to build a successful marriage out of the flotsam and jetsam of their old
one, then she really ought to start practising what she
preached: move forward and show him some support.

Her thoughts bore a striking resemblance to the theme of Rion's modest, inspiring and perfectly polished address. He spoke openly about the hard work that lay ahead, without dwelling on what had happened in the past, and shared his vision for the change that was possible, if everyone was willing, for a brighter and more equal future.

As his words turned into actions in the weeks that followed, Libby could well believe he'd been talking about more than just politics. Because after that night things within their marriage undoubtedly changed too. She understood the demands on his time, and why both his work and his political career meant so much to him. In return, to her delight, he began to invite her to accompany him in his duties—to the laying of the first brick for the new hospital, to the occasional meeting with his team. He even asked her to speak at one of them about how she felt the new set of guidelines aimed at restricting planning permission for luxury holiday homes would impact on the tourist industry.

And, though she had expected it to take time for him to fully understand how much having her own life meant to her, he purposely arranged a trip to Delikaris headquarters on the same day that she needed to return to Athens to make some arrangements for the first tour she was due to lead there at the end of the month. He didn't even bat an eyelid when she made a note on the calendar of the dates when she'd be away.

What was more, they made love—often.

Yet, to her distress, even though it seemed that he finally understood the importance of her having her own life, sharing his, the niggling uneasiness remained. In fact, though she'd tried to dismiss it as an old insecurity which would gradually work its way out, like a splinter coming to the body's surface, which only seemed to be getting deeper, causing her to lose more and more sleep.

So much so that one morning, four weeks after the election, Libby sat on the swing seat in front of the fig tree staring back at the house before the sun had even finished rising, and it was Saturday. At least during the week she could pretend to herself that she'd got up early to e-mail Kate before she opened the office for business. But today she had no such excuse.

The truth was that even though the timing finally felt right for them, she still wasn't happy. Because although they made love frequently it had never once been like it was that afternoon. Oh, he had pleasured her body in countless ways, but it always seemed to be about *her* enjoyment, never his. And when she tried to turn the tables—if she sidled down beside him, kissed the hollow by his hipbone and moved to take him in her mouth—he would encourage her away, only reaching what felt like nothing more than a perfunctory climax once she was satisfied.

Maybe it was a superficial reason to be discontent, especially as *he'd* never complained, but Libby had a horrible feeling that it masked something deeper. What if that day in the hallway, when their lovemaking had been so incredible, hadn't been evidence that her defiance had aroused him, but the end of the challenge of seducing her into staying—the age-old thrill of the chase? Then there *wouldn't* have been anything left to excite him the second she'd agreed to stay with him, would there? Just as there hadn't been after their wedding.

And that kind of excitement was never going to last in any marriage unless desire was kept stoked by love.

Libby swallowed down the lump in her throat. Yes, she'd pinned her hopes on that after he'd opened up to her in the walled garden, been convinced it could blossom if only they shared what was in their hearts, but since then they hadn't once talked properly about their relationship. To be perfectly frank, he was more closed off than ever.

Or at least that was how she saw it. But had she bothered to make him understand that and find out how he saw it? No. Libby flexed the soles of her flip-flops, annoyed that she still didn't seem to have learned not to jump to conclusions without consulting him.

Well, that wasn't strictly true. She *knew* she needed to talk to him, she was just afraid. Because what if he turned round and told her she had it spot-on? She couldn't bear it—not now. But the thought of repeating the mistakes of the past was worse. She took a deep breath and stood up.

He was in the kitchen when she came in through the back door. The sight of him wearing nothing but some pale lightweight trousers made her stomach contract.

'Up early again?' he asked, studying her for signs of

nausea. She did look pale. 'Sit down.' He pulled out one of the stools from beneath the breakfast bar. 'Coffee?'

'Umm…yes, thanks.' She wasn't in the least bit thirsty, but it occurred to her that having something to occupy her hands might be a good idea. As he turned to remove a mug from one of the cupboards on the opposite wall, she was grateful that it also gave her the chance to begin without his eyes boring into her. 'Rion, there's something I need to talk to you about.'

Rion stared into the open cupboard. It *had* happened, then. He'd guessed as much from all the early mornings. His heart began to swell with joy, but he forced himself to restrain it. Because, despite his best efforts to make her forget the pedigree he was lacking over the course of the last month, it was obvious from the look she'd worn as she'd walked in the back door that he hadn't succeeded. It was the same look that she'd worn inter-mittently ever since that night, and he knew this was anything but a joy to her.

'I can guess,' he said grimly, turning back round to face her.

'You can?' Libby blinked up at him, her heart starting to pound.

'It doesn't exactly require a detective, Libby.' He finished pouring the mug of coffee and slid it across the breakfast bar towards her.

So she hadn't imagined it. There *was* a gaping hole in their marriage. She knotted her hands around the mug and raised it to her lips, glad to have the opportunity to at least partially obscure her face for what was coming next.

'Then I need you to tell me how you feel about it.'
Tell me there's a chance there might not be a gaping hole for ever.

'I don't think *my* feelings are the issue, do you?'

Libby frowned. 'Of course they are.'

Rion shook his head. No, he knew what this was. She wanted him to come out and say that *he* wasn't a hundred per cent happy about it to stop her feeling guilty because that was how *she* felt. She was out of luck.

'I wanted a child five years ago, Libby. I still do.'

'*What?*' Libby choked on her coffee.

He did a double-take, suddenly aware that perhaps they'd been talking at cross purposes. 'You *did* want to talk to me about the fact that you're pregnant, didn't you?'

'That I'm…?' She looked at him, aghast, her mind struggling to process what he was saying. 'No, that it isn't… I'm not— Why would you think that?'

His swollen heart shrank and his voice became droll. 'It *is* a frequent outcome when two people have a lot of unprotected sex. Even two people as different as you and I.'

The objects of the room began to blur before her eyes. 'But we haven't been having unprotected sex. I told you, I'm—'

Horror coursed through Libby's veins. That night at the mayoral residence, when she'd said using a condom wasn't necessary, she hadn't actually spelt out why, had she? But surely he couldn't possibly have assumed that without discussion, when their relationship was still so fragile, she'd meant—?

'You're *what*?' he said impatiently.

Yes, she realised suddenly, he could have. Her head began to whirl. He'd spent the last month making love to her as though it was nothing but a functional exercise because that was precisely what it had been. He'd been trying to get her pregnant. And, much as she longed to believe that the reason he wanted that was because he loved her, the look on his face told her it categorically was not. For when had he ever promised any such thing? Never. He'd invited her here to play the role of his wife, and then he'd asked her to stay on. She realised now it was just an extension of their original agreement. Yes, maybe she had convinced him that an independent wife was better than a bland, clichéd one—yes, all his motives were honourable—but at the end of the day what mattered most was his electorate and showing them he was the ultimate family man in the most deliberate way there was.

'I'm on the pill,' she said wretchedly. 'I thought you realised when I said—'

'Of course,' Rion bit out, humiliation washing over him. 'How foolish of me. It should have been obvious that you'd do everything in your power to protect yourself from having my child.'

Libby shook her head. 'I was on the pill anyway. I have been for five years.'

His nostrils flared in disgust. The way she'd expected them to that night, when she'd naïvely taken his lack of reaction as a sign that their marriage was on the mend. She should have realised he hadn't understood what she was saying at all.

'For convenience,' she added. '*Never* for contraception.'

Never? Rion's head shot up. Her eyes met his unhesitantly. Was she saying…? Yes, he realised, she was. Part of him felt infinitely triumphant, yet the other part of him only grew angrier.

'So you've *always* known that no other man could bring you the pleasure that I do?' He slammed the jug of hot coffee down on the breakfast bar. 'Doesn't that tell you that Mother Nature never intended you to give a damn about class?'

Libby frowned. '*Class?*'

Rion exploded at her ingenuous expression. 'For God's sake, Libby! Isn't it about time you stopped pretending? Maybe the thought that you share the same prejudice as your father *does* make you ashamed, but I already know it's why you walked away. I know it's why you fought this for so long, and I know it's why the idea of having my child disgusts you.'

Libby's eyes frantically searched his face. She was hoping she'd misunderstood him. But for the first time in weeks his expression was one of openness and honesty. The kind of expression she'd longed to see but which she'd now do anything to make disappear.

Her mind traced back over the past—how obsessed he'd always been with bettering their situation in Athens, how reluctant he'd always been to discuss his past with her—had it really been because he believed she didn't think he was good enough?

It had been, hadn't it?

Libby's whole body began to shake. She was horrified that he'd spent all those years thinking she was wired that way, that it had never occurred to her that *that* was what was going on in his head, that he'd never told her. That in leaving she must have doubled the insecurities he'd battled with for so long.

'I've never thought that way, Rion. Not the day we met, not the day we married, not ever.'

He looked thoroughly unconvinced. But then she supposed he'd spent most of his life hearing people tell him he was worth nothing, hadn't he? The Spyros family, her father… Well, the latter at least she might be able to go some way to putting right.

'Anyway,' she added, 'if I did share my father's perspective I would have come back years ago.'

His head shot up a second time.

'When my father heard about the success of Delikaris Experiences he tracked me down and called me up, wanting a reconciliation with both of us.' Libby's voice turned sour, but she kept her eyes focussed on his face, not forgetting her purpose in relaying the story. 'When I informed him that we were separated, he promised that if I returned to you he would welcome us back with open arms and make you the heir to Ashworth Motors. When I refused, he swore he'd never speak to me again as long as he lived.'

Rion stared at her in disbelief. Thomas Ashworth had *wanted* her to stay married to him? Had come to consider him a worthy son-in-law regardless of his background because of what he'd achieved? Not long ago that would have felt like the ultimate accomplishment. Now her father's good opinion just felt like an insult. As hollow as defeating Spyros had felt.

Because, no matter how long he'd spent telling himself otherwise, the only person whose good opinion he really cared about was Libby's. He flicked his eyes up to meet hers, guilt forming a lump in his throat. Could it really be possible, then, that he'd had it all along? That he'd been wrong about everything?

'Are you telling me that…you have no objections to having my child?'

Libby looked up at him desperately, feeling the tears prick behind her eyes. If he'd told her that he loved her, that he wanted her to be the mother of his child, nothing would have made her happier. But he hadn't—because he didn't.

'I couldn't bring a child into this world unless he or she would be guaranteed two parents who want to be married to one another for the right reasons.'

Libby watched as Rion closed his eyes. When he opened them again they looked completely changed, as if he'd finally faced that whatever he'd once felt for her had withered away. It had returned briefly, when their relationship had been fresh and exciting again, but now it was gone.

'And that's never going to be us, is it?' he murmured.

Libby felt her heart shrivel and die inside her chest. She'd come inside to talk to him about the gaping hole in their marriage, to find out whether there was any chance he could ever truly love her. She hadn't asked that question but she had the answer, and it was as clear as the result of a landslide election.

'No,' she whispered brokenly, 'it's not.'

And that was why she had to leave.

CHAPTER THIRTEEN

THE muffled slide of a suitcase from beneath a bed, followed by the opening and closing of wardrobe doors, seemed to Rion to be the most depressing sound on earth. He strode to one side of the living room and then back again, afflicted for the first time in his life by an inability to keep still. He wanted to go up there and kiss her until she agreed to stay. But he understood now that that would be as cruel as locking a bird in a cage.

His eyes skimmed the table where she'd been working yesterday, its surface scattered with brochures and scribbled notes. How had he not realised that earlier? If not five years ago, then at least that night at Georgios's, when he'd seen for himself that she needed freedom like other people needed air. But he'd been so blinded by his own inferiority complex that it hadn't occurred to him that when she'd argued that the sensible thing to do was get divorced it had been because she didn't want to be married full-stop.

Now he understood that so long as she remained his wife, no matter how hard he tried to support her career or give her space to spread her wings, she was always going to feel trapped. Not because of his past, but because to her marriage itself was a prison. Or at least marriage to *him* was a prison. For a while there she must have believed there was a chance her feelings could change, that the desire she felt for him might grow into the right reason for wanting to stay, but he knew now there was no way it ever would, and so did she. He'd already done her too much wrong.

But he swore he'd do her no more, no matter how persistent the urge to take the stairs two at a time and haul her back into his arms. What was that phrase? If you loved someone, you should set them free? He raked a hand through his hair, the thought of letting her go excruciating. But, much as he believed in challenging accepted wisdom, he knew he should have heeded that advice a long time ago.

Rion reluctantly walked the short distance to his study and removed the sheaf of papers from the bottom drawer of his desk—the papers he'd placed there after she'd tossed them down the stairs at him, the ones she'd first pulled from her bag that day at his office in Athens. He'd been so determined not to sign them that he'd never read the small print. He didn't read it now. If it asked for anything he'd gladly give it to her, just so he never had to see that look of desolation on her face again. But he knew it didn't ask—knew nothing but walking out of his front door with the signed papers in her hand could ease her expression of torment.

And after that he'd never see her face again, he

thought dismally, glancing round his office at the photos of the latest progress on the hospital, at the plans for the new affordable houses. The things which ought to buoy him up but just left him feeling numb. Because, yes, he'd done everything that he'd sworn he would the day Jason died: made a success of himself, returned to Metameikos and fought for the position which would allow him to make sure nothing like that ever happened again. Only now did he realise that it had been at the expense of his own happiness, that life was only truly worth anything if you had love. Someone to share it with.

But he knew that he had realised it too late. Even if Libby had thought that she wanted to share her life with him once, he could never make her happy now. There was only one thing that could.

Rion looked back down at the papers before him and opened the glass cabinet next to his desk. He poured himself a measure of Scotch, knocked it back, then reached for his pen.

As Libby kneeled on the floor, pressing the mass of unfolded clothes into her suitcase, she could taste the salty drops of her tears. They weren't the hysterical tears of sudden grief, they were the resigned, silent kind, mourning a death that had been inevitable for months—in her case years—but that didn't make them any less painful.

Because all that time, even when she'd told herself not to, she'd kept hoping it wasn't terminal, that underneath it all he *had* wanted her to be his wife, for the same reason that she'd wanted him to be her husband: love.

But now there was no hope left, and she didn't know how to begin to live without it. Even locked in the cupboard under the stairs at Ashworth Manor, she'd had that much. Now all she had was a void in her heart where hope used to be.

'You'd better not go without this.'

She hadn't heard him ascend the stairs or enter the room behind her, but then her mind was such a mess it was a miracle that any of her senses were working at all. Quickly she brushed the tears from her cheeks. But before she could even move on to attempting the neurological function required to process what he'd said, he slid something onto the bed in front of her.

The divorce petition.

The *signed* divorce petition.

Her eyes dropped from the official court logo down to the 'O. Delikaris' scrawled without hesitation on the line. It was the only thing she'd come here originally to get—the thing she'd once imagined would bring with it a sense of closure. She'd never been more wrong about anything in her life. It felt as if she'd been torn open.

'You were right in the first place,' Rion said quietly, unnerved by the way she didn't even move her head, needing to fill the silence because he was afraid that if he didn't the temptation to press his lips to the back of her neck might overwhelm him. 'This is the right thing to do.'

'Thank you,' she choked. It felt as if she were trying to swallow a loaf of bread without chewing.

'I can fly you back to Athens,' he said stiltedly, 'or drive you to the airport if you'd rather?'

The thought of sitting beside him in the plane or next to him in the Bugatti was unbearable. She shook her head and found the courage to turn around, needing him to know she was grateful for the offer.

'If you could just call me a cab, I'll make the arrangements from there.'

Of course, Rion thought helplessly. Anything else would encroach on her independence. He nodded and turned on his heel. 'I'll let you know when it's here.'

The taxi arrived ten minutes later. She'd been watching out of the upstairs window for it to arrive, and was already halfway down the stairs with her suitcase when he called her. She knew it was rude not to have gone and waited with him once she'd finished packing, but she couldn't have trusted herself not to break down, nor have borne him awkwardly trying to comfort her if she had.

'Let me take that,' he insisted, swooping to grasp the handle of her suitcase.

'No, I'm fine, honest—'

He cut her off mid-sentence. 'Please. Allow me that much.'

Libby relinquished her grip, the feel of his hand moving over hers too agonising to even contemplate doing anything else, then followed him downstairs.

'So I guess this is it?' he breathed, placing the suitcase down on the marble.

She nodded, the irony of standing just metres away from the spot where they'd made the most incredible love not lost on her. 'I guess it is.'

The silence was deafening.

Rion fought the urge to offer her money, or the use of his apartment in Athens. 'You'll file the papers when you get back to the city?'

Libby felt her stomach lurch. He seemed so keen to have it all over with now.

She nodded. 'I'm sure the solicitor will send you copies, along with the decree absolute once it's finalised.'

'It should come through pretty quickly, since we're both in agreement.'

His voice seemed to Libby to go up at the end of his sentence, almost as if it was a question. But she told herself not to read anything into it. She'd spent six weeks reading things that weren't really there, that had never been there.

'I should go. The taxi's waiting.' She stepped forward and reclaimed her suitcase. 'I can take it from here.'

With great effort he forced himself to take a step backwards. 'Who knows? Maybe we might bump into each other if you run those excursions here some time.'

'Maybe,' she agreed. Though in her heart she'd already made up her mind to tell Kate there was no way she could carry on with the Greek tours. There was no point in pretending that her memories would do anything other than destroy her if she remained on Greek soil. Maybe even if she didn't.

'Well, in the meantime, I hope your tours in Athens go well.'

She wanted to look back. She wanted to give him a blithe smile and say *Thank you. Good luck running Metameikos too.* She wanted to be glad they understood each other now, if nothing else. But she wasn't, and she couldn't. It took everything she had to place her fingers around the door handle and wrench it open.

'Goodbye, *gineka*—' He stopped himself and sighed deeply. 'Goodbye, Libby.'

'Goodbye, Rion.'

If the sound of Libby packing her things had been the worst noise in the world to Rion, then the click of the door latch as she pulled it shut behind her was Libby's equivalent. Leaving him once had been hard enough— but then she'd been sure their marriage would have broken them both if she'd stayed, had been able to throw herself into discovering who she was and what she wanted. But now that she had, all her discoveries had led her to was the fact that she was completely and irrepressibly in love with him.

She swallowed hard, tears thick in the back of her throat. As much at the discovery that he'd spent all those years believing that in her eyes he'd never been good enough as for the end of their marriage.

But what would he believe now? she wondered. The thought made her whole body jolt forward. *Did* he fully understand that had never been an issue to her? She hadn't actually explained the real reason why she hadn't felt able to agree to have his baby, hadn't told him that a huge part of her wanted to. And, even though she knew it would change nothing, the thought that he might be in any doubt—now or in years to come—that maybe they *still* didn't fully understand one another, clawed at her heart.

She closed her eyes, contemplating whether she could

bear the pain involved in putting that right. She wasn't sure she could, but maybe that was why she *should*. Maybe, in the absence of any other kind of closure, just going back in and saying the words, leaving them there in the hallway, was the closest she was going to get.

'Are you ready to go, Kyria Delikaris?'

Libby's eyes flew open to see the taxi driver, looking at her from his vehicle with a mixture of perplexity and concern, and it suddenly occurred to her that standing outside Rion's front door with tears rolling down her cheeks was an exceptionally thoughtless thing to be doing. Whilst he'd have to publicly confess that they were getting divorced at some point, he didn't need speculation starting now.

'I just—need to do one last thing,' she replied, and without giving a second thought to the pros and cons she turned and rang the doorbell.

Rion opened the door instantly. If she hadn't known better she would have guessed that he'd been leaning up against it, contemplating whether to come after her.

He stared at her, hollow eyes wide. 'You've forgotten something?'

She hesitated for a moment. 'Yes.' She supposed you could put it that way.

Rion did a quick mental tour of the house. 'Of course—your work.' He stepped back, encouraging her to wait inside. 'It's still on the table in the lounge. I'll get it.'

'No—I mean—yes, please—in a minute. But that wasn't what I came back for.'

'Oh?'

'I just…need you to know something.'

He turned fully back to face her, and nodded to confirm that she had his undivided attention. Her misgivings quadrupled, but she forced herself to go on.

'I need you to know that the reason I said I didn't want to have your baby has nothing to do with your past.'

'I know,' he said softly.

Libby knotted her hands together self-consciously. 'Good, I just didn't want you to think—'

'I don't.'

An awkward silence descended.

'I'll get you those papers, then,' he said, disappearing from the hallway.

Libby looked at herself in the mirror on the opposite wall, appalled. *Oh, yes, Libby. Great job of expressing your feelings.*

He returned swiftly, his hands full of her brochures and notes, but she didn't even register them.

'In fact,' she bulldozed on, before she lost her nerve, 'there's no other man I would want to be the father of my children, if I had any. It was one of the reasons I married you then.' *And it's one of the reasons I'd marry you again tomorrow,* she almost said—until she realised how ridiculous that would sound, given that there was a taxi waiting outside to carry her and her suitcase containing their divorce papers away from him for ever.

One of the reasons I married you *then,* Rion noticed. Before she'd realised that marriage and a family couldn't make her happy. He felt a certain relief that it sounded as though she didn't foresee any other man being able to change her mind. Yet the thought that she'd never have any children, his or not, made him infinitely sad. She'd make a wonderful mother.

'You don't have to explain. I know that married life could never make you happy.' His voice grew self-critical. 'It's taken me too long, but I understand now that freedom and independence are the only things which can.'

She did a double-take, her heart beginning to pound in her ears. *That* was the reason why he thought she didn't want his child?

'Then you misunderstand, Rion.' She shook her head, relieved that she *had* turned around on the doorstep to set the record straight. 'Crazy, I know, but the only times in my life when I've felt truly free have been times when I was with you.' Their wedding day. Making love here in the hallway. Inside that lift.

Rion took a step towards her, the tempo of his breathing beginning to accelerate. 'Then why are you leaving?'

She dropped her eyes, tears hovering beneath their lids. 'Because the only times I've ever felt that kind of freedom have been times when I stupidly thought it was possible that you might love me as much as I love you…the way I've loved you ever since I was fifteen years old—so much that when I'm not with you it feels like I'm only half alive.'

'You think I don't love *you* that way?' Rion bit out, trying to stop his own tears from falling, almost unable to believe what he was hearing. But Libby wasn't looking at his face. She was staring at the floor, stifling her own sobs.

'I know you don't. Maybe you had a passing attrac-tion to me once, when I presented you with a chal-lenge, but—'

Rion's foot came into view, and she realised he'd taken another step forward and was now only inches away from her. He placed his forefinger under her chin, tilted her face upwards, and smoothed her hair away from her eyes before she had a chance to even try and hide behind it.

'A *passing attraction*?' he repeated in disbelief. 'You think what I feel for you is a passing attraction? I can't tell you how many times in the years since you left I've wished that was all it was—so I could just forget you, stop wishing you'd come back and move on.' He shook his head. 'I never could. Libby, I want you so much that when I'm with you I can barely control myself—so much that it makes me ashamed.'

'Ashamed?' Her eyes widened. 'Why ashamed?'

'Because you are my wife, and you do not deserve me taking my own pleasure like the boy from the streets that I am.'

Libby's mouth fell open and her heart-rate rocketed. Good God, had what she assumed was uninterest in her in bed really been him thinking he was showing her *respect*? Was it possible that it could always be the way it had been when they'd made love here, in this hallway?

'Rion, I *wanted* to bring you the pleasure you brought me. I didn't want to experience it alone; I wanted to ex-perience it *with* you. I wanted to experience *everything* with you. That's what marriage is about.'

Rion nodded with more than a hint of self-recrimination as he truly understood for the first time the damage he had done to his marriage all those nights he'd worked late, failing to see that she didn't care about money, that she just wanted to be with him.

'It took the thought of you leaving to make me realise that—to realise that you were right about me being obsessed with making it on my own. After Jason—' His voice was thick with emotion. 'After Jason's death I was so determined not to waste one moment of the life he'd been denied—to become a success and to prove men like Spyros wrong, to make sure that I was giving you the life you deserved—that it didn't occur to me that what really matters is sharing life's experiences with someone you love.'

She gave a sad smile and nodded, trying to contain her soaring heart. 'I bet if Jason could tell you what he missed the most it wouldn't be not having all of this, but not being here by your side, to share it with you.'

He managed the smallest of laughs. 'And trying to beat me at it.' The glazed look in his eyes cleared. 'I'm sorry I never let you share my life properly, Libby. I'm sorry I just assumed—so many things. And I wish…' He raised the brochures still clutched in his right hand before dejectedly placing them on the windowsill. 'I wish we could have lived out our dreams together.'

Libby looked up into his liquid brown eyes, and this time she let her heart soar. In doing so, all the wounds which had been inflicted upon it began to heal, as if it had been doused with a miracle cure. Hope returned. No—

more than hope, *faith*. She wasn't entirely sure how it was possible, but she knew it was real. She could feel it.

Slowly she pushed back against the door until the latch clicked behind her. This time the noise had never sounded better. Then she reached down into to the flat front pocket of her suitcase and pulled out the sheaf of divorce papers.

'And I'm sorry that I wasn't ready to share my life either, that I was so preoccupied with myself that I never tried to understand you. But I don't see any reason why we can't start now, do you?' she whispered.

His eyes blazed with delight in exactly the way she'd been hoping, and it was the final confirmation she needed. He hadn't signed the divorce petition because he'd wanted to. He'd signed it because he loved her, because he'd thought it was what *she* wanted. It wasn't. *This* was what she wanted, what she'd always wanted, only it had taken them five years to be ready to open their hearts and cherish it. Frantically, elatedly, she took the divorce petition in her hands and tore it into tiny pieces, flinging them in the air so they rained down on them like confetti. Or snow.

Rion's mouth slid into a wide, wide smile, and he reached his hands around her waist, closing the remaining distance between them.

'Wait!' she cried. 'I have these to go as well.' She reached down into the pocket of her suitcase again and produced a sheet of foiled pills.

Rion looked at her in shock and delight, but then his face grew sombre. 'You know, nothing would please me more than having a child with you, Libby, but…do you mind if we wait just for a little while?

Libby's expression faltered. 'Oh?'

'It's just there are so many things I want us to do together first.'

'Oh!' This time the sound was pure ecstasy on her lips. 'You mean we should research some Delikaris Experiences for two?' Her eyes danced. 'No, Rion, I don't mind at all.'

'You're certain about that?' He furrowed his brow in concern.

She snaked her arms around his neck and whispered in his ear. 'I've never been more certain of anything in my life.'

He drew back, just enough to look her in the eye, his voice deadly serious. 'Then clearly I have a lot of work to do.'

Libby cocked one eyebrow. 'Work?'

'Indeed—because there's one thing you should be more certain of than anything else in your life.' He grinned, catching her wrists and gently pressing her against the wall. 'And that's that this is a whole lot more than a passing attraction. This is love, *gineka mou*. But don't worry. I fully intend to spend the rest of my life convincing you of it.'

And with that he kissed her, with more passion than she'd ever dreamed possible. A passion that matched her own, and that was accompanied by the greatest sense of freedom Libby had ever known. The freedom of loving, and of truly being loved in return.

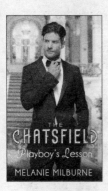

Hot reads!

These 3-in-1s will certainly get you feeling hot under the collar with their desert locations, billionaire tycoons and playboy princes.

**Now available at
www.millsandboon.co.uk/offers**

24 new stories from the leading lights of romantic fiction!

Featuring bestsellers Adele Parks, Katie Fforde, Carole Matthews and many more, *Truly, Madly, Deeply* **takes you on an exciting romantic adventure where love really is all you need.**

Now available at:

www.millsandboon.co.uk

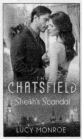

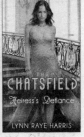

Discover more romance at

www.millsandboon.co.uk

- ❤ WIN great prizes in our exclusive competitions

- ❤ BUY new titles before they hit the shops

- ❤ BROWSE new books and REVIEW your favourites

- ❤ SAVE on new books with the Mills & Boon® Bookclub™

- ❤ DISCOVER new authors

PLUS, to chat about your favourite reads, get the latest news and find special offers:

- 🔲 Find us on facebook.com/millsandboon
- 🐦 Follow us on twitter.com/millsandboonuk
- ❤ Sign up to our newsletter at millsandboon.co.uk

The World of Mills & Boon

There's a Mills & Boon® series that's perfect for you. There are ten different series to choose from and new titles every month, so whether you're looking for glamorous seduction, Regency rakes, homespun heroes or sizzling erotica, we'll give you plenty of inspiration for your next read.

By Request
Back by popular demand!
12 stories every month

Cherish™
Experience the ultimate rush of falling in love.
12 new stories every month

INTRIGUE...
A seductive combination of danger and desire...
7 new stories every month

Desire™
Passionate and dramatic love stories
6 new stories every month

n o c t u r n e™
An exhilarating underworld of dark desires
3 new stories every month